Praise for *Day Brings Back the Night*

"A beautiful family love story set across generations. Duren hauntingly captures the heartbreaking impossibility of family—the love it demands and the love it destroys."

Junot Diaz, Pulitzer Prize-winning author of *The Brief Wondrous Life of Oscar Wao*

"Brian Duren has composed this novel as a song, a melody that carries from generation to generation the voices, visions, and scars a family has grown up with and will never leave behind."

Cass Dalglish, novelist, *Ring of Lions,* and poet, *Humming the Blues / Cantando los Blues (a boca cerrada).*

"Day Brings Back the Night is an eloquent story of family tragedy and its aftermath. Using myriad voices, Duren deftly conveys one woman's life and the pain and love she leaves in its wake. This novel is both an elegy and a triumph of a family's journey finding their way back to each other, and to love."

Cary Griffith, Minnesota Book Award winner and author of *Grizzly Narrows*

"This absorbing, intelligent family drama plays out between Minnesota's two polestars, the rich cultural life of Minneapolis, and escape to up-north cabin living. Duren's finely rendered story of love and grief proves a universal truth: our past is never fully behind us."

Will Weaver, award-winning author of *Power & Light* and *Black Dirt, Bright Stars*

DAY BRINGS BACK THE NIGHT

Minneapolis

First Edition 2026

10 9 8 7 6 5 4 3 2 1
ISBN: 978-1-962834-76-6

Cover and book design by Gary Lindberg

DAY
BRINGS BACK THE
NIGHT

Brian M. Duren

Minneapolis

Also by Brian M. Duren

Whiteout (2009)

Ivory Black (2023)

The Gravity of Love (2023)

I dedicate *Day Brings Back the Night* to my partner, Jane Bassuk; to my children, Neil, Michael, Daniel, and Cathy; and to all of the people in the world who provide love and support to others.

Part I: 1989
Helen prepares for a new life

"You only have to let the soft animal of your body love what it loves."

Mary Oliver, "Wild Geese"

I wake up in the morning, and my dreams evaporate before I open my eyes. But the feelings linger. They fill me, fill my heart, my mind, my lungs, as if I were breathing them, as if they provide the oxygen for the state that I'm in. I'm inside myself and have no desire to get outside. I could stay here until the end, and I would, if I didn't have Tom, if I didn't have my kids. They make me want to go on, and I do. Sooner or later, I always do. I get up and make breakfast and drink coffee and watch my family eat, listen to them talk and laugh, and listen to the radio and find myself alone again. And at night, every night, I become who I am, the person who haunts me, whose feelings permeate my body and my spirit as I sleep and dream.

* * *

Tom and the kids have already had lunch and left, and my mind is somewhere else, nowhere, really, until a cardinal sings, startles me as it whistles two or three times, like a boy at a pretty girl, and chirps, as if it were chuckling at what it has just done. I stand up from my bed, go to the open window and look out at the backyard, trying to find the bird among the leaves and pink blossoms in the crabapple tree, but can't, and wonder if it's still there, until I hear the little rascal whistle and chuckle again, and I hum as the whistles and chuckles warm my heart. I love spring, when the crabapple is in bloom. Some of its blossoms have already fallen, lie scattered on the ground, and within a few days all of them will fall and carpet the grass with dazzling pink petals. But, for now, the tree is still a bouquet, albeit one with a small red swing attached, a bucket swing for Nicky and Mandy when they were little. And then we got the swing set, where they could both swing at once, reach out with their legs and pull themselves toward the sky, grinning with excitement and screeching with laughter as they screamed, "Look at me! Look at me!" But now, at ten and eight, they've almost outgrown the swings.

We've outgrown this house. Our first house. I was so happy when we moved here five years ago, I went crazy with gardening, which I'd never done before, and planted all these flowers—the peonies near the house, with blossoms of every hue, from a soft white and a pale pink to a deep dark red, and the purple and yellow irises that line the fence on both sides, where the tiger lilies will bloom in July. I glance over at the screened-in porch, where we talk and laugh over lunches and dinners, catching a whiff of the perfume of the Asiatic lilies, of the hibiscus and of the other flowers that bloom in the summer, and hearing the whistles and chirps of the birds in the trees. I take another deep breath. It's time to let go, time to get back to work.

I return to the bed on which I stacked the pile of manila folders and papers and stare at the cardboard boxes on the floor. I've sorted through most of the papers and notebooks that I've accumulated over the last fifteen years, stacking what I want to keep on the bed and tossing the rest in the boxes, wondering again and again, Why in the world did I save this term paper, or that essay, or the papers I'd graded but hadn't been able to return to the students? Tom teases me about the difficulty I have letting go of things, and he's right, but I'm not a hoarder.

The other day he suggested I was, and I said, "Are you kidding?

People who are constantly moving from one place to another don't have the luxury of hoarding."

He said, "This is the first time we've moved in years."

And I said, "Look at these boxes full of papers I'm throwing away. Could a hoarder do that?"

"Of course not." He took me in his arms. He was teasing. We kissed, and if we'd been alone, we might've made love.

I look off toward the closet, where his clothes and mine still hang, and where the last box of papers sits on the floor, and then at my watch. It's almost two o'clock. He and the kids won't be back until five or six. I have time to take a break. I leave the room and walk past the bathroom to the kitchen, where the radio's broadcasting the news. My coffee cup's still on the table, along with my cigarettes, and the newspaper Tom set next to my place, when the kids ran upstairs to put on their bathing suits. I refill my cup, light a cigarette and look at the article Tom wanted to show me—a review of a new film called *Dead Poets Society.*

"This is a film you might want to see," he said, looking at me with that impish grin of his.

"*Dead Poets Society*? Sounds like a dark comedy about the poets from the sixties and seventies—Plath, Sexton, Berryman..." I nodded and scanned the first few paragraphs. "Stars Robin Williams, but it's certainly not a comedy."

"No, it's not."

I looked at Tom. "What's the last film we saw him in?"

He paused, and his playful spirit disappeared as he mumbled, "*Good Morning, Vietnam.*"

I could see his memory of his lost brother had seized him, a loss that had led him to become obsessed with films about Vietnam. He'd go through periods when he'd watch them repeatedly—*Apocalypse Now, The Deer Hunter, Platoon,* and *Good Morning, Vietnam.* And then he wouldn't watch them for a year or two. But he'd go back to them... He'd always go back.

He seemed to regain his spirit, smiled, nodded at the article about *Dead Poets Society* and said, "We should see it."

I smiled back. "We should." And our eyes held onto one another.

I hum, feeling the warmth I saw in his eyes, and drop the paper on the table. I take a drag of my cigarette and notice the reporters on National Public Radio are talking about Poland, Czechoslovakia, and Hungary pulling away from the Soviet Union and moving toward democracy. The people in those countries must feel so happy to rid themselves of their Soviet rulers and begin a new life. Begin a new life... That's what Tom and I are doing. It started the day we learned he'd gotten tenure at Macalester. All the anxiety that was stifling us, about what we'd do if he didn't get it, vanished as soon as we learned about the decision, and we celebrated, put our house up for sale and found a new one in Tangletown, just a short walk from campus. A big house, much bigger than this one, big enough so we can breathe, with a fireplace, chandeliers, beautiful woodwork, sculpted wood columns, built-in buffets, bookshelves with glass panes and lead-glass windows that filter the sunlight into rays of blue and green and red that illuminate the rooms and glow on the surface of the furniture and hardwood floors. The kind of house in which I can see us living out our lives.

I take one more drag of my cigarette, stub it out, turn off the radio, leave my coffee on the table and walk out of the kitchen, through the dining room and the foyer and into the living room. I head toward the back wall, sit down on the floor, in front of the stand with the turntable and the shelf beneath it, and flip through the albums, thinking maybe Patti Smith's *Horses,* or *Radio Ethiopia,* or Tina Turner's *Private Dancer,* and I hear her singing in my mind about love being a second-hand emotion. Her voice fades, and I stop going through the albums, feeling at once sad, happy, and nostalgic in this empty space. I stand up and look around the living room at the brick fireplace, the bare shelves, and the boxes on the floor, full of the books that had been on the shelves and the family photographs that had been on the mantelpiece. My gaze drifts to the mauve drapes, with a pattern of green stems and red, orange and blue flowers, and the couch and armchairs in front of them, where Tom and I would sit with Nicky and Mandy on our laps when they were little and read to them, and where the four of us now sometimes sit and read or watch TV. It's hard to let go of this room, full of memories, like every room in this house.

I wander back into the dining room and stop in front of the window where I stood after lunch, watching Tom and the kids, both wearing bathing suits and T-shirts, descend the front walk to our car parked in the street. Nicky got in the front passenger seat and Mandy in the back. Tom walked around the car, glanced up toward the house, saw me in the window and gave me a nod and a thumbs up, and I smiled as he opened the door and got in. Nicky looked toward Tom and back at me, and then he grinned and waved, and so did Mandy. I waved back and pursed my lips in a kiss, as if my darlings were within reach. All they were able to talk about at lunch was the fun they'd have at the swimming pool, doing cannon balls off the diving board, or seeing who could jump the furthest off their dad's shoulders as he stood in the water... Mandy's face was still turned toward me, her eyes, concealed behind the dark lenses in the pink plastic frame of her glasses, fixed on me... fixed in a way that made me pause and wonder, as I often do, What are you thinking? Why are you staring at me like that? I've been a good mother to you. I love you... The car pulled away, and my hand sunk to my side. I felt the silence of the empty house. And feel it now…

* * *

I sit on the edge of the bed, staring down at the box that I lugged from the closet and dropped to the floor. I haven't opened it since we moved into this house. What will I find? My Bachelor's and Master's English degree diplomas? A bunch of notebooks? Maybe some papers I wrote. I rip the tape off, pull back the flaps and see a red tin box, with gold and silver starbursts, resting on top of a bunch of notebooks. I have a vague memory of the box, but not of what's inside. I put it on my lap, take off the cover and discover piles of photographs, with pictures of Tom and me, and of the kids when they were infants and toddlers. And I recall that this is the box in which I decided to place the photos that Tom and I hadn't included in the albums we'd assembled, pictures I was too attached to to throw away. I look at shots of Nicky taking his first steps, holding on to Tom's fingers, who's standing behind him, and of Mandy, lying on her blankie on the floor, her head raised and her mouth open as she stares at the camera, and of Tom and me before the kids were born, of each of us standing alone in front of the townhouse we were renting, or in the backyard, in front of the porch, one of us photographing the other, he in his slacks and dress shirt, me in a blouse and black pants, the kind of pants I'd wear with a matching suit coat when I'd teach.

Looking at one photograph after another, reliving moments from our life, I come to a picture of the two of us in our early twenties, standing, leaning into one another, smiling, happy. The close-up features just us, just our happiness, and nothing of the world we were in, but I remember the room in which it was taken, and the house, and the parties in that house and the things that changed my life… I gaze at Tom, dressed in jeans and a short-sleeved shirt, with his light brown hair combed away from his forehead and barely covering his ears. He never seemed to want to stand out in any way. He might wear a T-shirt, with a picture of Led Zeppelin or the Grateful Dead, but never bell-bottoms, or wild colored jeans or shirts unbuttoned to his navel, and he never tried to be the center of attention at those parties, never tried to perform for an audience by telling stories, and probably never flashed a seductive smile at a girl. No, he was very reserved. Unremarkable. I wasn't attracted to him in the beginning.

We met in front of Walter Library, spring quarter of the year I graduated. He told me he'd moved into a big house just before the school year started, a house that he shared with three other guys, not far from campus. I asked him where, and he told me the name of the street and described the location. My stomach churned. I felt light-headed. I took a deep breath, tried to calm myself and asked, "What are they like, the guys you live with?"

As he described them, he said, "One of them is really cool. Witty, funny, loves to tell stories. Above all if he's got an audience. A real performer."

That's when my relationship with Tom started. We'd get together for coffee occasionally, and then dinner, and then started going to movies, and eventually he invited me to a party to celebrate the end of spring quarter and, for the first time in nearly a year, I returned to that house. I close my eyes, shake my head, take a deep breath and sigh, and open my eyes to the picture of Tom and me in the backyard and gaze at him. No, it wasn't love at first sight. When I started seeing him, I didn't realize what rare qualities his compassion and capacity for love were.

I place the picture on the pile next to me on the bed and continue going through the photos, trying to stay focused, not letting my mind wander, feeling apprehensive about returning into the past, into all that pain, and yet compelled to go on, until, tossing aside another picture, there it is, what I've been anticipating, dreading and... and desiring to see—a photo of Dick Rayburn and me. This one happens to be a profile view of us, facing each other, our heads turned toward the camera, as if someone just shouted, *Hey, over here!* I gaze at Dick's eyes that look back at me, at his sculpted face and his long, dark brown hair hanging to his shoulders. He's in jeans and the white tuxedo jacket he'd wear at parties when he'd do his Bogie thing, acting like Rick in *Casablanca.* He'd make martinis for his housemates, their girlfriends and the two of us before the others arrived, and then, when the crowd showed up, we'd switch to jug wine and keg beer, and smoke joints and groove to the music of the Stones and Led Zeppelin in the living room and dining room, where the furniture had been pushed to the side.

It was so many years ago when I met him, the winter quarter of my fourth year, in that course on American literature. I arrived late the first day of class and stopped in the doorway. The prof was writing something on the blackboard. I looked around the room and noticed an empty desk toward the middle of a row, squeezed past everyone, almost tripping over someone's boots, plopped onto the desk seat, sighed with relief, pulled my coat off and settled in, all before the prof turned around and resumed lecturing. I felt the guy sitting next to me staring at me and looked at him. He smiled, and then looked down at his notebook, at a drawing he'd started of a male figure, and wrote in large letters, at the top of the page, "You look like Faye Dunaway." And I thought, Oh, jeez, what a come-on! He smiled, arched his eyebrows and returned to his drawing of a male head, with a long nose, glasses perched at the end of it and bulging eyes. The professor started lecturing again, and when I looked up at him, I thought, Hmm, the drawing resembles him, and I glanced back at the notebook and watched, as Dick sketched a tall wispy figure, and realized he was doing a caricature of the prof and I bit my lip so I wouldn't giggle. Dick looked up at me with a mischievous grin and then back down at his notebook and wrote above the caricature, "The Ichabod teaching in Sleepy Hollow," and proceeded to sketch students asleep, their heads resting on their folded arms on their desks, or hanging back, their mouths agape.

From that day on, we sat next to one another. Sometimes, he'd write questions in his notebook and, as I became more comfortable sitting next to him, I would too. Questions about our names, where we were from and what we were interested in. Once he asked if I had a boyfriend, and I wrote, "No."

So, I asked him if he had a girlfriend, and he wrote, "Always. I'm a serial monogamist."

I stifled a laugh and wrote, "But not a murderer?"

And he gasped and wrote, "NO!"

Sometimes, after class, we'd have coffee together and, during our conversations, he'd refer to the class as Sleepy Hollow, claiming the instructor didn't have us read that story for an obvious reason. At the end of the quarter, Dick wrote in his notebook that he no longer had a girlfriend, and I drew exclamation points. We went out for coffee, and he invited me to a party he and his housemates were throwing at the end of final exam week.

His house was just a few blocks from Joyce's, the schoolteacher who rented one of her rooms to me, so I walked to his place. The sun was setting, and the warm red glow beyond the trees was fading to black by the time I rang his doorbell. One of his roommates gave me a big welcome and led me to the kitchen. There was Dick, in his white tuxedo jacket and blue jeans, making the martinis. Pretending to be surprised when he saw me, he said, "'Of all the gin joints in all the towns in all the world, she walks into mine.'" He sounded just like Bogie. His three housemates and their girlfriends laughed, and so did I. He introduced me, and we talked, joked and sipped our martinis. I noticed one of the girlfriends, Charlotte, kept gazing at him and, when she caught me staring at her, snorted, "Huh!" and rolled her eyes and looked away, leaving me to wonder, What the hell was that about?

The crowd arrived, and Dick and I mixed with them and danced, and then, after a song ended and he went off to use the bathroom, Charlotte appeared, standing next to me. She said, "He's going to take you up to the choir loft. Get you to sing your hallelujahs." She grinned, took a sip of wine and wandered off, just as Dick returned.

He glared at her as she walked away and asked what we were talking about.

"Oh, nothing," I shrugged. "Just the music."

That seemed to satisfy him, and we danced and drank more wine. And then he put his arm around my back and led me off, guiding me toward the stairs to the second floor. One of his housemates, who was talking to his girlfriend, paused to look at us as we passed and said something I couldn't quite understand with the music blasting, something that included the words "nooky nook." I looked at Dick and asked what he had said.

Dick shook his head and shrugged, as if he didn't know. He guided me up the stairs to his room, opened the door, and there stood his brass bed, and in my head I heard Bob Dylan's voice singing to a lady, telling her to lay across his big brass bed. I looked up at the red veil hanging around the overhead light, giving the room a kind of rosy glow, and felt like I was in a whore house or a strip joint. I knew the words I'd heard the roommate say were nooky nook, and that's what I'd entered. The door closed behind me, muting the sound from below, and I felt trapped. I'd be just another lay. I felt like leaving.

He came around from behind and faced me. I looked him in the eye and thought, We'll see, and walked past him, walked around looking at the walls, at everything that was meant to impress the girls he brought to his precious little nooky nook. There were caricatures everywhere, the most unforgettable one being a drawing of a prof that accentuated features of the man's head to make him look like a pig, with a snout for a nose, hams for cheeks and what appeared to be a pig's anus for a mouth. The words MIRACLE OF NATURE had been printed at the top of the drawing and, at the bottom, "An asshole from one end to the other." And there were posters of bands, like Led Zeppelin and Pink Floyd. Of course, Dick had attended their concerts, because he was always in on everything cool. Oh, and the Che Guevara poster, I can't forget that—the beret with the silver star, the long black hair and the intense eyes that seemed to be focused on something in the future—probably the revolution.

Dick so loved talking about revolutions—or "liberation movements," as he called them—and about when he'd become a history professor and he'd teach as his way of contributing to *the* revolution, which seemed imminent the way he'd talk about it. Rambling on, he'd get going about his father, the son of a miner who'd grown up poor in a mining town, had become an artist and had died young, in his forties, and Dick would go on and on about how his father had trained him to be an artist, from the time he was a little kid, and he'd look at his self-portrait—his head, facing the viewer, and his eyes looking off at something in the distance, or maybe in the future, like Che's eyes gazing at the revolution. Dick's face in that painting was huge, and when I told him I'd never seen a face that big, he said, "I find myself infinitely fascinating." He was joking, but it was true.

He liked to joke, play around with me, see what it would get him. Like with that poster for the film, *Taxi Driver*, with the picture of Robert de Niro, and the words at the bottom, "You talkin' to me?" I hadn't seen the film, so, earlier, when we were downstairs, talking with his friends, and he looked at me and snarled the words, I was confused and thought he was angry. But when I saw the poster, I realized he'd been playing with me again, and I turned to him and said, "So, when you said, 'You talkin' to me?' like you were angry, that just came from the movie."

He lit up the joint he'd been rolling, took a drag, stared at me with a crazy look in his eyes and said again, "You talkin' to me? Huh? You talkin' to me?"

I shook my head and laughed. I moved closer to him, dropped my purse on his bed, reached for the joint between his fingers, took a toke, and blew the smoke on his neck and chest and said, "You like to do that to me, don't you."

"Like to do what?" he asked, as he reached for the joint.

"Like to mess with me." I held onto the joint, took another toke and blew the smoke on him again.

"You're so much fun." And he reached again for the joint.

I pulled my hand back and grinned at him, and he grinned back and said, "Please," and I handed him the joint. While he inhaled, I grazed his cheek with my fingertips. We passed the joint back and forth until it was just a roach, and then he went to the head of the bed, stubbed it in an ashtray on the night table and turned toward me.

I looked down at the bed and my purse and then at him. He approached me, laid his hands on my shoulders and drew me close, but, when our lips were about to touch, I pushed back and stared at him. His hands slid down to my hips.

Looking into my eyes and trying to read me, he asked what was the matter.

"That roommate of yours we saw just before we came upstairs, he was asking if we were going up to the nooky nook, wasn't he? He seemed to think that was funny."

Dick grinned and pulled one of his stunts, comparing me again to Faye Dunaway, asking me if I'd seen *Chinatown*.

I removed his hands from my hips and said, "I've also heard your room referred to as the choir loft."

He pretended to be confused. "The choir loft?" When he saw I didn't buy his act, he shrugged and said, "Yeah, well, I guess a few girls have kind of... practiced their scales. Hit a few high notes. Some very high notes."

"In the nooky nook."

He nodded.

"Was one of those girls Charlotte?"

"Charlotte?"

"Yeah, Charlotte."

"Did she say something to you?"

"How high did she sing? Soprano high?" I was amused to see he looked a little pissed. "You're used to getting what you want in your little nooky nook." I grazed his chest with my fingertips. "You'd like to make me sing my hallelujahs, like I could feel the presence of the messiah." I glided my fingers up his neck and traced the line of his jaw.

"Now you're messing with me."

"Oh, I'm definitely messing with you." I peered into his eyes. "So why don't we just sit down on the bed and talk."

"Talk?"

"Talk. You know, utter words to one another."

He snorted a laugh.

"You can tell me all about that little town where you grew up in Colorado, and if you're a good boy, maybe you'll get what you want. And maybe not. Depends on what I want."

He looked baffled. And then he forced a smile, gestured toward the bed and said, "After you." I crawled onto the bed, slid across to the far side, put my purse in the middle to establish a boundary, and leaned back against the headboard and watched him sit down next to me, with a couple feet between us. I'd gotten out a cigarette and was about to light up, when he said, "Cigarettes will kill you. They killed my dad."

For once, I didn't feel he was playing with me. I said, "I'm sorry."

He looked away.

"I didn't mean to—"

"It's okay." He sighed, looked at me and started talking about the town in which he'd grown up, constantly returning to the subject of his father, as if his memories of him were a home that he carried inside. Not only did his father train him to be an artist, working with him in his studio, he also shared with him his love of old films, from the 1920s to the 1950s, and the two of them would watch them together on TV at night. Dick saw some of them so often he could perform scenes from them. That's what he'd do for his father. And he performed some lines from one of Bogie's films for me, trying to charm and seduce me. His imitation of Bogie's voice was so good, if my eyes had been closed and I'd opened them, I would've expected to see the movie star. What I did see was Dick's happiness mutate into a kind of sadness and nostalgia. Wanting to help him, I told him he could be almost anything—"An actor, an artist... "

"We had one artist in the family. One in any family is enough."

"Why do you say that?"

"The only thing my dad wanted to do was paint. That was his way of living. But he couldn't earn enough money to support a family, and my mother taught school and didn't make much either, so there was a lot of tension around money. And other things… My dad didn't talk much, except about painting and films. He was very quiet. What I remember most about his work was the silence. He usually painted empty city streets. Everything seemed still. And if someone did appear in a painting, the person was alone, and the buildings and the shadows they cast were so much taller, they dwarfed the person. His paintings were like dreams. You know, the kind of dream in which everything is still, and you can feel death. And you wake up scared out of your mind."

His eyes remained fixed on the wall across the room, his mouth open, as if there was something else he wanted to say, but couldn't. I remember an unbearable silence. It made me feel the weight of what was oppressing him. I said, "But an artist understands the kinds of things that go on inside people. You had someone you could talk to. You must've had conversations."

"My dad and I had movies. Above all, that last year, after he'd quit drinking and gone through AA. I'd perform scenes for him from the films we watched, do imitations of Bogie, Peter Lorre, and James Cagney, and he'd laugh." Dick's head fell back and he stared at the ceiling. "He died... at forty-three." He closed his eyes.

I moved my purse out of the way and pulled close to him.

"It felt like suicide." He rolled away from me.

I drew close to him again and asked if he was okay.

He took some deep breaths, like he was trying to control his emotions, and got up, walked a few steps and stopped, his head bowed.

I followed him, stood behind him, placed my hands on his arms and felt him take another deep breath. I asked him if he was all right.

He didn't answer. I was about to ask him again, when he spun around, glared at me and snarled, "You talkin' to me? Huh?"

I screamed, "Dick!" I was shocked, and then upset, and pounded him on the chest and started laughing, a crazy laugh that shattered my tension, and I collapsed against him, repeating his name, and he bent over and kissed me, and I kissed him back, and we staggered toward the bed.

* * *

I woke up happy in the morning, like I'd just come out of a beautiful dream. But I hadn't come out, I was still in it, in Dick's arms, and we made love again. We came, he rolled off, and I flopped my arms and sighed, a hum resonating through my whole body. Soon my fingers were touching his thigh, he rolled over toward me, and we started playing around again, until Dick saw the scars across the inside of one of my wrists and along my forearm. He looked at me, shocked, looked back at my arm, and then turned my other arm over and saw those scars. He stared at me, baffled, and asked, "What happened?" I was too ashamed to tell him. So much of the most painful parts of my life exposed on my forearms. But it was a memoir in code that only I could read. I said I'd had some painful issues when I was young, had seen therapists, and now I was fine, all that was in the past, and I didn't want to talk about it. I turned my arms over so he couldn't see the scars. He nodded, but continued to stare at me, like he was determined to try to read my mind, until he gave up and rolled away. We got dressed, went downstairs to the kitchen and there was Charlotte, sitting at the head of the table, next to Dick's roommate, Ken, her long blond waves splayed across her purple sweatshirt and her eyes fixed on me. I sat down at the other end, and Dick brought us each a cup of coffee and sat down close to me. Still feeling her eyes staring at me, I looked back at her, and she smirked, looked at Dick and asked, "Did you have a good night?"

Dick looked her in the eye, nodded and, after a pause, said, "Yeah, we had a great night. Didn't we, Helen."

Before I had a chance to respond, Charlotte said, "I was just wondering. I heard loud noises coming from your room. Sounded like someone was screaming... or singing hallelujah." She shook her head and furrowed her brow, as if mystified. "Weird!"

"Nothing weird about that," Ken said. "Hear it all the time."

He and Charlotte laughed.

Dick smiled and shook his head. "You clowns finished yet?"

They both chimed in with, "Oh, yeah, we're done, we're done."

Dick looked at me. "They think they're funny."

Charlotte gave me a look that seemed to say, *I told you so.*

I looked away from her and back at Dick. Our eyes met, he leaned forward as he sipped his coffee, and I felt his hand on my thigh. I was totally smitten.

But as I walked home, I thought about the night before, how we'd ended up in bed and how Dick had gotten what he'd wanted. I felt used. I wanted the same thing, but the way it had happened bugged me. I'd lost control. Lost it because I felt concern for him, afraid he was suffering, and opened myself to him and made myself vulnerable. He took hold of me and got what he wanted. He'd designed that room to help him get what he wanted. Everything he did with a woman, he did to get what he wanted.

* * *

I look down again at the photo of Dick and me, the two of us appearing so happy, and smile back at the beautiful lovers, until I remember what he did to me. What I allowed him to do. And I look away.

Another night we were together, he surprised me when he complained we were always talking about him and said, "What about you? You never talk about yourself." Of course, after seeing the scars, he would want me to talk about myself and give him a glimpse into my past and all the trauma that had led to those welts. I said I was just an ordinary girl from the burbs. My dad and my two brothers went to the U, and so I go there, too. And I turned our conversation back on him.

He was aware of my feeling of weakness, and that awareness gave him power over me. His performances amused, charmed, and suckered me, and he was performing from the day we met, in that course on American lit, and every day after, when I'd sit at his side, watch him sketch in his notebook, write his funny comments and glance at me with his sly smile. I'd look into his beautiful hazel eyes and see mischief sparkling, and sometimes our arms would touch, or our fingers, when I'd lay my hand on his notebook, pointing at something, and the touch would trigger a tremor in my heart. I'd begun falling in love with him before I even went to that party at his house and fell more deeply during the five months that followed. He was handsome, funny, and talented. But he needed a spectator, an audience for whom he could perform, do his imitations of actors, tell stories theatrically and show off his paintings and caricatures. It was as if he'd never stopped performing for his dead father, and I and all of Dick's friends and admirers were just surrogates for his dad.

I didn't always see his flaws for what they were. He'd defined himself from the beginning as a serial monogamist, and yet I believed the serialization had ended with me. I didn't begin to suspect the end until he and his housemate went on that easy-rider trip. *Easy Rider*. He talked about projecting that film when he was fifteen, working at a movie theater in his hometown and for years dreaming of doing his own easy-rider trip. He bought a motorcycle, had it chopped like the one Peter Fonda rode in the film, found a buckskin jacket with tassels like the one Dennis Hopper wore and, after he graduated, in August of the only summer we were together, went on the road with a housemate. The two of them traveled to the West Coast and down to San Francisco, where his friend's chopper was stolen, and the friend flew back alone. Dick called me every day, until he left San Francisco. Then I didn't hear from him for nearly a week. I was so scared that something horrible had happened to him. And then he called me from Austin, Texas. He was okay. His cycle had broken down, and he had to stay there a few days. Then I didn't hear anything again. And I began worrying all over. I'd rush home from work to see if he'd called, find he hadn't and spend the rest of the evening reading in the bedroom I was renting, or watching television in the living room with Joyce, while trying not to stare at the phone, trying to appear calm, so she wouldn't begin asking me if there was something wrong, because I was so tense, so brittle, I knew I'd shatter like glass.

Then one afternoon, when I was alone, he called. He was home. No joy in his voice, no playfulness. Nothing about missing me, wanting to be with me. Just a few words, a few pauses, and then he said, "We need to talk." I hung up and, as I stood there, stunned, lightheaded, knew his love for me was as dead as the hollow, cavernous tone of his voice. I collapsed in the armchair, took a deep breath, and another, and tears streamed as I shook my head and sobbed, "No, no, no." I cried until I had no more tears. I stared at the window, wondering what had happened, who was the serial monogamist's new lover. And then he showed up in his easy-rider jacket, walking toward the door. The bell rang. I got up, opened the door, and our eyes met. I could see in his face a plea for forgiveness for what he was about to say. I stepped aside, and he walked into the living room. I gestured toward the couch, and he sat down at one end and I at the other. When he looked at me again, I saw a scared little boy and almost felt sorry for him. He looked toward the front door, like he wanted to flee, and then down at the floor. In spite of all the practice he'd had, he didn't find it easy to tell me he was dumping me. Maybe his struggle proved he was human. I lost patience with his silence and said, "You've met someone else."

He looked up and nodded.

"I hope she'll make you happy. At least happier than I made you."

He shook his head and bit his lip, as if this was all too painful to talk about.

I added, "Which must not've been much." My eyes riveted his. "I loved you. I thought you loved me, too."

"I did." He nodded, and I saw tears in his eyes.

"So, what does the new one have that I don't? Is she prettier?"

He looked down.

"Sexier?"

He looked at me. "It's not—"

"Does she give you better blowjobs?"

He took a breath, sighed and wiped away his tears with the back of his hand.

"You scared?" I looked at the door and then back at him. "You wanna leave?" I laughed. "Go on. You can go." He didn't move. "Better get out of here before I go crazy." I glared at him. "Go on, run for it."

He shook his head and stood up and said, "I'm out of here," and headed for the door.

I stood up. "Run, little boy. Run for your life." And as he walked out the door, I shouted, "Run, run, run!"

I fell back onto the couch and cried until I was just taking deep breaths with every heave of my chest. As my breathing calmed, I looked down at my hands, resting on my knees, and turned my palms up and stared at the red lines across my wrists and forearms. The cuts I'd made when I was a little girl didn't leave any scars, but the later ones had. They'd bled a lot. The cuts and the bleeding always made me feel better. Cutting was a relief. It brought a kind of solace. I yearned for that peace. I got a paring knife from the kitchen, went upstairs to my room, sat on the bed, my back resting against the headboard, and, with my palm facing me, clenched my fist, held my breath and slashed my forearm. The cut stung like a deep burn, and my breath caught on a scream. I slashed again, and again, and slashed the other forearm, and leaned back and let go as tears flowed down my cheeks and blood down my arms. Eventually, my breathing calmed and I fell asleep knowing that, if I never woke up, I'd never be depressed again. I already felt at peace, and the peace brought a happiness that left a smile on my lips as I drifted off.

* * *

I become aware of the picture of Dick and me again, look at it one more time and toss it aside. And then I look at my arms, turn both forearms toward myself and stare at the scars, the memoir in code. When I met Dick, some of those welts were only a few years old, from when I was still with Vince. I shake my head. Vince…

We went to high school together, but the school was so big, with nearly five hundred kids in every graduating class, I didn't even notice him until my junior year. I'd see him in the halls, usually alone, but sometimes talking with someone, and if I looked away for a second and then back, he'd be gone. That's what it was like when I went with Debbie and our friends to the University of Minnesota campus and joined the march with thousands of other kids to the capital in St. Paul—the march against the war in Vietnam and the invasion of Cambodia. I'd catch a glimpse of him from time to time, walking with a couple of guys, and then he'd disappear and then I'd see him again. I don't know why I always looked for him. Maybe because he seemed hippier than anyone else in our suburb. He had dark blond hair that hung down to his neck and usually wore T-shirts with pictures of popular bands and singers—the Beatles, Neil Young, Bob Dylan. That march was the last time I remember seeing him in high school.

Near the end of our senior year, Debbie gave me a sly look from her locker right next to mine and asked if I remembered that "hippie guy" who had graduated the year before, the one I'd always had my eye on?

"I didn't always have my eye on him."

She shook her head and huffed, and then said, "Well, apparently, he's a musician and a singer. A really good one. And he's performing at a bar in Minneapolis called the Triangle. I've heard it's a really cool place to hang out. You wanna go?"

I was stunned. I didn't know he was a musician and a singer. He'd always seemed so quiet, so withdrawn, I couldn't imagine him talking to an audience, let alone performing for one. I had to see him.

I told my parents I was going to a movie with Debbie and my friends. We did a lot of partying, and when we couldn't party in someone's house or a motel room, we'd bring beer or whiskey into whatever car we were using and party at a drive-in theater or hang out at the bars that didn't card. If Vince was performing at the Triangle, then it was probably one of those bars.

Debbie came by, and then we picked up a couple of our girlfriends and drove to Minneapolis. I sat in the passenger seat and gave directions from a map. As we wandered the streets of the seedy neighborhoods, on the west bank of the Mississippi, I looked out at the weathered wood-frame houses, with their sagging roofs and porches, and at the two-story brick buildings, with bars and coffee shops on the first floor. We found the Triangle, an old building at the tip of the triangular convergence of two streets. We parked, walked in without anyone carding us at the door, and sat down at a table near the wall, across from the bar. We hunched close, so we could hear one another over the raucous voices and laughter, and looked off from time to time at the kids standing around, probably university students, and nearly all of them smoking, a thick cloud hovering above their heads. There were older people, too, guys and women who looked to be in their late twenties, some of the women wearing heavy make-up, and a few of the men looking like the kind you didn't want to mess with. A waitress came and we ordered whatever was on tap. I lit up, looked around and there was Vince on an elevated stage, at the tip of the bar's triangle. He was sitting on a chair, in front of a mic, in jeans and a black T-shirt, with a picture of Bob Dylan on the chest, footlights illuminating him as he tuned his guitar.

He adjusted the mic and tapped it, and each tap clicked and echoed in the smoke-fogged space. The crowd looked at him. He mumbled a greeting, and everyone hushed as he played and sang, "Mr. Tambourine Man." He performed a few songs by Dylan—"It's All Over Now, Baby Blue," "Lay Lady Lay," and "Just Like a Woman." But unlike Dylan's strong, nasal, twangy voice, Vince's was soft, diaphanous, and hypnotic.

When he sang his own songs, they felt even more like poems than Dylan's, poems about a lady who appears in blue light, like she's walking on the moon, or a lady named Red Lily, with her silent dog, who'd walk by on green mornings, an elusive, dream-like creature, whom he might ask, "Do you miss me, like you say you do?" And she'd stare off into space like a doll and repeat, "You're no good, you're no good, and I felt I wasn't understood." And he'd sing, as if consoling himself, "Drink up, fake your life, pretend you're there when you're not. She'll never know you, but you'll love her anyhow."

The yearning for love in those songs felt like a cavern filled with echoing cries of longing, pain, and despair. He sang the lyrics in a whisper, and a hush fell over the audience. His voice and the repetitive progression of the chords led me like a sorcerer into an intimate space, and I felt close to him, to his loneliness and melancholy, as he followed the elusive, wandering dream of love. The songs felt as if he'd written them for me, as if he'd given me his hand and led me into that cavern. Once, as he paused and scanned the audience, while talking about the next song he was going to perform, our eyes met, and I saw a glimmer of recognition that caused him to pause and brought a smile to his lips.

He continued singing one song after another, and I remained transfixed by the sight of his face as he gazed off, as if at someone who wasn't there, or shook his head and closed his eyes, or opened them and stared down at his fingers plucking the strings, or looked out at the audience to announce his next song, and then, finally, his last. He finished, leaned back and scanned the room, and the audience applauded, and he nodded and thanked everyone. I blinked and looked around the table, as if I were coming out of a dream. Debbie arched her eyebrows and pretended to scream, *She's back!* And the three of them cackled. I shook my head, faked a scowl, and got up and walked toward Vince. He'd stood the guitar on the floor, leaning it against his leg, and was looking at a sheet of paper as I weaved my way around the tables and through the crowd standing in front of the stage. I dropped a dollar in his tip jar and looked up at his eyes focused on the sheet. He noticed me and said, "Hi," and gazed at me.

"I love your music. You have such a beautiful voice."

"Thanks." He nodded, looking unsure of what to say. "I'm sorry, I know we went to the same high school, but I don't remember your name."

"Helen."

"I'm Vince."

"I know. You do this often?"

"Gigs? I wish. I got this one because someone had to cancel."

"I hope you get more. I'd love to see you perform again."

"I'd love to perform again for you." He folded the sheet of paper, slipped it into his shirt pocket, put the guitar in a black case, picked up an empty glass off the floor and walked toward the stairs, smiling at me, and I walked parallel to him, smiling back, and waited as he descended the steps.

He said, "I don't think I've ever seen you here before."

"This is the first time."

"Well," he smiled again, "you wanna get a drink?"

"Sure."

We walked over to the end of the bar. He flagged one of the bartenders, asked him to put his guitar away and give us a couple of taps. The guy set the case beneath the bar and served us each a glass of beer. We clinked glasses, drank and then hunched over the bar, shoulder to shoulder, staring at our beers, until our eyes connected again.

He took another drink and said, "So, you like music?"

I beamed. "I love music."

"And who do you like?"

"Oh, the Beatles, Crosby, Stills, Nash & Young, and Jefferson Airplane. I get high just listening to 'White Rabbit,' and 'Somebody to Love' gets me stoned every time. And Janis—love Janis. She's the greatest. How about you?"

"The same. And Neil Young. I love 'Down by the River' and 'Cowgirl in the Sand.' But, ah, Bob Dylan, *he's* the greatest. You know," Vince paused, looking awed by what he was about to say, "people used to get to see him perform for free at a coffee house in Dinkytown, called the

Ten O'Clock Scholar. At least until about ten years ago, when he left for New York. The Scholar moved to the West Bank and then went belly up. All the guys who used to perform there, and some of them with Dylan, they play here now. Spider John Koerner, Dave Ray, Willie Murphy. A whole lotta good musicians."

"And you."

He nodded and chuckled. "And me."

"What do you like about Dylan's music?"

"Well, first of all, I think it's really cool that Dylan's from here. He's one of us. Makes me feel it's possible to do what he did. But the music itself? His songs are like poems. They draw you in, carry you off, make you feel something... something that stays with you. And you keep on hearing that song in your head. That's what a song should do."

"I agree. But it bugs me he calls a woman a baby, and then says she breaks just like a little girl."

He laughed. "You don't like that, huh?"

"I think your songs are more interesting. They're like poems, too, but they seem more... more personal."

"Thanks." He nodded, looked down at his beer and then at me. "Dylan's special for me. I don't know if I would've learned to play guitar or would've started writing songs if I hadn't found him."

Vince fell silent, and the longer the silence lasted, the more I thought trying to talk about his lyrics would make him stay quiet, so I kept to myself the questions I wanted to ask and the things I wanted to say about the constant yearning for love in his songs, the despair of ever finding it, the feeling of being unworthy, and the need he felt to fake his life, pretend he's not suffering when he is. Those lyrics, the way he sang them, the way he picked the strings that made the songs resonate inside me, that's what drew me to him.

We finished our beers and he ordered another round. Just as he asked me what I planned on doing that summer, I asked him what he'd been doing since high school and we laughed.

"You go first," he said.

"I graduate in a couple weeks, going to continue working this summer as a cashier at a supermarket and, in the fall, I'm moving into a dorm and starting classes at the U. Okay," I smiled, "your turn."

"That sounds familiar. Last summer, I worked at a supermarket, packing groceries and stocking shelves, and started classes at the U last fall. But I dropped out after two quarters. I didn't see any sense in it. None of the guys who are doing what I want to do finished college. It's a waste of time."

"What about the draft?"

He chuckled. "Canada. I sure as hell have no intention of fighting in a war we were lied into."

"No one should."

He looked at me. "What do you want to do?"

"When I grow up, you mean?" I laughed, and he laughed with me.

"Yeah, when you grow up."

"I know what I don't want to do. I don't want to get married and have kids, live in a suburb, go to church every Sunday and... and be like my mother. Oh, no. I'm going to do what I want to do, just the way a man gets to decide what he wants to do. Like you got to decide. But I haven't decided yet. I love to read, so maybe I'll become a teacher."

"A teacher?" He arched his eyebrows. "What would you teach?"

"Probably English. I like to read novels and poetry. And books about women. But I don't know yet. I want to travel, too. Maybe I'll get a job as an airline stewardess. Or maybe I'll just be a tramp." I laughed, and he laughed with me.

I felt someone staring at me and glanced over at the table where my friends were sitting, and Debbie raised her wrist, pointed at her watch and mouthed the words, "We gotta go." I looked back at him, saw his eyes had followed mine and he'd gotten the message.

"Well," he said.

"Yeah."

"Maybe I could, ah, pick you up sometime, and we could come back here and watch Koerner or Ray perform."

I nodded. "I'd love to."

He nodded.

"Would you like my phone number?"

"Oh, yeah." He pulled the paper out of his pocket, spread it out in front of him on the bar and asked if I had a pen.

I rummaged through my purse and found one. He wrote my number at the top of his list of songs, returned the pen and looked down at the number again. I laid my hand on his and, as he looked at me, said, "Please don't lose it." We gazed at one another, until I felt the eyes of my friends on me. I said, "Well, I'd better go." Just as I started to turn away from him, he touched my arm, a touch so gentle it felt like a caress, and I looked back at him, at his radiant eyes. He said, "I'll call you tomorrow."

His smile, his voice and his haunting lyrics stayed with me that night, and I fell asleep happy, dreaming of him. Fell into a deep sleep... unlike so many nights in that house, a dark space that echoed with anxiety and fear. Even when I was little, I'd wake up and find myself staring at the ceiling, or at a dark form that made me feel afraid and that I'd realize after a minute was just the chest of drawers, or at the closed door I'd watch out of fear that it would open. I'd lie still, listening to the silence, feeling alone, even more alone than I did during the day, when I could watch *The Flintstones* or *Mister Rogers*, or read about Madeline and Pepito, or Eloise in Moscow or Paris, or play with my doll, Amy, with the long blonde hair. And sometimes, as I lay there listening, I'd hear Mother's voice and remember conversations she'd had with friends on the phone, or smoking and drinking coffee with them at the kitchen table, and she'd talk about the life she'd have someday, when she and Daddy would be able to travel, go to places like London or Rome, once the last of her kids would be grown up and gone, and I'd feel her eyes fix on me and hear her sigh, as if she were disappointed to find I was still there, still hampering her life. Or I'd hear her comments about my brothers, about the older one playing on his high school football, basketball, and baseball teams. Such a talented boy, everyone liked him, and, oh, he was going to go to the U, get his degree and join his father's business. And the younger one, he looked like he'd follow in his brother's footsteps. She could go on and on about my brothers, but she rarely talked about me. Or to me. At night, she'd tuck me in, read to me, even kiss me on the forehead and then turn away, without looking at me, at my eyes fixed on her. Her mind was somewhere else. She was just being a mother.

That was when I still called my parents Mama and Daddy, still hoped they loved me. But I didn't talk much to them. Instead, I'd talk in my head, or to Amy. I'd hold her, facing me, look into her blue eyes and say, "Do you love me?" And I'd whisper, "Of course I love you." And I'd say, "Why?" And she'd say, "Because you're the best little girl in the whole world." "Does Mama love me? Does Daddy love me?" And Amy would always tell me, "Yes, of course they do."

I talked with Amy about my brothers, too… the way they treated me... like that day on the farm. I was about six, and my brothers about twelve and fourteen, when Mama and Daddy took us there. I was in the house with my parents and grandparents, who were watching television and talking about stuff that meant nothing to me. I got bored talking to Amy, or looking out the window at the trees that lined the gravel driveway and the field on the other side, so I set her down on the windowsill and walked outside. No one looked away from what they were doing to yell, Hey, where are you going? So, I kept going. I pulled myself up onto the wooden seat of the lone swing that hung from a limb of the gnarled old tree in the yard and stretched and pumped with my legs, until I could feel my hair drifting away from my neck as I reached with my feet for the sky. The sun was bright, the day still, and I could hear birds chirping.

I noticed my brothers a hundred feet away, BB guns in their hands, their heads bowed. They were kicking through the tall grass near a barbed wire fence, searching for something. I wondered what it could be. I stopped pumping and, when the swing came to a near stop, slid off the seat and walked toward the fence. Still wearing the dress Mother had put on me for church, I kept my eyes fixed on the grass that brushed against my skin, anxious about what might be crawling or scurrying around down there. I neared the fence and looked up to see a snake hanging limp by its tail from a post, its body shredded and its head gone. I looked off to where my brothers were poking through the grass. One of them stomped the ground, and stomped again and again, pursuing something. And then he stopped, and the other brother bent over to pick something up—a garter snake that he held by the neck, turning its head so they could look at its face and cackle. They rushed through the grass to a fence post and leaned their guns against the wire. One of them pressed the snake's tail against the post, and the other hammered a nail through the tail, and they pointed at the snake, joked and laughed as it writhed. They picked up their guns, backed off and, as the snake whipped its head one way and another, shot at it and continued shooting until it hung lifeless. I followed them as they walked over to the post. One of them lifted the limp head in his hand, the shredded body barely hanging together, and they both started laughing.

As I stared, shocked by their cruelty, they noticed me and asked what I was doing there. One of them said, "You think she can run fast enough to get away?"

The other one grinned. "Let's find out."

"Hey Helen, let's see how fast you can run. Come on."

They raised their guns, pointed them at me, and one of them said, "You better run, little girl. Better run, run, run. Come on." And he shot his gun at me. He didn't hit me, but I was scared and backed up. He shot again, and I turned, ran and felt the sting of the BBs hit my back and my butt, while hearing my brothers laugh, and by the time I ran into the house, I was sobbing. My parents and grandparents stopped whatever they were doing and stared at me. I froze, and my breath caught as I looked back at them through the mist of my tears.

Mama said, "What's the matter?" She said those words in the same tone of voice she would've used if she'd said, What is it now?

Before I could respond to those blank stares, the screen door slammed, and I turned and saw my brothers looking at me and at my parents and grandparents, and then at one another, acting as if they were wondering what could be going on.

Mother asked, "Why are you crying?"

Between my hiccupped sobs I said, "They shot me."

One of my brothers cried, "No, we didn't. We wouldn't do that."

And the other one said, "We pretended we were going to shoot at her and told her she'd better run home. We just didn't want her coming with us, that's all."

"Yeah, that's all."

Mama looked at me, shook her head, opened her arms and said, "Come here." The tone of her voice almost duped me into believing she pitied me, but her heavy sigh made it clear it was my brothers she believed, not me.

I ran upstairs and threw myself on the bed. I knew all Mother would do if I'd gone to her was say, Everything will be all right. Now just stop crying. That was always her response. Everything will be all right. All I needed to do was shut up. I thought about that as I lay on the bed, whimpering, and my feelings changed from hurt, really hurt, to anger and resentment. A while later, Mother called me downstairs for dinner. I sat next to one of my brothers. When no one was watching, he looked down at me and smirked. And they both sneered at me a few times that night, on our way home, when we sat in the backseat of the car, with me in the middle. But, once it got dark, they looked out their windows and left me alone with my feelings.

What happened during the day must've returned to me in my sleep that night, because when I woke up in the morning, I felt so... so sad... The only word I knew to describe my feelings. Today, I'd probably say depressed... How common is depression for a six-year-old?... I went downstairs for breakfast. Mama was leaning back in her chair, at one end of the kitchen table, reading the paper and smoking, her coffee cup nearby. The boys' cereal bowls were still clean, so they hadn't come down yet. I walked over to my place, next to hers. She glanced at me, said good morning, and went back to reading her paper. I sat down, looked at the boxes of cereal, selected one and filled my bowl. I noticed a paring knife and a half-eaten banana lying next to Mother's bowl. I stared at the banana for a while.

"Mama."

She looked over at me.

"Can I have some banana?"

She followed my eyes to the banana, sighed, put her cigarette on the ashtray, pulled my bowl toward her, sliced the fruit onto the cereal, placed the bowl back in front of me and picked up her cigarette and her paper. I started eating the cereal, while staring at the knife, wondering, What was it like to cut something? I'd never cut anything. Never even held a sharp knife. I was still eating, when she stubbed her cigarette out and went downstairs. Hearing the doors to the washer and dryer open and slam shut, I got up, went around to her place, took the knife, and ran the tip of my finger up and down the blade, feeling how sharp it was. And then I gently ran the blade across the inside of my wrist, and ran it again, and again, each time applying a little more pressure, to see if it would hurt. At first, it didn't. But with the fifth or sixth try, the blade sliced my skin, and I felt a stinging sensation as a thin streak of blood appeared. I stared at it. The sting disappeared, and, instead of pain, I felt relief. I felt better than I had when I'd wakened. I learned that the pain of the cutting is always less than the pain that triggered it. I gazed at the blood. When I heard Mother climbing the stairs, I licked the blade clean, went upstairs to the bathroom, closed and locked the door, and sat on the toilet and held toilet paper to my wrist until the bleeding stopped.

* * *

Wanting something to warm me, someone to hold me and make me feel loved, I stand up and walk down the hall, turn into the dining room and then the foyer, stop in front of the closet, open the door and scan the coats hanging in front of me. I push a clump of them aside, the hangers grating on the rod, and another clump, until I come to Mother's fur coat, the only thing of hers I wanted when she and Father decided to downsize and buy an apartment. I wrap it around me and pull the red fox fur, with its long, silky hairs and soft, dense underfur, pull it close to my neck, so its softness touches my face and caresses my skin, as I raise and lower my chin and rotate my head. The warmth of the fur feels like love, just as it did when I was little, when Mother would be gone, and I'd get her coat out of the closet, wrap myself from head to toe in it and feel as if all the love missing in my life had wrapped itself around me. I feel so good I hum, purr like a cat and recite the line from one of Mary Oliver's poems, "'You only have to let the soft animal of your body love what it loves.'"

I close the closet door and see myself in the mirror, see the happiness in my smile. Feeling playful, I strike a pose, thrusting my chest forward and looking to the side, while glancing back at the mirror and seeing my face in profile. There's something about wearing a fur coat that makes me want to behave like a model. Or like Mother. When I was little, I'd stand in the entrance to her bedroom and watch her looking at herself in the mirror of her vanity, tapping powder on her cheeks, applying eyeshadow, penciling her eyebrows and brushing her lashes with mascara to create the dark, romantic eyes that complemented her blonde bombshell look. And she'd layer her lips with lipstick that matched the polish on her fingernails, put on a gold necklace and matching earrings, and then turn her head and peer from different angles at her face and the necklace on her chest, the upper part of her breasts revealed by her low-cut black dress. She'd get up and walk toward me, as I stood in the doorway, maybe looking down at me as she passed, maybe giving me a faint smile, patting my head, or ignoring me. I'd turn and follow her down the hall and through the living room to the foyer, where she'd open the closet door, put on the soft, warm red fox fur, close the door and gaze at herself in the mirror. And then she'd turn her head to the side, while looking at the reflection of her face in profile, and raise her chin, as if she were being photographed for a fashion magazine. Father might appear, wrap his arms around her and kiss her. He was so proud of her in this coat, as she brandished his success by strutting around in it. Wow, he had the money to buy his wife a fur! It wasn't mink, sable, or silver fox, but still, red fox was more expensive and classier than most furs. I shake my head as I gaze at the mirror and think of the animals that had died, the horrendous way they'd been killed and flayed, so Father and Mother could buy their skins to flaunt their status.

Of course, they wanted their sons to be successful and be able to give their wives fur coats, too. Father liked to talk about being the first in his family to go to college, thanks to the G.I. Bill, and the first to start his own business—an insurance office. He wanted his boys to follow in his footsteps, get a college education, join him as partners, and get married and have a family. And if one of the boys were to meet a woman in college and make her his bride, well, that would be wonderful. "But," Father said once, as he paused while repeating his spiel to smile down at me, "a woman certainly doesn't need a college education to get married and have children. Look at your mother. She's done just fine. Better than fine. All you need to do is find a man who can earn a good living and support you." And he looked at Mother and said, nodding toward me, "She certainly doesn't need a college education to be in the family way." Mother grinned and shook her head, and one of my brothers said, "I don't think they even offer a course on getting pregnant," and the other chimed in, "But she can always get an MRS," and everyone laughed but me. Yeah, I think, as I shake my head. I become aware of the mirror and see the look of disgust on my face, all a woman needed to be happy was a prick and a fur coat.

I continue staring at my face. I try smiling, but can't. I'd like to feel I'm a better mother than she was, but sometimes I wonder. I turn away from the mirror, go into the living room, plop onto one of the armchairs, glance down, notice my sleeves have ridden up enough to reveal my wrists and turn them over to look at the inside and the scars and wonder, What kind of a mother have I been for my kids? I pull one of the sleeves up my forearm to my elbow and gaze at the scars. A record of my life, of my desire to be loved and of the pain I've felt when I knew I wasn't worthy of being loved. Yes, the pain that precipitates cutting is so much worse than the pain of the cutting itself. I can't talk about that with my kids. When Mandy and I would sit squeezed together in this armchair as I read to her, she'd stare at the scars if my forearms weren't covered, and I'd turn them downward. A few months ago, she traced one with her fingertip and asked how I got it. I smiled and answered, "Oh, I just cut myself," as if the cut had been an accident, nothing more. Sometimes, at the kitchen table, or when I'd be giving her a towel after her bath, or tucking her in at night, I'd see her staring at the scars and pretend not to notice. She'd look up at me and follow me with her eyes, and I knew she was wondering, What are you hiding? What kind of mother are you? Her eyes still follow me, still fix on the scars any time they show. Someday, she's going to ask about them again, and she'll want more than, Oh, I just cut myself. She'll want the history they've recorded.

And I'll have to tell her about the family I grew up in, about her grandparents and the two uncles she rarely sees, and the way they treated me. I'll tell her about the Catholic grade school and high school I attended, about wearing a uniform, marching in line, getting indoctrinated in religion every year, learning how to behave, how to be a good girl, a girl who went to confession every Saturday and Mass every Sunday, and who worked hard and got good grades, said and did the right things, gave smiles and hugs, and always tried to appear happy, because if I didn't, I might hurt my parents' feelings, might make them feel I wasn't grateful for all they'd done for me, for my proper education and upbringing. And what do you do with an ungrateful child? Well, you look her in the eye and tell her she's an ungrateful little thing, has no appreciation for all that she's been given, how dare she behave like that, with that smirk on her face, and you slap her, you smack that smirk right off her lips. And if she still has the gall to look back at you, look you in the eye like she thinks she knows more than you, like she looks down on you, despises you, well, then you whack her so hard you knock that look off her face and that thought out of her head and you teach her a lesson. You teach her to respect you.

That's how I learned to be proper. And to conceal myself. And be alone within myself. And as I didn't enjoy watching television in the living room with my parents and brothers, I spent much of my time alone in my room, reading books, mostly stories about girls and women—*Little Women, Jane Eyre, Emma, To Kill a Mockingbird.*

But in the spring of my first year in high school, some of my girlfriends and I participated in an anti-war demonstration, chanting,

"'Hey, hey, LBJ, how many kids did you kill today?'" And when Mama and Daddy found out, they were furious. They called me a peacenik and said people like me were disloyal to the country. Look at your brothers, they'd say. Can you imagine them doing something like that—demonstrating against their own country? Of course, my brothers had deferments all the way through college, and married and had kids soon after, so my parents didn't worry about them getting sent off to the war.

When I was a sophomore, the burgeoning woman in me split open the husk of the proper little girl, and I started expressing my thoughts in school, questioning things like the virgin birth and a sexless Christ, and proclaiming that the Vietnam War was based on lies, and Tricky Dick was an even bigger liar than LBJ and people were dying because of their lies. The nuns branded me a rebel, and at the end of the year, my parents met with the principal, and then informed me I'd shamed them and didn't deserve to go back to that school in the fall, I'd be going to the public school, as if that were a punishment. That was about the time I started calling my parents Mother and Father, instead of Mama and Daddy.

That summer I got the cashier job, so I wouldn't have to ask them for money, and in the evenings I went out with Debbie, whose parents had also been informed she wasn't allowed to return to the Catholic school, and we'd sneak booze out of our parents' liquor cabinets, or get older friends to buy us whiskey or gin, and go to drive-ins, motels, and the houses of friends whose parents were gone, and drink, smoke, party, and have sex with boys. By then I'd chosen to be deflowered and would go with the boys, toe to toe, nose to nose, and let them know what I wanted. I talked more freely at home, too, saying things like, "Women should be able to dress the way they want, and not how men want them to, and they shouldn't have to wear bras if they don't want to," and Mother would slap me and sneer at me, and I'd stay in my room and read books, like *Anna Karenina, The Bell Jar, Ariel,* and *I Know Why the Caged Bird Sings.* Everyone saw me as a rebel, a peacenik, and a hippie, but inside there was still the child who felt unworthy of being loved and found relief by cutting herself. And then Vince came into my life.

I hum and roll my head to feel the warm fur caress my cheeks as I smile at the thought of him. I'd already fallen for him by the time we went out on our first date. I let him in the front door, and Mother looked askance at his hippie hair and Bob Dylan T-shirt and glared at me when she noticed I wasn't wearing a bra. I led him out before she could do anything to ruin our evening, got into his black Chevy, and looked back and saw her in the picture window, staring at us. When he got in the car, I said, "Let's get out of here." He looked at me, startled, and I said, "Let's go!" After we pulled away, I explained that Mother hated peaceniks and hippies, and I didn't like the way she stared at my friends. I don't remember what film we saw at the drive-in, because we spent most of our time talking and making love. I'd been dreaming of making love with him, so, after a lot of kissing and caressing, I unbuttoned his shirt, unzipped his pants, and lived my dream.

Nearly every evening that I didn't work, he'd come by the house to pick me up, and I'd be ready to go out to the car, so he wouldn't have to deal with my parents. And if I was working, he'd pick me up at the supermarket at the end of my shift. We'd go to a drive-in movie, or to the Triangle, where we'd drink and listen to music, and every once in a while, he'd get a gig there, or somewhere else, and I'd be part of his audience, and he'd look at me as if he were performing for me and his voice would carry me off. Sometimes, we'd just go to his place, a one-bedroom duplex in an old sagging, two-story house, walking-distance to the Triangle and a lot of other bars. He'd furnished it with stuff he'd gotten for little or nothing—the mattress at the Salvation Army, the old couch he'd found by the curb in the neighborhood, and the wooden display shelves he'd discovered on a sidewalk, in front of a nearby retail store that was renovating. A friend had helped him lug the shelves home, and Vince had stood his LPs and his books on the bottom shelf, piled his papers and notebooks and some of his clothes on the second, and set his turntable and the picture of him performing alone at the Triangle on the third. We often hung out there, sitting on the couch and talking, or lying on the mattress and making love. After we'd come, we'd talk and smoke, and I'd trace designs with my fingernails on his chest and belly, until he'd get erect and we'd make love again.

We'd started seeing one another a few weeks before I graduated high school and, during that time, I'd come home late, after everyone was in bed, and the next day Mother would confront me, demanding, "Where were you? What have you been up to? Who do you think you are?" And she'd get frustrated with my answers, if I gave any, and say, "You listen here, young lady. If you want to continue living in this house—" And I'd stomp off to my room, and she'd pursue me, shouting, "Don't you walk away from me!" And I'd slam the door, and she'd barge in and insist I listen to what she had to say, and I'd glare at her and, when she'd finish, I'd ask, "Are you done?" And then I'd claim I had homework to do, or I had to get ready for school, or go to work.

What I was really getting ready to do was to leave. For good. That summer, on a Sunday, a few days after my eighteenth birthday, I sat in an armchair in the living room, reading *The Female Eunuch*, occasionally glancing out the picture window. Mother sat on another armchair, knitting, and Father sat on the couch, leaning toward the coffee table, where he'd spread the newspaper. When I saw Vince's car pull to a stop in front of the house, I went to my room, slung my purse over my shoulder, grabbed my suitcase, and walked through the living room, while my parents stared at me. I picked up my book, opened the door, paused to look back at them, their mouths agape, and said, "I'll come back someday for the rest of my things," and left. Vince got out of the car, came around, opened the back door, wrapped his arm around my back and kissed me, and I tossed my suitcase and book on the seat, got in the front and looked at the house, where my parents stood on the steps, gawking at me. I didn't wave, didn't smile, just stared back at them, feeling no regrets, no fear. I moved in with Vince, expecting we'd be happy together...

* * *

When the two of us were in the apartment, we'd often sit at the table in the dining room, and Vince would compose songs, writing the lyrics in a notebook, pausing to lift his guitar off the table, pick a few chords and sing the lyrics to himself in a whispery voice as he gazed off, listening, and then set the guitar back down, grab his pen and continue his composition, and I'd sit on the other side of the table, reading, or trying to write a poem, thinking I was the next Sylvia Plath. I'd never had a relationship like that, the two of us being close to one another as we each did our own thing, sometimes for hours, and had never felt such a strong attraction for anyone before. His lyrics, the way he sang them, it was like he'd composed the music as an accompaniment to my life. Like he understood who I was, what I'd lived through and the feelings I'd kept hidden. And when he'd lean back and take a break, we'd start talking, and I'd do something I normally didn't do—I'd open up about growing up in a family that didn't love me, with a mother who probably wished I'd never been born and might've had an abortion if she hadn't been so subservient to the Church, and a father for whom I didn't exist, and my dear brothers, who'd left home years before me to go to college, get married, have kids, work in my father's business, and buy their wives fur coats, and who'd been so cruel, they probably would've shot me again if they hadn't received .22 caliber rifles for Christmas and indulged themselves instead in the thrill of killing rabbits, squirrels, and who knows what else.

The more I opened myself up to Vince, the more he opened himself up to me, telling me about his family, and how, when he was a little boy, he'd hear his father in the late afternoon close the door of their apartment, and he'd run into the living room screaming, "Daddy!" and throw his arms around his legs, and his father would pick him up and toss him in the air, and Vince would shriek with joy as he fell into his father's arms. And, when he was a little older, he'd walk into the living room and say, "Hi Dad," and grin, happy, because he knew his father had finished attending classes and studying at the U for the day, and they could go out in the yard behind the apartment building and throw a baseball back and forth or kick a soccer ball.

But then things started to change. He'd wake up at night to the sound of angry voices coming from his parents' room, the voices sometimes shrieking, and then hushing. Then arguments started to erupt during dinner, and his parents would scream at one another about the cost of his father going to medical school and the stress on his mother of having to support the family, and Vince would focus all his attention on a little toy soldier he'd brought to the table. And then his parents divorced. And Vince became an angry kid, who loved to break things. And when he was about thirteen, he got drunk for the first time. He loved getting drunk. Didn't feel any pain. All the hurt was gone. He just wanted to drink and drink and leave it all behind. As he told me once, "Just fucking fly and soar above all of life's shit."

One night, we were sitting on the couch and, after a rambling monologue about my father, I said, "He wasn't mean to me. Just indifferent. Pretty much left me in my mother's hands. After all, I didn't have a prick, I wasn't going to have a career in his business, and I didn't need to buy a fur coat for a wife."

Vince nodded, humphed, and mumbled, "Fathers," and shook his head. I looked at him and saw his jaw had clenched. He stared straight ahead for a while, then told me that after the divorce, his father moved to New York and worked at a clinic in upper Manhattan. So after Vince graduated high school, he used some of the money he'd saved for college to fly to New York and stay at a YMCA. He went to the clinic and told the receptionist he'd like to see Dr. Walker, that Dr. Walker was his father. The receptionist left and, when she returned, she told Vince his father would be out soon and he could sit down. When his father appeared, he didn't seem to see Vince until he stood up. And then his father came over, studied his face and said, "Vincent?" Vince nodded. And his father asked him what he could do for him. Vince told his father he didn't know what he could do for him. When his father tried to lay his hand on Vince's shoulder, Vince pulled away. His father looked scared. He took a business card out of his pocket, wrote his phone number on the back, gave it to him and told him to call him that night, he had to get back to his patients. When Vince called, his father invited him over to his house the next afternoon.

Vince remembered standing in the foyer of the house, when his father's wife and their little boy appeared. The way the wife looked Vince over, he could tell she knew all about him. She guided the boy out the door, as he waved, "Goodbye, Daddy." Daddy smiled. The door closed, and Vince and his father stood there, looking at one another. His father led him into the living room, and they sat down and talked. When Vince told him he was going to the U in the fall, his father said, "Well, if you need help with money—" Vince cut him off, told him he didn't need his help. His father asked him what he wanted to talk about, and Vince said, "Why didn't you ever contact me? Did you ever wonder how I was? What happened to me?" His father just talked about all the stress he went through with the separation and divorce while he was in med school, and then the move to New York. He said he was sorry.

Vince reminded him of the life they'd had before the fighting, the separation, and the divorce and how much he missed that father. His father just said it wasn't easy for him, either. And then he asked Vince what he wanted, and Vince said, "I want us to get together again and be close." His father told him he was happy to help him with money for school, or for something else, if he needed help, but he wasn't letting the past back into his life.

Vince said, "So you're happy to pay me to stay away. Is that what you're saying?"

"If that's how you want to interpret what I'm saying, then, yeah, I'm happy to pay you to stay away."

And then Vince exploded, swore at him and ran out of the house. And never spoke to him again.

Tears flowed down Vince's cheeks as I climbed onto the couch, sat on my folded legs, and put my arms around him and pulled him toward me. He rested his head on my chest, and his body trembled as he sobbed.

As Vince came to trust me more, he'd repeat the story about the father who'd pay him to stay away… or allude to it in our conversations... or fall silent, and I could tell he was thinking about it. It was always with him. And with me, too. I identified with him, with his pain, to the point that his story became mine. Maybe that's why I loved him.

* * *

Vince told me other stories at the table, a bottle of Jack in the center, a glass in his hand resting near his notebook and guitar, and a glass in mine, near my sketchpad, the two of us drinking 'til all we could do was stagger into our room, fall into bed and make love, if we weren't too drunk. Some of the stories had to do with leaving both of his fathers behind. The second father was a businessman his mother married a few years after the divorce. She had two kids with him. He had money and a rambler in a suburb, and Vince suspected that had a lot to do with his mother's decision to marry the guy, because she wanted a good home for herself and her son. Vince despised him. He'd sneer with contempt as he'd repeat a comment his stepfather had made to him once, when he was trying to be funny, "Women, they're all the same upside down." That was how the man treated Vince's mother, like a sex object, casually sliding his hand across her breasts or her ass, and she'd look around, blushing, to see if her children were watching. The stepfather had a volatile temper and was quick to whack any of the kids who misbehaved, and Vince seemed to get caught misbehaving far more often than the other two. And if he should cry, the stepfather would say something like "Aw, look at the baby cry."

Vince's way out was music. His mother helped him with presents she'd give him for his birthday and Christmas, presents she'd say were from her and his dad. Vince knew the money might've come from his stepfather, but not the love. She bought Vince a turntable that played LPs, and then a guitar, a cheap one, and then a nicer one, and so on. And he'd spend nearly all his time at home in his room, listening to music, teaching himself to play guitar, writing songs, and staying away from his stepfather. When he was old enough, he got a part-time job so he could buy more records and take lessons, and by the time he graduated high school, he was an accomplished musician and songwriter. He left home, got an apartment on the West Bank, started classes at the U, and returned home only when he knew his stepfather wouldn't be there.

Vince and I would drink, talk about our families, get low and drink some more to forget. And in the middle of the night, I might wake up, or maybe I'd dream, and feel like I was walking down a dark hallway, anxious about what was ahead, and the hall would turn, and turn again, and again, like in a maze, and I'd see light from an open doorway, and walk toward it, wondering if I should continue, or turn around and run. Or I might find myself standing in the doorway and looking at Mama, sitting at her vanity, gazing at herself in the mirror; or see myself on the couch in the living room, wrapped up in Mama's fur coat, in the warmth of the love I so desired, whimpering as I hear her screaming that I'm never to take that coat out of the closet. "Do you hear? Never!" Or I might see Mama hitting me with a wooden yardstick as I cringe, beating me as if I weren't any more important to her than the pigs on her parents' farm. Or the door might open onto a dark room, and I'd see myself lying in bed, staring at the ceiling, hurt, sad, unable to sleep. Or I might go running down one of those halls, running away from someone shouting at me and into a room where Mama's sitting, and throw myself onto her lap, and try to hug her, as she looks past me at whomever I'm running from, and feel her body stiffen as she pushes me away, and hear Daddy say, "Now what's the matter? There's always something going on with that kid."

And sometimes I'd feel there were no halls, just a space that might expand and go on forever, an immense, vacuous space, in which I'm alone, and there's no love, nothing to contain me, to hold me, and the echoes of voices crying, or whimpering and whispering, would come from an unfathomable distance. Or the space might contract, walls close in around me, and I'd hear voices say things like, "Oh, just grow up and be a big girl and stop your whining, you worthless little thing, worthless little thing, worthless little thing." And the walls closing in on me compressed this absence of love, this feeling of unworthiness, until the blood in my head throbbed like the veins would burst and I'd clutch Amy close to me.

I might've left the house in which I'd grown up, but I hadn't left it behind. It came with me. When the night would fade and morning arrive, I'd lie awake next to Vince, and remnants of memories might return, and the feelings would stay with me, and I'd get up and they'd still be with me, sometimes for days.

* * *

One Sunday morning, not long before the beginning of fall classes at the University, dreams had troubled my sleep and clouded my mind. I opened my eyes and stared at the ceiling in the gray darkness of the room, lit by slivers of daylight, from the sides of the window shades. Finally, I sighed, giving up hope of getting any rest, and extended my hand toward Vince's side of the bed and discovered him gone. I lay still, wishing I could sleep. I finally got up, put on my bathrobe and walked past the bathroom to the kitchen, where I saw the red light glowing on the coffeepot stand. I poured myself a cup and went into the dining room, where Vince sat, his elbows resting on the table, his chin on his intertwined fingers, his long hair covering the side of his face, his eyes staring at a point beyond the open notebook in front of him. He didn't respond to my presence. I waited, but he didn't even look at me. I went into the living room, sat down on the armchair and gazed through the windows at the sidewalk, at the cars parked in the street, and at the houses with their sloping roofs and porches on the other side. What was I going to do? Try to talk with him? Write? Read? Draw? Make breakfast? Everything seemed a waste of... whatever. I had no desire. Maybe I could just sit there for the day, staring out the window, my mind sinking into a dark place inside myself. But I couldn't take it anymore. I rushed past Vince, who was frowning at his notebook, his head resting on his fist, his elbow on the table, his other hand tapping the surface with a pen. I slammed the cup on the kitchen counter, went into the bedroom, yanked one of the shades up so I could see, found my jeans, threw my robe onto the bed, indifferent to anyone who might see me through the window in just my underpants, and pulled on my pants and a T-shirt and left, slamming the door behind me.

I walked down the sidewalk, my head bent, wondering, Why do I love him? He can't see beyond himself. He writes those songs that make me feel he knows what it is to be me, but he's so fucked-up, he's not even aware I'm there, right next to him. I thought I needed to be in a relationship with someone who knows what it's like to be me, but he's so obsessed with himself. This is all a mistake. I need to get out. I raised my head as I walked past Savran's Bookstore on Cedar Avenue and turned at the corner onto the street that heads toward Wilson Library, rehashing the same thoughts, not finding any clarity, looking up at the trees that line the street as the wind blew the limbs. I continued past the university library out onto the top of the double-deck bridge across the Mississippi, looking over the railing at the river far below. A gust of wind whipped me, and I bent my head, crossed my forearms over my chest and grasped my upper arms. A stronger gust hit me, and I turned, stopped, huddled against the railing and looked down at the river, its surging black waves frothing at the end of each burst. As I stared at the waves, something in the rhythm and endless repetition of their surge and collapse hypnotized me, dissipated the clouds in my mind and filled me with a strange kind of peace. Gazing at the waves, lulled by the rhythm of their flow, I felt so calm... like I could just let myself go... and fall and feel peace... forever.

I was probably standing within a few feet of where John Berryman would stand four months later, the day he lifted himself onto the railing, waved to the people staring at him, and jumped... and found peace... It was just a couple months before he killed himself that I stopped by during his office hours to tell him how much I loved his poetry, to try to talk to him about my poems and to ask him if he would like to read them. I only had a few. I'd started writing poetry about a year before, but, working at the library while being a full-time student, I had little time to write. I was anxious, wondering, What in the hell was I thinking, coming to the office of this great poet? Why would he want to read my poems? I was shocked when this icon of the confessional poets, with his scraggly grayish beard, smiled and said, "Yes, let me look at them." I took them out of a folder and handed them to him, and he leaned back in his chair and read them, smoking his cigarette, sometimes arching his brows above his glasses, or nodding his head, as if he were agreeing with what I'd written. He handed them back to me and said, "There's always something, or someone, haunting your character." I nodded. And he said, "This is very good work. Keep on writing." I told him I couldn't wait to take one of his courses, but, unfortunately, I was in my first year at the University and couldn't register for one of them until next year. He told me he was looking forward to working with me. I left his office, ecstatic, feeling I'd found my way. And then a couple months later, he jumped off the bridge.

I continued staring at the river, until I no longer felt hypnotized by its flow. The rest of the world around me began to reenter my conscious mind, and I started walking back. The wind had died, the day was getting warmer, and it felt good to walk among people and hear cheerful voices. When I reached Savran's, with the amusing wall painting next to the door of the life-size Jewish man, in a heavy black coat, with a big black beard, black hat, black-rimmed spectacles and a white face, holding a book in his hands, looking as if he were welcoming book lovers, I decided to duck in and browse. I leafed through the novels and books of poetry by writers from all over the country and other parts of the world, and by local writers, and came across a copy of *The Dream Songs*. There was just one left on the shelf. I decided I wanted my own copy, instead of continuing to check one out from the library, so I could always have it close to me. I had little money, but I bought the book... *The Dream Songs*... I loved the title.

I was expecting to see Vince at the table when I got home and was relieved to find he wasn't. Nor was he in our bedroom. I remembered he had to work at that music store, the Electric Fetus, and wouldn't be home before six, so I wouldn't have to put up with his self-infatuation. I set the book on the table, made lunch, sat down and read some of the poems, but ended up staring at Vince's notebook, pen, and guitar. He always seemed to benefit somehow from the kinds of feelings that pulled me down. He didn't have it all that bad. His mother must've loved him, even though she didn't communicate often with him, or he with her. Why else would she have given him the record player and the guitars? But he always seemed to feel sorry for himself. Feeling the need to express my feelings, I got my notebook and pen out of our room, returned to the table and tried to write a poem, but what I composed didn't really express the feelings that had driven me to the bridge. Not in the way I wanted. I ripped out the page on which I'd written and crumpled it into a ball. Plath didn't need to worry about me ever knocking her off her throne as the greatest woman poet of the century. But dead people never have to worry. I got up, went into our room, pulled *Ariel* out from the pile of books on my side of the bed, lay down and tried to read a few poems, but nothing fit my mood. My mind wandered, and I drifted off.

* * *

The sound of a door slamming startled me awake. I gasped and, after a few beats, realized I'd been sleeping. I listened to Vince move around the apartment. I got up and went to the dining room, where I saw him standing by the table, a nearly empty glass of whiskey in one hand, the notebook with his songs in the other. He finally noticed me, dropped the notebook onto the table, next to a bottle of Jack, took a drink, stared at me and asked, "What happened to you this morning?"

I didn't bother to answer him. I went to the kitchen, got a glass, returned to the dining room, poured myself some Jack, and took a drink.

He refilled his glass. "Well?"

I took another drink. "I didn't feel well."

"Yeah. The amount of whiskey you drank last night."

"Didn't drink as much as you. Anyway, it wasn't that." I took another drink, paused and stared in the direction of the living room, thinking about the morning. "I had some weird dreams. Woke up a couple times and had a hard time getting back to sleep." I looked at him. He was staring at his notebook on the table. "You're not even paying attention."

"Sorry." He looked at me and sighed. "I didn't have a very good morning. Woke up with what I thought was a song in my head and worked on the damn thing until I had to leave. Didn't get anywhere." He took a drink.

"You will. You always do." I heard the resentment in my voice. I thought about the poem I'd tried writing, and that came to the same end many of my poems did—a crumpled ball of paper. I took a drink.

"You sound angry," he said.

"Oh, yeah? What could I possibly be angry about?"

"You tell me."

I felt disgusted and shook my head. I walked away from him and into the living room and sat down on the couch. He followed me, sat down at the other end, set the bottle he'd brought with him on the floor, turned toward me, pulled his feet up on the cushion and took a drink. I felt like leaving.

"So," he said, "what's going on?"

"What do you mean?"

"What are you angry about?"

I was going to take a drink, noticed my glass was empty, and extended it toward him. He picked up the bottle and refilled my glass and his.

I stared off, feeling irritated by his question. "Sometimes I think you don't give a shit about me."

"That's not true."

"I felt down this morning. Alone. Depressed. And you totally ignored me. Wrapped up in yourself, as always."

"Sorry. I was trying to write a song."

"Couldn't pay attention to me?"

"What were you so depressed about?"

"Now you want to know?"

"Yeah, I want to know."

I took a deep breath and sighed. "I can't remember the dreams. I just remember the feeling they left me with. Not being loved, not being worthy of love. Always the same old shit."

He set his glass on the floor, slid over next to me, put his arm around my shoulder and pulled me toward him, and I let my body lean into his.

Tears trickled down my face. I wiped them away, feeling relieved and happy to be held, and lay my head on his chest, until there were no more tears, and my body had begun to ache from leaning. I pulled away and sat up, and he leaned toward me and kissed me, and I smiled as he pulled back. And then I remembered what he'd said about his frustration at not being able to finish his song and asked, "The song you were working on this morning, what's it about? You remember any of the lyrics?"

"Oh, I remember a hodgepodge of lines. I was going to call it, 'Drink up, my love.' Some of the lines went, 'Drink up, my love, and let's forget the pain of going home. Drink up, my love, and let's forget the feeling of being alone. Drink up, my love and…'

and so on. A lot of lines that went nowhere. That was the problem. It just seemed to repeat the same old shit."

"I assume I'm the 'love' in your song, so I guess I should drink up."

He chuckled and raised his glass to me. We drank, and then he refilled our glasses.

I felt a shift in my mood. Didn't say anything for a while, just thought about the lines. Finally, I said, "These things I need to forget, they must make you miserable, if you're asking me to forget them."

"The people in the song aren't necessarily us. They could be—"

"Oh, come on, Vince, you know damned well they're us."

"And it's not *you*, it's *us*. 'Let us forget.'"

"Well, it sounds like what I tell you about myself becomes a burden for you. But a burden that provides you with material for a song."

He gave me a suspicious look. "What are you getting at?"

"You're profiting from our relationship. Or from my problems."

"I'm not profiting."

"I'll get to listen to you perform songs about me at the Triangle. Or maybe on your LP. And maybe it'll sell really well. That's making a profit off me."

"Again, it's not just *you,* it's *us*."

"Yeah, well, why don't you just make it about *you*. Don't drag me into your shit."

"My songs are shit?"

"All your songs are about misery. Misery, misery, misery. You love to wallow in it. Maybe you should write a song to Miss Misery, a never-ending litany of all your shit."

"You told me before that my songs make you feel close to me."

"Maybe they did. But there's only so much crap anyone can take. I mean, they're sick."

"So, I'm sick?"

"You said it, I didn't."

His mouth hung open, and he shook his head, like he couldn't understand what the hell was happening. "Well, if I'm sick, why do you stay with me?"

I finished my whiskey, lifted the bottle off the floor, poured myself another glass, took a drink and said, "Because I'm fucking stupid."

Tears trickled down his cheeks. "Why don't you just fucking leave?"

"That's what I did this morning. I shouldn't have come back. Stupid! But there was nowhere for me to go, so I wasn't leaving." I looked at him, saw his tears, and shook my head. "You're such a baby. Never grew up."

I ridiculed and belittled him until I had him bawling. It felt so good to inflict pain and make him feel worthless. Because I knew that if I didn't make him feel worthless, if I didn't make him feel the pain I felt, if I didn't turn it on him, I was going to turn it on myself. I was going to attack myself, ridicule myself, and cut, and the deeper the pain, the greater the need for relief, and the deeper the cuts. The cuts that would bring the relief that felt so good, and I would smile as I bled and lost consciousness.

* * *

I become aware of myself in the living room and look down at the red fox fur covering my arms, at my wrists and forearms lying on the armrests and turned toward me, and at my scars, and I cringe at the memory of the vicious person I often became when I was drinking. That night, like many others, I slammed the bedroom door on him and told him to stay out, leave me alone, and I slept on the bed and he slept on the couch. There were days when *he'd* find ways to get revenge and ridicule me, and nights when *I'd* sleep on the couch. If we hadn't drunk the way we did, hadn't used booze to stoke the flames inside, hadn't inflicted so much pain on one another... If we'd been able to understand our pain and control our emotions, we might've been able to help one another. But we were just kids. I might've understood, at some level, that I was envious of him, of his success, which wasn't that much, but I hadn't had any, other than getting good grades and being admitted to college with a scholarship. I was obsessed by the idea that he was using me, but if I could've written some good poems that fed off his suffering, maybe I wouldn't have cared. We didn't help each other. I knew he was bad for me, knew the best thing to do was to stay away from him, and he probably knew the same. But we did the opposite of what was best. He was an addiction for me, as I was for him.

And then in April, he got an offer to perform every weekend for a month at the Triangle. He was ecstatic. I was, too. I loved to watch him perform, loved to feel proud of him, feel a little of his glory shine on me, and listen to my girlfriends tell me I was lucky to have a guy like him and hear the envy in their voices. The first Friday night, I invited some friends to join me at the Triangle. By the time my three girlfriends showed up, Vince was already sitting on stage and tuning his guitar in front of the mic. The bar, as always on a weekend night, was packed and raucous, but as soon as he began singing, the crowd fell silent and gazed at him as if they were hypnotized by his soft, thin voice. Between songs, one of my girlfriends told me again that I was so lucky to have such a talented man, the others chimed in and agreed with her, and they asked questions about what it was like to live with him, and I told them about how we'd work together at the table, and about his growing number of music friends, who'd come over sometimes with their instruments and they'd all play together, and about the bars where we'd listen to his friends perform, and the after-hours parties. And then Vince took a break, came over and joined us. My friends told him how beautiful they thought his music was and asked, "What made you want to become a composer? A musician? A singer? Will you be coming out with an album soon? What other gigs do you have coming up?" And all the while, I sat next to him, proud, glancing over and smiling at him as we remained squeezed together. And then he went back onstage.

The evening was going so well, and I was so happy, until, during a pause between songs, I noticed a woman, sitting at a table a few feet away, her eyes fixed on Vince. At first, I thought nothing of it. Women often gazed at him like that. But she rarely took her eyes off him to talk to the people at her table. By that time, the bar was full of thick clouds of smoke that had accumulated and created a haze, and beyond that haze sat Vince, who looked like he was endowed with an aura of pure light. When he finished his performance for the night, she got up, went to the edge of the stage, slipped some cash into his tip jar, looked up at him and said something. He smiled down at her and leaned forward, and they talked for a minute. And then he stood up, put his guitar in the case, picked up the tip jar and, carrying the case and the jar, walked toward the top of the stairs, while she walked parallel to him, looking up at him, waited for him at the bottom and then accompanied him to the bar, just as I had done eleven months before. He stood at the end of the bar, where I could see him in profile, and she sat around the corner, her back turned toward me and her head toward him, and I imagined her gazing at him, totally infatuated. He took the money out of the jar and, when the bartender came over, handed him the case and the jar, and the bartender went to prepare their drinks. Vince and the woman continued talking and, after the barman served them, started drinking.

I got up, threaded my way around the tables and the clusters of drinkers to the bar, stepped in between Vince and the woman, looked at him and said, "Hon, I loved your performance tonight."

He beamed and thanked me. And then he seemed to remember the other woman and said, "Oh, let me introduce you to... " He paused and said, "I'm sorry, what's your name?"

I looked the woman over, from her dark eyes and her long brown hair to her low-cut blouse and the points where her nipples projected, and arched my eyebrows, as if to say, *Who the fuck are you?*

She repeated her name to Vince, he completed the introduction, and she said, "I need to rejoin my friends." She glanced over at one of the tables and looked back at Vince. "It was wonderful talking to you, Vince. I'll be on the lookout for your album."

I watched her walk back to the table, sit down, and glance at us. Her eyes met mine, and she abruptly looked away. I stared at Vince. He was drinking his whiskey. I said, "She seemed very interested in you."

"Yeah. She came over to the stage and told me how much she loved my music. And guess what."

"What?"

"Someone put a five-dollar bill in the jar." He grinned. "Might've been her."

"Really? How about that." The tone of my voice caused him to look at me. "Maybe she's rich." I chuckled.

"Being able to put a five-dollar bill in a tip jar doesn't mean you're rich. What's going on, Helen?"

"Oh, I was just wondering if… "

"If I was attracted to her?"

"Yeah."

"The only girl I'm attracted to is you."

He wrapped his arm around me and pulled me close. I felt tears well up, felt like a fragile, stupid little girl. I looked up to see him smiling at me as his face drew close and he kissed me. He held me, we peered into one another's eyes, rubbed noses and laughed. And then we sat down with my friends. From time to time, I'd look off and see the woman was still there with her friends. The last time I looked, she was gone, and my anger and anxiety faded. I felt I could breathe, live, and have fun.

* * *

Bright lights jolted us. It was closing time. I was struck by the shabbiness of the bar—the filthy floor covered with drink stains and cigarette butts, and the dull paint peeling off the walls all the way to the ceiling.

Vince gave me a warm smile. "Hey, what do you say we go to a party and have some fun?"

After the tension that woman had caused, I needed some. I said, "I'd love to. Where is it?"

"At this weird place I've never taken you to before. It's hosted by a guy named Red. He's a real character. Used to be one of the owners of the Ten O'Clock Scholar, when it moved from the East Bank to the West Bank. He got to know all the musicians who performed there, even the ones who hung out at the Scholar before it moved. Like Dylan. So, when he throws a party, everyone shows up."

That was enough to make me want to go. We got into Vince's car, drove a few blocks, turned down a desolate street where all the buildings on one side had been torn down, leaving a barren space, while on the other stood narrow, wood-frame houses, with sloping roofs and porches, and not a light in any of them. No one anywhere, nothing but a few parked cars. We pulled to a stop and got out. Vince said, "It's over there," and pointed across the street at an old gray-stone building that rose from the ground like a huge tombstone, with two black windows on the second floor looking like dead eyes. Someone put a candle in one dead eye, and then in the other, and with the little glowing lights the eyes looked even more sinister. As we crossed the street and got closer to the building, I could see two huge doors on the main floor, in the center. We were about to enter through a small door at one side of the building, when I stopped, looked up and down the cold, dark street and said, "This looks like Desolation Row."

Vince sang a couple of Dylan's lines about going to the carnival on Desolation Row.

I laughed. "That puts me in a carnival spirit."

He responded with a grin, opened the door, and we went in. He flipped a switch, and lights on the ceiling lit up an open space with a gray concrete floor, huge, square wood columns rising to the second floor, a ceiling of wood planks and a few windows on each side wall.

He said, "I heard this used to be a barn, like eighty years ago. But it's been used for a lot of other things since. I don't know what exactly."

He flipped the switch off, and the only light left was the one shining like a beacon at the top of the stairs. We climbed the wood steps leading to the light, my hand clinging to the thin metal railing, and entered another large space, with junk furniture, the kind of second- and third-hand couches and armchairs that everyone on the West Bank had, and a few floor lamps here and there that gave off a dim light and massive wood columns that rose through the holes in the floor to the ceiling. At the end of the room, I glimpsed in the dark the contours of a bed and some other furniture. I thought if I lived in a space like this, I'd feel abandoned and depressed and was happy I had a home with Vince.

A voice said, "Hey, man. Glad you could make it."

I turned and saw a guy with red wavy hair come up and grab Vince's shoulder with one hand and shake his hand with the other. He said he'd heard Vince's performance was great, wished he could've been there, but he'd be there the next night. Vince put his arm around my shoulder and introduced me to Red, and I felt he was proud to have me next to him. While Red and Vince talked about Dylan and his latest album, I scanned the half-dozen scattered groups of people, looking for someone I might know, but didn't see anyone. I noticed a table that held a keg of beer and bottles and jugs of wine and thought I'd have a pacifier to get me through the conversations, in which I wouldn't have much to say.

There was a burst of shouting behind me. "Red. Hey, how are you?" Vince and I glanced back at a group just arriving. After Red clapped Vince on the shoulder and said, "Hey, good talking to you, man," Vince and I went to the drinks table and helped ourselves to wine.

We looked around, and he said, "Hey, there's Spider John and Tony." I followed his eyes and saw lanky John Koerner and Tony Little Sun Glover standing near a wall in a dimly lit area of the room. I knew Vince would want to spend most of the evening with them, and I'd stand there and listen to them talk about music and their musician friends, so, laughing, I refilled our plastic cups to the brim. We joined Koerner and Glover, and they raised their cups to us and said they'd heard Vince's gig had gone really well and they'd be there the next night. They mentioned they'd been talking to Dave about getting together to record another album, and when I asked, "Dave?" Koerner said, with a big grin, "Dave Snaker Ray," and I responded, "Oh, yeah," and wondered, How could I've forgotten Dave Snaker Ray? The three of them—Spider, Snaker, and Little Sun—were continuing a tradition of nicknames they'd inherited from the musicians and singers they admired and loved to talk about, like Lead Belly, Lightnin' Hopkins, Tampa Red, and Blind Lemon—musicians and singers I probably remember because of their nicknames.

I knew Vince and his friends wouldn't miss me if I were to wander off, so I headed back to the table to refill my glass, weaving around clusters of people, feeling a little tipsy, occasionally bumping into someone and excusing myself. A floor lamp stood behind the table that held the bottles and provided enough light so I could see which ones still had some wine in them. I thought, Maybe I shouldn't, maybe I've had too much already, but I ignored that thought and refilled my cup. As I was about to put the bottle down, a voice said, "I'll have some too, if you don't mind." A woman with frizzy red hair was smiling at me and holding up a plastic cup. I filled it, she thanked me, looked around the room and back at me and asked, "You ever been here before?"

"First time."

"Me, too. It's weird." She looked up toward the ceiling lost in the dark and back down at me. "Great place to film a horror movie."

I laughed, "Yeah." And nodded toward the other end of the room and the barely visible furniture and looked back at her and murmured, "Can you imagine living here?"

"Oh my God! Creepy."

Other people were practically pushing us out of the way to get to the booze, so we stepped aside.

"You here with anyone?" I asked.

"Some friends brought me." She nodded in the direction of one of the groups in front of us. "How about you?"

"Oh, I came with my boyfriend." I wanted to see how she'd respond, so I added, "Vince Walker."

"Oh, you're with him!"

"Yeah. You can't see him. He's on the other side of the crowd."

"Wow, that's cool!" She stood on her tiptoes and strained her neck, trying to see above and around the groups in front of us and gave up. She said, "He's a fantastic guitarist. And such a beautiful voice. It's just... hypnotic!"

"Yeah." I beamed with pride. "And he loves performing at the Triangle. He's gotten to be really good friends with Spider John Koerner, Tony Glover, Leo Kottke, and all those guys."

I was so proud of myself and Vince as I responded to her questions about what musicians had influenced him and how old he was, and when I said he'd just turned twenty, she looked amazed and exclaimed, "He's so young!" I grinned as she said I was lucky to have such a man and asked how long we'd been together and if we planned on getting married. And I said, "Oh, we've talked about it."

Every once in a while, I'd look to see if people might have migrated and Vince had come into view, and the third or fourth time, as the woman continued talking and asking questions, I glanced Vince's way and saw him standing in the semi-darkness, and a woman with long brown hair looking up at him. My happiness sank into my gut, and I clenched my teeth. The eyes of Vince, John, and Tony were fixed on the woman, who appeared to be telling a story. The men threw their heads back and laughed, and then Vince leaned toward her while pointing at someone or something behind her and off to the side, and she turned her head to look, and I recognized the woman who'd latched onto him at the bar.

I told the woman I was with that I had to take care of something. I walked over to the table, filled my cup, and headed for Vince and the woman, trying not to spill. I went up to Vince, standing next to the woman, and said, "Hi, hon," and smiled at him, and looked to the side, and exclaimed, "Oh!" and pretended to have been shocked by her presence, and that shock jolted my body, and my hand holding the cup jerked upward and the red wine splashed all over her face and chest, and I said, in a sarcastic tone, "Oh, I'm so sorry!" and burst into laughter.

"You bitch," she said, as she wiped her face with the back of her hand. She glared at me and hissed, "Fuck you!" And turned and headed toward a group of people, who were probably her friends.

"What the fuck are you doing?" Vince snapped.

I looked up at him, while hearing the other two muttering, "Jesus Christ!" and "Holy fuck!" as they shook their heads and snickered.

I said, "I didn't notice her until—"

"Oh, bullshit!"

John and Tony moved off.

"Well," I said, "what the hell is she doing here? Did you invite her to the party? Did you tell her how to get here?"

"I have no idea how she got here." He glared at me. "What the fuck is wrong with you?"

"What's wrong with me? What's wrong with you? You've been playing along with that bitch all night."

"Oh, come on." He shook his head. "You're jealous about nothing."

"Oh, yeah? Well, what was so fascinating about her?"

"Nothing. She's a bullshitter, a funny bullshitter. Okay? I wasn't thinking of jumping into bed with her."

"Really. And if I hadn't been here, what would you have done? Huh?"

He glared at me. "Nothing."

I stared at him, and he stared back, and I realized he was telling the truth. I felt stupid, so stupid. Such a loser! Oh, God, I thought, what have I done? I whimpered, "I'm sorry. I'm so sorry."

He put his arm around me, said it was time to go and, as I bowed my head in shame, walked me out of the building to the car. I felt his anger in the silence and cried as I stared out the window, watching everything pass by in a haze. We arrived home, and I went straight to bed. The next day, I woke, and he was gone. I looked at the alarm clock. Almost noon. I took a shower, got dressed, straightened up the apartment and did everything I could to busy myself and not think of what had happened, but memories still came back, and I felt ashamed. He came home in the late afternoon, and when I asked where he'd been, he said he'd gone over to a friend's house. I could see he was still upset. I didn't ask any more questions. I prepared dinner, and we ate in silence. Sometime afterward, he gave me a perfunctory hug, and I murmured, "I'll be there soon," peering up at his eyes that looked away as his arms released me. He grabbed his guitar case and left for the Triangle.

By the time I walked down our street, the sun had disappeared and it was getting cold. I zipped my jacket and focused my gaze on the sidewalk. In my mind, I continued returning to the previous night, but my thoughts took a new turn—or rather, they returned to their original way. Was it so crazy of me to think something was going on between Vince and that woman? Why did I give in so quickly and believe what he said? I thought of the way she'd latched onto him at the Triangle and then at the party, and the more I relived what I'd seen, the more I felt I wasn't crazy and had reason to be jealous. I entered the Triangle and saw Vince sitting onstage, tuning his guitar. A lot of people lined the bar, but there were still a few empty tables. I sat down at one against the wall, near the stage, and gazed up at him, hoping he'd look at me, but he didn't. A server stopped by, said she was happy to see me and was looking forward to watching Vince perform again, he was so talented, and we talked for a few seconds, and then she left to get my drink. It felt good to be welcomed by someone. I took off my jacket, draped it over my chair, and looked around and saw John, Tony, Red, and a couple more of Vince's friends standing at the end of the bar near the stage, talking, laughing, and drinking. John's eyes happened to meet mine, and I smiled, he smiled back, and so, too, did Tony, whose eyes had followed John's. I nodded toward the space next to me, inviting them to join me, but John just raised his bottle to me, took a drink, and the two of them went back to their conversation. I looked away and focused on the stage.

Vince raised his head and was about to say something in the mic, when our eyes met, he paused and for a second his face remained expressionless. And then he smiled, and for the first time that day I felt some hope and beamed back my love. He looked past me at his audience, greeted them and introduced the song he was about to sing. The waitress came with my glass of beer. I had my money ready so I could pay her and not take my eyes off him. He began playing his guitar, and his voice, as soft and warm as the fur on this coat, filled the space. He finished the first song, people applauded, and he sang another. The bar was getting packed, and I began to feel self-conscious about having a table to myself.

I looked around to see if I might recognize someone who could join me, didn't see anyone, and then, just as my eyes were returning to the stage, I noticed, about ten feet away, the woman from the night before. She was sitting with friends, at a table a little further from the bar. One of her friends, who had been blocking my view, had left, and now I could see her, and all the emotion of the preceding night's drama gushed back. I looked away and up at the stage and fixed my eyes on Vince. He was gazing off at some point above and beyond the people in the room as he sang into the mic, and I watched him, feeling deeply moved by his song about the lady walking in blue light, when he glanced down at his guitar and back at the audience, and his eyes fixed on someone for a second. He seemed to smile at that person, and I followed his gaze to the face of the woman, the woman from the night before, who was smiling back at him. The connection of their eyes couldn't have lasted more than a few seconds, but I felt as if it would go on forever. I was on the verge of sobbing. I blinked several times, tried to catch my breath, stared down at the table and thought, Don't do this to yourself. Just because he smiled at her doesn't mean he's attracted to her. Doing my best to rationalize what I'd seen and convince myself there was nothing there, I looked up and saw her smiling at Vince, and looked at him and saw his eyes settle on her and then look away. I looked back at her, but the friend who'd left had returned and was blocking my view.

I took some deep breaths, and as I thought about the night before and what had just happened, my pain morphed into anger, and then rage, and I wanted revenge. I didn't need to come up with a plan for that, because one presented itself, in the sound of a voice saying, "Do you mind if I join you?" I looked up to see a guy about my age, with intense eyes and a playful smile, bending over the empty chair next to me, a glass of beer in his hand. I said, "Go ahead." He sat down, and we started to talk. I didn't really pay attention to him, except to respond in ways that encouraged him to think I found him interesting, so he would keep on talking and drinking with me. And soon we were leaning close to one another, bending our heads so they were nearly touching, and we could hear one another over Vince's singing, and then from time to time we'd rock back and forth in laughter at a joke one or the other of us had made, disrespecting Vince and everyone trying to listen to his music.

When I'd look up at Vince, his eyes would be directed away from me, except once, between songs, when I saw his eyes fixed on us as we laughed at a joke my revenge tool had cracked. Vince took a break, went down to the bar, got a glass of beer and joined his musician friends. I noticed him and his friends staring at me and the guy next to me, and I knew they were talking about us. And then they looked away and seemed to ignore us. About ten minutes later, Vince went back on stage and performed the second half of his set. By the time he'd finished, the guy and I were touching heads as we talked and laughed.

It was during one of those intimate moments that I recognized Vince's purple blazer and black shirt as he stood in front of the table. I looked up to see him glaring down at me, while ignoring the guy.

"You ready to go?" Vince asked.

The guy leaned back in his chair, I glanced over and saw his mouth agape and, beyond him, the woman my wine had sullied staring at Vince and me. I leaned back, returned Vince's glare and said, "You sure you want *me* to go with you?"

Vince and I continued staring at one another.

"Are you two together?" the guy asked.

Vince said, "Yeah, we're together. She was just using you to piss me off."

The guy looked at me, saw my eyes focused on Vince and blurted, "Oh, fuck!" He stood up, glared at me and said, "Asshole!" And then he headed for the door.

I glanced over at that woman, saw she was still watching, and looked at Vince.

"You ready to go?" he asked again.

I emptied my glass of beer, stood up and put on my jacket, and we left.

We hardly said a word during the short drive. When we got home, I tossed my jacket and purse onto the dining-room table and plopped down on the couch in the living room. He went to the kitchen, came back to the dining room, stood there with a glass of Jack in one hand and the bottle in the other and drank and stared at me.

"Why didn't you get me a glass, too?" I asked.

He ignored me.

I went to the kitchen, got a glass and returned to find him sitting at one end of the couch, the bottle of Jack by his feet, like he was the only one who was going to drink. I filled my glass, set the bottle on the floor near the middle of the couch, sat down at the other end, took a drink and said, "Well, how did it feel?" When he didn't answer, I laughed and said, "Come on, Vince, how did it feel?"

"You seem happy. You like to hurt me." The way he looked at me, I could see he was really pissed. He took a drink.

"I just wanted you to know how it feels."

He shook his head, emptied his glass, refilled it and said, "I wasn't trying to hurt you last night."

"Well, you did. You hurt me a lot."

"You need to get used to the fact there's always going to be someone in an audience who develops a thing for whoever's performing. That's just the way it is." He glared at me. "You went totally fucking nuts last night. And you earned yourself a reputation. People look at you now and say, 'Don't get near her, she might go crazy and throw a glass of wine at you.' What do you think John, Tony, and all those guys were talking about? Crazy Helen. Crazy fucking Helen." He drank some more.

"That's what they call me now? Crazy Helen?"

"I didn't set out to hurt you last night, but you intended to hurt me tonight."

"Your friends call me crazy fucking Helen? And I intentionally hurt you?"

"Yeah, you did."

I stared straight ahead. "Why did you want me to come home? So you could hurt me back?"

"So I could help you get your fucking head straightened out." "My head's the problem?"

"So people will stop calling you Crazy Helen."

"I'm the problem? You weren't flirting with that bitch?"

"I hardly noticed her."

"Don't bullshit me."

"You're the one who's doling out the shit."

"You fucking liar!" I tossed my whiskey into his eyes.

He screamed and dropped his glass. He tried rubbing the whiskey out of his eyes and shouted, "You Goddamn bitch!" And reared back and swung at me, his fist hitting me on the side of my head, and pain shot through my brain. I pulled my legs up, covered my face with my hands and cowered into a ball.

He screamed, "Get out of here, you fucking bitch! Get out!"

I leaped up, ran a few steps, stopped, turned to look down at him on the couch and watched him blink repeatedly, trying to see, and then cover his eyes again. I rushed to the dining room, grabbed my purse and jacket off the table and ran outside into the cold night. Trembling, I wiped my tears with the side of my hand and hugged myself, while my mind ping-ponged from one thing to another—the sight of him standing in the dining room, glaring at me, as if the very sight of me disgusted him; his screech, when the whiskey splashed and burned his eyes; his mouth wide open as he screamed and reared back to hit me; the blur of his fist, the blow to my head, and the throbbing pain. No, I couldn't go back there. I kept on walking, panting, almost out of breath as I fled the images, the cries, and the fear and panic that had seized me. I reached an intersection, stopped, looked back down the street and realized I'd already gone two blocks. I checked my watch. It was after two. I gazed up at the gray clouds and the dimmed glow of the moon and wondered, What should I do? I thought of waiting a while, then going back to the apartment and sneaking in to see if Vince was asleep, but decided it was too dangerous. So where could I go? I looked around at the dark forms of the trees, the parked cars and the sidewalk ahead of me, where at any moment I felt someone might appear out of nowhere. I headed for a busy street, where there would be more light. I arrived at Cedar Avenue, with its rows of streetlamps on both sides, and turned down the sidewalk. A car would pass from time to time, and I'd keep my eyes fixed on the sidewalk in front of me, afraid the driver might slow down and try to pick me up, or worse. I crossed Riverside Avenue, glanced off at the Triangle a couple hundred feet away, passed Savran's Bookstore and the Mixers and continued on Cedar to the Tenth Avenue bridge across the Mississippi. I stopped halfway across the bridge, moved close to the railing, and looked down at the black river a couple hundred feet below. Out here, all alone, shivering from the cold, my forearms crossing my chest as I clutched my arms and watched the river and its hypnotic flow, I felt terrified and calm—the calm, the peace that awaits us at the end of our lives.

* * *

Remembering that bridge, the cold, the fear, the temptation to pull myself over the railing and plunge into that black water, I pull the collar of the fur coat close to my face and feel its softness and warmth. Everyone needs the warmth of love. Everyone. I tell my children every day I love them. Every time they leave the house, every night before they fall asleep and every morning when they wake up, I tell them I love them. I don't want them to ever feel what I felt growing up, what I felt that night on the bridge, or what I was feeling when I walked back to the apartment, found Vince passed out on the bed, the empty bottle of Jack on the floor, and wondered, Why go on? I had no reason to. I lower my arms and pull up the sleeves and turn my forearms up and look at the scars, at my story written with knives.

That night, I added to the story. I left the bedroom, got a knife in the kitchen, went to the bathroom, filled the tub, lay down in the warm water and cut myself again and again. My pain flowed with my blood that turned the bath red, and I smiled as I lost consciousness.

* * *

After the ER and the ICU, I was taken to the Psych Ward. The doctors didn't want to release me, unless I had a safe place to go, so I called Debbie. She came, convinced them I'd be safe with her and took me to her apartment. The next day, she drove me to Vince's place, helped me gather up my things and carry them out. He tried talking to me, but I wouldn't answer, and Debbie told him to leave me alone, or she'd call the police.

I saw him again a few weeks later, the day of the demonstration against Nixon's order to mine North Vietnam's harbors. Debbie and I and some friends joined the march from the Minneapolis campus of the university to the state capitol in St. Paul and, while Eugene McCarthy was addressing the thousands of demonstrators who were sitting on the lawns or standing in the streets, his voice the only sound in the still afternoon, I noticed Vince sitting next to the woman, the one on whom I'd splashed the wine. She was leaning into him, and he into her. I looked away, and every once in a while, as McCarthy and then others spoke, I'd look at Vince and the woman, until he noticed me. They got up and left. I saw him a few more times. We'd run into one another in a bar, begin talking, and, thinking we could make it work, go back to his place and make love. And I might stay for a day or two, and then we'd get nasty and fight, and one of us would try to reduce the other to tears. And then, after another break-up, he disappeared. I rarely saw any of his friends again and, when I did, didn't try to find out what had happened to him. I just assumed he'd done what he'd always said he wanted to do, what Dylan had done—gone to New York to make a reputation for himself.

* * *

About two and a half years later, the night before the big party that Dick and his housemates were throwing to celebrate the end of the academic year, we rode across the Tenth Street bridge on his chopper to the West Bank, went to the Mixers, and then walked down to the Triangle. As we approached the open door, I heard Spider John's folksy voice and then saw him sitting onstage, plucking his twelve-string guitar and singing into the mic. Dick held onto my hand, so I wouldn't get tangled in the crowd, and pulled me along as he weaved around people. When he left me to get our drinks, I turned to watch John. I hadn't seen him onstage since the days when Vince and I were still together. I remembered the happiness I'd found with Vince, and for which I felt a strange combination of sorrow and regret. I reminded myself of the pain we'd inflicted on one another and wished we'd had the sense to try to get help. Dick came back and handed me a beer and wrapped his arm around my back, and I leaned into him. The crowd was bobbing to the music, and the bar was raucous and vibrant with joy. I smiled up at Dick and caught a kiss, and then, as I lowered my head and looked away, I glimpsed a guy sitting at the bar, hunched forward, with long dark blond hair hanging in thick strands to his neck, and wearing a faded green army field jacket.

I leaned one way and another to try to get a good look at him. He turned his head to the side, and I saw Vince's face, his mouth agape, his eye drooped, like he was drugged. I had to go to him, I had to, and started pushing, trying to get through the mass of people between us, but they pushed back. Dick asked, "What's the matter?" I panicked and realized I had to get out of there. I pulled away from him, bored through the crowd toward the door, rushed down the street to Cedar, and turned and headed toward the Mixers, thoughts throbbing through my brain. What happened to Vince? Why was he wearing that army jacket? Why did he look totally wasted? Dick caught up, grabbed my arm and tried to talk, but I kept my head lowered and plowed ahead. I had to get away, had to protect myself. When we got to his place, I went straight to bed and lay with my back turned toward him until I fell asleep. The next day, Dick prepared breakfast, but I couldn't eat. He kept on asking, in the nicest way possible, "What's the matter?" All I could do was shake my head and tell him, "I don't know. I don't know." There was a maelstrom of thoughts and emotions churning inside me. I got up and left. No explanation. Just headed to the door and ran out.

I rushed the few blocks home from Dick's house and found Joyce was gone. I called every one of Vince's friends who I could find a number for in my address book, but only got through to one of them. I told him who I was, and he said, "Crazy Helen!" and laughed, and added, "Sorry, didn't mean to offend you." I told him I'd seen Vince at the Triangle and he looked half-dead, and I was scared for him and asked if he had a phone number for him. He didn't, but he had the address of the woman he was living with.

All the while I was driving to south Minneapolis, I was thinking of Vince in that fatigues jacket, seeing images from the film footage of the war that appeared every night on the news and hearing the voices of the reporters. I remembered the stories of friends sent to Viet Nam and the hell they'd gone through, the atrocities they'd experienced, and the way the war and the drugs had come home with them. Stories had circulated about vets drinking themselves to death or OD'ing, and I was afraid that's where Vince was headed. I saw the address, pulled over, rushed to the house and rang the bell. And rang it again, and was about to ring it a third time when the door opened. A woman stood staring at me through the screen, a befuddled look on her face. "Yes?"

"I'm a friend of Vince's."

"Oh? What's your name?"

"Helen."

She nodded. "He's talked about you. Come on in."

She pushed the screen door a few inches, and I pulled it open and followed her into the living room, where she pointed toward a couch.

I sat down, and she sat on a chair nearby. A brunette in jeans, with a shirt with the sleeves rolled half-way up her forearms, and wearing sandals. She gazed at me with a kind, patient look. I sighed, scanned the room and saw an acoustic guitar on a stand near a wall. My eyes returned to the woman, still gazing at me.

She told me her name, which didn't register in my frenzied brain, and asked why I wanted to see Vince.

"Last night, I saw him at the Triangle. He was wearing an army jacket, and looked depressed. I mean, really depressed. Totally out of it. Like he'd come back from Vietnam and—"

"Vince wasn't drafted. He didn't go to Vietnam."

"Oh, thank God!"

"But he is at war with what's going on inside him."

"What do you mean?"

"When did you last see him?"

"Fall of '72."

"That's when I met him. We were together that fall, off and on, and the following winter and spring. And then he moved to New York. I'm sure he'd talked to you about Bob Dylan being from here, going to New York and—"

"Many times."

We both nodded. I took a deep breath, sighed, and felt my body relax a little.

"In the beginning," she said, "things went well in New York. He continued writing songs, performing in coffee shops down in the village, and getting whatever gigs he could by himself, or with a band. I'd visit my older sister in New York from time to time, and we'd go to the coffee shops and bars to see him. I got to know some of his friends and gave them my phone number, should things go wrong. They did. Instead of recording an album and building a career, he used the money he earned to buy whiskey, and then coke, and he'd end up broke and unable to pay his rent. He'd pawn whatever he could, and sometimes that was his guitar, and then instead of using the pawn money to pay his living expenses, he'd use it on alcohol and drugs, and someone would have to bail him out. Or he'd steal, and because of his stealing, some of his friends didn't want him to stay with them anymore. When he did perform, he was often hung over, wasn't himself, and people lost confidence in him. And his father... he was no help. Wouldn't have anything to do with him. Nothing."

“Did he tell you about the time he went to his father’s house?

“Oh, yeah. More than once. The father who offered to pay him to stay away.”

From the look of despair in her eyes, I could see she’d found that story as devastating as I had.

“His mother’s very different. She was worried sick about him and sent him money for a plane ticket to come home.” She shook her head. “You don’t send money to an alcoholic to buy a plane ticket.” She paused and then continued. “The second time he ended up in the ER for drinking, he’d drunk enough to have the blood alcohol count of a corpse. I went to New York, brought him to my sister’s place and then back here.” She shook her head again, her voice trembling as she murmured, “If I hadn’t done that, he’d be dead.” She bit her lip, and tears welled. She took a deep breath and sighed. “Sometimes he starts crying, calling himself a failure, saying he’s destroyed everything in his life and he’s nothing but a piece of shit. If there was no one with him, no one to love him, he’d end his life. I know he would. I got him to see a therapist, and he’s going through AA. He relapsed and disappeared for a few days, but... ” She looked lost. She knew he could turn on a dime, drink and drug himself to death.

“Thank you for loving him,” I said.

She took another breath and wiped away her tears. “Would you like to see him?”

Her question stunned me. “Sure.”

We stood up, and she led me through the dining room, past the bathroom to a closed door, stopped, very gently opened it and stepped aside. Vince was sprawled on his belly on the double bed, his legs spread, his arms raised on each side, as if to try to break his fall when he collapsed.

She whispered, “He’d been missing for two days, when I got a call from the bartender at the Triangle last night, telling me Vince had passed out in the bathroom. A friend helped me bring him home.”

Her voice woke him. He lifted his head, turned his eyes toward us, saw me and said, “Who the fuck?” His brows furrowed, and he cried, “What the fuck are you doing here? What the fuck’s going on?”

The woman said, “She just stopped by to visit. We’ll let you sleep.”

He mumbled another fuck, she closed the door, and we headed for the living room. We stopped near the front door, and I looked into her eyes, took her hand in mine and said, “Thank you. Thank you for caring for him.”

She smiled. “Don’t be surprised if you see an album with his name on it someday. Music has helped him survive. It’s part of his therapy.”

As I drove home, I felt relieved. I had confidence in her. And in him. He needed someone to love him the way she did. And I felt guilty, guilty about having failed Vince, about having failed us. But, I reminded myself, we failed each other. I realized too that I still loved him, even though that night, I would attend the party at Dick’s house, and after the party, when we were in bed, I’d tell Dick about Vince, and then I’d tell him... tell him twice... “I love you.” He was the second man to whom I’d said that. I loved him so much. And three months later, he returned from his easy-rider trip, and the serial monogamist told me he’d met another woman. And I went crazy and screamed, “I love you. I thought you loved me, too.” And then I got the knife, went to my room and recorded my feelings.

* * *

I become aware of myself staring down again at the sleeves of the fur coat and at the scars on my forearms, take a deep breath and sigh. I look up toward the back wall of the living room, the turntable and the shelf beneath that’s full of albums and think of listening to one of Vince’s records, and the thought brings a smile to my lips. He’s come a long way. And I know how long that way is. Oh, God, I know. I get up and take a few steps toward the shelf and think, If I listen to his songs, they’ll take me back again to where I’ve just been. I stop and check my watch. It’s going on five o’clock. I need to finish sorting through the photographs, if nothing else. I go to the foyer, stop in front of the mirror, smile at myself, caress my cheek one more time with the fur and think, I’m so lucky to have you, Tom, so lucky to have your love. I hang up the coat, go through the dining room and down the hall to the bedroom, where the red tin box sits on the bed, pictures scattered next to it.

I sit down, glance at one of the pictures, the one of Tom and me, standing in the backyard of that house, and remember him telling me about living there with a bunch of guys, and one of them was a real performer. I knew he must be referring to Dick. That was about five years after Vince and I had split, after I'd been taken to the ER for the first time, and the psychiatrist put me on an antidepressant that I took for a few weeks, just long enough to make it to the end of the quarter and earn the grades I needed to hang onto the scholarship that paid my tuition. After that I quit taking the meds, because, if I hadn't quit, I wouldn't have been able to down more than a couple drinks without nodding off. I got to be too much for Debbie to handle, so I moved out of her apartment and into another one, with other friends. And now I'm Crazy Helen, the woman with the scars all over her forearms, reading and reciting the confessional poets—Plath, Sexton, and Berryman—and drinking and doing drugs and fucking, and I make it clear to every guy I fuck that I decide if and when and how we fuck. And if they act as if they don't get it, I rivet them with my eyes and repeat, *I decide*.

I make my second trip to the ER. I come back to life again, get another shrink and more prescriptions, and again I stop seeing the shrink and taking the meds, and start drinking even more. I feel the emptiness inside, the pain, the cries, and the lie that echoes through me—I love you. The echoes fill me with anger, with rage, and I defy every attempt to control me. I drink, dominate, and take what I want. I strip in the most casual way, tell men to take their clothes off and get down on their knees, and I bury each one's face in my cunt. I tell him what I want him to do and, when I'm ready, I command him to lie down and I straddle him, and I do what I want.

I read and reread Sylvia's poem, "Lady Lazarus," and realize that's who I am, Lady Lazarus, come back to life a second time. And when the guy I'm drinking with, the guy I'm snorting coke with, stares at my scars, I rivet him with my eyes and chant, "'Dying / Is an art, like everything else. / I do it exceptionally well. / I do it so it feels like hell. / I do it so it feels real. / I guess you could say I've a call.'" And I laugh uproariously, and sometimes the guy laughs with me, and sometimes he looks baffled, or scared, and I drink, snort, and laugh some more. And if one of those guys should look disgusted and call me a crazy bitch, I say, "Well, 'There is a charge / For the eyeing of my scars, there is a charge / For the hearing of my heart.'" And sometimes, when I'm straddling a guy, and I'm really stoned and want to freak him out, or make him laugh like he's crazy too, I bulge my eyes, like I'm in *Eraserhead*, and chant, "'Out of the ash / I rise with my red hair / And I eat men like air'"—only I chant "blonde hair" instead of "red." And laugh like I'm insane, and hear him call me Crazy Fucking Helen. And if he doesn't throw me off and put on his clothes and run off, if he doesn't slap me around and ridicule me, and I wake up in the morning and find him lying next to me, I sit up, stare down at him and think, I'm lucky I haven't brought home any murderers or thieves—yet.

I read somewhere that Sylvia, like her character in *The Bell Jar*, loved vodka, and so I gave it a try. I found I loved it, too, and made it my drink of choice. It was like a magic potion. It made me feel even more gutsy, more powerful, like I could take on anyone or anything and win. When I was drunk, I never felt weak. Never felt there was something lacking, something missing in me that... But that wasn't true. I'd given my heart to Dick. I didn't have one anymore. You can't live without a heart. I didn't intend to. Lady Lazarus was only going to make one more trip to the ER. But first, she'd visit Dick. Tom would bring me back to that house.

* * *

If it hadn't been for that breathtaking song a bird was singing, a bird somewhere high up in one of the elms that lined the sidewalk, I might've never met Tom. It was evening, I'd finished working in Walter Library, on the main campus, and had started walking down the mall toward home, when I heard the song. I stopped and looked up, my eyes searching the branches high above. The bird chirped and sang again, and I heard a voice say, "Beautiful! Isn't it?" I looked over and saw a young man smiling at me, a man about my age, in jeans and a short-sleeve shirt, with long brown hair, but not hippie long, smiling in a way that warmed my heart every bit as much as the song. And feeling that warmth, I smiled back and said, "Yes, it is beautiful. What kind of bird do you think it is?"

"I don't know," he said. "Just know its song makes me feel good."

"Feels like the bird's singing for all of us."

"A feel-good song. We need that. After everything we've been through."

"Everything we've been through?"

"The war." He paused. "I'm sorry. It's kind of an obsession. I need to get over it."

"We all do," I said. The war had ended about two years before, but everyone had been affected, everyone knew of someone who'd died, or who'd come back damaged. Or had never come back.

I looked around. Students and faculty, who appeared to be done for the day and on their way home, walked on the sidewalks that crossed the mall or bordered the length of it. My eyes returned to the man gazing at me. He asked where I was headed. I said I had an apartment on the other side of Dinkytown. He lived on the other side, too, and asked, "You mind if I walk with you?" As we headed for Dinkytown, I answered his questions and told him I lived with a roommate in a duplex, was going to graduate at the end of the quarter with a major in English, after six years of working part-time jobs, like the one at the library, and was starting graduate school in the fall. And then I'd work as a TA and teach Freshman English. By the time I asked, "And how about you?" we'd left the campus behind and reached the blocks with two-story buildings, with shops on the first floor and apartments above.

He, too, was going to graduate at the end of the quarter, had done his degree in history in five years, and planned on getting a Ph.D. and becoming a professor. We were approaching Fourth Street, in the middle of Dinkytown. Although he was nice, I didn't find him attractive. I was wondering whether to go straight ahead at the intersection, or turn and walk with him, when he mentioned that he lived in a large house, with three friends. I asked him where the house was, and he said about six blocks down Fourth Street and a couple blocks over. And when I asked him what his housemates were like, he said they loved to party, and one of them was an incredible performer. A guy who loved to joke around and always got a crowd. We reached Fourth Street and, instead of saying goodbye and going straight, I turned down the street with him.

Trying to sound as if I were just casually interested, I asked, "Your housemate who's a performer, what does he do when he performs?"

I could hear the tension in my voice, but Tom didn't seem to notice it. He described Dick doing his Bogie imitations and some of his other routines.

I felt light-headed. I took a deep breath and asked, "Well, why do you think he likes to perform so much?"

"Huh! He loves to be the center of attention. And he used to be a real ladies' man. My housemates told me he'd sleep with one woman for a few months, dump her, bring a new one to a party, get her plastered and seduce her, and go through one after another. But now, he's been with the same woman since last summer. That's about eight months."

"I wonder if I know him. What's his name?"

"Dick Rayburn. Ring any bells?"

"Nope." I shook my head, thinking, What are the odds? I try to appear calm and ask, "How long have you known him?"

"I met him when I moved in last summer. Or actually, I moved in while he was gone on a motorcycle trip, with the housemate I replaced. Dick returned after I'd settled in. Guess what the first thing was that he did when he got home."

"No idea."

"Broke up with his girlfriend, because he'd found someone else on the trip."

"What an asshole!" The anger in my voice caught Tom's attention. I took a deep breath, sighed, and tried to sound calm as I said, "Well, I'm glad I haven't had to deal with someone like that."

He nodded and, after a pause, said, "Tell me more about you."

I talked about the kinds of things that might impress a guy interested in becoming a professor, such as my love of books, and in particular fiction and poetry, and some of my favorite writers. After we'd walked about three blocks, I stopped, nodded off to the side and said, "I live that way."

He looked across the street, then back at me and said, "I enjoyed talking with you. Would you like to get together sometime?"

"I'd like that. Very much."

"Well, I don't have anything specific in mind, but maybe... Are you working at the library again tomorrow?"

"Yeah. And I finish about the same time."

"Maybe I could meet you at the entrance, and we could go to Dinkytown and have a burger at Annie's Parlor?"

"Sounds wonderful."

We smiled at one another, and he said, "Okay," and I replied, "Okay," and he nodded, and I nodded, and we smiled some more and went our separate ways.

As I walked home, taking deep breaths, grinding my teeth and staring blindly ahead, I imagined confronting Dick, and the things that I would say to hurt him. I could see the shock and pain on his face as I brought him to his knees, ridiculing, mocking, belittling that piece of shit and reveling in my total dominance. Tom was my ticket to that show. I'd be able to watch it repeatedly in my mind—a Super-8 brain film, full of laughs.

But by the time I entered my apartment and plopped down on the couch, I was thinking about Tom. In spite of the painful memories his words had revived and the rage those memories had rekindled, something in the way he'd looked at me and smiled, in the kindness and warmth I could see in his eyes, something in all of that calmed me and made me feel happy.

The next day, when I came out of the library, I saw him sitting on a concrete bench, just a few feet from where I'd stopped the day before to look for the bird singing in the tree. It was again a lovely evening, the sun was descending behind the buildings that lined the west side of the mall, the light had softened to a golden glow, and I felt the peace that comes when the day's work is done, and everyone seems happy to pack up and go home. Tom leaped up when he saw me, and the warmth I'd seen the day before in his eyes and his smile illuminated his face again, and I felt that warmth radiate through me as he came close.

We walked to Annie's Parlor, ordered cheeseburgers, fries, and malts, and talked. I never forgot that Tom was my ticket to the house where he and Dick lived, and I intended to captivate Tom so he would do what I wanted. I sat across from him, my eyes fixed on him, as if he were the most fascinating person I'd ever met and asked him questions that would make him feel I was interested in him. I found it ironic I should be dating someone who wanted to be a history professor, the same profession Dick had chosen, so I asked Tom why? He said he'd always had an interest in history and, from the time he was about twelve, loved reading history books and historical fiction. So, of course, he'd love to teach history. But there was something else. His older brother had been drafted and sent to Vietnam. He came home once, went through hell, re-enlisted, and got sent back. And went MIA. Never returned. And his parents were never the same. "Never," he repeated, looking down, shaking his head. Then he looked at me with determination in his eyes and said, "One thing I'm going to do is develop a course on the Viet Nam War and reveal the truth about our government's lies." It turned out he and I had participated in some of the same demonstrations. If my parents had seen Tom and me at Annie's that night, they would've grumbled, "She found another goddamn peacenik." But maybe not. They might've started seeing things differently by then.

After Tom and I had talked for a couple hours, he invited me to his house for a glass of wine. I panicked, while maintaining a calm demeanor. I wasn't ready to confront Dick. If I did, that might mean the end of my relationship with Tom. I felt I needed more control over Tom before I went to the house. So, I told him my roommate stayed at her boyfriend's apartment, and we'd have my place all to ourselves. I blushed, because I realized he might interpret that as an invitation to go to bed with me, and I wasn't ready to reveal my scars.

We walked to my house, he stayed for a while, and we talked, laughed and drank wine. Normally all I had to drink was vodka, but I didn't want him to know I was a boozer. Someone had left a bottle of wine one night, so offering a glass seemed the perfect cover. Spending the evening at my place quickly became a routine. And then one night, we started making out, and pretty soon we were pulling one another's clothes off and heading for my bed. Making love with Tom was different from fucking the other men I'd been with since Dick. I wasn't drunk, stoned, and didn't morph into Lady Lazarus. No. Because of the way he drew close to me, and the gentleness and affection in his touches and caresses, and the way his lips grazed my skin and whispered my name, his breath making my skin tingle, I let myself go, gave myself entirely to him and experienced the most heavenly orgasm. But, in the morning, I woke to find him lying on his side and staring at me.

"What?" I asked, wondering what he was thinking.

He reached across my belly, traced one of the scars on my forearm with his fingertip, and asked, "What happened?" He didn't look like he was judging me, didn't look disgusted. He just seemed concerned. The moment I hadn't wanted to think about had arrived. He gave me a smile that reassured me and said, "You can trust me."

"I need to sit up," I said. We pushed ourselves up and leaned against the headboard, the side of my leg and hip and arm nearly touching his. I looked straight ahead and said, "I don't like to talk about them… I have problems with low self-esteem and insecurity... that go back to when I was a kid…." Did I really want to tell him? I looked at him and saw compassion in his eyes. "I didn't feel loved by my parents or brothers when I was growing up. That made me feel worthless… That hurts. Still hurts… This might seem crazy to you, but the way I learned to deal with that feeling when I was a little girl was to cut myself, because the pain that led me to cut was always greater than the pain of the cutting itself.

In a strange way, cutting relieves pain. It would flow right out of me with the blood."

He nodded and, as he stared at my arms, said, "A few of those scars look recent."

"I have a hard time dealing with rejection. With breakups. Some have happened within the last few years. I also have problems with alcohol and drugs. And I'm most likely to cut myself when I've been drinking. A lot, not just a couple glasses of wine."

He gazed at me. "Well, that's all I've seen you drink."

I nodded and looked away. I was afraid if I told him everything at once, he might think I was just too crazy and leave me. I hesitated, and then blurted, "I've seen a couple psychiatrists and therapists over the last five years. But I'm not seeing one now."

He continued gazing at me for what felt like a long time and then said, "I'll do whatever I can to help you."

I saw compassion in his eyes. We kissed and made love again.

* * *

Over the next few weeks, Tom and I were happy. He'd bring a bottle of wine over, we'd have dinner, sometimes we'd go out, sometimes we'd stay home, and he often spent the night. When we did go out, I'd suggest a movie or a play, one where we weren't likely to encounter Dick. When we stayed home, we'd sit on the couch in the living room, or at the kitchen table, and talk about what interested us—works by poets, fiction writers, historians, filmmakers, and our memories and feelings about the war. The warmth in his eyes as he'd look into mine while talking to me, and the way he'd listen to what I had to say, without trying to talk over me or cut me off, made me feel he treasured being with me and getting to know who I am. His presence was like a balm that calmed my spirit and made me feel at peace, and I looked forward to our nights together.

But one Friday evening, things changed. I was making a salad, when I heard him come in the front door and call out, "It's me!" He entered the kitchen with a big smile, a bottle of wine and a boxed pizza, set the pizza and the bottle on the table, and took me in his arms and kissed me. He poured the wine, and we clinked our glasses and drank. I returned to slicing vegetables for the salad, and we were talking about how our day had gone, when he said, "And guess what?"

"What?" I asked as I finished slicing a tomato.

"My housemates and I are going to throw a party to celebrate the end of the academic year. And my graduation." I looked and saw him smiling at me. "And we'll celebrate yours, too." He took a drink, while I stared. "There'll probably be a lot of people. And you'll finally get to meet my roommates."

I bit my lip as I thought, I have to tell him. I set the knife down and said, "Tom."

He saw the look in my eyes, and the joy vanished from his. "What's the matter?"

"There's something I've been meaning to tell you."

"What?"

I paused and thought, He's going to learn the truth, whether I tell him or not. And it would be better if I told him. I said, "I know your housemates. And Dick, in particular." Tom stared at me, his mouth agape. "I was the woman Dick dumped last September, when he got back from his trip."

Tom looked baffled. "You?" He shook his head. "Why did you keep this from me?"

"When I met you, I still felt a lot of anger toward him. A lot. He told me he loved me. We'd even started talking about getting married. And then he went on that trip. He called me every night. And then he stopped. Every day, I worried, worried to the point I'd feel sick." I took a deep breath and continued. "One day, he called. He was home, and wanted to come over and see me. There was no love, no affection in his voice." I paused and took another deep breath. "What he had to say was that our relationship was over. All the love," I shook my head, "all the love I thought had been there... was gone. I felt worthless. And pissed. After he left, I went to the kitchen, got a knife, went upstairs to my room, and cut myself. Here." I extended my arms and showed him the largest, most recent scars, and watched his eyes fix on them. "And I woke up in the ICU."

"What an asshole!" He shook his head. "What a goddamned asshole!" And then he got a puzzled look on his face. "But I still don't get it. Why didn't you tell me this before?"

I closed my eyes, opened them, saw his eyes fixed on me and knew I couldn't lie.

"I wanted revenge. Wanted to ridicule him, make him feel like shit. Wanted to tell him, in the presence of his housemates, that he's still—and will always be—nothing but a little boy performing for his daddy. All of us who make up his audience, we're just substitutes for Daddy. And without us, without Daddy, he's nothing. And the reason he's a serial monogamist, as he likes to say, is because he's a scared little boy, who doesn't have the courage to grow up and have a relationship that is more than just performing and seeing himself in someone's eyes. I wanted to make... I wanted to see him suffer on his own stage."

"You started a relationship with me so you could do that to him?"

"In the beginning, that's—"

"You didn't find me interesting in any way. You just wanted to use me."

"That's not how I feel now."

He shook his head and mumbled, "Just wanted to use me."

Seeing the pain in his eyes, I took a deep breath and pushed out the truth: "I still had so much anger in me. Anger and pain. And they weren't going away. When I left the hospital last September, I started drinking more than ever before. I was guzzling vodka from the bottle, like it was pop. Joyce, the schoolteacher I was living with, she found me in my blood-soaked bed, called 911, and then came with me to the hospital, visited me and brought me home. She finally got fed up with my drinking and told me she couldn't take it anymore. I had to quit or move out. So, I moved here and started drinking even more." I paused as I gazed at the shock and disbelief in Tom's eyes, wondering if I should continue. What I was saying was hurting him, but, in the long run, silence hurts most. "The more I drank, the more I felt the pain from what Dick had done, the more my anger raged inside me and the more I wanted revenge. I took my anger out on every man who drank, did drugs, and had sex with me. I brought men here to fuck, and I'd tell them how I wanted to fuck, and anytime a man showed a weakness, if he was sentimental about anything, anything at all, I'd make fun of him. I'd ridicule him. And every time I did that and got away with it—some guys didn't put up with my behavior and struck back—but when I got away with abusing those men, it got me hyped. I'd be in a frenzy, and then I'd feel relief. I'd feel calm. And I'd fall into a deep sleep. And then, the next day, it would start all over. But now... " I could feel tears welling up. I took a deep breath and then continued. "Since I've been seeing you... " I had to pause and take another breath... "Just doing the things we do, that has calmed me so much. I don't feel as anxious, as insecure, and... and I no longer feel, if I were to die, no one would care. I know you would. You're the only man I've ever been with who really seems to care about me. About my happiness. I don't feel I need the vodka anymore. Don't feel I need the sense of power that it gave me, because you've made me feel loved". I smiled. "Although, come to think of it, you've never said you love me. But I feel you do."

Tom stepped forward and put his arms around me and said, "I do love you."

* * *

Tom and I talked during the days that followed about my problems with alcohol, depression, breakups, and the feeling of worthlessness that always haunted me. And the two suicide attempts. I felt embarrassed, humiliated, and sometimes I'd choke up, close my eyes, take a few deep breaths and wipe away the tears, and he'd put his arms around me, and I'd continue. I trusted him, and for the first time, I was completely open with someone about my problems, far more than I'd been with the two psychiatrists I'd seen. I even told Tom about the vodka in the refrigerator, and that sometimes I'd sneak a drink when he was asleep. Always having a bottle in the refrigerator made me feel more secure, and I'd open the door and look at it just to reassure myself that my vodka was still there. Even though I wasn't drinking as much as before, the thought of not drinking at all terrified me. It would be like a cripple losing her crutches. But sometimes I'd see the bottle, look at my scars and feel terrified, because I knew I never would've ended up in the ER if I hadn't been drinking. And I also knew, if I didn't quit, what had been my plan would become real—Lady Lazarus would end up in the ER again, but wouldn't survive.

Tom talked to me about his aunt who was an alcoholic, and about AA and the twelve steps. I'd heard most of what he had to say before, but this time, I listened. I said, "Maybe I should enter AA, as soon as the quarter ends," and he took my hand in his and said, "I'll do whatever I can to support you." That night, as Tom lay asleep, I lay next to him, thinking about my vodka. I got up, went to the kitchen, took it out of the refrigerator and stared at it. I unscrewed the cap, poured the vodka down the drain, went back to bed, spooned Tom and held onto him like I was in deep water and he was the log keeping me afloat.

But the weekend before I would finally start AA, there was the party at the house where Tom and Dick and their roommates lived. The night of the party, just before Tom and I left, he said, "We don't have to go, you know. We can just go see a movie instead."

"No. I want to go. Even though it'll be weird being in that house again. And confronting Dick for the first time in nine months."

"You still want your revenge?"

"A serial monogamist hurts a lot of women, and I think he should pay for what he's done, but... "

"But?"

I was almost shaking. Finally, I said, "Let's just see how it goes."

A few minutes later we parked, entered the house and walked into the kitchen, and there was Dick, in his white tuxedo jacket, blue jeans, and a black Led Zeppelin T-shirt, standing on the side of the counter that divided the kitchen in half and pouring gin into a shaker. I glanced at the two housemates and their girlfriends, on the other side of the counter, and saw Charlotte, toward the opposite far end, staring at me, a shocked look on her face. I smiled, and she smiled back. And then I fixed my eyes on Dick. It was strange to see him without a woman close to him. Noticing everyone was looking off to the side, he glanced over, saw Tom and me, froze and stared for what seemed forever. And then his eyes lit up, and he said, "Of all the gin joints in all the towns in all the world, she walks into mine." Everyone cracked up and then fell silent, their eyes darting back and forth from Dick to me. I felt my heart beating.

"Welcome back," he said, smiling as he peered into my eyes.

I smiled, too, trying to appear calm.

"I was wondering if Tom's Helen was the same one I'd known." He looked around at his roommates and corrected himself: "We'd known."

Charlotte nodded, appearing very amused by what she was witnessing.

"Well, how are you?" Dick asked.

Tom put his arm around my back, and I leaned into him and said, "I'm happy. I've found a wonderful man."

Dick nodded. "Good. Well, I guess I should add some more gin. We're going to need enough for... for seven martinis."

I said, "You don't need to make one for me. We're on our way to see a film. Just wanted to stop by to say hello."

"Yeah," Tom said. "I'll pass, too."

"Well," I said, "it's good to see you." I nodded again as I scanned the group, some of them still looking baffled.

I was about to turn away when Charlotte exclaimed, "Wait! Before you leave, I want to take a picture of the two of you." She reached over, picked up a camera on the counter, came around to Dick's side and had him move over so she could position herself in front of us. She said, "Smile just as beautifully as you did a minute ago," and aimed her Polaroid at us. The light flashed, the picture flowed out of the camera, and she took a look at it and handed it to me. "It'll take a few minutes to fully develop. Put it in your glove compartment."

Tom and I looked at it and saw our image—the first photograph of us ever—gradually coming into existence.

"You're a survivor!" Charlotte laughed.

I looked at her big grin and laughed back. No explanation was needed.

As Tom and I left the house, I realized that I got the revenge I'd wanted, which was no revenge at all, but simply the ability to walk back into that house, see Dick, and know that I could walk out, leave him behind and take my heart with me. My future was with Tom. I went through AA, did the twelve steps, made amends, suffered relapses, went through hell and started all over again. And again.

* * *

As I place the picture of Tom and me back in the tin box, I hear a cardinal whistling and chirping again, walk to the window and gaze at the crabapple tree and the flowers. Here we are, Tom and I, ready to make another big move in our lives. I've come such a long way since those days with Vince and Dick. I have so much to be proud of, so much to be happy about. My life with my family is beautiful. As beautiful as these flowers. They remind me of that woman in my composition course, the one with the tattoos, the green stems and leaves and delicate pink and blue blossoms that cover her arms from her shoulders to her wrists. I'd look at her and see a woman who isn't afraid to have feelings and splay them across her skin. When I'd have the students read something to themselves—a composition or an article—I'd gaze at her tattoos, fascinated by their beauty, and fantasize what one can do with tattoos. One day, she looked up, our eyes met, and I smiled and looked away. As she was walking by me on her way out of class, I told her I thought her tattoos were lovely, and she thanked me.

A few days later, we ran into each other at the cafeteria and ended up eating lunch together. She mentioned the name of the tattoo artist and said he'd talked to her about tattooing as an art that went back thousands of years and showed her pictures of tattoos from around the world and from different periods in history. I asked her how long it took him to do her tattoos, and if it was painful. She said she had to return for three or four sittings, and yes, it hurt, but it was worth it to use her skin as a canvas and transform it into a living work of art. And then she grinned and asked, "Why do you want to know all this? You want to get tattooed?" The question felt like a dare. I chuckled and told her I might want to. She took a piece of paper out of her purse, wrote the name of the artist and his address, handed it to me and said she couldn't wait to see what kind of tattoos I'd have done. I said it might be a while.

That was a month ago. Since then, I've thought about the artist transforming the scars on the inside of my forearms into stems by adding green leaves and blood red roses—or maybe peonies, or lilies, or chrysanthemums. Or luminous pink crabapple blossoms. Maybe there could be bees, butterflies, and hummingbirds, so the plants could be seen as giving life to other creatures. And then, when Mandy stares at my scars, she'll also see everything beautiful that has grown from them. And so will Nicky. And maybe I'll be able to talk to them about my feelings that led me to cut myself and everything I've done to be who I am today.

I find myself in a boisterous, Janis Joplin mood and see myself flaunting my flowers and singing, "Oh Lord, won't you buy me a Mercedes Benz." I love this feeling, this fantasy of myself as an irreverent, gutsy Janis singing on stage, asking the Lord to buy the next round and a night on the town. But I no longer do nights on the town or rounds in bars. I need a new song, one that will complement the beautiful flowers my scars will bear.

As I imagine those flowers, I hear Nicky and Mandy scream, "Mom, we're home." And I think, Yes, yes, I will talk to them.

Part II: 2006
Tom and Amanda drive to the Boundary Waters

"I wak'd, she fled, and day brought back my night."

Milton, "On His Deceased Wife"

Waiting on the front porch, looking at the garden on the other side of the balustrade, gazing at the Oriental lilies Helen planted, after we'd moved into this house, seventeen years ago... Seventeen years... A hummingbird swoops in, hovers above one of the milk-white blossoms of the Casa Blanca lilies, and then darts to another, its wings beating so fast they're just a blur. Like a beautiful lost soul seeking... seeking what? Helen would have an answer. A poetic one. She loved hummingbirds... They seem to prefer the Casa Blancas to the Stargazers, the Josephines, the hibiscus, and the other flowers. The bird darts to yet another blossom. I take a deep breath and hum as I exhale. I love to sit here on the porch, read, drink coffee, and breathe the air permeated with the intoxicating perfume of the Casa Blancas. Is it the fragrance that attracts the hummingbirds? Do they have a sense of smell? This one flutters off, and I try to follow it with my eyes, but it disappears. Gone. My gaze lands on the garden farther away from the house, the one full of roses near the sidewalk. The colors of the blossoms range from milk-white and baby-pink to a red as vibrant as blood flowing from a wound, and to another red so dark it's almost black. I sigh. These gardens are thick with weeds. They're almost as tall as the lilies. I keep telling myself I've got to find a gardener. I'll do it when we get back. Huh! I've told myself that before.

The front door closes behind me. I turn and see Amanda, in her up-north clothes—jeans, T-shirt, and running shoes—and notice the purse she went looking for in the house is slung over her shoulder and her jacket draped over her arm. "I'm ready," she says, as she walks toward me, her beautiful brown eyes beaming at me. Her mother's eyes. "What's that grin about, Dad?"

"I'm just happy. That's all. Happy you're here and... and we're going up to the cabin." I hug her.

"I'm happy, too," she says, smiling back at me, her voice resonating with excitement.

I go back to lock the door and turn around to see her looking at the gardens. I draw close to her.

"They're so beautiful," she says. "Every time I look at them, I think of Mom."

I take a deep breath and sigh, "Yeah."

We gaze at them for a while. And then she looks at me and says, "Dad, those weeds, they're going to choke the flowers if you don't—"

"Yeah, yeah. I'm going to deal with it."

She smiles and shakes her head.

We pick up our suitcases, head for the car, and drive off.

"You want to listen to the radio?" I ask, as we pass our neighbors' houses.

"No. I'd rather talk."

Her response surprises me. She's always been the quiet one in the family, the one you look at and wonder, What's she thinking? Soon we're on a thoroughfare. But rather than talk to me, she stares out her window at the houses, while I navigate traffic on our way to the freeway. When we reach it, I let out a big sigh. "Finally! On our way."

"Yeah. Feels good to be on the road." She looks at me. "I wish my plane hadn't arrived so late. We hardly got a chance to talk last night."

"It's too bad you couldn't have flown in yesterday morning, or sometime Friday. Then we could've all ridden together."

"Well, like I said, I had that appointment for financial aid scheduled for Friday and didn't feel comfortable trying to reschedule it. You know, asking for more aid than they'd already offered... and what they'd offered was pretty generous. And by the time that appointment was confirmed, it was too late to make a reservation for yesterday morning. The tickets were all sold out. So, I had to fly in last night. I'm sorry, Dad."

"It's not a problem." But I wonder, Why did you wait so long to schedule the appointment, if you'd received the offer from the Financial Aid office four months before?

"Besides," she says, "this way I get you all to myself."

I feel her smiling at me. I look at her and say, "Well, we can talk now." I look back at the road. "We've got about four hours to go. Five hours, if you want to take the scenic route along the North Shore. More than five hours if we stop. You want to do that?"

"You know I love the drive along Lake Superior."

"Oh, I forgot. I heard something on Minnesota Public Radio this morning about thunderstorms that started yesterday up there and might continue today."

"I don't see any clouds here. I'd rather take the North Shore, even if there is some rain. It's always so beautiful."

"Okay, we'll do it."

As I'm thinking about how wonderful it is to have this time alone with my daughter, I hear her repeat, "Five hours." I look and see her warm gaze fixed on me and ask, "What's that look about?"

"What look?" Her eyes sparkle. "How's Grace?"

"She's good. Busy with work. She's been looking forward to a week at the cabin. Seemed pretty happy to leave yesterday morning with Nick and his girlfriend."

"And Nicky?"

"He's fine. He surprised me when he called to tell me he and Jessie would be coming. I didn't think he'd take time off from the campaign. But he seems pretty confident his candidate will win, so maybe that's why."

"What's his girlfriend like?"

"Kind of laid back. You know how Nick talks when he gets going on politics. Looks you in the eye, like he's got ninety seconds to convince you of what the world needs." I glance over and see Amanda looking back at me, with a bit of a smirk. I turn my attention back to the road, wondering what that was all about, but then Nick and Jessie come back into my thoughts. "Well, when he got going the other night, Jessie sat there and nodded and smiled. She rolled her eyes once, and I knew exactly what she was thinking." I chuckle, as I remember her glimpsing my grin, and the recognition I saw in her eyes. "But she seems to love him. I think she's calmed him down. He's been living in Portland now for over a year. That's the longest he's stayed anywhere since he graduated college." I pause, remembering the years he spent wandering around the country, from city to city, job to job, while I worried, wondering if he'd ever find his way.

"It sounds like he's happy," she says. "I can't wait to see them."

I hesitate, wondering if I should, given the tension that usually surrounds the question, and then decide, Why not? "How about you? You seeing anyone?"

"I see someone every day."

"Okay." I laugh at her joke. "But you never bring anyone home."

"I will. When the time's right. Now, I just want to focus on school." She looks at me. "Thanks again, Dad, for helping me with the money."

"Sure. I'm happy to." I look at her and then back at the road, while my mind detours to worrying about money. Putting her through college in New York and Nicholas in Portland cost me everything I had. They both started out at Macalester College, and if they'd continued there, I'd be in good shape financially. But they wanted to move. They needed to get away. Too many memories. I've felt at times like leaving, too, but I couldn't. I can't.

I become aware of the freeway and the suburban neighborhoods we're driving through. Not much traffic. We're moving fast. I notice Amanda staring out her window. I check the road, then look at her again and ask, "How does it feel to be going back to school, after three years of working?"

"I'm looking forward to it."

"If you go on to get a PhD, after you complete your master's, there'll be another Dr. Faust in the family."

She laughs. "Yep."

"Did I ever tell you about the time your mother and I were at a party, and she was joking with friends and said, 'Whenever someone refers to him as Dr. Faust, I think of myself as Helen of Troy.' And she struck a dramatic pose and said, 'He's always asking me to make him immortal with a kiss.'"

Amanda sighs and smiles. "You've mentioned that a few times, Dad."

"And then she said she'd given me a kiss, I was already immortal, and I could at least thank her. And everyone laughed." I chuckle as I remember Helen caressing my cheek with her hand while grinning at the circle of friends, a glass of wine in her other hand. She could really come alive at parties and charm people with her jokes, her wit. Until she drank too much. Then we'd have to leave. I sigh as I remember holding her, feeling her hair and her tears against my cheek and comforting her...

* * *

Coming out of my thoughts and realizing I haven't heard anything from Amanda for some time, I glance over and see her staring ahead. I look at the road, then back at her and ask, "What's going through your mind?"

"Every time I see those gardens, I think of her."

"I do too, sweetheart. I do, too."

* * *

We leave the suburbs, and now it's just warehouses, shopping centers, isolated houses, farms, fields, and clusters of woodland. I recognize the

Dairy Queen sign at the end of an exit we're approaching and remember the time I had Nick and Amanda in the back seat. They were fighting and whining, calling one another stupid and mean, and I couldn't get them to stop. And then I noticed up ahead the exit, and the signs for a gas station and the DQ at the end of it, and I said, "Hey, if you guys can be nice to one another, after I fill up the tank, we'll get Dairy Queen. Okay?" I filled the tank, we got our Dairy Queens, sat at a picnic table and ate our treats, and I got them to talk about what they wanted to do when we got to the cabin, the one at the resort we go to every summer. Of course, swimming. Canoeing. Making s'mores. Playing board games at night. And maybe going on a camping trip again, and portaging from one lake to another, and returning to the one with the Native American pictographs on the cliff walls that date back hundreds of years. And they remembered waking one morning to a pack of wolves howling, each eerie howl launched at a different second and in a different key. Just the memory left them speechless for a moment, their mouths hanging open. When we got back on the road, I had Nick sit in the front seat and Amanda in the back, where she read her book in peace. The entire drive, from St. Paul to the North Shore, to the two-lane highway to Ely, and from there to the resort, I've done so often, that the buildings and exits have become landmarks that tell me where we are and how much further we have to go. The DQ means we still have four hours.

* * *

I slow down as the two lanes of traffic heading north merge into one, orange barrels with white stripes forcing the merge. It's Sunday, so whatever construction needs to be done on the blocked lane will probably start tomorrow. The cars are still driving fast, but closer now. I tense up.

"Dad." Amanda's voice startles me.

"Yeah?"

"Are you looking forward to teaching this fall?"

"I always look forward to teaching. Keeps me out of trouble." I glance over and see her smiling.

"What are you teaching?"

"The usual. And my course on the war in Vietnam."

She remains silent for a minute, and then says, "You've taught that several times."

"Yeah. I think it's important."

"Why?"

"Because of how we got into that war and stayed in it, even when we knew we shouldn't have gone to war and should've ended it long before we did. That's just one of many reasons." I could hear the anger in my voice.

"Well, how do you feel about the war in Iraq? Are you going to teach a course on it?"

"As a matter of fact, I am. Spring semester. Just finished writing a review of Tom Ricks's *Fiasco: The American Military Adventure in Iraq*. Have you read it?"

"No."

"He was interviewed on NPR the other day. Said the invasion of Iraq was the greatest blunder in the history of American foreign policy. The greatest blunder. And yet we know damned well some of those senators who voted for it will run for president. And if the subject comes up, they'll claim they didn't know the Iraqis didn't have WMDs, even though there was never any evidence they did. They'll say they made the best decision possible with the information they had. They'll tell one lie after another to get elected." I clench my teeth and take a deep breath.

"You always sound angry when you talk about those wars. Do you get upset in class, too?"

"No, I don't. And why all the questions?"

"Oh, I've been thinking."

She's smiling at me.

"Here I am, about to start working on a master's in psychology, with the intention of becoming a therapist and using talk therapy, and I come from a family in which no one likes to talk."

"Above all, you."

She grins back and shakes her head. "Oh, I think we're both pretty quiet, Dad. It would be good for us to talk. And we've got plenty of time."

It would be good for us to talk? I've often felt her staring at me and wondered what was going through her mind. But she obviously wonders what goes through mine, too. And now we're trapped in this car for five hours.

She says, "I think it's interesting that you usually avoid talking about those wars, and yet, you've developed and teach courses on them. And when you do talk about them, it's with the passion of the anti-war activist you've said you were when you were young." She pauses and looks at me. "If you're interested in those wars, if you can teach them, why don't you talk about them?"

"I haven't taught a course on the Iraq War yet."

"Okay. Well, if you can teach a course on the war in Vietnam, why don't you talk about it?"

I don't respond.

"Dad?"

I shake my head. "There's something different about lecturing on a war, or discussing it in class, and talking about it... " I take a deep breath. "Talking about it with one of my kids."

"Is that true for all wars, or just the Vietnam War?"

"Vietnam."

"Huh!" She falls silent, and then says, "I remember, when I was little, and you used to watch those films about the war over and over."

"Not over and over. I'd watch them, but—"

"Well, often enough so I could be sitting close by and hear Jim Morrison singing that weird line about all the children being insane, or one of the characters talking, like the one who says, 'I love the smell of napalm in the morning,' and I'd know where you were in the film, how much longer it would go on. And when I'd hear that voice rasp, 'The horror. The horror,' I knew the film was over." She pauses, takes a breath. "Sometimes, you'd get angry, really angry. Like when you'd watch that film in which the Vietnamese father cries about his wife and kids being killed in a bombing of his village and yells at the filmmaker that his beautiful, eight-year-old daughter was killed right here, she was feeding the pigs, she was so sweet, and he says, 'I'll give you my daughter's beautiful shirt, and you can take it back to the United States and throw it in Nixon's face, tell the murderer she was only a little girl.'"

I nod, remembering how upset I'd get when I'd watch *Hearts and Minds*.

"I was around five the first time I heard that man mourning his dead daughter. I stopped playing with my doll, walked over close to you and stared at the TV."

"If I watched those films when you were present, then I wasn't being a good father."

"No." She shakes her head. "You were obsessed. You watched those films every time you taught that course." She waits for me to respond, but I don't. "Do you think it was because of Bobby?"

I stare at the car ahead, feeling her eyes on me. That car passes the one in front of it, and I realize the orange-and-white barrels have disappeared and both lanes are open. No words come to mind, just cries from years before that still echo inside me.

Her voice says, "Grandma and Grandpa have those high school graduation pictures of you and Bobby on their mantelpiece. And that picture of him in his military uniform."

I see Bobby's face beaming at a world he was eager to explore. And, in the other picture, the stone face of the young man in the uniform.

"And you've always had that picture on your chest of drawers in your bedroom, of you and Bobby when you were teenagers. You look so happy together... grinning, your arms around each other's backs. Well, your arm around his back. He has his two fingers sticking up from behind your head."

I nod, nod at the picture I can see of Bobby and me that's greeted me every day for the last thirty-some years.

"I didn't even know you had a brother until I was seven or eight. One day, Mom and I were sitting on the edge of the bed in your room, and while she was talking, I noticed the picture on your chest of drawers. I'd seen it before and wondered, Who are those boys? When I asked, she said, 'Well, one of them you know.' And when I looked at her, perplexed, she said, 'The one on the left is your dad.' And I remember looking at that little boy, with his big grin, and thinking, Wow! That's Dad? Then I asked who the other boy was, and she said, 'That's your dad's brother, Bobby.' I asked why we never see him. She kind of smiled and said, 'No one sees him, sweetie. He went away to a country called Vietnam a long time ago, before you were born.' And when I kept on asking questions, she just said, 'You need to talk to your dad.'" She looks at me. "We both know how that went. You don't like to talk about personal things." Her eyes remain fixed on me. "When you and Mom would have guests at the house, she'd always do most of the talking. You'd hardly say a word, unless the subject of the war came up, and *then* you'd talk."

"He should've never gone to that war. No one should've." I take a deep breath and grip the steering wheel as I stare ahead.

"Are you okay, Dad?"

I take a couple more breaths, my hands relax and I say, "Yeah."

After a pause she asks, "Do you mind talking about Bobby?"

I don't respond.

"Dad?"

"What do you want to know?"

"Whatever you'd like to tell me."

"Huh. Well... " I hesitate. "He was two years older than me."

"Okay." She nods.

"We played together when we were kids." I pause, feeling memories coming back. "We loved to throw a ball around in our backyard, or go to a field with our buddies and play football, baseball. We'd bike a couple of miles in the summer to Lake Josephine, to this private beach where we'd pay a dime, or maybe a quarter, to get in. The lake was at the bottom of a long slope, covered with grass and shaded by trees. And there was a huge house at the top of the hill, off to the side. Not far from the house, there was this flat area, exposed to the sun, and that's where Bobby and I would go, where the cool kids—the kids who were going to be seniors in high school, or who'd already graduated—that's where they hung out, sprawling on their towels, smoking, horsing around, telling dumbass jokes, bullshitting one another and getting into towel fights. Some of the guys and their girlfriends would lie there and make out, in front of everyone, and then stop to light up and look around at the rest of us." I chuckle at the memory. "I'm sure they thought they were really cool." I chuckle again. "That's where Bobby started hanging out after his junior year. And he brought me with him. That was, what, the year I turned fifteen."

I see myself lying on my towel, my head resting on my hands, the sun shining down through the clearing between the trees and blades of grass in front of my eyes. Bobby gets up, a couple of his buddies stand up and follow him, and I follow them as they all trot down the slope, past the concession cabin and the green picnic tables, to the sandy beach and the dock that juts out into the lake, and we begin running, fly off the end, swim to the raft, climb up and wrestle and push one another off. We climb back onto the raft, jump onto the diving board, cannonball, swim toward shore, wade through the shallow water to the beach and walk up to the top of the hill, where we lie down on our towels. My head resting on my hands, I feel the sun warm my body. I'm in a lazy, sun-drenched stupor, just gazing at what's in view—a girl, lying a few feet away. Her shoulders raised, she's resting on her elbows and smoking a cigarette, her head turned to the side as she talks to the guy lying next to her. The top of her bikini is untied. I stare at her breasts, revealed except for the nipples. As she continues talking to the guy, I remain still, afraid my slightest movement might draw her attention to me and what I'm doing. She takes another drag, looks straight ahead as she flicks her ashes and notices my eyes ogling her. She stares back at me, scowls, jabs her cigarette into the ground and says something to the guy, and they both glare at me. I feel caught and look away.

"Dad?"

I start, glance over to see Amanda staring at me, and look back at the road. "What was I saying?"

"When you were fifteen, you began going to a lake with Bobby and his friends."

"Oh, yeah." I pause. "You know, the amazing thing about Bobby is he always stood up for me. Always ready to protect me and help me any way he could... I remember, this one time, the two of us were at that lake with a couple of his buddies. We'd gone swimming and were lying in the sun. This guy, who was lying next to his girlfriend a few feet away from me, he got up, came over and stood above me. I looked up from his feet in front of me and saw him sneering down at me. He was big, built like a boxer. Not the kind of guy you mess with. He said, 'Why are you staring at my girlfriend?' I said, 'I'm not staring at her.' He said, 'Yeah you are, you little creep.' And he stepped on my shoulder, put all his weight on me. I screamed. It hurt like hell. Bobby leaped up and pushed the guy off me. Threw himself at him and knocked him to the ground, and the two of them started fighting. Everyone gathered around. And then the manager of the beach showed up, had some guys grab hold of them and pull them apart, and told Bobby and the other guy to knock it off or he'd have them thrown out." I shake my head. "I think one of the reasons I remember this so clearly is the guy who stepped on my shoulder," I pause to look at Amanda and then back at the road, "he was huge. And Bobby, he was just a tall, lanky kid. The fact he took on that guy to protect me, his little brother... " I shake my head. "That was so like him."

After a brief silence, Amanda says, "So, were you staring at the guy's girlfriend?"

I glance at Amanda and see a sly look on her face. "Well, I looked at her, but... "

Amanda snickers.

"The guy was a bully. I was just an excuse for him to show his girlfriend how tough he was. It was all theater. But, getting back to Bobby. When we were little, if we got into trouble, he'd stand in front of me and do the talking for both of us. This one time, we were playing in the backyard, I think we were about seven and five, and we decided we wanted a treat. We knew there was a bag of Oreo cookies in a cupboard in the kitchen. So, we snuck into the house, slid a chair over toward a counter, and Bobby climbed up, opened the cupboard door and pulled out the bag, and we were just about to slide the chair back, when Mom came into the kitchen and caught us." I pause as I remember how I jumped with fright and cowered behind Bobby when Mom demanded to know what we were doing. "He stood in front of me and did the talking. And I knew he was ready to take the punishment if any came."

"Maybe that's why you're so quiet. He'd talk for you when you were little."

"Maybe." I smile as I think of how I looked up to him. And then, as I see the flash of playfulness in his eyes, I feel his absence, and it pulls the plug on my happiness that drains right out of me, and anger fills the void. "When Bobby graduated high school, he got a job at a car dealership, running cars through the car wash, delivering them to people, and to other lots that belonged to his employer. And then he got drafted and sent to Vietnam." I pause. "There were no champagne squadrons for ordinary people. Just for the rich. The rich and the well-connected." I take a deep breath. I can't talk about Bobby without getting angry. Just as I can't feel his presence without feeling his absence.

I stare at the car a hundred feet ahead, glance in the mirror and see another car far behind. Billboards, fields, cattle grazing, woods scattered here and there. Another exit sign appears, this one for Hinckley, famous for the fire that flashed through the town in the 1890s, with the force of an atomic bomb, as one of the displays in the town's museum says. In four hours, hundreds of thousands of acres burned, and hundreds of people died. How did that firestorm compare to those in Vietnam, the ones ignited by our napalm bombs? When Bobby came back from the war, he talked about the bombings and the sea of fire that could engulf a village and a wood in seconds, and I'd think of the people burning in that sea, the flames searing their lungs as they tried to breathe. When the films about Vietnam started coming out, they confirmed everything he'd said. I take a breath and try to calm myself. We've just passed the turnoff for Hinckley. Three and a half hours to go.

"Dad? Dad?"

I glance at Amanda. She's staring at me, her mouth open. "What?"

"Are you okay?"

"Yeah. I'm fine."

She gazes at my face, until she seems assured. After a pause, she says, "I imagine you talk about the champagne squadrons in your course. Do you mention the current president as one of those who benefitted?"

"You bet I do. And I mention others, too." I glance over, see her eyes still fixed on me and look back at the road. "When I teach that course, I have my students read traditional history books that deal with politics, battles and all that. But I also have them read memoirs and fiction by people who fought in the war—*Going after Cacciato*, *The Things They Carried*, *A Rumor of War*. Or by Vietnamese authors, like *The Sorrow of War*. And we watch films—documentaries and fiction films. Even surreal ones, like *Apocalypse Now*. And films that deal with how it felt for the Americans forced or conned into going, like *The Deer Hunter* and *Born on the Fourth of July…* People have raised questions about me using fiction and memoir in a history course, but I want my students to learn what it was like for the men who didn't get to party in a champagne squadron and got shipped off to Vietnam, as well as for the Vietnamese.

"And people have criticized me for the films I've chosen, because they're not realistic. Like *The Deer Hunter*. The Vietnamese playing Russian Roulette? That's absurd! But you see the randomness of destruction and death in the section of the film that's set in Vietnam, and then you watch someone put a bullet in the chamber of a gun, spin the cylinder and hand the gun to a soldier, who holds it to his head and struggles to cock the hammer, and you see the anxiety in the man's face, and then he closes his eyes and pulls the trigger, and you hear a click, or a bang. And you feel what life was like in that war, with its guerilla tactics. Some invisible being puts a bullet in a chamber, spins the cylinder, holds the gun to your head, and you feel it, you hear the hammer click, the gun's ready to fire, and then... you set out on patrol, walk through fields, paddies and villages, along rivers and streams, and across bridges, and you try to get through the day, knowing that invisible being might pull the trigger at any second. Or might not. You never know. Think of the anxiety and the stress. The character played by Christopher Walken is so traumatized by the experience, he becomes addicted to the game, chooses to remain in Vietnam, continue putting the gun to his head and pulling the trigger—until he kills himself. He had the option to go home, but he couldn't.

"The main character in *Apocalypse Now* has already served in Vietnam, gone home, gone through a divorce, and returned, because he can't stay away. Can't stay away from the trauma. The stress you can hear in the drone of the helicopters, of their blades whacking the air." I shake my head. "If I hear that sound in the real world, I think of the opening sequence in the film, of the choppers flying back and forth and of the threat of imminent death. And then the cut to the main character lying on his back, opening his eyes, seeing the blades of the fan circling above him, hearing the thumping of the helicopter blades and awakening to the world that has already traumatized him."

I stare at the car far ahead of us and wonder again, Is that what it was like for you, Bobby? My mind drifts, until I hear Amanda say, "Did you ever talk to Bobby about the war?"

"A few times. Once he got home."

"He came home?"

"Yeah. After his first tour."

"Wait a minute. I'm confused. I thought he died in Vietnam."

"He chose to go back. And a year later, he was reported MIA."

"Oh my God!"

"When my parents first told me he was reported missing, I thought, At least he's alive. And that's the way I thought about his MIA status for the first few years. But, as time passed, I came to accept that MIA meant dead. And yet, I still have moments when I catch myself thinking about him as if he were alive. Like you and I might pull off the road to a restaurant to get some lunch and find him sitting at a table, grinning at us and saying, 'It's about time you got here.' I can see him doing that."

I smile at the thought. "He might've died over thirty years ago, but he'll live as long as I do."

After a long pause, I hear Amanda say, "Do you ever talk about Bobby with anyone?"

"No."

"Why not?"

"It doesn't help." I look over and find her gazing at me. I know what she's thinking. "I saw a therapist years ago. It might've helped a little with the pain, getting it out there, but... it's still there."

"Teaching the course, does that help? It's obvious one of the reasons you teach it so often and put so much work into it is because of Bobby. Am I right?"

I nod and continue staring at the road, while in my mind I find myself sitting in the living room with my parents. We're waiting for Bobby to call so we can pick him up at the airport. Mom's sewing something, Dad's got his nose in the newspaper and I'm trying to read *The Quiet American*. Bobby's arrival time comes and goes, but no call. I keep on checking my watch and staring at the phone on the table, next to the couch where Mom's sitting, until I can't sit still anymore. I get up, walk around and look out the window at the sidewalk and the cars parked in the street. I plop back down in the armchair and try to focus on my book. I'm curious about Vietnam and want to know more than what's been in the news, want to be able to talk with Bobby about it. If he wants to talk. Will he? I wrote to him often, telling him about the four dead in Ohio, the anti-war demonstrations all over the country, the rage so many of us felt against the politicians who'd lied to lead us into the war and I wondered what he was thinking, feeling. The few times he responded he didn't say. I kept on writing, not as often as in the beginning, but I couldn't let go of him. I'd try to imagine what he was going through, how he felt about being in the war and how I would've felt if I'd been drafted and forced to go fight in a war I didn't support. That was the impression I'd had when he'd left, that he didn't support the war. He'd participated in demonstrations, but maybe he'd changed his mind. I looked again at the phone, as if staring at it could make it ring, and got up and walked to the window.

There he was, in his uniform. He'd just gotten out of a cab and was coming toward the house. I shouted, "He's here!" And rushed to the door and down the walk. He stopped, grinned and dropped his satchel, and we threw our arms around one another. And then I heard Mom and Dad shouting and running toward us and stepped aside so they could hug him, too. Mom was wiping tears away as she cried, "Thank God! Oh, thank God you're here!" And Dad held him and said, "Welcome home, son. Welcome home." I took Bobby's bag, and we walked him into the house and the living room. Mom said, "Sit down, I've got coffee ready in the kitchen," and left. And Dad said, "Make yourself comfortable." Bobby sat down, took his service cap off and set it on the table. I grinned at him like a kid who'd just gotten the best present of his life—his big brother, home from the war.

"Well, son, you happy to be home?"

Bobby nodded. "Sure, Dad. Of course."

"We've got a fantastic dinner planned for you. I'm going to grill some sirloin steaks and corn on the cob, and your mom's made potato salad and chocolate cake, and we'll have some ice cream with that. And, ah... " Dad, his eyes radiating joy, beamed at Bobby as he said, "It's so good to have you home, son. So damn good."

"It's good to be home, Dad."

Mom arrived carrying a tray with the coffee pot, cups, and saucers. She set it down on the coffee table, in front of Bobby, sat down next to him, poured for him and asked, "No milk or sugar?"

"That's right, Mom. Thanks."

She handed him his cup, served Dad, me and herself, and we gazed at Bobby as we all sipped our coffee. He set his cup down and leaned back, looking very formal in his uniform.

"I'm sorry," Dad said, "I totally forgot. I should've asked if you'd like a beer. Or maybe a glass of whiskey."

"Wow!" Bobby exclaimed, a startled look on his face. "You've never asked me that before. Would I like a beer or a whiskey? Yeah," he nodded, "whiskey sounds good."

Dad went to the cabinet in the dining room, got a bottle of whiskey and a glass, set them on the table in front of Bobby, poured him a couple fingers and sat back down. Bobby took a sip and said, "Tastes good, Dad. Haven't had a whiskey since, ah... since I was on the plane."

We all laughed.

"Glad to see you haven't lost your sense of humor," Dad said.

"Yeah," Mom said, her eyes sparkling with love through a glaze of tears. "It's wonderful to have you home. We've missed you so much."

Dad nodded and said, "Our world feels right again."

"Thanks, Mom. Dad. I'm really happy to be home."

Dad cleared his throat and wiped his eyes, and Mom wiped hers, too, and took a sip of coffee.

I said, "So, Bobby, what's the first thing you wanna do?"

He looked around at us and said, "Spend time with you guys."

"What else?"

"See Shirley."

"Oh, is she coming for dinner?" Mom asked.

"No, she couldn't come. But I'm going to see her after dinner."

"Oh, wonderful! She can join us tomorrow night if she wants. We have something special planned." She paused and smiled, looking excited as she said, "We're going to have dinner at the Lexington with Mary and Jack and your cousins to celebrate your homecoming." She paused again, probably expecting to see a look of amazement on Bobby's face, given what a ritzy restaurant the Lexington was, but he just smiled, nodded and said, "Okay," like it was no big deal.

He downed his whiskey, stood up and was about to pick up his glass and cup, when Mom said, "No, no, sweetie, I'll take care of that."

"Thanks, Mom." He smiled. "I think I'd like to get out of this uniform and put on some normal clothes."

"Your room's just as you left it."

He picked up his satchel and left. My eyes followed him until he disappeared. I looked at Mom and Dad. They seemed as puzzled by his calm as I was. We sat there for a while, and then Dad picked up the newspaper he'd been reading, Mom took up her sewing and I returned to my novel, but couldn't focus on it. There was something off with Bobby, something that made me wonder if he *was* happy to be home. Mom put down her sewing, stared at it for a while, and then got up and carried the tray with the pot, the cups and Bobby's glass to the kitchen. I went upstairs to my room, lay down on my bed and found myself listening for sounds on the other side of the wall that might suggest what Bobby was doing, but heard nothing. I went to his room and knocked on his door. He opened and stood there, in jeans and a short-sleeved shirt. "What's up?" he asked, as he smiled at me.

"I thought maybe we could talk for a while."

"Sure. Come on in."

He stepped aside, and I walked into his room and looked around at the familiar pictures—of him in his high school football uniform; of the two of us, grinning at the camera, my arm around his back, his two fingers sticking up from the back of my head; and of Shirley in her prom dress and him in his rented tuxedo, the two of them posing in the living room. He'd graduated, gotten a job and started saving money, but instead of getting his own apartment and marrying Shirley, he got drafted. I missed him so much, I'd go into his room, put the Beatles or the Stones on his record player, lie on his bed, stare at the ceiling and listen to his music, while thinking of the things we used to do together, before he went off to the war.

I sat down on the bed. Bobby walked past me to his desk, pulled the chair out, swung it around so its back faced me, sat down, offered me a cigarette and took one himself. He extended his lighter, and I leaned forward and lit up.

"So," I said, as I exhaled, "you're going to go see Shirley after dinner."

"She's expecting me." He beamed and took a drag and, for the first time since he'd gotten home, he looked happy. "She says she can't wait to see me. We'll spend some time with her parents and then go somewhere we can be alone." I could see the joy he anticipated in his smile. He grabbed the metal wastebasket next to his desk, pulled it between us, tapped his cigarette on the edge and asked, "You got the keys?"

"The keys?"

"For the car."

"Oh, yeah. Sure." I handed him his keys. "It's all ready to go. Got it tuned up and filled the tank."

"Hope you had some fun with it."

"Lotsa dates." I grinned.

"Great!" He looked at the keys, as if he were refamiliarizing himself with them, or the life he'd been living before he went to Vietnam, and then put them in his pocket. "So, this fall, you're going to the U."

"You read my letter?"

"I read all your letters. I know all about you, Tom." He laughed and then got a serious look. "I'm happy you're going to get a deferment. Won't have to go to this fucking war." He took a drag and jabbed his cigarette against the inside of the basket.

"What's it like over there?"

He shook his head. "That's a loaded question." He snickered. "Better than a loaded gun." His amused look faded. "It's war. People kill and get killed."

I took a drag, stubbed out my cigarette and looked down at the floor, wishing I hadn't asked. I didn't know what to say.

"Your buddies get killed. You don't make friends with the new guys, because they'll probably end up dead, too. You give them all nicknames, so you don't even begin to get to know them. Sooner or later, you're alone… Like I said, glad you're getting a deferment."

"As long as I'm a full-time student, I should be okay."

"Good."

We stared at one another, and then he gave me a faint smile, nodded and looked down at the basket. We were so close to one another, but a world apart.

There was a knock at the door. Mom looked in and said, "Your dad's grilling the steaks. We'll be ready to eat in a few minutes."

"Thanks, Mom." Bobby smiled back at her. "We'll be right down."

"Okay." She closed the door.

"What are your plans for tonight?" he asked.

"Don't really have any."

"You got a girlfriend?"

"Nah. Can't seem to find the right girl."

"Well, you want the right one. I didn't find Shirley until just a few months before I graduated."

"That's great. I mean that you found her."

"Yeah," he nodded, his eyes warm with his love for her. "Well, you hungry?"

"Yeah. We should go down."

We entered the dining room and sat at our usual places at the table, as if Bobby had never left. Mom disappeared into the kitchen and returned with the potato salad, and then with a platter piled with corn on the cob, followed by Dad with the steaks. He asked Bobby if he'd like a beer, went back to the kitchen and returned with beers for both of them. He sat down at his end, with Bobby at the other, while Mom and I sat across from one another. Dad raised his beer to toast Bobby's return, and we welcomed him home again. While we dug in, Mom talked about how delicious the corn had been that summer, and Dad about how expensive the steaks were—rib eye steaks, the best money could buy. And then the conversation turned to Bobby, with Dad asking him what the food was like in Vietnam, and Mom if he'd gotten to know any of the people over there and Bobby responding with vague answers—the food was good, and, no, he hadn't really gotten to know any of the people. He responded to a few more questions about Vietnam with similar answers that didn't reveal much and didn't lead to a conversation, and his responses to questions about what he wanted to do now that he was home suggested he hadn't thought much about it. We stopped asking questions and, by the end of the meal, the only thing left to talk about was how good Mom's cake was. Then we sat in silence, in front of our plates covered with smears of chocolate frosting and vanilla ice cream.

Bobby looked around at us and said, "Well, Shirley's expecting me, so I need to get going. Dad, thanks for grilling the steaks and the corn.

They were great. And Mom, the potato salad and cake were fantastic. Best meal I've had since I left home." He stood up.

"I'm glad you liked it," Mom said. "When do you think you'll be home?"

"I don't know. Might be late."

"I'll leave the light on for you, sweetie."

"Thanks, Mom." He looked around at us, said, "I'll see you in the morning," and headed for the door.

The rest of us remained seated, following him with our eyes until he disappeared. The door closed, and no one spoke. Mom sighed, got up and cleared our dessert dishes, and I followed her into the kitchen, where she set the dishes on the counter next to the sink and said, "I'll take care of these in the morning."

She went upstairs. I returned to the living room and found Dad had disappeared. I didn't know what to do, having planned on spending the evening with Bobby, so I turned on the TV and watched something, while thinking about Bobby's absence, like he hadn't really come home. I went back upstairs to my room, lay down on my bed and continued reading *The Quiet American.* I read for a couple hours, started drifting off, and decided to go downstairs and watch TV until Bobby got home. When I reached the stairs, I noticed light coming from the living room. I stopped at the entrance to the room when I saw him sitting in one of the armchairs, staring straight ahead, a glass of whiskey in his hand. He looked lost. After a few seconds, he glanced at me, his mouth hanging open and his eyes red. He looked away, wiped them, and looked back at me.

"You okay?" I asked.

"Yeah." He took a drink.

"When did you get home?"

He mumbled, "I don't know." He stared at the floor and seemed to forget I was there. After a while, he looked at me and took another drink.

"How did your evening go?" I asked.

"Huh! How did it go?" He shook his head. "She's got a new guy."

"A new guy?"

"Yeah. That's why she didn't want to join us for dinner." He picked up the bottle standing on the table next to his chair, poured and drank. "It would've been awkward for her to come here and tell me she's fucking another guy. I guess I should be grateful she didn't come." He sighed. "That's why she stopped writing a couple months ago. I was too stupid to figure it out." He paused. "Nah, that wasn't it. I just didn't want to admit the obvious." He took a drink and stared off. He seemed to become aware of the glass in his hand, saw it was empty and poured himself another. He looked at me. "How was your night? Couldn't have been as bad as mine."

"I'm sorry, Bobby."

"Yeah." He fell silent, like he was in a trance. After a while, he became aware of my presence again and asked, "So, what did you do tonight?"

"I stayed home. I'm reading *The Quiet American*."

"What's that?"

"A novel set in Vietnam."

"Never heard of it." He gulped the rest of his whiskey. "Well, I'm going to bed. I think I've drunk enough booze to get some sleep."

He stood up, swayed, stepped back and regained his balance.

"You okay?" I asked.

"I'm fine." He chuckled. "Just fucking fine." He headed for the foyer and clomped up the stairs.

I shook my head. What a shitty homecoming! After everything he must've gone through in Vietnam, and then he comes back to this. I looked at the bottle. It was nearly empty. I put it away, took the glass to the kitchen, rinsed it, and went to bed.

The next day, a Saturday, I looked around for Bobby, but couldn't find him. Mom said he'd driven off somewhere. She thought he'd be back soon. I got my book from upstairs and read in the living room, hoping for an opportunity to hang out with him. I was finishing the last page when I heard the front door close. I got up, walked over to the foyer and saw him in the dining room, squatting in front of the china cabinet, next to a brown paper bag, setting a bottle of whiskey on the bottom shelf. He looked up and said, "Hey, Tom."

"Why are you wearing your uniform?"

He grabbed the bag as he stood up, and I heard bottles clink inside. He closed the cabinet door and turned toward me. "Because no one's going to card a veteran." He grinned. "Old enough to die in a war, but not to buy whiskey." He went up to his room. My mind repeats his words as I think of the irony.

* * *

I start, as I remember Amanda. I've forgotten about her. I glance over to see her staring out her window at a dense wood and feel a need to connect. "It's beautiful," I say.

She looks at me and shakes her head. "That's the way you've always been, Dad. Disappear, sometimes for days, and then you're back."

I nod and sigh as I think, Yeah, I still do that. The bad father. And I wonder why my kids moved off to the coasts. "Let's see. We were talking about Bobby. Right?"

"We were. You said he'd come home from the war. And then he chose to go back." She looks at me. "Remember?"

I nod. I hear the warmth in her voice and know I'm forgiven. I was just Dad being Dad. "I remember," I say.

"Why would he do that?"

"I've wondered about that for years." I pause, feeling the question that has haunted me. "There were probably a lot of reasons. One might've been that his first evening home, his girlfriend, who he'd planned on marrying, told him she'd found a new guy."

"That sucks."

"Yeah. That was his first gut-punch." I pause again, remembering his pain. "Another might've been the way some of the people our age treated him. The second night he was home, Mom, Dad, Bobby and I met up with my mom's older sister, her husband, and their two kids for dinner at the Lexington."

"The Lexington? Really? Grandma and Grandpa dining at the Lexington?"

"Yeah. I know. A ritzy restaurant like that?" I laugh, and then the amusement I feel evaporates as the memory comes back. "I'll never forget the look on the face of my cousin, Denny, when he saw Bobby in his Army uniform. His condescending smile. He shook Bobby's hand, patted him on the shoulder and welcomed him home, but that smirk didn't leave his face. The two of them were close when we were little. Denny lived just a few blocks away, and Mom used to take us over to her sister's house, and we'd play with him, or he'd come to our place. And then my aunt and uncle and their kids moved into a huge house on Cathedral Hill, and we moved to the suburbs. Rarely saw them after that. So... Where was I?"

"The Lexington?"

"Oh, yeah. Yeah. We arrived and sat down. When the waitress came to take drink orders, she stared at Bobby, wondering perhaps if he was old enough, and then wrote down his order. She ignored me and moved on to the adults at the table. The drinks came, Dad interrupted the conversation to raise a toast to Bobby and then we all went back to talking to one another. Denny started asking Bobby questions about what he'd seen in Vietnam. If Bobby said he didn't feel like talking about something, like whether or not he'd seen people massacred, then Denny seemed to get suspicious and asked him more questions. He kept on bugging Bobby, and Bobby kept on drinking and flagging the waitress when she walked by to order another whiskey. When she served our dinners, he ordered yet another, and Dad stared at him and cleared his throat. When he caught Bobby's attention, he gave him a look that said, Don't you think you've had enough? Bobby told the waitress to put his whiskey on a separate check and, after she left, looked Dad in the eye, took a drink and started eating. Then Denny asked him how he could've gone to Vietnam, and when Bobby said he didn't have a choice, he'd been drafted, Denny said, 'Well, you could've gone to Canada. I have a friend who did. He sneaks home all the time.' Bobby answered, 'I guess I just didn't have the guts.' Then Denny said something about the Pentagon Papers proving we'd been lied into the war, and how did he feel about that? And when Bobby shook his head and mumbled something like, 'Who gives a shit?' Denny started talking about the anti-war movement and said Bobby could get involved and do some good. You know, like he'd done nothing but evil all the time he'd been in Vietnam and needed to atone for his sins. Well, Bobby stood up, went over to Dad, handed him some money, probably to pay for his drinks, and walked off. I followed him out of the restaurant, caught up to him and tried to talk to him, but he said he wanted to be alone."

I shake my head, as I stare at the road and think about how shitty Bobby must've felt. I hear Amanda say, "I don't remember anyone named Denny when I was growing up."

"That's because I never had any desire to see him again."

"It's amazing how much I don't know about our family."

"There's always something you don't know about your family. I thought I knew Bobby, but after he came back… " I shake my head. "He was nice to my parents and me. He'd offer to help out—mow the lawn, set the table, do the dishes, whatever. He'd talk about his long walks, running into neighbors who'd welcomed him home and the conversations they'd had. But he didn't talk about the war, about what was going on inside him—at least, not in the beginning. Or about how he felt when he learned Shirley had a new boyfriend. Mom and Dad told him how sorry they were about what had happened, but he just said, 'I'm fine.'" I shake my head. "Yeah, he was always fine. He'd have dinner with us and then go out, and we wouldn't see him again until the next morning."

"That must've been very difficult for you. And for Grandma and Grandpa."

"Yeah. Probably more for them than for me. Because Bobby and I would spend time together before dinner, after I got home from work. I had a summer job at a warehouse, and when I'd get home, I'd go up to my room, totally exhausted, and lie down. One day, while lying on my bed, I heard Bobby moving around in his room. I went out into the hall and saw his door was closed. I hesitated. He never seemed to want to have anyone in his room. But I wanted to see him and talk with him. So, I knocked. No response. I was wondering, Do I knock again, or respect his desire to be alone? And then he said, 'Come in.' I opened the door and saw him standing near his desk, holding a half-empty glass of whiskey and looking as if to say, Well, what do you want? I saw a bottle on his desk, looked at him and he said, 'If Dad finds out I'm giving you whiskey, he'll get pissed.' I assured him Dad wouldn't find out. He poured me some and said, 'Be ready to toss it down the hatch if anyone comes to the door.' I sat on his bed, and we started to talk.

"That got to be a routine—a glass of whiskey before dinner, and Bobby talking about his nights out. Most of the time, he hung out in bars with guys he knew from high school who'd got sent off to Vietnam, or vets he'd met in those bars. When he was with them, it was easier to say what was on his mind. He didn't talk much about the war. It was more about men coming home. And what they came home to. Girlfriends who'd dumped them for someone else. Friends and family members who sometimes looked at them suspiciously, as if they were wondering, What did you do over there? And everyone raging about the lies and the politics of the war. Bobby said the guys in the bars would shake their heads and grumble, 'Should anyone be surprised we were lied to? Does anyone give a fuck at this point? What difference does it make?' They just thought about what they needed to keep them going—booze, drugs, and sex. Because they were going to live with that war to the end. Live with the feeling they'd been used, and no one cared.

"He told me about a vet in a wheelchair who'd gotten both of his lower legs blown off. The guy was beginning to learn how to walk on artificial legs, but he'd decided to take a break, because of the pain, so he was in his chair when Bobby met him. I remember Bobby shaking his head, a look of disgust on his face, and mumbling, 'Artificial limbs. I bet that's a booming industry.' And then he looked at me and said, 'It's good you got a deferment. You don't wanna go to that fucking war. There's nothing heroic about it. Nothing heroic about killing people. Or surviving. What does that even mean, to survive? Life has no purpose, no meaning. Why go on?'"

I fall silent and stare ahead, and a memory returns… of the two of us in his car at a drive-in theater, watching *McCabe and Mrs. Miller*, while drinking whiskey out of paper cups. At one point in the film, he looked at me and asked, "You ever been with a hooker?"

"Nope."

He chuckled. "You know what the great thing is about prostitutes?"

I shook my head.

"You don't have to talk. Don't have to tell them what you're thinking, what you're feeling. Don't have to tell them shit about what's going on inside you, the way you do with a girlfriend. It's just a simple transaction. You give her money, she gives you a good time." And then his face lit up and he smiled. "The prostitutes in Vietnam are fantastic. Whenever we took a break from the patrols to go back to Saigon or the other cities, first thing I'd do is look for a brothel. It was the best escape from the war, from the constant tension, the feeling that, at any time, you could be hit—" he snapped his fingers "—and gone. We'd all been through it... Those brothels, man, there would always be dope, or heroin, and toward the end, amphetamines. I'd get stoned and lie with a woman, who'd be nude, or in some thin silky robe. There'd be candles and incense, and she'd hold me in her arms, or spread me out on the bed and lie on top of me, and every touch, every caress—oh, my God!" He was gazing at the film projected in his mind, his mouth hanging open, his eyes shining.

Amanda's voice penetrates my silence. "That's really upsetting, what Bobby went through. And his despair. Did he try to get any help? Any therapy? Did the military offer him anything?"

"Not to my knowledge."

"I'm sorry, Dad." She pauses. "But I agree with Bobby—I'm happy you got the deferment and didn't go to that war. Nicky and I wouldn't exist without you."

"And your mother." I glance over, and our eyes connect. The warmth in her face fades, and she looks away.

"And Mom," she says, in a reflective voice. I sense what she's feeling. Eventually she says, "So, it was Bobby's despair that somehow drove him back to the war?"

"I didn't know what to think, then. Now, it's obvious to me he'd been traumatized. Things were falling into place for him to rebuild his life. He got his old job back and started working again. Mom and Dad told him he could continue living at home and encouraged him to apply for admission at the U. And eventually he would've met a woman with whom he could've had a relationship. But," I shake my head, "one day, after he'd been home for a few months, we were drinking in his room before dinner, and he looked at me and said, 'You've asked me what it's like over there... You see people get killed. Blown up and burned alive. Women and children murdered. Your friends die right in front of you. You kill people. You have blood on your hands. You do things you never dreamed you were capable of doing. You wonder, Who am I? And that thought keeps coming back. *Who am I?* You fall asleep and think you're safe. You can rest in peace. But it all comes back. Morning arrives, you wake up to a new day, a new beginning... But it's like you wake up with a hangover. And the only thing that can get you out of that hangover is more of the same.' He fell silent for a while... and then said, 'I'm going back. I signed up for another tour.' He looked at me and said, 'It's been good to spend time with you, Tom.' That was it. He told Mom and Dad. They cried. Pleaded, 'Why? Why?' All he'd say was he needed to return." I take a deep breath and sigh. "He was gone in a week."

"That must've traumatized *you*," Amanda says.

"I've never stopped wondering, Why did you feel you had to go back? Where are you today? Are you still alive? Who are you? Who were you then, and what did you become? When he said, 'You do things you never dreamed you were capable of,' what did he mean?"

"Dad, if you're still asking yourself these questions, then you need to see someone."

"I told you, I did that. The therapy helped with the pain, but it didn't provide answers to the questions that are always in the back of my mind."

"A therapist can't tell you—"

"I know." I regret the sharp tone of my voice cutting her off. I take a deep breath, sigh, and say, "I'm sorry."

"It's all right, Dad."

"It's just... seeing a therapist brings back all the memories."

"I understand."

I glance over and see sympathy in her eyes.

I stare at the road, then look off to the other side, where an island of trees and tall grass now separates the lanes heading north from those going south and conceals the southbound lanes. My gaze passes over the trees flashing by in a blur and back to the road. Soon we'll reach Duluth, drive along the shore of Lake Superior, then cut cross-country on a narrow, winding highway, past woods and lakes, across bridges spanning rivers and creeks and eventually we'll head down the narrow dirt road to the log cabin that faces the lake. It seems as if I've been doing this annual migration north all my life. Now it's to the Boundary Waters, but when I was a kid, it was to the lakes in the Brainerd area, with Mom and Dad.

Bobby and I would ride in the backseat, entertaining ourselves with toy soldiers and airplanes, and later with comic books and card games, but we'd get bored and start whining and fussing, because the trip seemed so long, even though it only took about half the time it takes to drive to the Boundary Waters. I remember the relief of seeing the log cabin ahead of us and then to the side as our car gently pulled to a stop in the shade beneath the limbs of a white pine.

Bobby and I would jump out of the car, like prisoners breaking out of jail, and dash across the carpet of brown pine needles toward the lake and the aluminum rowboats pulled up on shore on either side of the dock. I pause on the dock to gaze down at the water in which I see the shimmering forms of sunfish or bluegills and look up to see a couple of mallards waddling along the edge of the water, stretching their necks and pecking at things I can't see. I stare down at the fish for a while, which continue to swim toward the surface, as if curious to see who I am, or if I'm going to feed them, and then I look around at the lakeshore, at the pines and birches, at the other docks that extend into the lake, and I hear a bird sing somewhere in a tree. I turn, walk toward Bobby standing at the end of the dock, stop next to him and look down at the deep, opaque water and up at the blue sky and the afternoon sun that make life feel as if everything were in slow motion. I take a deep breath and relax, knowing Bobby and I have a whole week to swim in the lake, go fishing with Dad and explore the shores. And in the evening, I might hear what I've heard so often, the most beautiful sound in the world—a loon calling across the lake to another loon, a call that sounds like a cry of hope, longing, and melancholy. A cry like the one I feel for Bobby. And as the car flies down the freeway, I see us standing close to one another at the end of the dock, looking off at the lake.

I'm still going after you, my Cacciato. I started within days after you left to go back to the war, writing you a letter and telling you how much I missed you and wanted you to return. And I kept on writing, over the following weeks and months. The first thing I'd do when I'd get home from class or work was check the mail. Nothing. Always nothing. I stopped writing but continued talking to you in my head. I'd ask, What made you go back? What haunts you?

I followed you the only way I could, through the stories of others—the news reports on television, with footage of our soldiers in Vietnam, and books and films about the war. Two years after you'd left home for the last time, *If I Die in a Combat Zone* came out. Its Minnesota author was drafted the same year as you, the year the My Lai Massacre was revealed. The war games Tim O'Brien described playing as a boy resembled the ones we used to play, and the descriptions of his experiences in Vietnam, like the constant danger of mines, made me think of your stories. About a year later, when I was at the U, I saw *Hearts and Minds*, which revealed the lies of Nixon and previous presidents about our role in the twenty-year war in Vietnam and represented Americans as counterrevolutionaries and imperialists. The title evokes LBJ's comment that ultimate victory will depend on the hearts and minds of the Vietnamese people, while the film shows what we did to their hearts and minds by blowing up, burning alive, and riddling with bullets mothers, fathers, children and grandparents.

Watching that film, I seethed with rage and disgust and began planning in my mind the course on the Vietnam War that I would teach when I became a professor. I wanted that course to affect my students so deeply they would oppose every new war that politicians might try to lie us into. I read the books and watched the films on Vietnam as they came out and integrated the best of them into the course that I would finally teach my second year at Macalester.

But all the while I was developing that course, I was going after you, Bobby. Did you behave like some of the characters in those books? In those films? Did you set fire to the thatched roofs of homes in a hamlet? Interrogate a prisoner, bully him with the tip of your gun, throw him from a helicopter? Go crazy and murder unarmed civilians? No. No, of course not. You'd never do any of those things. But every memoir, every novel I read, every film I watched, showed me that war changes people.

As time went by, as more memoirs, novels and films came out, and as I contemplated the possibility that you might have done some of the things the characters in those films and books had done, you faded into the stories and became a mystery for me. I don't know if you're alive or dead. Maybe you followed the path Cacciato took to Paris. Maybe you're living somewhere in the United States. Maybe, when Amanda and I pull over for lunch, we'll walk into a restaurant and find you sitting in a booth, with a big smile, and you'll say, It's about time you guys got here. What took you so long? And I'll hear myself answer, What do you mean, so long? It's just been a little over thirty years. And we'll laugh.

Yeah, Bobby, you've taken me on quite a trip. I never found you, but maybe I found myself. Or maybe I became who I am by following you. See, you're still my big brother, influencing my life, even though you've disappeared. Gone for over thirty years. Time. We learn who we are by living through time. It forms us. Reveals what we might not have even suspected when we were teenagers. When I thought I knew you. When I thought I knew myself…

* * *

"Dad! Dad!" Just as I look at Amanda and see panic in her eyes, a car behind me honks, and honks again, an angry blare, and I look at the road, realize I've drifted into the left lane. I cut back into mine. The car speeds past, the driver shaking his head, sneering at me, like he's thinking of giving me the finger. I glance at the speedometer and see that I'm driving over the speed limit, but not fast enough for him. I feel Amanda's eyes on me, feel the tension and look at her. She shakes her head and sighs, as if she's given up on me, and looks away and stares at an open field and a dense wood a couple hundred feet off. I focus on the pavement of I-35, feeling as if I just woke up, and wonder if I've been silent for a long time, if she said something to me and I didn't hear her. I have no idea how far we've come and don't see a sign indicating the number of miles to Duluth. But I notice there are more hills with long, gradual slopes covered with woods. I want to get her to talk with me, but not about Bobby, or psychotherapy, or the master's she's going to do in psychology, so I say, "Are you seeing someone?" And immediately think, That was a dumb question.

"You asked me that already, Dad."

"Yeah. Sorry."

After a pause, she says, "I *am* seeing someone. His name is Chris."

I look over at her and see a wry smile on her lips. "Well, tell me about him."

"What would you like to know?"

She seems reluctant to talk about him, so I give her an easy question. "How long have you been seeing one another?"

"About a year."

"Well, how come I haven't heard about him?"

"Oh, you know, relationships start and stop. I guess I just didn't feel like talking to you about someone who might be gone the next day. Or the next month."

"If you've been seeing Chris for a year... sounds serious." I glance at the smile still dimpling her cheek as she gazes forward. "Tell me about him."

"He's... a very warm, affectionate, loving person."

"Then I'm happy you found him. How did the two of you meet?"

"After I'd get home from work, I'd go for a run in the park. And I'd see him running, too. I started looking forward to seeing him every time I ran. One day, the sun was shining and the birds were chirping, but I was a little tired, so I sat on a bench and just breathed the air and listened to the birds. And then he appeared. He caught my eye and smiled at me, stopped and said, 'It's a beautiful day.' And I said, 'It's such a lovely day, I had to sit down so I could take it in.' 'Yeah,' he said, with a big smile. We introduced ourselves, and I invited him to sit with me. He admitted he'd been looking for an opportunity to talk to me, so, as soon as he saw me sitting there... I told him if I'd known that, I would've sat down a lot sooner." She chuckles. "We started running together, and then going to a café, and one thing led to another. Now, we see each other all the time." She takes a breath and hums as she exhales. "I love him. I don't think I can live without him."

"Well, you should've invited him. I would've loved to have met him. I'm sure Grace and Nick would've too."

"I did, but he was working on something and couldn't take time off."

"Too bad."

"But maybe next summer."

"Yeah, definitely." I pause. "I'm curious. What attracted you to him?"

"Oh, I don't know, Dad. I've just always enjoyed being with him. Because when I am, I feel his love wraps around me and keeps me warm, like a fur coat."

"Hmm. That's an interesting analogy."

I glance over and see she's looking off to the side, where dense stands of yellow flowers border the freeway. I've seen those flowers with little button-like blossoms in round clusters so often in northern Minnesota, but I can't remember what they're called. I wish I could. Helen knew. I see her standing on the edge of the gravel road near our cabin, bending over those flowers, talking about them, how beautiful they are. But what did she say they're called?

Amanda's voice startles me. "And you, what attracted you to Grace?" I glance over again and see her eyebrows arch as she says, "Well?" While I'm thinking about how to answer, she says, "She's about eleven or twelve years younger than you. Right?"

"Is that too young? You think I robbed the cradle?"

"That's a horrible thought. No, I'm just wondering how the two of you met."

"I told you. I saw her at an anti-war demonstration a couple years ago, we started talking, and one thing led to another. Kind of like you and Chris."

"Yeah, but what was it about her that attracted you?"

"Well, she's a librarian, she has a special interest in ancient manuscripts, which means she has an interest in history, and we're both opposed to the Iraq War. We have a lot to talk about." I smile, hoping she's finished with her questioning.

"Yeah. I'm sure." She looks away, and then back at me. "Probably more, I suppose, than with all those women you dated." She grins.

"I didn't date a lot of women. I dated a few. And mostly because I had friends who were worried about me being alone, and they wanted to help me find someone who would be a... a good companion. It was just... " I take a deep breath and sigh. "They were all nice women. I wasn't attracted to them. That's all."

"But then Grace came along, and you were attracted to her."

"Yeah."

"So, what did she have that—"

"I told you. We have common interests."

"Okay! God!"

She's shaking her head. I return my attention to the freeway, where we're alone, the two lanes stretching out ahead of us. I think, Just follow the road. Dense woods of pine and birch fly by, the trees so close to one another the sunlight can't penetrate the darkness. I imagine the silence, like the silence in which I'm driving. I hear distant voices chanting, "One-two-three-four, what the hell we fighting for? Oil, oil, spoils and trouble." I'm in St. Paul, standing on Summit Avenue, at the edge of Macalester's campus, watching demonstrators file by, carrying signs and banners on which they'd scrawled and spray-painted slogans—"US out of Iraq," "Impeach the Shrub," "Drop Bush Not Bombs," and "No Blood for Oil." The demonstrators appear to be in their teens, twenties, and thirties. Their chanting is loud and defiant. I remember marching against the Vietnam War, and the energy that came from feeling we were the people, we had power, we'd win, we'd stop that fucking war.

A man's voice says, "This is going to stop a war?" I turn to my side and see one of my colleagues, a professor from another department. "You're a historian," he says. "What do you think?"

"There's power in numbers. When enough people do the right thing, they can change the world."

"I don't see the tens of thousands we had in the demonstrations against the Vietnam War."

"I'm guessing there's a thousand."

I notice some of my students marching. My eyes connect with one of them, and she waves, elbows the kid next to her and points at me, and he waves and I wave back as they pass. And then I see Helen. My breath catches. I stare. She hasn't aged. She looks the same—the same blonde hair, the same vibrant eyes, the same energy and the same rebel. *She's there!* She passes me. I step into the street, walk with the row of people behind her, push my way toward her until I'm walking next to her and look at her and say, "Helen." She ignores me. I say, "Helen, it's me! Tom."

She frowns and says, "My name isn't Helen."

"Oh," I laugh. "Come on, Helen."

She glares at me as she pulls away. "I'm not Helen! Leave me alone!"

She looks a little different from Helen. Maybe she's not Helen. No. No, she is.

She flows with the crowd, and I feel left behind. I decide to pursue her, staying close enough so she's always in sight, and continue following her after the rally and the speeches at the capital, weaving through the crowd, as she walks over to Grand Avenue. She turns onto Grand, while the people walking close to her cross the street, leaving her alone. I walk faster, until I'm just a couple feet behind her, and say, "Helen. Please."

She glances over her shoulder, and I realize her eyes are blue, not brown. "You again?"

I stop for a minute, stare at her as she continues walking, realizing the woman might not be Helen. But, still, I don't want to lose her. I catch up to her and say, "I want to apologize. I wasn't trying to come on to you. I mistook you for someone else. That's all. I'm really sorry."

"Okay. You made a mistake."

"I don't normally follow women. I'm not a creepy person." She ignored me. "I'm a professor. A history professor."

"Oh! A professor! I guess I'd better pay attention, then."

"I just happened to be watching the demonstrators march by, saw you, and literally thought I was seeing someone else. The resemblance is just... uncanny. But, I'm not crazy. Okay? I'm a very ordinary, sane human being." I tap my temple with my fingers and grin at her.

"It's weird, knowing I resemble someone that much."

"Yeah. And, again, I apologize. I didn't mean any—"

"Don't worry about it."

We stop at a red light, and I say, "You know, there are a lot of good restaurants on Grand." I look off to the side. "There's one right up the street. La Cucaracha. They serve great margaritas. You like margaritas?" She doesn't answer. "How about having dinner?" I smile. "My treat. Just to make amends."

"You don't need to."

"I know. I want to."

She hesitates, looks around, hesitates some more and says, "Okay."

La Cucaracha's packed with demonstrators drinking, celebrating at the bar and eating at the tables. We get a table toward the back of the dining room, where people pass by on their way to the restrooms. As she looks at the menu, I gaze at her and see her hair's a darker blond than Helen's and her face is more round, but still, the resemblance is so powerful, I feel Helen has returned. She's here, in this woman. She feels my eyes on her, takes a deep breath, sighs and says, "You know, maybe this is a mistake. I don't want to be sitting with someone who wants me to be someone else."

"That's not it."

"Really?"

"I find you attractive, and I, ah... I want to make amends. Want you to have a good time."

"What's my name?"

I shake my head. "I don't know."

"You never even thought to ask."

"I'm sorry. What's your name?"

She stares at me, as if contemplating whether or not to tell me. Finally, she says, "Grace."

"That's a beautiful name."

"Really? What's beautiful about it?"

"Grace is something that comes from God. Right?"

She snickers. "You're going to tell me I'm a gift from God? That's pretty heavy-handed."

I shrug and smile. "Maybe you are a gift from God. You want to know my name?"

"Sure."

"Tom. As in, 'Every Tom, Dick, and Harry.' Now that's about as ordinary as you can get."

"Maybe." She pauses. "You said you're a history professor."

"Yeah."

"Where do you teach?"

I tell her about my experience teaching at Macalester and go on about myself, painting a picture of a happy childhood and adolescence, of the anti-war activist I became, of the things I'm happy to talk about. Seeing she's feeling more relaxed and open, I ask her questions, and she smiles and looks into my eyes as she tells me about herself, about her name, which came from her mother's birthing experience, which Grace had learned about years before, when she'd asked her mother, "Why did you give me that name?" And her mother revealed the hell she'd gone through giving birth, her delivery that lasted twenty hours, the terrifying complications, the C-section, her fear that she or her infant or both of them might die, and her crying and praying and, when it was over, her whimpering that if her baby survived her birth, it was by the grace of God, and so she named her Grace. Because of the ordeal she'd experienced giving birth, she decided not to get pregnant again.

So, Grace grew up an only child, loved by her parents, who took her on trips, visiting resorts up north and national parks, coastal beaches in the United States and on the Mediterranean, and cities and museums in France and Italy. She fell in love with Paris, majored in French as an undergraduate and, when it came time to make that decision about what to do when approaching the precipice of graduation, decided she didn't want to be a teacher or a professor. "Oh no, definitely not a professor," she shook her head. She'd heard stories about what they go through to get tenure, and she didn't want to spend the rest of her life being a specialist of one thing or another, nor did she want to teach high school, as her father had, or elementary school, as had her mother, that could be stressful. But she didn't want to go out and get a job in what people call the real world either, so she decided to get a master's degree in library science, because she loved books, loved to read, reading is the best thing to do when you aren't traveling, visiting Paris or Venice, or going to plays, movies and restaurants. As a librarian she could earn enough to be independent and free to do whatever she liked. She nods and smiles and says, "That's it, that's my life."

And I smile back, still sense something of Helen in Grace's face, the way she looks at me, the way she tilts her head, and in the excitement in her voice and in her gestures, and in her curious, adventurous spirit, and I know that while it was Grace's physical resemblance to Helen that led me to her, it was her spirit that made me feel Helen's presence.

As the evening progressed, we both seemed increasingly in tune with the raucous spirit of the crowd, laughing and smiling at one another over the table, Grace drinking her margaritas, and me, feeling I'd found Helen's reincarnation. We took a cab to my place, and then I drove her to where she'd parked her car, before joining the demonstration. When it was time for her to get into her car and go home, she hesitated, looked at me and said, "Well, I guess this is, ah... " I leaned toward her, put my arm around her and we kissed. I told her I'd call her, maybe we could do something together the next day. And we did. And every day after that. And soon we were sleeping together. And then she sold her place and moved into my house, into the home that Helen and I had created. I couldn't let go of it. Too many memories—the gardens, where I can breathe in her presence; the crabapple tree that would transform into a dazzling bouquet of beautiful pink blossoms that would captivate her, and she'd gaze at that bouquet for long periods of time, as if she'd been hypnotized; the porch, where we ate in the summer, while talking, laughing and listening to the birds chirp; every room in our house, so full of memories... and family pictures... and Helen, the heart of our family. Before Grace and I married, I replaced a few of the photos with new pictures, but some of the old ones have remained. They'll always be there. I love Grace, but I know that Helen's spirit lives on in her. Maybe somehow they've become one. And when I make love to Grace, I make love to Helen, too…

* * *

I see we're passing a marsh filled with tall reeds and cattails, and a few short, skeletal, leafless trees. I feel Amanda's gaze on me.

She says, "I'm sorry for being a pest."

"Being a pest? What do you mean?"

"The way I kept going after you about what attracted you to Grace. I shouldn't have done that."

"You're no more a pest than I am."

"It's just that, what attracts us to someone, why we fall in love with someone, it's so personal, there's nothing wrong with keeping it to ourselves." She gives me an apologetic smile.

I nod. She's right, of course. It is personal. When I think of what my love for Helen, for Grace reveals about me...

A little later, Amanda says, "I'm going to rest. Let me know when we get to Thompson Hill."

"Okay," I say, glancing over and seeing her lean her head back and close her eyes.

* * *

The woods between the northbound and southbound lanes of the freeway have disappeared, and just an island of grass separates them. We cross the bridge over the St. Louis River. We're not far from Duluth. The hills are more mountainous, with long gradual slopes, broad valleys, and open fields. As we ascend a hill, I expect to attain from the summit a magnificent view of wooded slopes and extended valleys, but when we reach the crest and begin our descent, I'm confronted by a gray mist hovering among the trees ahead and blurring the valley. We reach the crest of the next hill. As we descend, I let up a little on the accelerator and continue to let up as we reach the bottom of the hill and cross the valley. The almost blind ascent of the next slope feels like it extends for miles, and I suspect we're approaching the crest of Thompson Hill. When we reach it, I don't see the city of Duluth and its bridges that connect the Twin Ports far below, but rather a dense gray fog. I follow the freeway as it snakes down the slope, focusing on the taillights of the shrouded car ahead as we descend into the fog, almost losing sight of the red lights as the gray thickens, and decelerating even more, on the alert for whatever might appear ahead of us.

"Amanda," I say. No response. "Amanda."

"What?"

"You asked me to let you know when we reach Thompson Hill."

"Oh my God!"

I see her startled expression as she stares into the fog.

We reach the city and ride above the neighborhoods on the elevated freeway. I follow taillights from a distance, while looking down at the roofs, appearing and disappearing in the fog, and over at the tall buildings that fade and reappear, and up at the maze of bridges as they emerge above us from the thick gray cloud. The fog makes the city feel foreign and dangerous. A shrouded world, through which we grope, half-blind.

Lucky for us, we have a road to follow. What must it have been like for a captain navigating a ship through dense fog on Lake Superior, back in the day when he'd have to rely on nothing but a compass? Sailing blind, with no idea of what might emerge from the murky clouds. The only sound he hears, that of the waves crashing against the hull, the constant reverberation making him feel the fragility of his ship and his isolation. His vulnerability. He'd be peering into the fog, looking for a rock formation, or another ship, a collision that would send him and his crew to the bottom of one of the deepest lakes in the world.

The right signal light on the car ahead flashes, and the taillights exit the freeway. My grip on the steering wheel tightens. I have nothing to follow through the fog but what I can see of the road. The roofs of houses no longer appear beneath us, nor do bridges above our heads, and I sense we must've left the freeway and are closer to the lake. Yes, we're approaching the west side of the lake, what Minnesotans call the North Shore. Two ghostly glimmers of light appear ahead to my left and slowly emerge through the mist. They pass, leaving me again to lean forward, peering into the dense fog.

Amanda is also leaning forward. Wanting to engage her, I say, "This weather makes me think of all the shipwrecks in Lake Superior. Can you imagine what it must've been like for a captain, navigating a ship through the fog, back in the day when he would've had nothing but a compass to guide him? And maybe a foghorn or a bell on shore?" I shake my head. "Makes me think of that song, 'The Wreck of the Edmund Fitzgerald.' You remember? I used to have the CD in the car."

"Oh, yeah. The one about the witch of November who's come to drown all the men. Of course, it would be a woman who'd do that." She shakes her head and snickers.

"Okay." I laugh back. "A witch didn't have anything to do with the sinking of the ship."

"There are no witches."

"Right. I was just thinking what it must've been like to navigate."

"Scary."

The fog billows, and the silence thickens. I can't even see fifteen feet ahead. The tension I'm feeling tightens its grip on me, and we continue gliding on the invisible road into this unfathomable gray shroud, my foot ready to hit the brake, my hands ready to spin the wheel. Finally, the fog begins to thin, and I take a few deep breaths, sigh and loosen my grip. A sign appears, indicating we're now on Highway 61, and I remember how Helen would grin at me when we reached the highway and say, "Let's listen to it." Keeping my eyes on the road, I say to Amanda, "You know, whenever your mother and I drove through Duluth, she'd want to play that CD, *Highway 61 Revisited.* It was one of our favorite albums." I take another breath and relax a little more. "One time we were listening to Dylan sing 'Desolation Row,' and I asked her if she knew what those lines on selling postcards of the hanging and the circus being in town were about, and she told me about the lynching of the three Black carnival workers in Duluth... nearly sixty years before." I nod. "I was shocked. And angry. And asked, 'Why in the hell didn't I learn about that in school?' And your mom said, 'That's the same question I asked, when I first heard about it a few years ago.'"

Instead of responding, Amanda stares in the direction of the lake. We continue in silence.

The fog has thinned to wisps, and we pick up speed. A sign announcing the Glensheen Mansion appears and disappears. I slow down, hoping we can get a look at it. "Hey," I say, "can you see the mansion?"

"What mansion?"

"Glensheen." I get a fleeting glimpse of the three-story red brick building, a gust of wind coming off the lake buffeting the fog around it. "I think every time we've driven by, I've said it would be fun to stop and visit it, but we never do." I add, in a hyper dramatic tone, "The mansion, where old Miss Congdon and her nurse were murdered... in the middle of the night... by none other than Miss Congdon's adopted daughter, and the daughter's husband." And then I say, in my normal voice, "Just think of what Hitchcock could do with that." I grin, thinking I've pulled off a good joke.

"Hitchcock's dead."

"Yeah. Well, still, I can imagine what a great filmmaker could do with that story, and that mansion for a setting."

As we continue along the highway, I glance over from time to time to see her staring at the houses that appear and disappear among the billows of fog and wonder why she was so happy to have me to herself for five hours—at least six, with this weather—if she's not going to talk to me. She's as quiet as she was when she was eleven or twelve, or a teenager. I'd feel her staring, her eyes boring into mine, and I'd say, "What's going through your mind, sweetheart?" "Nothing," she'd say. Sometimes she'd blush, and I'd try to coax her into talking, but she'd shake her head and try to get away from me, leaving me to wander through my thoughts.

* * *

After driving for what seems like an hour since we entered the fog, a gas station emerges on one side of the road and a motel on the other. We coast past houses, a supermarket, shops and, between the road and the lake, what appears to be a park. I remember the restaurant where I took Amanda and Nick once and ask, "You want to get some lunch?"

"Yeah." She smiles at me for the first time since she woke up. "Lunch would be good."

I turn off the main road and, after passing a couple blocks of houses, pull to a stop in the parking lot of a log-cabin-style building. We get out, and I stretch and groan. I follow Amanda into the restaurant and look around at the tables arranged along the walls and across the open floor. Only a few are occupied. The waitress smiles as she approaches with menus in her hand and says, "Take any table. No one seems to want to come out in this weather." We choose one by the front window that looks out on the fog and sit. I scan the menu, until I notice Amanda gazing at a rose in a tall narrow vase on the table, near the window. She touches the flower, her fingertip slowly gliding down and up the edge of a petal.

"Every time I see a rose, I think of Mom. The tattoos on her arms."

I nod, seeing the red roses and green leaves on Helen's arms.

Amanda's finger stops and hovers at the tip of a petal. She takes a deep breath, sighs, pulls back her hand, looks at me and says, in an apologetic tone, "I lied to you about Chris. I didn't invite him to come. He could've. And I thought of inviting him."

"Why didn't you? If it was a question of money, I could've helped."

"It wasn't money, Dad. He wanted to come, but I decided not to bring him. I wanted to make it clear to him that, ah"—she takes a deep breath and looks me in the eye—"that I'm perfectly capable of traveling without him. Of living without him."

"I'm sure you are."

"He's very supportive, I owe him that." She nods. "And affectionate. And he makes me feel loved. But... "

"But?"

"Sometimes he treats me as if I'm broken into a thousand pieces, and without him there to hold those pieces together, I'm nothing. So, I decided I'd show him." She takes another deep breath. "And now"—she shakes her head—"now I'm worried he won't be there when I get home."

The waitress sets two glasses of water on the table and asks, "Have you decided yet what you'd like to order?"

Stunned by her words, I look up at her. "I think, ah... " I look at Amanda. She's biting her lip, and tears have welled up in her eyes. She mumbles, "Let's go."

"I think we're going to leave. Ah, nothing to do with the restaurant, or your service. We just need to go."

The waitress, startled, says, "Okay," and nods, and we leave.

We pause outside the restaurant, and I take Amanda in my arms and hug her. I feel a tremor in her breathing and pull back so I can see her. She looks away and brushes tears from her eyes. "Sorry."

"You have nothing to apologize for."

"I just… " She shakes her head as she looks at me, her eyes revealing her pain. She takes a deep breath, tries to pull herself together, and looks toward the lake and the fog.

"You want to go for a walk?"

"Yeah." She chuckles. "The fog might feel good."

I nod. "Maybe."

I walk close to her as we head down the sidewalk in the mist to the sound of waves crashing in a hypnotic rhythm, the wind billowing the brume in front of us, yielding an occasional glimpse of the lake.

"This Chris, do you live with him?"

"He lives with me." She shakes her head. "He doesn't just live with me. He takes up all the space in my life. Fills my whole apartment with his voice. Talks and talks about himself, his family. And when we have friends over, he talks louder than anyone else, until everyone shuts up and listens to him go on and on about his performances on stage, the classes he's taking at Tisch, his father's life as a classical musician in Boston. And, oh, everyone should be so impressed by this actor who's on his way to Broadway, and by his father, a world-renowned violinist—who no one's ever heard of. Chris has to have an audience. And that's why he can't live without me."

Her face wrinkles with disgust.

"Little, subservient me. I'm silent. I listen. I'm very good at listening. Watching. Paying attention. I've been doing it all my life. Since I was a little girl, with Mom."

She is staring ahead, jaw clenched.

"But *she* was able to get along without *me*." The anger in her voice pricks my anxiety and makes me wonder what's simmering inside her.

The sidewalk ends, and we cross the street to a gravel path that leads to the lake.

"Well," she says, "I guess for Chris and me, it works both ways. I can't get along without him, either. He loves me, and I need his love. Need to be able to curl up inside of it, like a little animal in its burrow."

She falls silent for several steps. "He was furious when he learned he wasn't coming. He said, 'You never want to acknowledge all that I do for you. Where would you be without me? Huh?' And I wonder, Where would I be? Where?" She shakes her head.

"Amanda... Amanda?"

She looks at me.

"What does he do for you?"

She stops. "There are times when I don't feel confident in myself, and I just... " She shakes her head. "I'm afraid to try."

I take her in my arms and hug her.

After I pull back, she says, "When I was considering getting a master's in psychology, and maybe a PhD, I was wondering if I was smart enough to do that."

"What?" I see the consternated look on her face.

She turns away, wiping her eyes, and starts walking and I walk with her.

She takes a deep breath. "Chris said, 'Oh, you're smart. Very smart. Your father's a professor. Come on, you've got what it takes.' When we meet up with some of his friends, if I feel insecure, he'll look at me and say, 'Don't forget, you're one of the sharpest people I know.'"

"He's right. You are smart."

"But now, when he does that sort of thing, it feels like it's his way of making me dependent on him. His performance to reassure me. He loves to perform for women. Sometimes, when we're at parties, I'll watch him crack jokes, or do impersonations of famous actors, like Christopher Walken, or Robert de Niro, or reenact some scene he'd done recently in a play, anything to capture a woman's attention."

I see Dick Rayburn, dressed in his black T-shirt, white tuxedo jacket and blue jeans, looking at Helen as she stands next to me and saying, "'Of all the gin joints in all the towns in all the world, she walks into mine.'" And I remember how deeply that serial monogamist hurt her, the scars that recorded her pain.

"I was watching him perform for a couple of women at a party the other night and I thought, If he hasn't slept with someone else since we've been together, it's just a matter of time until he does. He needs every woman to be infatuated with him."

"Amanda, you've got to end this relationship. Get rid of him. If he's that kind of a performer, he's a serial lover. He'll go from one woman to the next, living off their infatuation for him and indifferent to the pain he's inflicting on them."

She doesn't respond. The path comes to an end. We stop. She looks into the mist above the bay. I look in the same direction and see off to the side two ore docks that resemble monstrous phantom ships, so huge they feel threatening as they emerge from the fog. A gull screeches high above us, the only sound other than the rhythmic crashing of the iron-gray waves rolling into shore and splaying across the basalt lava, almost to our feet. I turn away from the docks, see a dim light glowing through the fog and remember the lighthouse at the tip of the distant breakwater, two or three hundred feet from shore, at the other end of the bay.

I breathe deeply, trying to calm myself, and look back at her. "You okay with walking along the shore?"

"Yeah. Why not?"

We start walking in the direction of the breakwater, the wind spiriting the clouds that shift their shapes as if some kind of ghostly life animates them.

After a few steps she says, "I can't help but wonder, What do I really mean to him?... I'm always afraid people are going to leave me... I feel so alone."

I grit my teeth. I'd love to beat the shit out of that jerk for what he's done to her. I take a breath again to try to calm myself. "Where were you before you met him? You had a job, right?" Her face is a little obscured by the mist.

"Yeah."

"And you were paying your living expenses and taking care of yourself."

"Yeah."

"So, you know where you would be without him."

"I know. But... I'm so afraid he'll be gone when I get home." She takes a deep breath. "He knows that. He knows I'm afraid. And he uses what he knows to manipulate me. Exploit me... I'm like his servant. And his guardian... the person responsible for everything. I'm the one who pays the rent, pays the utilities and picks up the check when we go to a bar or a restaurant. Unless we're with other people. Then he pays. And he likes them to see he's paying. He'll say, 'I'll get it,' and reach across the table in such a way that everyone sees him pick up the check. Or he'll flag the waitress over." She falls silent and then says, her voice tense with anger, "I hope he's gone when I get home. I don't ever want to see him again."

"Amanda, you've got to get him out of your life."

"I know." She sighs. "But I still love him. And I'm still afraid."

"You don't need him. I'm confident in you." I pause. "You start school in the fall. You've got a lot to look forward to." I look at her. "Someday, you're going to be Dr. Faust. I know you are."

She gives me a fleeting smile. "There you go again, Dad."

"Joking aside, I really do believe you've got a good life ahead of you. You're smart. You've done the right things. Continued seeing a therapist. Doing what you need to do to move on and find happiness." I look at her. "You're still seeing a therapist, right?"

She nods. "Doesn't everyone?"

"Yeah. A therapist seeing a therapist."

"I'm not one yet."

The wind crashes a wave so hard against the shore we get sprayed, flinch, and step further from the water's edge.

I catch my breath. "You want to continue?"

"Yeah. I'm not ready to get back into the car yet."

We continue walking, while maintaining a greater distance from the shoreline.

"Dad, the invitation I said I'd offered to Chris... "

"Yeah?"

"That's not the only lie I told you. I also lied about the financial aid meeting. There was no meeting."

"What?"

"I lied to you because I wanted an excuse to arrive late. I wanted Grace to go with Nicky and his girlfriend to the cabin, so I could have you to myself."

"Why?"

"There are... there are things I need to talk to you about."

I think, Here we go.

"Chris isn't the first man with whom I've had a sick relationship. There've been others." She reflects for a second. "The guy I lived with when I was a senior in college." She pauses again and then continues. "I went through his emails one day. Wasn't looking for anything he'd done wrong. Just curious. Anxious. He'd gone to a conference in Florida, said he'd call me every day he was gone, but he didn't. Just called the day he arrived at the hotel. So, I checked his emails to make sure he was okay... and discovered his correspondence with another woman. He talked about what a great time they'd had in bed. I started calling him and, when I finally got him on the phone, asked him who was this woman. I was crying. I couldn't control myself."

I look over and see she has clenched her teeth as she shakes her head.

"He blamed me. Said I was such an introvert. So withdrawn, so uninteresting, if he was having a relationship with another woman, it was because of me. I only had myself to blame." She pauses, and then her voice quivers as she says, "But the previous time we'd talked, he'd told me he loved me."

"What an asshole!"

"And Brandon, in high school. You remember him?"

"Oh yeah."

"I thought, since most of the kids in high school didn't know me, it would be easier than grade school. But it wasn't. It was hard to make friends. I felt so insecure. And then, when I was a junior, Brandon started at the school. He caught me looking at him a couple times in the hall. One day I was standing in front of my locker, and he came up to me and said, 'You've been staring at me.' And I said, 'No, I haven't.' And he said,

'You wanna go on a date with me?' And I said, 'I don't know where you got that idea.' And he said, 'It's obvious. Why don't you just tell me you do. If you want to, tell me. Come on. Are you afraid?' And I said, 'No, I'm not afraid.' Even though I was. And then I said, 'Okay, I want to go on a date.' And he said, 'Good, so do I.' And I laughed. It all seemed so easy. What had I been so uptight about? Our first date, he took me to a drive-in movie. I had such a crush on him, we... we had sex." She shakes her head. "I thought I'd found the love of my life. I was so happy when I was with him. And I wanted to be with him whenever I wasn't."

She falls silent for a few steps. "And then one day, he showed up at my locker. Upset. He said, 'Someone who knew you in grade school told me the truth about your mom. She didn't die of cancer. Why did you lie to me?' The kids nearby were staring at us. Everyone in school would find out if I told him. I slammed my locker shut, like I could leave the truth hidden inside, and tried to walk away, but he grabbed my arm and repeated, 'Why did you lie?' I looked at the kids watching us and then at him and said, 'Let's go outside.' When we got outside, I told him what had happened, and what it had been like for me in grade school after Mom died. Being with my friend in her house and watching her talk with her mom and feeling the absence of mine and knowing I'd never see her again, never talk to her again. And wondering, Why? Why?'... My friends pulled away from me. Some of the boys in school made jokes in front of me. One day, a kid at school pretended there was a noose around his neck and pulled at the imaginary rope while choking. And another kid acted like he'd been stabbed and started staggering, his hands reaching toward a friend who faked a scream, like he was in a horror film."

I grit my teeth, feeling again the wrath I felt then. "As soon as I got that call, I cancelled my class and rushed home and found you crying in your room. You told me everything." I take a couple breaths. "We met with the principal the next day." I shake my head. "I don't think anyone was punished."

"I remember kids avoiding me even more. Girls looking at me like I reeked of death and turning away." She falls silent for a few steps. "I think some kids were afraid to be my friends, because they thought the others would ridicule them. That's what happened to the one friend I still had. The other kids made fun of her. And I lost her. And then I was alone." She falls silent for a few steps. "I've wondered if it was my feelings about myself that caused the girls to avoid me. Maybe they shunned me because I was so afraid something was wrong with me that I distanced myself. I might've made them uncomfortable the way I avoided them. I'll never know." She pauses. "That was fifth grade. And then you took me out of that school."

"I couldn't let you go back there."

"And I went to the other grade school, and then middle school and then high school. And met Brandon. And after that conversation we had, when I told him the truth about Mom, he looked at me like he felt my pain, and said he felt sorry for me... But he pulled away. Any time I'd try to talk to him, he'd say, 'I gotta go.' And then he started hanging out with another girl. When we were together, before he learned the truth, I felt I was with a boy who loved me. And then his love was gone. I confronted him one day. I said, 'So, when you started school here, were you just looking for someone easy? Is that what I was for you? Just low-hanging fruit, ripe for picking?' At first, he ignored me. But then he lost his temper and said, 'Yeah, plucked and fucked!' And left. I fled the school, calling myself a loner. Loner, loner, loner. Always ready to throw myself at anyone who would take me and give me what I craved."

"You never told me this before." I look over and see her staring down at the wet rock. "I found you lying on your bed when I got home. Tried to get you to talk, but you wouldn't. All I could do was rub your back. I suspected it had something to do with Brandon."

"Sometimes I wonder if men have a sixth sense that enables them to find women like me. Women they can use and abuse."

I take a deep breath and sigh. "I failed you."

"We all failed. Failed ourselves and one another. We were broken. Mom's death was a black hole, and I struggled every day to climb out of it. I didn't want to get up in the morning, didn't want to go to school, didn't want to stay home, didn't want to do anything. Some days I didn't struggle at all. I just cried. And moped. And felt like shit."

I nod, remembering those days. "And Nick… he'd been so quiet before, but after your mom's death, he'd get angry, scream, and throw things. Get into fights at school, talk back to teachers and refuse to do his homework. Or lie and tell me he'd done it, when he hadn't. Those years were hell. We were all seeing therapists." I shook my head. "The therapy probably helped, but none of us were ever the same."

"Dad, you tried to make everything right for us. You held us and hugged us, and we wept. But… part of you had died." She pauses. "You remember that time, about three years ago, you came to New York to visit me? And we went to see that play, *Metamorphoses.*"

"Yes."

"There's that scene, where Orpheus is leading Eurydice out of the underworld. The god of the underworld told him to not look back at her, and he doesn't, until he reaches the entrance. And then he looks back and loses her. The scene is repeated over and over. He sees her hands stretched toward him and the fear in her eyes, and each time he reaches toward her, she's further away. And further away. And then the last time he looks, she's a long way off. She isn't extending her hands anymore, isn't imploring him to save her, to bring her back. She turns away, as if she's forgotten him."

I see Orpheus turning toward Eurydice, and turning again, and again, and remember the pain I felt and feel it now.

"When we were watching that scene," Amanda looks at me, "you started to cry. And when it ended, you got up and left. I panicked and followed you. Found you sitting on a chair in the lobby, your face in your hands, shaking. I knelt down in front of you and asked, 'What's the matter?'"

"And I told you that scene brought back the dreams I'd been having for years. I'd find her every night." I take a deep breath. "And lose her every morning." I shake my head and feel tears welling up. I look at her and try to smile. "But I had you. And Nick. Until he left for Lewis and Clark, and you for NYU."

"We had to leave. I get so fucked up in that house. I can't be in it without thinking of Mom. And Nick feels the same way." She pauses. "Last night I thought I saw her out of the corner of my eye, but when I looked, she was gone. And this morning... the gardens, the roses... Everything makes me think of her. Even the books in my room." She looks at me. "Why don't you get rid of them?"

"Maybe I'm hoping you'll have children someday."

"And pass all this onto them?" She sighs. "I don't think you can give anything away that Mom touched. And she touched those books when she read them to me. Hans Christian Andersen. The Ramona books."

She's smiling.

"My favorite was *Ramona and Her Mother.*" She takes a breath. "I reread all those books on my own. My love for reading, I got that from Mom. And you."

I nod.

"I remember Mom reading 'The Little Mermaid' to me. And 'The Snow Queen.' 'The Little Match Girl.'"

I smile at the memory of little Amanda curled up on Helen's lap.

"Sometimes, I'd notice the scars as she read and wonder, What was Mom's story? Will she read me a tale someday about a girl whose arms had been clawed by a witch?"

"I thought witches don't exist."

She smiles. "Only in fairy tales."

"Your mother was a lot more than just those scars."

"I know. I have wonderful memories of Mom. The way she used to cuddle me. And my dolls. Talk to them as if they were real." She chuckles. "We'd mother them together." She smiles and repeats, "Mother them." She hums at the happy memory. "She loved taking Nicky and me swimming, just joyful to be near us." She takes a breath. "Nicky and I were lucky. We meant everything to her. That was obvious. I can still feel her warmth, hear her reading to me." She sighs. "She's always with me."

We come to a large rectangular crevice in the rock that blocks our path. It's filled with gray water, nearly a foot deep. Beyond the crevice, the rock has broken into slabs lying at different angles, with grass growing between them. I peer into the mist and see the breakwater, still about a hundred feet away, and at its tip, the lighthouse, its light glowing through the fog. A drop of water strikes my forehead, and another, and I see the rain striking the surface of the water in the crevice.

"Dad, I think we'd better head back."

"Yeah. Let's go."

As we return through the mist the rain strikes my face, and within seconds we find ourselves in a downpour. We rush forward, bending our heads, while trying to see the basalt rock in front of us. By the time we reach the gravel path, we're soaked. We rush up the path to the sidewalk and the car, and Amanda stands by her door, shuddering, as I grope for the keys in my pocket. I open her door, and then hurry around to the other side and get in. My hair is drenched, water streams down my face and my shirt sticks to me. Amanda reaches into the backseat for her jacket, which she wraps over her chest like a blanket. I turn on the ignition and the heat. Warm air circulates and the glass mists up.

We pull away from the curb, and I lean forward, peering into the rain, rattled by the exploding thunder, the windshield wipers swishing back and forth.

* * *

The wind and rain suddenly decrease as we follow Highway 61 between the granite walls of a passage dynamited out of a hill, only to pummel us again the second we're in the open. After a few miles of searching, I find the turnoff onto the narrow, winding highway that will take us to Ely, the little town on the edge of the Boundary Waters. Rain continues to fall and the wipers swish, as I clutch the wheel, hoping this damned downpour will end. I glance over, see Amanda leaning back in her seat, staring ahead, and wonder what she's thinking. I look at the road, then back at her. Now she's looking off to the side, through the water rippling on her window at the rain pummeling the trees. I focus on the road again and turn the wheel just in time to avoid flying off a curve. The blurred landscape varies from dense woods to open stretches of grass, reeds, and occasional marshes. I continue to grip the wheel, more alert to the curves and to the possibility of a deer leaping out from the woods.

"Dad, you know one thing I'll always remember about Mom?"

"What?"

"The scars."

I wish she remembered something else.

"I'd look at them and wonder, How did you get them?... I was probably around seven, right about the time we were getting ready to move from our old house to the new one, when I first caught myself thinking, Could you have done this to yourself? Why would you? It would've hurt." She falls silent, and then says, "Whenever Mom saw me staring at her scars, she'd turn her arms so I couldn't see them. Or she'd pull her sleeves down, or move away… But then, after she got tattooed, she showed me her arms and the flowers and said, 'Aren't they beautiful?' They were beautiful. Using the welts as stems, adding the green leaves and the gorgeous flowers. Transforming all that suffering I'd begun to suspect into something so beautiful. I was shocked. It was like a miracle. I didn't know what to say. She looked me in the eye and said, 'I've accomplished a lot. An awful lot. Someday I'll explain. For now, I just want you to know, I'm very proud. And you should be, too.' She never explained why she was proud, or what she'd accomplished. And we never talked about it again. I was confused. I still am."

I nod. Helen had a hard time talking to me about her past, about what seemed to haunt her and drive her to drink. How could she have possibly talked about that with our little girl?

Amanda continues, "She had the tattoos done just a few months after we'd moved into our new house. That was such a great time. Everyone was so happy. She started working in the gardens that summer, planting flowers. And then school started, and she'd make breakfast for Nicky and me and see us off. And then get to work on her dissertation. She told me it was about courageous women poets—Emily Dickinson, Sylvia Plath, Anne Sexton, Mary Oliver, Maya Angelou. She loved to talk about them and read their poems to me, even though I was too young to understand."

I remember Helen reading their poems to me, as well.

"And when Nicky and I got home from school, she'd always have a snack ready for us. If we had homework, we'd go to our rooms and get it done. But if we didn't, we'd go out and play. By the time we came in, you'd be home, and Mom would be in the kitchen making dinner. And after dinner we'd sit together on the couch and watch *The Simpsons*. And when we'd go to bed, you'd both come into our rooms and hug us and kiss us and wish us good night and happy dreams." She looks at me. "We were happy."

"We were," I sigh and take a breath. "Your mother had stopped teaching, so she could focus on her dissertation during the day and you and Nick at night. She had a future to look forward to as a professor. And we started going out more."

"But, after a while, she seemed to become more absorbed by her work. When she wasn't making meals or spending time with us, she'd be in the study, her desk piled high with books and papers."

"That's right."

"And your desk had stuff piled on it, too."

"Yeah. Always writing articles, preparing lectures, grading papers."

"I remember thinking I had parents who lived in a world of books. I wanted to be in that world, too, because both of you were so deep into it. It's like nothing else existed."

"No! You kids existed. You were everything to us."

"Oh, I don't know, Dad. I can remember walking into that room, and you and Mom were working, and neither of you even noticed I was there. I could've gone in there and danced and sung hallelujah, and you wouldn't have noticed."

"That's not true." I glance over, see her staring straight ahead, ignoring me, and look back at the splattering rain and the road and mumble, "Not true."

"And then Mom started to change. The papers and books on her desk mostly stayed in the same place. She'd sit there, stare at her computer, and sometimes she'd type. Type a lot. And other times, she'd just stare."

Amanda falls silent. The only sound, the pummeling of the rain, the swish of the wipers.

"One night, I woke up. I felt anxious. I lay still and listened but couldn't hear a thing. I got up and walked to my door. Looked around the hall. And noticed the door to the guest room was open. I went over and looked inside. I saw Mom, saw her silhouette in the dark, in front of the window, sitting in the rocking chair, just staring ahead. I watched her for a while. She never moved. I wondered, Is she awake? If she is, then what's she staring at? What's going through her mind?"

Silence again, filled with the sound of splattering rain and wipers swishing.

"I watched her a little longer and then went back to my room and tried to sleep. I never talked to her about that night. I felt I wasn't supposed to have seen anything... That happened a few more times. I woke up with that weird, anxious feeling, got up, went to the guest room and always saw the same thing—the silhouette of Mom, like a ghost, sitting in the rocking chair in the dark, in front of the window. But, after a while, waking up with that weird feeling no longer made me anxious. I'd watch her, sitting like a statue in the dark, and, for some odd reason, I felt reassured, as if her being there was normal... During the day, she was a zombie. I can remember saying to her once, 'Mom. Mom?' And finally shouting, 'Mom!' And she looked at me like she just woke up." Amanda's eyes fix on me. "Did you know this was happening?"

"Yeah."

"You did?"

I nod.

"Did you ever try to talk to her, Dad? Ask her why she was doing that?"

"I did. I woke up one night and she wasn't beside me. At first, I didn't think anything of it. Just tried to get back to sleep." I pause, struggling to see the road blurred by the downpour. "But... but when she didn't come back to bed, I got up and found her in the guest room. She was so still, I wondered if she was somehow sleeping while sitting up. As

I continued watching her, I saw her eyes were open. I said, 'Helen,' but she didn't respond. I repeated, 'Helen,' as I walked toward her. I bent over in front of her, took her by her shoulders, and repeated her name again. Finally, she realized I was there. She looked surprised. Said she couldn't sleep. When I asked why, she said, 'The things I have on my mind.' I asked, 'What things?' She said, 'Memories.' I asked, 'What memories?' She just shook her head. I tried several times to talk to her about her insomnia. Never really succeeded. And she wouldn't see a doctor about it, or a therapist."

Amanda sighs. "She's a total mystery."

"I saw you one night, standing in the doorway, staring at her. I thought of going over and standing with you, but I knew you'd ask questions, for which I had no answers. Toward the end, your mother was a mystery to me, too."

"That's one of the most horrible things about our family. The silence... Didn't you feel you had to understand? You had to do something? I mean, those last few weeks, she just stopped talking. Why?"

I shake my head as I peer through the downpour, still feeling baffled. "I tried talking to her. Told her you kids missed her, she meant everything to you. Tried to engage her every way I could. Asked her how she was coming with her dissertation, even though I suspected she'd given up on it. Talked to her about the job possibilities, hoping to rekindle her dreams. Reminded her of the cities we'd always wanted to visit—London, Paris, Rome. That had been our dream—to become a traveling family."

Amanda murmurs, "Dreams... She loved dreams. Certain kinds of dreams. I remember one day, I was lying on my bed, reading, and I felt Mom's eyes on me and looked over and saw her standing in the entrance to my room, smiling. She said she had great news for Nicky and me. She left, and a couple minutes later I heard her say, 'Come on, Nicky, come on.' She coaxed him into my room. He looked confused. I was, too. Because all of a sudden, there's Mom—happy, excited, eager to talk to us. She had him sit down next to me on my bed and said, 'You remember the story of *Beauty and the Beast*?' And we said, 'Yeah.' And she said she'd read an article about the new film adaptation of the story. 'It's supposed to be the most beautiful one ever made. You remember how much you liked *The Little Mermaid*?' We nodded. 'Well, this *Beauty and the Beast* is supposed to be a much better film. People say it's gorgeous. It's like a dream.' So, we all went to see it that Sunday afternoon. And then we went to a restaurant and talked about it. Everyone loved it. But the more we talked, the more Mom's excitement seemed to wane. She became quiet and calm, in a weird way. Kind of somber. I remember our eyes connecting, and her smiling at me—a smile that seemed to say, It's good to see you happy. A smile that left me a little sad, and anxious, because there was something strange going on. And four days later... "

I bite my lip and shake my head. All the pain is still inside me.

"Four days later, Nicky and I... " She pauses, takes a deep breath, and continues. "We got off the bus and started walking up the sidewalk. Police cars were parked in front of our house. Neighbors were walking through our front yard toward the back. I knew something was wrong. Nicky started to run, and I ran after him. When we got to the side of the house, we saw the neighbors rushing toward the alley, where an ambulance was parked, its lights flashing, a crowd standing around it. We ran to the crowd and pushed our way through, and when people looked down and saw who we were, they gasped and stepped aside. And then we saw you, standing just outside the garage door, and we screamed, 'Dad! Dad!' And you turned. And the look on your face... " She shakes her head. "You took me in your arms, pulled Nicky close to you and you cried. And we cried, too, even though we didn't know what had happened. But we knew it was something horrible. And then the paramedics pushed a gurney with a long black bag toward us, and I stared at that bag and realized, Mom is in it. She's dead! And I screamed, Mom! Mom! You held me close, while the paramedics wheeled her past us, put her in the ambulance and drove away. I cried and cried. You hugged me and cried, too. Some police officers and our neighbor guided us into the house. But I have no memory of what happened after that. I couldn't stop thinking, Mom is dead. She's dead. And all I could see was that black bag on the gurney passing in front of me... Mom is dead."

My breath trembles as I peer past the swishing wipers through the downpour. Amanda is gaping, as if she were staring at the body bag. Maybe she is staring at it. I want to say something, but can't find the words, and look back at the road.

"After the police and our neighbor left, you sat down on the couch with us, and we cried. And cried. And Nicky and I begged you to tell us what had happened. You said, 'Your mother died.' We asked, 'Why?' You shook your head and said, 'I don't know. Sometimes people die for reasons no one can understand.'" She takes a deep breath and sighs. "We kept on crying. After a while, you carried us to your room. And you had us lie down on the bed and sat next to us. I fell asleep. A few hours later, I woke up in the middle of the night. Nicky was still sleeping, but you were gone. I got up. Went to the guest room, hoping to find Mom sitting in the rocking chair. But instead, I found you. I couldn't really see you, just your silhouette."

I remember sitting in that chair and staring at Helen's body in the car.

"You were never open with Nicky and me about Mom's death."

I hear the anger in her voice, shake my head and say, "How could I? At the wake, before anyone arrived, I brought the two of you to her coffin, so you could see her. Have time alone with her. I remember how calm your mother looked. Maybe she had found happiness. But you have to be alive to be happy."

"You didn't tell us how she died."

"I did tell you." I pause. Fifteen years later, I still find the words difficult to say. "She committed suicide."

"You told us that later. But you never said how she committed suicide."

"I told you she poisoned herself."

"You were always very vague."

"Does it make a difference?"

I feel her eyes riveting me. "She's my mother. I have a right to know."

I feel I can't continue driving if we're going to talk about this, but we're crossing through low-lying areas, where the water along the side of the road is rising, creating puddles that might eventually become deep enough to flood the road, too deep to be able to just splash through, and I don't want us to be stranded here through the night on a flooded highway, so I continue driving, my eyes riveted to the blurred road, while my mind is riveted to the impact that I fear the details about Helen's suicide would have on Amanda. "I didn't tell you, because I thought it might destroy you."

After a few swishes of the wipers, she says, "Silence generates questions. And not getting answers makes everything more painful."

Had it been wrong of me not to tell them the depressing details? And if I tell her now? I shake my head. She's twenty-four, for Christ's sake. Tell her!

"Fine. That day… I got home from my classes and looked around for her. Walked through the rooms on the first floor shouting, 'I'm home!' No answer. I went upstairs to the study. She wasn't there. I looked through the whole house. No sign of her. I went out into the backyard... and when I looked at the window in the garage, I saw smoke. I heard a faint humming sound and thought it might be a car idling in the garage." I take a deep breath and sigh. "I ran to the door, opened it, and saw the garage was full of fumes. I rushed to the other end of the garage, pulled up the door and opened the window, and as the fumes began to escape and fresh air entered the garage, I saw the car was idling... and someone was sitting in it. Your mom. I opened the car door. Her face was turned toward me, and her eyes... her eyes were open... glazed over... staring at nothing. I touched her face. It was cold. Stone cold." I take a deep breath, as I remember touching Helen's skin. "I turned off the motor. And cried. And hugged her. And... " I feel my anger swelling inside me. "And smelled the alcohol. There was a bottle of vodka on the seat. She'd started drinking again."

"Why? Why did she do it?"

"I've asked myself a million times... After you and Nick fell asleep in my bed that night, I looked all over the house. Didn't find any alcohol.

Just that half-empty bottle in the car. She might've started drinking that day. Or maybe long before. I don't know. She knew how to hide things. I sat in the guest room, in the rocking chair, where she used to sit, wondering, Why? Why?"

I want to weep, but I have to continue peering through the rain and focusing on the road. I choke back my sorrow and look at Amanda. Her eyes are closed and her face is wet. I continue. "The only explanation for her suicide I've ever been able to come up with is... she started drinking again because of her depression. And her depression... " I take a deep breath and shake my head. "When I found your mother, she was wearing her fur coat."

"Her fur coat? That doesn't make sense. It was warm. She didn't need a coat."

"It was her mother's."

"I didn't know that."

"When her parents moved into their retirement home, they gave a lot of their things away. All your mother wanted was the coat. I remember her telling me that when she was a little girl, she loved to wrap herself in it and feel its warmth. That's how she imagined love feeling."

"Huh... I remember her rubbing her cheeks against the fur when she'd wear it."

"One morning, not long before she... I woke up and found her gone. At first, I didn't think anything of it. I got up and went downstairs to the kitchen, thinking she might be making coffee, but she wasn't. I went through the dining room to the living room, but she wasn't there either. I walked back through the dining room and was going to go upstairs, when I noticed the door to the back porch was open. I walked over and saw her standing in front of the screens, wearing her mom's coat. When she heard me walking toward her, she looked at me, gave me a big smile and said, 'I've been listening to this cardinal sing. It's so beautiful.' The cardinal chirped again, and it was beautiful. Or maybe what I found beautiful was seeing your mother happy. She said, 'It's going to be a beautiful day.' She leaned her head back and rotated it around, pressing her skin against the fur collar, and repeated her favorite lines of poetry—'You only have to let the soft animal of your body / love what it loves.'"

"I remember those lines."

As I nod, I remember Helen taking me by the hand and leading me to our bedroom. I closed the door and watched her spread the coat on our bed, pull off her nightgown, and lie down on her back on the coat and caress her breasts with the fur, grinning and humming. And I lay down on her and we made love, and I felt the soft animal of her body and the warmth of the fur.

"Was it cold…? Dad…?"

"Cold? Ah… no. It was a spring morning. A little cool, but she didn't need a coat. She wanted that feeling of love." I continue peering through the rain, the only sound the slosh of the wipers.

After a silence, Amanda says, "When I went back into the house today to get my purse, I thought of how cold it can get at night in the Boundary Waters, even in August. So I looked in the closet for my jacket and found her coat. I couldn't resist putting it on... and rubbing my cheeks against the fur, the way Mom used to. I can see why she did that. It does feel like love."

Seeing Amanda smile, as if she could feel that love now, makes me smile, and almost brings tears to my eyes. I look back at the road.

She says, "The coat has some bald spots, you know. And holes in the leather. I guess the moths have gotten to it."

"Yeah. But I'm not going to get rid of it."

"It's part of Mom."

I nod. "It's part of Mom." I see Helen sitting in the car, in the fur coat, her head leaning back, and her eyes open, dead. I grit my teeth, shake my head and feel a flash of anger. And then sadness. "Like I said, the coat belonged to your grandmother, and your mother loved to wear it. But she hated her mother."

"I didn't know that."

"It's not surprising. Your mother didn't want to be around her mother, and she didn't want you kids to be around her, either. So, you rarely saw her... But she never stopped missing her mother's love, the love that was never there. She despised her, and yet she yearned for her love." I shake my head.

"Pretty confusing, Dad. Why did she hate her?"

"Wasn't just her mother. She hated her whole family. Her parents didn't seem to feel any love for her, and sometimes they seemed to despise her, just because she'd do things like participate in anti-war demonstrations. And her older brothers, who her parents adored, liked to bully and ridicule your mom." I look at her. "I think that had a lot to do with her cutting herself. From what she told me, it all started when she was a little girl. She tried to project the image of someone who was tough, but she was easily hurt."

"I don't know her family."

"Yeah. Well, you've rarely seen them." I shake my head. "The way they treated her when she was a kid... Her brothers were abusive toward her, and her parents always let them get away with it. By the time she started high school, she'd become a rebel, questioning the things she'd been taught, getting expelled from the Catholic school her parents hoped would straighten her out, becoming a peacenik and a feminist, who never wore a bra." I smile as I remember how much she enjoyed telling me about her rebellious behavior. "And the way she left home, a few days after her eighteenth birthday... walking through the living room, her suitcase in one hand and a copy of *The Female Eunuch* in the other, and her parents just sitting there, gawking at her... She told them she'd come back someday to get the rest of her things and left. I don't know if she ever did. She told me that story more than once. I think she liked reliving it, reliving the day she gained her independence." I nod. "She was quite a woman—smart, gutsy, compassionate. She loved you and Nick so much. You meant everything to her."

Amanda doesn't respond.

"She wanted you to have what she didn't get—love. That was important to her."

I glance over and see Amanda staring off to the side at the blurred trees drenched with rain. I look at the clock on the dashboard. It's almost five o'clock.

* * *

Leaning forward, struggling to see the road, I'm startled by Amanda's voice.

"Did she think about us? Did she ever think about what her suicide would do to us?... What if Nick and I had gotten home before you? Can you imagine? How could a nine-year-old child deal with that? Her mother dead, in a fur coat, in a car full of carbon monoxide. With a bottle of vodka."

"I don't know. I—"

"I hated her. Hated her for what she did to me. And to Nicky. The suffering she caused us... How were we supposed to go on living?"

"You did." I look at her and see she's crying. "Somehow you did."

I look back at the road and see we're heading right into the trees and scream, "Oh shit!" and swing the steering wheel and hit the brake. The front bumper crushes the tall grass on the side of the road, muddy water splatters across the windshield, and the rear end swerves, but I've got the car headed in the right direction. I step on the gas, the front wheels get traction on the blacktop, and we pull forward. I gasp, "Jesus Christ!" I take one deep breath after another.

Amanda laughs—an insane, sobbing laugh. "I guess you wanted to end the conversation."

I shake my head, still panting. "No!" I sigh, "No. I... "

"That felt good! Weird, but good. I'd almost rather be dead than talk about this... I hated her. And then I hated myself."

"You had no reason to."

"Maybe if I'd been a better daughter... If I'd done more to make Mom happy... If I hadn't stared at her scars the way I did." I hear the tremor in each breath she takes. "If I'd made her feel loved... Mothers love their children. They don't abandon them. If she abandoned me, maybe it's because I didn't love her enough."

"Your mother didn't commit suicide because of you."

"There had to be a reason for which she abandoned me. There had to be something wrong with me. Something... something pretty awful.

Disgusting. Repulsive. Something that made her feel I wasn't any good… I wasn't any good."

"What killed your mother was the feeling that *she* wasn't any good. That *she* wasn't worthy of being loved. That's why she cut herself. Why she used to say, 'The pain that precipitates the cutting is always worse than the pain of the cutting itself.' That's why she was so obsessed with that fur coat. Its softness and warmth made her feel the love she so desired when she was a child. But, unlike your mother, *you* were loved. She *did* love you. I love you. Your brother loves you."

"Then why did she abandon me?"

"She didn't abandon you. It's not that simple."

"Yes, she did." Amanda glares at me. "She abandoned all of us. Maybe we all failed her." She looks away and mumbles. "Maybe none of us gave her what she needed. None of us were worthy of her love." She takes a deep breath and sighs. "This family is so fucked up."

"Our family experienced a tragic loss. But it is not fucked up."

"Really? Then why did Nicky and I decide to move as far away as we could? Nicky can't stand being in that house. And neither can I. And for the same reason. It brings everything back. And we can't live with that."

"What do you want me to do? Sell the house? You think that'll make it easier for us to go on living?"

"Nicky and I might come home more often. And maybe Grace will be happier. I can't imagine what it's like, being married to a man who can't let go of his dead wife. It's like *Rebecca* all over again. Welcome to our home full of memories of my dead wife!" She laughs.

"Amanda! That's… " I shake my head. "That's mean. Really mean."

"Is it? I remember you telling me once that what first attracted you to Grace was that you'd mistaken her for Mom. And then you mentioned *Vertigo* and laughed, and said, 'Well, what do you expect from a Hitchcock lover?'"

"I was joking."

"I know. But the fact is, Dad, much of the time, you're gone. You've always been that way. A million miles away. Fixated on something in your head. Maybe it's Bobby. I feel for you. I'm sure it was horrible to have your brother disappear like that. But, after Mom's death, it really got worse. You abandoned me. And you abandoned Nicky. How do you think that made us feel? I know how it made me feel. Like I didn't exist. Like I wasn't worthy of your love. And I know Nicky felt the same way. Your silence toward us was an affirmation that Mom was right not to love us."

I catch my breath, on the verge of crying. "I love both of you, and I did everything, everything I could to make you feel loved."

"You can't love someone if you can't be with them. And much of the time, *you* can't be with anyone, other than the dead who live inside you."

"When your mother died, I lost all reason to live."

"I know. I know that Nicky and I couldn't be your reason to go on living. We didn't mean enough to you."

"You mean everything to me."

"That's not what you just said. You said that when Mom died, you lost all reason to live."

"You and your brother are the reason I go on living."

"I wonder how Grace would feel about that. Doesn't she count for anything?"

"All three of you mean everything to me!"

"Really? It took a lot to get that out of you. But I'm not convinced."

"I love all of you."

"Huh! Maybe, when you're not obsessing about the dead you carry inside you."

"You just aren't going to listen to me, are you?"

I feel her staring at me. I glance over, she glares, shakes her head, and looks the other away. I look back at the road, feeling I've fucked everything up. Maybe she's right, maybe I am such a fucked-up mess I can't be a good father or a good husband. I don't know what to say to her.

I continue driving in silence, peering through the downpour, while her words repeat in my mind and grate against my nerves. Wanting this conversation to end, I put a little more pressure on the accelerator, and we pick up speed. We're probably close to Ely, maybe an hour from the cabin.

Amanda breaks the silence. "I can't stop wondering, Did she think about us? About what her death would do to us?" She takes a deep breath. "Will we ever reach a point where we stop wondering, Why? Why did she do it?"

"I don't know."

"But you must have some sense of why she did it."

"You think I haven't wondered? I thought she was happy with our new house, with having a family, with going back to school to finish her PhD and become a professor. She seemed to be doing so well."

"So, what could've caused her to do it?"

"Maybe she went off her medications. Maybe her mother's death affected her. She died just a few months before. Or maybe her sense of shame. She had all those beautiful tattoos on her forearms, but she knew why they were there, and it wasn't just to celebrate what she'd accomplished. It was also to conceal the scars. She was hyper self-conscious about people staring at her arms, afraid that somehow they could see all the madness, suffering, and pain she'd experienced, in spite of the beautiful flowers. She even talked once about having her arms amputated."

Amanda gasps, "You're kidding!"

I shake my head. "I'm not." And then I wonder, Do I really want to express the thought that has so frequently entered my mind, and that I've always kept to myself? I pause, anxious about what I'm about to say, and then decide to say it. "You know, she might've been seduced by what she seemed to perceive as the attractiveness of death."

"What!"

"She saw something very seductive, almost beautiful, in death." I pause, as a conversation comes back to me. "I remember one night, before you kids were born. We were sitting in bed. Smoking. Relaxed." I smile as I remember we'd just made love. I take a deep breath and go on. "I kept on looking at her scars. Couldn't ignore them. I'd asked her about them before, but she'd always answered by saying, 'I don't want to talk about it.' I decided to ask her again. This time, I got an answer. She talked about the cuttings, and once she got going, it was like she was entranced. And she talked about death being so beautiful. 'You'll never suffer again, never be depressed again. Death is the total absence of suffering, of pain. Absolute peace. That's what makes it beautiful.' She was staring off, saying these words, like she was in a kind of rapture." I take a deep breath and hear the tremor. "That day, when she got in the car in the garage, she might've been seduced by her thoughts about death. That she would never suffer again. Never be depressed again." I take another deep breath. "I don't know. We'll never know."

"She found death more attractive than life with us?"

"She might not have been able to see the choice she was making. See the consequences. The pain."

"This is never going to end. Never."

I hear her weeping, sniffling, catching her breath. I want to tell her it will end, but I know it won't. I want to plead with her to please, please don't ever harm yourself, don't ever think of death as a way to end your pain, your suffering. But I can't. I might put that idea into her head. I want to tell her to never forget what her mother's death did to her, but she lives with that every day. Neither she, nor Nick, nor I will ever be whole again. I'll never stop missing Helen, never stop loving her, even though I have Grace. I'm lucky to have found Grace. I think Nick will find someone to love, someone compassionate who can love him. He might've found her already. But Amanda? Will she find someone? Someone whose love can bridge the gorge inside her and give her a chance to live?

The rain is beginning to stop, and only tears blur my vision. The sun reappears, its light splaying like a deep puddle of blood across the tips of trees as the road curves again. I step on the gas, eager to end this trip and get us to the cabin. I glance over and see Amanda's body trembling, her head bowed as she sobs, and catch my breath. I look back at the road, and there's a deer, frozen still, staring at me. I slam on the brake and spin the wheel, and the car swerves, and the trees and the sun flash by until my head slams against the steering wheel.

* * *

I wake to the sound of birds chirping. My brain is throbbing with pain, and each breath feels like a knife stabbing the inside of my chest. I see the road off to the side and the trees beyond it. I lift my head, feeling my neck crack, and look ahead and see the sun has sunk further behind the trees, the puddle of blood splayed thinner across their tips. I stare at the puddle for a while, and then notice the windshield on Amanda's side has been smashed by a broken limb. I see her face covered with blood, her head leaning back away from the limb, her mouth agape.

Part III: 2023
The family reunites in the Boundary Waters

> *"The past is the present, isn't it? It's the future, too. We all try to lie out of that but life won't let us."*
>
> Eugene O'Neill, *Long Day's Journey Into Night*

Day 1, Saturday

Tom has graced me with such a beautiful life, I think, smiling at my pun as I sit here, so happy to be back, gazing at the lake, from the balcony of our cabin. *Cabin.* Huh! Every time that word enters my mind, I shake my head and laugh. This cabin feels more like the chalet in the French Alps, where Mom and Dad and I stayed when I was in college. Only this one's on a lake in the Boundary Waters, with balconies and a view of the entire inlet—the evening sun glowing like warm gold on the water, and ripples shimmering like diamonds; the small island in the middle, with those granite slabs and boulders, and a few scraggly pines rising from the crevices between them; the boat house on the other side, with the deck, standing above the water; the cabins and their docks that line the shore; and the lodge and the cabins further back, nestled among the birch and pine trees that cover the slopes surrounding the inlet. The sun is still above the tips of the trees on the ridge behind those cabins. It'll set in a couple hours.

Tom, Amanda, Nick, and Sarah and their boys should be back by now. I hope they didn't decide to portage to another lake. Tom would probably insist on trying to carry one of those canoes on his shoulders, the way he did last year, when it was just the two of us, and he lost his balance, fell and slammed his head against the side of the canoe. I had to help him to the shore we'd been heading for, then go back, get the canoe and drag it to where I'd left him. God, that was hard. He convinced me he was fine, hadn't suffered any major injuries, and we paddled back to the cabin. At sixty-nine, he's too old and doesn't have the sense of balance needed to hoist a canoe onto his shoulders and walk those narrow paths around boulders and through the woods. I warned Nick before they left, warned him he had to protect his dad. But Tom's so excited about his grandkids being here, and that excitement energizes him so much, I can see him getting carried away and forgetting he can't do everything he used to do... But he doesn't always forget. Sometimes, I wish he could... wish he could forget the past. Be free of it. Just be happy. And Amanda and Nick, too. If only they could all forget.

Oh my God! A loon wailing. Such a haunting cry. A cry of loss, of mourning. A wail of pain. Longing. The most beautiful sound I've ever heard. Like a cry expressing a profound need, a desire, beseeching a response—perhaps from its mate. There it is again! I jump up and rush to the banister, hoping to see the loon. I search the inlet, so large it's like a lake of its own, but can't find the bird. I hurry around the corner of the cabin, rush down the steps and across the grass and descend the steep path, my eyes on the ground so I don't trip or lose my footing. I follow the path as it weaves back and forth, around boulders and shrubs and trees, until I reach the bottom. The loon wails again. I freeze, scan the lake's surface, and continue scanning it as I walk toward the end of the dock, where I stop and look. There it is! Its black head a few inches above the metallic-blue water, its body a bump on the surface, a couple hundred feet away, near the opening of the inlet onto another part of the lake. The loon dips its head underwater and plunges. I watch where it disappeared, and watch, and survey the area within about a hundred feet, knowing it could reappear anywhere within minutes. Could it have resurfaced already? My eyes wander to the resort's main dock and back across the inlet. And then I see the loon, about a hundred feet from where it disappeared. It has passed the entrance to the inlet now. Soon it will be gone. It wails one more time as it continues its journey, gradually disappearing in the long shadows cast by the trees along the distant shore.

I take a deep breath and sigh, and my gaze drifts toward the small inlet in which I stand and settles on the lily pads, the reeds and the dark water. Some of the reeds rise a foot or two above the surface, while others lie flat across it, perhaps blown down by winds. I glance at the shore near the foot of the dock and see the grooves carved in the sandy soil by the two canoes when they beached. And where hopefully they'll beach again soon. Tom, Amanda, Nick, Sarah and the kids, they'll want to get back before sunset. I look down at the clear water near my feet, notice a couple of rocks partially buried in the dirt at the bottom and a small fish swimming back and forth, just beneath the surface, and then another. And another. They might be crappies, bluegills, or sunfish, I don't know which.

Oh! The loon wails again. How can the cry of a bird evoke such a strong feeling of mourning and longing, and yet be so beautiful? Even from a distance, it seems so charged with emotion, it feels human. I look across the lake and see the sun has begun to bleed a red glow along the top of the trees. I'll wait on the balcony where I've got a better view of the lake.

I turn and look up at the bluff, at the boulders and rocks emerging from it, and at the scrawny pines and skinny birches protruding from the crevices, and I think of the power of the glaciers that carved out the lake beds in the Boundary Waters and pushed the dirt and rock to form the shores and ridges. My eyes drift upward toward the tall peaked cabin, with balconies on the first and second floors, and the two granite-gray boulders that conceal part of the first-floor balcony. I cross the beach and the grass and begin to work my way up the path, stopping from time to time to catch my breath, and then begin climbing again, until the main floor of the cabin, resting on the huge wood posts that elevate it above the rocks and vegetation, comes into view.

I mount the steps, follow the wraparound balcony to the front, and return to the railing where I stood searching for the loon. I scan the lake, on the lookout for the two canoes. The luminous blood of the setting sun is spreading and darkening, while the trees along the ridge across the lake have merged to form a dark wall. I listen, hoping to hear my family talking, maybe laughing. Or maybe a paddle bumping or scraping against the side of one of the canoes. I look down at the lake, but can only see the dock, much of the shore hidden beneath the bluff. I continue listening, while gazing at the clusters of flowers with yellow, white, purple, and orange blossoms that grow amidst the grass, the rocks and the moss-covered boulders below my feet. The lake, the sunsets, the woods, the flowers—all of the beauty around me feels new again.

I sit back down on the chair where I was resting, when I first heard the loon, pick up my book and open it, and just as I begin reading, the loon wails again, a long way off. A haunting cry, so charged with emotion, it feels like it's coming from years ago. The kind of cry I felt coming from deep within Tom… imploring Helen to return. To not abandon him. His longing for her so intense, he couldn't stop seeking her, even years after she'd ended her life. And the only reason he was attracted to me… because he'd mistaken me for her.

That's what he said the day we met, twenty-five years ago. He called me Helen. And the look in his eyes—it was scary. So intense. He seemed at once shocked and ecstatic. Kept on calling me Helen, until I yelled at him, "I'm not Helen! That's not my name!" He stopped, but soon I felt him following me. When I found myself alone at an intersection, he stood next to me and apologized, told me he'd confused me with someone else, someone whom I resembled so much. I looked up at him, and he smiled and said, "I'm not crazy. Really." And then he said, "I'm a professor." As if a professor couldn't be crazy. He offered to take me out to dinner as a way of making amends. I believed him and accepted his offer, but then it felt like just a weird come-on, and I thought of walking away, but he seemed sincere, seemed to care about me, and so we had dinner at La Cucaracha and talked, and he told me about how he became a professor, and then got me going about my life growing up, my love for traveling, and why I became a librarian. But he didn't say anything more about Helen.

When it was time to leave, he called a cab. I thought he'd try to entice me into going to his house for a drink, so he could get me drunk and seduce me, but he didn't. He had the cab drive us to his place, and then he drove me to where I'd parked my car. Just as I was about to get out, he asked if he could see me again. Maybe for dinner the next night. I accepted his invitation. I wanted to see him. It was strange—feeling the intensity of his emotions made me want to be part of his life. And as I drove home, I felt I already wanted him to love me the way he loved this woman named Helen.

The next night, he took me out to that fancy restaurant. What's it called? Chez... Chez Jacques. That's it! It's been gone for years, but back then, it was probably the most chic place in Minneapolis. I'll never forget walking toward that statue of the nude woman, with her hands raised and one knee bent, and that joyful expression on her face that made her look as if she were dancing on the rock in the middle of the fountain, or perhaps startled by the jets of water spraying her. So beautiful, she could've been sculpted by Rodin. I was thrilled as we walked past her and into the restaurant and the wood-paneled dining room lit up by chandeliers and full of diners being served by waiters in tuxedos. As we sipped our martinis, he told me he'd heard that Jack—yeah, Jack, not Jacques—had started out as an aspiring bootlegger in the 1930s, before switching to a safer career. That got a laugh out of me. He said he'd heard a few stories about Jack and his careers. They might've been propagated by Jack himself. I asked Tom if he came here often. He shook his head and said it had been years since he'd come. And I responded, "Only special occasions?" He grinned and nodded. And I wondered if the special occasions all involved Helen.

At times, as we ate our dinner, I'd notice his eyes fixed on me, just like the night before, as if he were hypnotized by my face, and I'd wonder what he was seeing, and if the only reason we were together was because he wanted to stare at me, like my face was the opening to a different world. And what was that world? When I finally confronted him about it, he apologized, said he was just so attracted to me, but didn't mean to stare. When we finished our dinner, we ordered cognac. After I'd taken a sip, I asked, "Who's Helen?"

His smile disappeared. He took a deep breath and said, "She's my wife."

"Your wife? Well, why are you here with me?"

He looked down at the table. "She *was* my wife. But she... "

"Is? Was? Which is it?"

He shook his head and sighed. "She died several years ago."

"Oh, no! I'm so sorry, Tom."

"Yeah. It was horrible. For me and the kids."

"You have kids?"

He nodded. "Nick and Amanda. They were devastated."

"I'm sorry." I laid my hand on his. "Your wife... Helen... she must've been young."

He nodded and said, "Thirty-seven."

"Oh my God! What did she die of?"

He appeared lost as he stared at the table. Finally, he looked at me and said, "I really can't continue talking about this. Not here."

"I'm sorry. We don't need to talk about it."

"I'd like to leave. Do you mind?"

"Of course not."

"I just can't... " He shook his head, looking like he was on the verge of crying.

We left and, as we drove off, he asked, "How about a walk down by the river?"

"Sure."

About fifteen minutes later, we pulled into a parking lot next to the blacktop path along the Mississippi and got out. The sun above the trees on the opposite shore glowed on the river's surface. As we walked next to one another, I took his hand. Finally, he looked at me, took a deep breath, and said, "Helen committed suicide." And then it all came out—the loss, the pain, the trauma that he and Nick and Amanda had experienced, and his inability to protect his kids, who left home several years later and started new lives for themselves. Helen's suicide still haunted them. And Tom's desire to be with her haunted him. I sensed in Tom a capacity for love that seemed unlike anything I'd ever encountered in a man and I wanted to help him recover from his loss. I wanted to replace Helen. I wanted his love. He put his arm around me and pulled me even closer. I didn't realize then that I would never be able to replace her. No one could. Not completely. She would never disappear from his mind, his heart.

After we'd walked for a while, he let me go, took my hand and said, "There's something very calming about walking along the river. Sometimes it flows so smoothly, you hardly notice the flow."

"And the sun glows on the surface, and you feel its warmth."

"Yeah… Hey, there's a bench up ahead. Shall we sit?"

I looked over and saw him smiling at me. His mood seemed to be changing. "Yeah. Let's."

We sat down. He put his arm around my shoulder, I leaned into him, and we sat in silence, watching the river. And then he said, "Tell me more about yourself."

"What do you want to know?"

"You said last night that your parents used to take you on great trips when you were a kid."

"And all the way through high school."

"Wow! Well, what was the best trip they took you on?"

I told him about the trip my parents and I took to a French town on the Atlantic, called Le Croisic. We stayed in a seventeenth century granite house that Mom and Dad had rented. It was located toward the tip of this long, narrow peninsula and looked out on the gulf and the ocean, and all day and all night I could hear the constant, rhythmic crashing of the waves on the shore, a hypnotic rhythm that relaxed me and induced me into a deep sleep at night. We'd spend our days at the sandy beaches swimming in the ocean, or walking along the bay in town, looking at the shops on one side and the boats at anchor on the other, and stopping to eat at the restaurants, where I had the best *moules frites* of my life. We went for hikes along the rocky shores and the cliffs, and visited places like

Mont St. Michel, a three-hour drive."

But, as I described to Tom the experience of walking up the steep road that wound around the mountainous island and led to the monastery at the top, I recalled Dad having to pause, lean against a wall and catch his breath, and Mom, with a panicked look, her hand on his shoulder, her face close to his, asking him if he was okay, and Dad, gasping, nodding, and finally sighing and saying he was. And then the image of Mont St. Michel faded, and I remembered the day Mom called me and told me Dad had died.

"Between her sobs and mine, she managed to tell me he'd gone on a bike ride, and after he got back, he went into their room to take a nap and never woke up." I looked at Tom. "Just four years ago. Four years." I looked off, staring at nothing. "Except for that day on Mont St. Michel, Dad had always seemed so healthy. I used to go on bike rides with him and Mom when I was a little girl and a teenager. Healthy, happy, and then... gone... I was so worried about Mom, I offered to move home and live with her, but she insisted I continue my life, she could manage on her own. She taught for a few more years and then retired, sold the house, and moved into a retirement home, still insisting I shouldn't worry about her. I'm lucky to have had such loving parents, but when one of them died, the loss was... unbearable. But you know"—I looked at Tom and saw his eyes focused on me—"I always feel that Dad is still with me. I mean, literally, I can feel his presence. He'll always be with me, and his presence gives me strength."

"Someone who's gone, but still present, and his presence gives you strength... you're very fortunate."

"I am." I smiled at him, and he kissed me.

The sun was starting to set behind the trees on the opposite side of the river, and he suggested we should leave. He drove me back to my house and parked in front. It was dark, but I could sense his eyes fixed on my face. He leaned over, and we kissed again. And again. And then, when our breathing became really intense, he stopped and, still holding me, whispered in my ear, "I need to leave. I'd like to see you again tomorrow night."

Surprised that he was ending the evening so soon, that the kissing and hugging weren't a prelude to getting into bed, I pulled back, looked into his eyes and saw... a warmth that felt like love, and I smiled and said, "I would, too. What would you like to do?"

"I haven't even thought about it."

"Well, I enjoyed tonight. How about we do dinner again tomorrow night, and then... do whatever we feel like doing. And this time, I'll make the reservation and pick you up. And I'll pick up the tab, too."

"Okay." He laughed. "A total reversal of roles. Where are we going?"

"That'll be a surprise."

"Sounds like fun."

We kissed, and I got out of the car, walked up to my house, closed the door, and heard him drive away. I sat down in the living room, gazed out the window at the moonlight and was amazed again that he'd made no attempt to seduce me and get me into bed. He seemed fascinated by me, but maybe he needed time to adapt to a new person in his life. And that made me feel even more that his love wasn't just bound up with sex. It was real love.

The next evening, I pulled up in front of his house and saw him sitting on the front porch, waiting for me. I waved, and he got up and walked past the flowers—the lilies, phlox, hibiscus, and beautiful roses. He got in the car, and we kissed, as if we were already a couple. As I was driving us to the restaurant, he asked where we were going for dinner. I told him again it was a surprise. We joked and talked about our day, and he said he'd just finished reading Molly Ivins' *Who Let the Dogs In*? I laughed at the title, and he kept me laughing as he repeated Ivins' comments about Dubya, the legacy life he'd led, and how he'd escaped serving in the war in Vietnam by joining the FANGers.

"The FANGers?" I asked. "What are they?"

"That's the special unit of the Fucking Air National Guard reserved for the rich and powerful in Texas, so they never had to serve in Vietnam. But, when they weren't partying, they did a great job protecting the U.S. border from an invasion by Mexico." I could hear the sarcasm in his voice evolve into anger as he continued to repeat some of Ivins's hilarious and contemptuous comments about the Shrub.

And then, as the Lexington came into view, he fell silent. I parked, turned off the motor, and looked at him, expecting to see him happy—maybe even impressed—that I was taking him to such a chic restaurant, but found his face devoid of expression. I asked, "What's the matter?" He just shook his head. I pleaded with him to tell me, and finally everything came out about his brother, Bobby, and the time Bobby came home from the war, and the family went out to dinner at the Lexington with Tom and Bobby's aunt and uncle and their two kids, and one of the cousins treated Bobby so horribly, and everything else that happened, until Bobby signed up again and returned to Vietnam, never to come back.

By the time Tom had finished talking about Bobby, his sorrow and tears had drained him of energy. He seemed weak, distraught, and so I brought him back to my house and scrounged up something for us to eat. And then I took him upstairs to my room, had him lie down on my bed and lay down with him and held him in my arms, holding him like he was my little boy. He slowly became more aware of my presence, and my compassion for him evolved into passion, and we made love and, after gasping for air and resting, made love again.

Our passion for one another was so intense, I couldn't imagine an obstacle to us being together. I was ecstatic the night he picked me up to go to the Jeune Lune Theater to see a performance of *The Miser*, and was even more excited after the play, when he invited me to his place for a drink. As we talked about the play on the way, my mind wandered, and I wondered what I would see at his house. I felt we'd already bonded and I had nothing to fear, and that we would spend another night passionately making love. We parked in front, walked past the gardens in the dark, entered the house and went into the living room. While he poured our cognac, I moved around the room, looking at the photos on one of the walls—high school graduation portraits of Nick and Amanda; a picture of them when they were little kids, and, standing behind them, of Tom and a woman, whom I assumed to be Helen; and a picture of Tom and Helen, standing in front of a lake, their arms around one another's backs as they leaned into one another, smiling at the camera. I stared at the photographs in which Helen appeared, not seeing any resemblance between her and me, aside from our blonde hair, although mine was darker than hers. He must've been unconsciously seeking Helen and been desperate to find her to have confused me with her. I felt scared. His wife was dead, but she was still present, and in his mind, too. I wondered if there was room for me in his life. But when he handed me my drink, put his arm around me and kissed me, he assuaged my fear, and the picture disappeared as we kissed and caressed one another and made love on the carpet, and then went up to his room and made love again.

I woke up in the morning and found myself lying next to him. I extended my hand to his thigh and remembered the excitement I'd felt as his body pressed against mine, as he penetrated me, groaned, and almost laughed as he came. I smiled at the ceiling, rolled onto my side, lay my head on his chest and breathed deeply, as if I could inhale him, until I noticed on his night stand a close-up of Helen's face pressed against his as they smiled at the camera. I lay there staring at the picture and remembered the other photos. I pulled away from him, sat up and looked around the room at the pictures of his family and Bobby on the wall, the chests of drawers and Helen's vanity and thought, His life is full. There's no place for me. I gathered my clothes from off the floor, got dressed and was about to go when I heard him say, "You're leaving?"

I turned around and saw him sitting up in bed, a panicked look on his face, and I said, "You don't have room for me in your life. Or for any woman, other than Helen. She's... " I looked around at the pictures and back at him. "She's everywhere. And she's in your mind."

"You're in my mind. This is the first time in… in years I've really wanted to be with a woman."

"A woman other than Helen?"

He nodded. "Yeah."

"But you want a woman who makes you feel you're with Helen."

"Please, please, give me a chance. Helen's death was... a lot of pain, but I've moved on." His eyes beseeched me. He got out of bed, naked, and came over and took me in his arms. "Please stay." He looked into my eyes and smiled and said, "We can at least have breakfast together." And we did, and after we made love again.

As the days went by, I began to realize this wasn't going to be just another relationship with a man. I was starting to feel I needed Tom, needed him to fill a hole in my spirit. After Dad's death, I'd spend a day or two every week with Mom, because I needed her as much as I felt she needed me. But as the months went by, I saw her less, and after she sold her house and moved into the retirement home, I'd see her once or twice a month, and just briefly, because she always had things planned with her friends there. I knew I was very fortunate to have had parents whose love had given me a kind of inner strength and a sense of self-confidence, but at the same time, their absence increased my need for love, my need for someone who wanted to be with me now, now and forever, and I felt Tom offered me that. And I offered him what he needed, too—someone who could live in Helen's place, who could provide him with the love he yearned for. But I also wanted to be who I am, and not *just* another version of her. I wanted his love and was prepared to do whatever was necessary to obtain it, as long as I didn't have to lose myself.

I hear the sharp sound of a paddle clank against the side of a canoe and resonate across the surface of the water, and then the echo of the voice of one of the boys, and, feeling ecstatic, leap up, rush to the edge of the balcony, and scan the lake, the inlet off to the left, listening, staring at the water that reflects the blood-red light of the sun above the trees on the opposite side. I hear a shout. And laughter. And then silence. And again a clank, and then voices speaking. And silence. And then the first canoe emerges from around the edge of the inlet, and I see Ethan paddling at the bow, Amanda behind him and Tom at the stern. And then the second canoe appears, with Sarah at the bow, little Luke in the middle and Nick at the stern. As they head toward our small inlet, Sarah points toward me and looks back at Luke and cries, "There's Grandma!" Everyone looks, searching for me, and finally Ethan shouts, "Hi, Grandma!" I smile, happy at the thought the boys think of me as their grandmother, even though I've never given birth to a child. In no time the first canoe strikes the shore below and scrapes across the sandy soil as it grooves its way, and then the other canoe pulls in next to it. Ethan and Sarah climb out of the bows and pull the canoes forward, and then Amanda and Luke get out and, with two at each bow, they pull the canoes further onto the shore, so Tom and Nick can disembark. Tense, holding my breath, I watch Tom, bent over, ultra cautious, grip the gunwales, take a step forward, pause as the canoe wobbles, take another step, and another, and then grab Nick's forearm and step out onto land, and I sigh with relief. The boys are already rushing up the winding path, shouting with excitement, and Sarah and Amanda follow side by side, talking to one another, and then Amanda follows Sarah up the narrow path, while Nick holds onto Tom's arm until they reach the path, and then Tom takes the lead and Nick follows close behind.

I follow the balcony around to the steps on the side and get a loud "Hi, Grandma!" as the boys, each wearing a bathing suit and a blue lifejacket over their soccer jerseys, run up the steps in their bare feet.

"Hey," I cry, extending my arms, "don't I get a hug?"

"I gotta pee," Ethan shouts.

"I gotta pee, too," cries Luke, as he runs by and catches the screen door and follows his older brother into the cabin, the door slamming behind him.

I look back and see Sarah, in her bathing suit and life vest, has reached the top of the bluff. Her eyes, sparkling beneath the broad-brimmed straw hat she's wearing, catch mine, and she greets me with a big smile and a heavy "Ooof!" as she shakes her head. "What a climb!"

"Welcome back!" I say, as we greet one another with a hug, and I feel the heat of the sun in her skin. "Did you have a good time?"

"We had a great time. Nick guided us to an entry to the Boundary Waters that has a sandy shore, like a beach, and we went swimming. I took a break for a while and sat on the grass, and a flock of mallards came walking along the shore, staring at us like they were wondering what we were doing there. They got pretty close, pausing from time to time, looking away and then at us, like they were thinking, Are you going to feed us pretty soon? It was fun."

"Yeah, it was fun," Amanda says, as she draws up next to Sarah, smiling, looking at me through her sunglasses, which are large enough to conceal part of her scar. "No portaging today. Just paddled around to the inlets, the islands and down the river and said hello to the lake and the animals. A pair of loons accompanied us for a while. And we saw an osprey. And a moose, down by the shore."

Sarah says, "I'm glad you and Nick and your dad know your way around. If I were out there alone, I'd get lost. I mean, this is supposedly one lake, but"—she shakes her head—"it's got all those huge inlets. It feels like you're going from one lake to another. And then, when you come back, everything looks different."

"Yeah, it does," Tom says, smiling at us as he slips off his lifejacket. "Wish you could've come." He draws close and puts his arm around me and kisses me on the forehead, and I look up and see the joy radiating from his eyes. After not seeing his kids and grandkids for five years, they're finally here with him.

"Hi, Grace." I hear Nick's voice. He stops behind his father, off to the side.

"Hi, Nick. I heard you went swimming."

"Yeah. We had a great time. We passed some guys jumping off a cliff into the water, and the boys wanted to do that, too, but I said, Nope. Too dangerous. They settled for a regular swim." He looks at Tom and says, "They got to swim with Grandpa." He laughs.

Tom grins. "For what that's worth."

We all laugh.

Nick walks past us, wraps his arm around Sarah, and Tom and I follow them and Amanda into the cabin and past the long table and the windows in the dining room that look out onto the balcony and the lake. While I stop and glance at the table on one side and the kitchen on the other, Tom lets go of me, continues past the front door to the living room, and heads for one of the armchairs to join Nick, who has plopped onto the other chair and leaned his head back, basking in the evening sun that floods the room, which also looks out onto the lake. I announce, "I'll get dinner ready," and Amanda offers to help, while Sarah heads past the kitchen and down the hall to the boys' room.

Amanda and I enter the kitchen, and when I turn to talk to her about what I'd planned on preparing, I see she has taken off her sunglasses and am struck—as I often am—by the long, deep jagged scar across her forehead, from the left brow to the end of her right brow, and by the sag of her eyelid over her artificial eye, and I remember that evening years ago, when Nick, his girlfriend, and I were in the cabin, going crazy worrying about Tom and Amanda, because it was so late, they should've arrived from St. Paul hours before, and we hadn't been able to reach them, because we didn't have Wi-Fi. And then the owner of the lodge pounded on our door and told us—with a panicked look on his face—that Tom had called him and said he and Amanda were in the hospital, they'd been in a car accident, and he'd tried to contact us but couldn't. Nick drove us in the dark to Ely, and we rushed into the hospital, found the ER, and asked at the reception desk about Tom and Amanda. They'd been transferred by helicopter to Duluth. I called Tom, got through to him and asked if he was okay. He started crying. Amanda had lost her eye, and her forehead had been horribly gashed. He sobbed as he described how the blood had gushed from her wound and flooded her face. And I cried with him. And as I remember the pain we felt, I notice Amanda looking into my eyes, as if wondering if I'm still here, and I panic, because I don't want to reveal what I'm thinking.

"Are you okay?" she asks, in a suspicious tone.

"Yeah. Yeah, I'm sorry. I just... I got distracted. Ah, let's—"

"Is there something... ?"

"No, no. Let's just talk about dinner. I've… ah... I've already prepared some wild rice. We can just warm that up in the microwave. And we've got those walleye filets. And I thought maybe a salad, and fruit for dessert. What do you think?"

"Yeah. I'll cook the filets."

"Great! I'll get started on the salad."

I sigh, relieved we'll be focusing on something that will help me not to think of that night so many years ago. And all the pain—the pain that led to the accident, and the pain that followed. Tom and I just want Amanda, Nick and his family to have a good time, so they'll come back. Tom can't live without them.

Amanda has taken out the flour, the spices, and the eggs she needs to prepare the breading and has begun working on one of the counters. I scoop up the vegetables, set them in a colander in the sink, rinse them off, get a knife and a cutting board, and begin slicing on the other counter. As I work, I recall Amanda getting a phone call early this morning from an editor, just as we were about to leave home, and wonder what it was about.

Sarah walks in, looks around, and says, "Can I help with anything?"

I ask, "Do you need any help, Amanda?"

"No. Thank you. I've got everything under control."

"Well," I look at Sarah, "you can help me cut up vegetables for the salad, if you like."

"Okay."

"Why don't you use this knife and board, and I'll warm up the wild rice and prepare the salad dressing." As I get the bottle of olive oil and vinegar to prepare the dressing, I say, "The kids sure looked happy when they ran up the bluff. They must have had a good time."

"Oh, they did!" Sarah exclaims. "They needed that canoe trip and the swim after the long ride up here. Nick kept on reminding them of all the things they'd get to do—canoeing, fishing, swimming, and seeing deer and moose, and wolves and bears. But by the time we reached the supermarket in Ely, they were going crazy in the backseat. And I mean *crazy*."

"Oh!" I shake my head. "When you pulled up next to us in the parking lot, I heard all that ruckus and thought, Oh my God! You and Nick are such wonderful parents. I don't know if I could handle that."

"Nick is a great dad," Sarah says. "He really is." She stops slicing a cucumber as she reflects. "You know, that's probably his biggest problem—he tries to be the perfect father. He always pays attention to his boys. He's always supportive. Coaches them in soccer, attends all their games, and helps them with their homework." She shakes her head. "But he always seems to find something he should've done better." She shakes her head and starts cutting the cucumber again.

"Hmm," Amanda hums. "I wonder where that comes from?"

I pause in front of the microwave, glance at her, and see an ironic smile on her lips. I know what's triggering that smile but decide to remain silent and keep the peace.

"I have no idea," says Sarah.

I take the bowl of wild rice out of the microwave, carry it to the dining room table, return to the kitchen, and see Amanda frying the filets and Sarah slicing tomatoes. I get out another knife and cutting board, help Sarah finish preparing the salad, and she carries the bowl into the dining room.

I look at Amanda, who has already finished cooking a panful of filets that she has laid out on a serving plate and is laying a second batch in the sizzling oil. She sets her spatula down, looks back at me and says, "You know, I love Nick and Sarah's kids, but when they pulled up next to us in the parking lot, and I heard those kids screaming in the back seat, I felt I'd made the right decision to ride with you and Dad."

I thought she was going to say she'd made the right decision never to have children. I continue smiling as I nod and respond, "They can be a handful."

"They sure can."

Hearing Sarah talk with Nick and Tom in the living room, and feeling Amanda has opened things up a little between us with her comment about the kids, I say, "When Sarah said something about Nick getting obsessed with how he could be a better father, you said, 'I wonder where that comes from?' I'm wondering what you meant."

"What did I mean?" She looks at me, as if considering whether she should tell me, and then says, "Well, I think it's pretty obvious. Our parents have a lot to do with who we become, and Dad... " She shakes her head, while staring at me, as if wondering, Do I really want to tell her this? And then she says, "Dad loved Nick and me, and when we were growing up, he was probably as good of a father as he could be."

"But?"

"But he was obsessed by... Well, you know what I'm going to say. He was obsessed by my mother's death and by his brother's disappearance. So obsessed, he didn't realize he often disappeared for us. And sometimes when we really needed him."

"But I'm sure he tried his best. He loves you and Nick so much."

"Oh, I know. Now. But I didn't always feel that during the years following my mother's death. And Nick didn't either." She pauses, and then says, "Dad was gone much of the time. His head was somewhere else." She nods and smiles, the same ironic smile as before. "Normal, for what he'd been through." After a couple beats, she adds, "What Dad, Nick, and I experienced during those years, we'll never really get over it. Therapy can help, but it doesn't put an end to what haunts you. It just helps you live with it." She smiles. "I don't need to tell you that."

"No, you don't. But I think your dad is much healthier now."

"Maybe. Maybe not... But the damage has already been done. Nick still lives likewith the father we had thirty-five years ago. He'll always live with him." She pauses for a couple beats. "When I made that comment, I was thinking that Nick didn't want to be the kind of father our dad had been for us. That's all."

Sarah enters the kitchen and exclaims, "Oh my God! Those filets are burning."

Amanda pivots toward the stove and turns off the gas. "They're okay!" She scrapes the filets out of the pan with the spatula, while whiffs of smoke drift through the screen a few feet away and disappear. "I got 'em out just in time."

"Well," Sarah says, "I'll let the boys know we can eat." She heads down the hall toward their room.

I follow Amanda, as she takes the platter with the filets and heads toward the dining room table, but stops behind the couch in the living room that faces Tom and Nick, resting in their armchairs, and stares at them. We both feel the tension in their voices as they talk to one another over the end table between them.

"I know, Dad," Nick says.

"It drives me nuts," Tom says. "Just drives me nuts, that now, when the planet is going through its sixth extinction, we have so many goddamn corrupt leaders focused on things like invading other countries, murdering demonstrators, amassing wealth by screwing the people they're supposed to be serving—"

"Yeah, yeah." Nick heaves a big sigh and smiles at Tom. "I know, Dad. I know."

"Well," I say, "I hate to interrupt you two"—I smile at them as they look at me—"but dinner's ready!"

Nick smiles, arches his eyebrows and nods, looking relieved, and says, "Thank you, Grace."

"Mom said we're having fish for dinner," Ethan says, as he stands next to the couch and looks up at me. "Are we going to eat fish every day?"

I smile at him. He's so cute in his white soccer jersey and shorts. And tall. The top of his head reaches my shoulder, and he's only eleven years old. "Well, I think that depends on how many fish you guys catch. You'll have to go fishing every day."

He turns toward Nick and says, "Dad, are we gonna go fishing every day?"

"Well," Nick says, "if you guys want to go fishing every day, we can. We'll become fish junkies."

"I want to be a fish junkie!" exclaims Luke, grinning, as he pulls up next to his big brother.

Sarah, Amanda, and I burst out laughing.

With a big smile, Tom exclaims, "Let's eat!"

We take our places at the dining room table. I sit at one end, facing Tom at the other, and glance back and forth from Amanda and Sarah on one side, to Nick and the boys on the other. Nick gets dinner started by serving the boys. Everyone's talking as we start eating, until Tom clinks his glass with his knife, and we fall silent.

"Well, I want to make a toast"—he pauses as he lifts his glass of water—"to my grandsons, Ethan and Luke, the two greatest soccer players of the future!"

We adults all laugh and shout, "To the two greatest soccer players of the future!" and drink our water, while Ethan gives us a huge, cocky grin, revealing the braces on his teeth, and Luke, with a shy smile, shrinks down into his chair.

"Grandma and I sent you those jerseys for Christmas last year. But we don't know anything about the names on the back. Who are those guys? Ethan, you go first."

Ethan hops off his chair and turns around so we can see the name on the back of his jersey and, looking over his shoulder, proclaims, "Manuel Neuer plays for Munich and he's the greatest goalie in the world!"

"And," Tom responds, in a loud boisterous voice, "I bet he's looking over his shoulder and wondering how much longer he's got before you arrive."

Ethan nods his head and keeps on grinning.

Sarah smiles at Ethan, beaming her love for him, and looks at Nick, who is laughing and shaking his head.

"Now, Luke," Tom continues, "tell us about the guy whose name is on *your* jersey."

Luke bends his head forward and murmurs, in a monotone voice, as if repeating a script, "Cristiano Ronaldo is Portuguese and he's the greatest forward in the world."

"And," says Tom, "I bet he's—"

Nick interjects, "Looking over his shoulder, scared to death that Luke is going to dethrone him." Nick chuckles, puts his arm around Luke, and looks at Tom. "Ronaldo is already in his late thirties, Dad, so, ah... " He glances down at Luke, who has collapsed into his side.

"I just wanted to toast these two wonderful little guys," Tom says. "I have been denied the pleasure of their company for so long. And that brings me to my second toast: to my family, to all of you. I am so happy that after five years... " he shakes his head and repeats, "five years... we're finally all back together."

We drink our water, and the boys drink their milk.

As we resume eating, Nick looks at his dad and says, "We did get to see one another on Zoom a few times. That's better than nothing."

"I never want to do another Zoom meeting as long as I live," Tom says. "It's just not the same as getting together." He shakes his head. "No way."

We all nod in agreement.

Tom smiles at Amanda as she is about to put a forkful of salad in her mouth. "And Dr. Faust... "

She holds the fork near her mouth as she smiles back. "Yes, Dr. Faust?" She puts the salad in her mouth.

"I'm so happy you're here."

She swallows and takes a sip of water. "Thank you, Dad. I'm happy to be here."

Tom continues eating as he says, "I wish your husband could've come, too. We'd love to meet him."

"Tony would've liked to, but his play is opening on Broadway in three weeks. It's his first Broadway production, and he just couldn't take the time off."

"That's too bad. But you got married three years ago." He pauses, holding his fork and knife over his plate, reflects for a few beats and says, "Three years, right?"

Amanda nods.

Tom stares at her as if stunned. "And you still haven't brought him home." He lowers his hands and rests them on the table. I'm wondering when Amanda will remind Tom that there are daily flights to New York, if he should ever decide to visit.

Nick asks, "What's the play about?"

"The title is *Putin the Great.*"

Nick bursts into laughter, and Sarah and I look at him and at Amanda and at one another and repeat, "*Putin the Great*?"

Amanda says, "Putin compared himself once to Peter the Great, so Tony couldn't resist the opportunity. It's a satire. I think it'll get a lot of laughs. Oh, one thing you learn in the play is that *putain* in French means 'whore.'"

"So," Nick asks, "the French are constantly calling him a whore?"

"No," Amanda says. "They spell his name differently."

I laugh. "They spell it p-o-u-t-i-n-e. *Poutine.*"

"Well," Tom says, who seems to have returned to our world after a brief disappearance, "I assume the play attacks Putin for what he's doing in Ukraine."

"Oh, it attacks him!" Amanda says.

"Good! Well, I look forward to meeting him." Tom smiles. "Your husband. Not Putin."

"Maybe next year," Amanda says.

Tom nods and repeats, staring down at his plate, "Maybe next year."

I take another mouthful of fish and savor its taste as I look around the table, everyone eating and talking, except Tom, who continues to stare down. "Tom," I say. He doesn't seem to hear me. I repeat his name, louder this time, and he looks up at me and gives me a blank stare. I say, "Maybe we should go to New York this fall and see the play. Sounds like something you'd enjoy. It would be fun."

He nods his head and feigns a smile.

"Tom… "

Everyone pauses and looks back and forth at him and me. I wish I hadn't said anything.

He looks around the table and says, in a somber tone, "The last time we were all here together was in 2018." He pauses, making sure everyone gets his message. "In 2019, no one came. And in 2020…"

Nick sighs and drops his fork, which clinks against his plate. "Covid arrived. There was no way we were going to take a plane and risk getting Covid." He shakes his head.

"Way too dangerous," Amanda agrees, and then continues eating.

"One of my colleagues died of Covid," Sarah says, as she pauses, her fork in her hand, remembering.

I feel anxious, like this is the beginning of something I've already witnessed, and I don't want to see it again.

"In 2021," Tom says, "the fires in the Boundary Waters kept you away."

"We don't bring our kids near forests that are burning down," says Nick, who glares at Tom.

"Everything I read about the fires was terrifying," Amanda says, shaking her head.

"And in 2022," Tom glares back at Nick, "you had to focus on getting elected."

"Is there something wrong with that, Dad?"

"Just makes me wonder."

"Wonder what?"

"How important family is to you."

"Oh, Dad. I wouldn't be here... " Nick looks around the table and back at Tom. "We wouldn't be here, if you guys weren't important to us."

Tom nods, as if simply acknowledging what Nick has said.

"And getting elected is not easy," Sarah says. "Nick was working at it all the time. And helping him and trying to take care of the kids was like having two full-time jobs."

"Yeah," Tom nods, a sarcastic look in his eye. "I bet it was." And then he turns to Amanda. "And you didn't come because... "

"Because I was concerned about getting Covid. Some of my friends and colleagues had gotten it."

He smiles. "You came at Christmas."

"Yes, I came at Christmas." She smiles back and nods.

"But that was just to do research."

"I'm sorry I wasn't able to spend more time with you, Dad."

"What was the research for?"

"I told you—an article I was writing."

"And you had to come home to do the research? You had to access your mother's computer?"

"Yes." Amanda stares at him. "And this is not the time to talk about it."

"Well," I say, "I want to make a toast now"—I grin at Tom—"if I may... "

He shakes his head and glares at me. "No. You may not."

"What!" I exclaim.

"Nick," Sarah says, "I'm going to take the boys for a walk."

She's about to stand up, when I say, "No. That's not necessary, Sarah. We prepared such a wonderful meal, I think you and Nick and Amanda and the boys should stay here and enjoy your dinner. Tom and I are going to go for a walk."

"I don't want to go for a walk."

"Well, then we can go sit by the dock and talk." I rivet him with my eyes, so he knows I mean business. "Come on, Tom."

I get up, walk to the other end of the table, put my hands on his shoulders and murmur, "Come on. Let's go for a walk." He doesn't respond. I realize what I'm doing might be humiliating for him, but I know this has to end now. I murmur again, "Come on, sweetie."

He finally gets up, and I take him by the hand and guide him out the side door and down the steps toward the steep, winding path to the grassy shore. We sit down on the plastic chairs facing the dock and the lake. The blood-red glow of the sun has darkened, and much of the remaining sunlight is blocked by the trees on the ridge, on the other side of the inlet. It will be dark soon.

After staring at the red glow on the black water for a few beats, I say, "I know that your feelings were hurt when Amanda and Nick and his family left early, back in 2018, and then didn't come back for four years. And I know you think they're just using Covid and the fires as an excuse, and they didn't want to come because they were still upset about what happened that year. But if you continue to just focus on your suspicions, on your anger, and you accuse them of this and that, they aren't going to want to come back. They just might pick up and leave. And then where will we be?"

He stares at the lake and doesn't speak.

"And our grandkids... When your anger and your pain take control of you, and you vent in front of them, they're going to get scared, and Nick is going to get angry with you. That's what happened in 2018. Okay?"

He nods.

"Tom, we want them to come back next year, and the year after and the year after that. But that's not going to happen if you don't forgive them. If you don't engage them. Talk about something they might want to talk about. Be kind to them. At some point, maybe everyone will be able to open up and say what they think and feel. But we're not there yet. And it might take more than just a week at the cabin."

He continues to remain silent.

"If we make it to the end of the week, and everyone's happy, and they all want to come back next year, then we're getting what we want."

He nods again.

"You love your kids, your daughter-in-law, and your grandkids. And they love you. You can be happy, if you can let go of the past."

"I know... I know." He extends his hand and takes hold of mine. "Thanks, Grace. This hasn't been easy."

We lean over and kiss. I settle back in my chair and gaze at the light from the few stars and the moon that have begun to shine on the dark water. I look over at him, see the profile of his face, and say, "You think we can make it up the path in the dark?"

He laughs. "We don't have much choice, do we? Unless you want to sleep here."

"I'd rather sleep in our bed."

We get up and hold hands as we head toward the path and stop when we see a flashlight, and then another, heading down the path toward us. And I hear the voices of Nick and Amanda, repeating, "Dad! Grace!"

Day 2, Sunday

Standing in front of the kitchen sink, coffee mug in hand, looking out the window at the view of the lake between the weeping willow and the three birch trees, feeling the warmth of the morning sun on the still water and imagining Nick and Amanda running out the door in their bathing suits and down to the beach to spend the day playing with their friends, I feel Helen's fingers graze my back and look to catch a glimpse of the smile she gives me as she walks away. I watch her—in her red T-shirt and denim shorts—enter the dining area, where Amanda, in her bathing suit and T-shirt, sits on one side of the wooden table, her back to the windows, and Nick, also in his bathing suit and T-shirt, sits on the other. I smile at the sight of the kids grinning with excitement as they anticipate eating the pancakes Helen is about to serve. She stops at the end of the table, looks from Amanda to Nick and back and says, "Ladies first!" And walks around Amanda's side of the table, serves her a pancake, bends over and kisses the top of her head and runs her fingers across her blonde hair, an even lighter blonde than her own. She walks around to Nick's side, serves him his pancake and, bending over, with her face close to his, says, "You're first tomorrow." She kisses the top of his head, rubs his messy brown hair, sets the platter piled with pancakes on the table and looks at me. "Well, are you going to join us?"

"Mom," Nick says, "where's the syrup?"

"Oh," Helen says, "how can one eat pancakes without syrup?" She laughs. "I'll get it!" She walks toward me, her warm brown eyes gazing at me as she moves closer, and closer, and closer, until our lips touch, and we kiss, and I hold her, feeling her body press against mine.

* * *

I open my eyes, stare at the pinewood ceiling and see Helen's body, covered in the fur coat, her head leaning back and to the side against the car seat, her eyes open. I grab the bed sheet and close my eyes, but the image is still there. I clutch the sheet so hard I can feel my nails pierce the cloth and the palms of my hands. I take a deep breath, extend one hand down toward my side and feel Grace's naked leg. I take another deep breath, roll over on my side, wrap my other arm around her and pull close, breathing in the scent of her body, sighing as I feel my body relax, hoping I can fall back to sleep.

But the memory won't let go. I get up, head for the kitchen, make some coffee, and while it's percolating, rinse some dishes left in the sink and put them in the dishwasher. The percolating stops. I pour myself a mug and head for the balcony, where I sit and stare at the top of the bluff, in the shadow cast by the cabin, and at the lake, the still water warming in the early morning light, and remember the view of the other lake, between the weeping willow and the birch trees.

I hear the screen door open and look over to see Grace, in her bathrobe, coming onto the porch. She bends over, and I raise my head for a kiss. And then she stands up straight, her hand caressing the back of my head and my neck.

"You had a dream this morning," she says.

"Yeah."

"Never forget that I love you."

I lean into her and put my arm around her hip, my eyes wet with tears.

* * *

I open the cupboard, find my favorite mug, the one with the two loons floating next to each other on blue water, pour myself some coffee, and head for the door to the balcony. The screen door closes behind me, and I look at the lake glittering in the morning sun and see the two canoes off to my left, leaving the large inlet and following the opposite shore, dense with pine and birch, heading toward another inlet, where Tom and Nick have always loved to fish. I smile as I remember fishing with them there, on the edge of an aqua-field of water lilies, five years ago. I hope Tom finds happiness today... enough to leave that dream behind.

And what was the dream? It could've been of Helen. Could've been of me. Or neither one of us. But he was spooning me, clinging to me, like he would've sunk if I hadn't been there. Sunk into what? A sea of sorrow? Time? Or maybe he just wanted to be close to me.

I glance down at the shadow of the cabin, cast across the patches of dirt and wildflowers in front of the balcony, and then to my right, where I see Amanda sitting on one of the wicker chairs, her hands on her lap, holding her coffee mug as she watches the canoes.

"Mind if I join you?" I ask.

Amanda smiles up at me. "Please do."

I place my coffee on the table between us and sit, lean back against the groaning wicker and look at the canoes that are getting smaller and wonder, How can I engage Amanda? Finally, I say, "Tom is so happy that you're all here. That's why he wanted to make breakfast for you."

"Oh! That was such a surprise. The table set, that huge stack of pancakes in the middle, and a bowl over them to keep them warm. And the coffee, too."

I nod and smile... and remember the incident yesterday and say, "I'm sorry about your dad's, ah... "

"Inquisition?"

"Well, I wouldn't use that word, but... "

"There's nothing that surprises Nick and me about Dad giving us a hard time about not coming to the cabin during those years. We've been dealing with that kind of thing for a long time."

"He really misses you."

"I know, I know. We are among his obsessions."

I smile. "His good obsessions."

Amanda smiles back.

As I think about where to go with the conversation, I notice the canoes have disappeared. "Well, *I* also missed you and Nick. And his family." I glance over and see Amanda sipping her coffee. "It's good to be with you. We seldom get to talk." She continues staring at the lake. "When you came home for Christmas, you seemed very occupied by your research."

Amanda smiles at me. "You're beginning to sound like Dad."

"Oh, dear!" I laugh, and then remain silent for a few beats. "I'm very curious about something."

Amanda eyes me. "Yes?"

"Yesterday morning, before we left, I heard you talking on your phone to someone you referred to as an editor. Was that call connected to the research you did?"

She arches her eyebrows. "You're very observant, Grace."

"Thank you." I smile back at her.

"Yes. The editor talked with me about an article I'd done that he's going to publish. And it's based on that research."

"What's it about? If I may ask."

"You may. It's entitled, 'Dead Poets Society.'"

"That's weird," I say, shaking my head as I glimpse Amanda's ironic smile.

"Yes, it is, isn't it. It's actually the title of a film that was very popular a little over thirty-five years ago." After a few beats, she adds, "Titles can't be copyrighted, and I found it perfect for what I was writing, so... "

"And what were you writing?"

"An article about my mother's growing obsession with the confessional poets." She pauses and looks at me. "Do you know them?"

"I've heard of them, but I don't really know anything about them."

"It was a literary movement back in the 1950s, '60s, and '70s. The biggest names were Sylvia Plath, Anne Sexton, Robert Lowell, John Berryman, and W. D. Snodgrass." Amanda looks at me. "Snodgrass. What a name, huh?"

"Yeah."

"Of those five, three committed suicide—Plath, Sexton, and Berryman. All within a period of about eleven years."

"Oh my god!" I shake my head. "How did your mother get interested in them?"

"Well, that's complicated." Amanda glances at me. "I wanted to learn more about her, so I came home at Christmas to go through her documents on her computer—which, of course, Dad still has."

"Oh, yeah," I nod, remembering how Tom clung to Helen's things and still clings to some of them.

"And I found her dissertation. She set out to write about courageous American women poets, who had overcome all kinds of barriers to make the voices of women heard. Poets like Emily Dickenson, Maya Angelou, Sylvia Plath, Anne Sexton, Adrienne Rich, and a few others."

"So, it was sort of a feminist dissertation."

"Yeah." After a few beats, Amanda looks at me and smiles. "I'm sure my father has told you the story about my mother walking past her parents in the living room and out of the house, with her suitcase in one hand and *The Female Eunuch* in the other."

"Oh, yeah," I nod and smile.

"Well, she never finished her dissertation. I wanted to find out why. So, I started reading it. The first few chapters were very focused, very well structured, with a lot of interesting observations. But then her carefully constructed chapters evolved into notes that rambled on and on, primarily about the work of Plath and Sexton. Instead of focusing on the way women poets had asserted a place for women in society as something other than just wives, mothers, housekeepers, and sex objects, she seemed to have become obsessed with those two poets' expressions of their obsessions, their madness, and everything that haunted them. And eventually the dissertation became a kind of journal, in which Mom continued talking about Plath and Sexton, but also about her own growing sense of isolation, loneliness, and depression. She talked a few times about Plath's poem 'Lady Lazarus,' and how obsessed she used to be with sex, which was like a drug for her, gave her a sense of power, and every orgasm was a thrilling death. She joked about dying over and over. And she talked about Dad, and his love, which seemed to calm her. And about having children. And about how much she loved Nicky and me.

"But, as she continued, she wrote increasingly about how isolated and alone she felt. And everything was I, I, I. Like she'd forgotten us. Like she'd forgotten she wasn't alone. We loved her. Dad, Nicky, and I, we wanted to be with her." She shakes her head. "She struggled with this... this something in her, that drew her into a lonely, isolated place. It was so powerful. Eventually, she seemed to see death as something beautiful. She would never feel isolated and alone again. Never again feel depressed." She shakes her head. "Never again feel anything."

"Wow. That's a lot to deal with, Amanda."

"Yeah." Staring at the lake, she says, "Dad told me pretty much the same thing, when we were driving to the cabin, seventeen years ago, just before we crashed... Mom had found something seductive in death. Something beautiful. Because death is the end of suffering." She pauses, takes a deep breath, and wipes tears from her eyes. "She even wrote a poem, about a lady in a fur coat, who sits dead, with a smile on her lips, a glass of vodka in her hand, and her eyes wide open." She shakes her head and sighs.

"Oh, God. I'm so sorry, Amanda."

"Thirty-two years later, and I still don't know if she had a smile on her lips when Dad found her. I do know she'd dropped her glass of vodka." She falls silent again for what feels like a long time, and then says, "I thought if I understood her better... but understanding better doesn't make me feel better. And there's still a lot I don't understand." She looks down toward the outer edge of the balcony.

Realizing I'm staring at her, I look at the lake. As the silence lingers, I feel I have to get her talking again. "I didn't know your mother wrote poetry. Was she actually a poet?"

"Oh, yes and no. She published a few poems, but... " Amanda sighs. "She had a tough life. She felt she was of no interest to her parents. That really came out in her notes. And in what Dad told me that day… the day of the crash." She runs her fingertips across the huge scar above her eye. "I don't think Mom ever returned to her parents' house, after she left. At least, to live there. She had to work her way through school, and that left her very little time for composing poetry. After writing about Plath and Sexton in her notes, she also started writing about John Berryman, who had, of course, nothing to do with feminist poetry. She'd started reading his work when she was a freshman at the University of Minnesota and was really excited about a course she was going to take with him the following academic year. And then, near the beginning of winter quarter, he jumped off the Washington Avenue Bridge."

"Oh my God!"

"Yeah." Amanda shakes her head. "He apparently waved to people on the bridge just as he was about to fall. She'd gone to visit him in his office toward the end of fall quarter, to see if he would look at some of her poems, and he did, and encouraged her to keep on writing, and told her he was looking forward to having her as one of his students. And then he killed himself." She pauses. "She read his obituary and articles about him and discovered he had three kids. She'd learned from his poems about his father committing suicide and the effect it had on him and wondered, How could you do that, knowing how your father's suicide had traumatized you?

"And that became a theme in her journal, just as it was in my article. Berryman committing suicide, knowing what his father's suicide had done to him. The blindness of these poets to the effects of their deaths on the people who loved them. Sylvia Plath, trying to protect her two children—who were about a year and two years old—by simply taping the doorframe to the room in which they were sleeping and cramming towels into the gap between the bottom of the kitchen door and the floor, so she could feel confident her kids would be safe when she turned on the gas and stuck her head in the oven. Did she think of the possibility that all that gas could explode, and her children die in the fire? Did she wonder about the possibility her kids could be so haunted by her death that they might kill themselves? Which is exactly what her son did. And, you know, when I think of the fact that her son, as an adult, left England to live in Alaska, and her daughter left England to live in Australia, I can't help but think of Nick living in Portland and me in New York, so far away from where Mom killed herself... No, there's no getting over this... Anne Sexton's daughter has written, what, two books about coping with her mother's suicide, and I'm sure she's still grappling with it... You know, you might be able to understand it with your mind... but never with your heart." She sighs. "So, the Dead Poets Society, I think of that as including Plath, Sexton, and Berryman, who all felt isolated, alone, depressed, and were obsessed with their isolation and depression, and with themselves, and eventually they couldn't think of anything but themselves, and that's what they had in common—that's what you needed to join the club. And that's how Mom qualified for admission."

I look over and see Amanda facing the lake, gazing at it as if she were looking at a projection of her thoughts.

"Sometimes she comes back to me in a dream, and I feel so happy, and then I wake up and she's gone. And I remember that line by Milton she used to repeat—'I wak'd, she fled, and day brought back my night.'" Amanda looks at me. "Some people think of writing poetry as a kind of therapy. If anything, writing poetry isolates you. You get your feelings onto the page, but if you're alone, isolated, and you can't be with others..." She shakes her head. "It's not therapy. That's what I learned from reading the confessional poets."

"You don't write poetry?"

"No, I don't. Occasional articles, but no poetry."

"And you don't feel that sense of isolation, of loneliness that your mother felt."

Amanda remains silent. I wonder if I'm pushing her too much. Tom has worried about her being isolated and alone in New York, even though she's married. But, I remind myself, as I'm not her mother, there are limits... "I'm sorry. I shouldn't be asking you all these questions. We can talk about something else, if you prefer." Amanda continues staring at the lake. "It's been a few years since we've actually talked. When you came home at Christmas, you were constantly busy doing your research."

Amanda nods. "You asked me if I feel that sense of isolation and loneliness my mother felt... When I was a little girl, I was obsessed by the scars on her forearms. I'm sure Dad has told you about them."

"He has."

"I was always wondering what happened. Who cut her? And why? Well, that obsession became more intense after her suicide. I ended up scarred, too. And lost an eye. So, my mother definitely left her mark on me. And on Dad. And Nicky. And she's not done with us."

I feel her anger. "The article that you wrote about her—did it help you understand her better?"

She nods. "Understanding... " She sighs. "Understanding is the first step toward a good life. But I still have a lot of anger... I'm sure you can hear it... I haven't forgiven her. I'm not there." She shakes her head. "If I can forgive her, I can let go of her. But I've been obsessed with her... trying to understand her, since I was a little girl. I've tried to get as much out of Dad as I could. I even contacted Mom's two brothers, whom I'd never met. They didn't seem to have much interest in communicating with me. When I talked to them on the phone, neither one of them seemed upset about her death. I really felt what it must have been like for her, having brothers who... who didn't give a shit about her. I'm lucky to have a brother like Nicky, who cares about me… Isolation and loneliness are something you carry inside yourself. I can be in a crowd, I can be with a group of friends, I can be with my husband and talk and laugh and still... still feel isolated and alone. During the last year of Mom's life, I sensed that's what she was experiencing. Even when she was with us. Even when she seemed happy." She becomes aware of me staring at her and looks at me and says, while shaking her head, "You married into a crazy family, Grace."

"Isn't every family a little crazy? The important thing is, can you be happy in your family?"

As Amanda gazes at the lake, I wonder how she's going to respond. She looks at me and says, "Are you happy?"

"Am I happy?"

"Yeah. In this family."

"Yes, I am."

Amanda looks back at the lake.

"Why do you ask?"

Amanda says, "I remember Dad referring to you a couple times as Helen. That must've been difficult."

I nod, remembering how often that used to happen and what a problem it became. The first few times, I just smiled and ignored his gaffe and told myself he really loved his first wife, it was natural for her to still be in his thoughts, and it was sort of a compliment for me, that he'd refer to me by Helen's name. But after a while, I started wondering if he really did love me, if he could love anyone other than Helen, if I was just a screen on which he projected his love for her.

"That didn't seem to upset you," Amanda says, pulling me out of my thoughts.

I take a deep breath and formulate my response. "Your father really loved your mother. That kind of love never ends."

"That's true. But… "

I look at her. "Yes?"

"You remember the first time we met? I came home for Christmas. You and Dad had recently married, and you'd moved into the house. He wanted to take the two of us out for a good time, so we could start getting to know one another. He proposed taking us to the Dakota Club, to see a band called Davina and the Vagabonds. And I remember getting dressed up and coming into the living room, all excited by what I anticipated was going to be a wonderful evening, and seeing you and Dad, waiting for me, smiling at me… and I froze. You were wearing a little black dress, with long sleeves, shoulder pads, and a collar around the neck."

I tense.

"It was Mom's dress."

I nod, biting my lower lip.

"Do you know Hitchcock's film, *Vertigo*?"

I clear my throat. "It's in our DVD collection."

"Well, when I saw you in that dress, I thought of the way Jimmy Stewart's character—I think his name's Scotty—I thought of the way he treated the Kim Novak character, the way he forced her to wear that gray suit to make her look even more like the woman he'd fallen in love with, the woman he thought had committed suicide."

I nod.

"Scotty disgusted me for doing that, and I was disgusted with my dad, too. Treating a woman like a doll, that's so inhumane. And Scotty's only attracted to her because of her resemblance to that woman—I can't remember… "

"Madeleine," I murmur, as I remember that night, and how conflicted I felt, as Tom pleaded with me to wear that dress, which he'd given to Helen as a gift. He loved it, and he wanted to give it to me, because he loved me, because he wanted to show me his love, and I wanted to keep peace in the family, and so I wore it, even though it was extremely uncomfortable, so tight around my waist and hips. But looking in the mirror, I thought it made me appear at once sexy and strong, even dominant, perhaps because of the shoulder pads, and I liked the power that it enabled me to project, even as a voice in the back of my mind told me I'd just given up my power.

"Yeah," says Amanda, "Madeleine. He wants to bring his Madeleine back from the dead, and that woman is nothing but a doll for his imagination. A doll to dress up and do what he tells it to do."

I remain silent, hoping Amanda will abandon this subject.

"I felt sorry for you," she says, "to be subjected to that kind of treatment. And it surprised me, because I'd found a lot of my mom's clothes hanging in my closet and packed in boxes that Dad had left in my room. He asked me to go through them and take back to New York everything I wanted. I thought all of her clothes were there, but then I saw you wearing her dress and I… " She shakes her head. "A few nights later, I heard the two of you fighting about another one of Mom's dresses that he wanted you to wear, and I thought, This marriage is not going to last! "

"Why are you bringing all this up?"

"I just want you to know that I have a lot of respect for you. I can imagine all the fights the two of you have probably had and the hell you've been through, but you've survived, you've helped Dad survive, you've helped all of us survive. You've kind of… held our family together."

"Thank you, Amanda." After wiping away the tears that have welled up and trying to shape my thoughts, I look at her and say, "You're right about the fights. They were intense. And I did accuse him of treating me like a doll. And other things. I threatened to leave him. I think the possibility of losing me brought him to realize how important I was to him… that it would be difficult for him to go on living without me. Just as it would've been difficult for me to go on living without him. He hasn't treated me like a doll in years. But I know that your mother is somehow always going to be with him. If I've learned anything from your father, it's that we can love the dead and the living. Human beings are complex. We can draw a line between the past and the present, but in our minds, in our hearts, the line often disappears."

Amanda places her hand on mine and holds it tightly. After a long silence, she takes a deep breath and says, "I'm going to go for a swim. Do you want to join me?"

I smile at her. "Oh, I think I'll just stay here and enjoy the sun. It feels so good. But thanks for asking."

Day 3, Monday

Sitting in the stern of the canoe behind Luke, gazing at the dense field of lily pads and white blossoms floating on the still water, beyond the bobber for my fishing line, I remember the resort on Lake Vermilion, and the cabin where Mom and Dad used to take Mandy and me when we were little, when I was about ten, and Mandy, eight. We'd spend our days on the beach, with the kids from the other cabins, wading in the water and splashing one another... swimming to the raft and climbing on and jumping off... digging moats in the sand and constructing castles... lying on our towels and telling stories, laughing at our lies. I'd glimpse Mom and Dad off to the side, sitting on the Adirondack chairs in front of the cabin, talking and laughing, and staring at us through their sunglasses. Sometimes they'd just look straight ahead at the lake and at that huge weeping willow, the tips of its branches floating on the water... And then Mom killed herself... We never returned. Never saw those kids again. Never saw the lake again. And we didn't go anywhere the following summer. Dad couldn't get it together. Couldn't get outside of himself. Most of the time, he lived in a world of silence, and so did we. The silence into which I could see Mom disappearing during the last few months of her life, when I'd wonder what was going on in her mind.

And then one summer, Dad brought us here, to the Boundary Waters. Forty, fifty miles east of Lake Vermilion. Brought us every summer, and never talked about the other cabin. Maybe he didn't want us to remember. Maybe *he* didn't want to remember. Too painful. Way too painful. And that's probably why he changed our route, too, the route that we could've taken most of the way to both lakes. Instead, we'd drive all the way to Duluth and then follow Highway 61 along the shore of Lake Superior.

And he started a new tradition, a tradition of music, to fill the silence in which we'd lived after Mom's death. He started playing Bob Dylan's album, *Highway 61 Revisited.* He'd turn on the CD right about the time we'd enter Duluth. The music was so loud and so much fun, I didn't even notice how crazy some of the lyrics were, like the one about Abraham telling God he wasn't gonna go kill him a son... But Dad didn't buy that CD for the trip. I'd already seen it in the collection he kept in the car. He probably just remembered it, when we were driving in silence to Duluth, and feeling the weight of that silence, decided to play it. An impulsive decision. Whatever it was, we listened to it every year. Kind of a ritual, as we'd drive on the elevated highway above the Duluth neighborhoods and along the North Shore. It was usually over by the time we got to Highway 1 and turned west and continued north to Ely. He was trying to bring us all into a different world, one that wasn't full of memories of Mom. But maybe he had memories of her that were associated with Dylan's album. I'll never know. It's the kind of thing we're never going to talk about. We leave the past buried in silence. The world of silence that Mandy and I have tried to escape.

That's what I was trying to do, a couple summers later, when I turned fifteen and took control of the CD player. I'd started buying my own CDs and I'd play them, and we'd listen to songs like Radiohead's "Creep." That's what I felt like, a creep. The child of a woman who'd killed herself and of a dad who was often dead to me. When we'd get close to Duluth, Dad would ask me to play his *Highway 61 Revisited*, and I would, but, as soon as it ended, I'd play my CDs. And Mandy started getting her own, and I'd play them, too. We weren't going to live in a world of silence, and we weren't going to let Dad decide what we'd listen to. We used music to create our own world. Maybe we still lived in silence as we listened to the music, but it was our silence, our world... Oh, Christ! Every time I think about this, I grit my goddamn teeth. I can still feel my determination to escape that world of silence.

I gaze at the surface of the water. Its stillness calms me. The silence of nature is so different from the silence I wanted to escape. I take a deep breath and sigh and shake my head. Jesus Christ! Oh, well, at least Dad introduced us to a good album—*Highway 61 Revisited.* I grin, but my happiness fades as I remember something.

Dad used to play Dylan's album in the car when Mandy and I were little, when I was about six or seven, and Mom was still with us. They'd play it when they drove up Highway 61, along Lake Superior to that lodge, the one with the dining room walls and ceiling covered with Native American designs, painted in bright red, blue, and yellow. We must've gone there more than once, because I can see it so clearly...I remember one evening, looking up at the designs painted on the barrel-vaulted ceiling in the dining room and feeling like I was in a huge upside-down canoe. I was so fascinated by the designs and the colors that I kept on looking until I got dizzy. And then, while we were waiting for our dinner, Mom saw a couple she knew and waved to them. They stopped by our table, talked with Mom and Dad, said something about having some really good stuff and Mom and Dad should come by, and they all grinned at one another. And that night, after Amanda fell asleep lying next to me, Mom and Dad each gave me a goodnight kiss as I lay in bed, said they were going to go visit their friends and would be back in just a little while, and turned off the light next to the bed and snuck out the door. I lay there, listening to the waves in the distance rolling against the shore. After a while I got up, went to the window, stared at the dark lawn, the Adirondack chairs, the black lake and the waves crashing against the rocks and boulders... and felt so alone.

I got back in bed, closed my eyes and eventually fell asleep next to Mandy. But later, she woke me up, grabbing my shoulder, crying and screaming, "Mommy and Daddy are gone! They're gone!" I sat up as she cried repeatedly, "Where are they?" I told her they said they'd be back in a little while and tried to hold her and calm her, but she squirmed out of my arms, grabbed her blankie and her doll, clung to them as she lay down, curled up and continued crying. I turned on the light next to the bed and looked at the clock. It was after midnight. I stared at the door, hoping it would open soon and Mom and Dad would enter, while Mandy kept on crying and repeating, "Where are they?" I thought maybe we could go looking for them, but I imagined the empty halls that I'd seen, with all the closed doors, and wondered how we could find them. There was nothing I could do to make her feel safe. This went on for a while, until there was a knock. Mandy stopped crying, and we both stared at the door. There was another knock, louder this time.

I got up, went to the door and said, "Who is it?"

A woman said, "It's your neighbor. Are you okay?"

I didn't know what to say. I looked at Mandy. She was staring at me, her mouth open, her eyes bulging with fear.

The woman knocked again.

I said, "We're okay."

She said, "May I come in?"

I hesitated, and then opened the door enough so I could see her. She was wearing pajamas and a red silk robe and had a very ordinary face.

She smiled at me through the narrow opening and said again, "May I come in?"

I opened the door slowly and stepped aside.

She came in, looked around and then at me and said, in a soft, warm voice, "Where are your parents?"

"They're with some friends. They'll be back soon."

"I thought I heard a little girl crying."

I looked over at the bed and saw that Mandy had disappeared. "I have a sister, but I think she's hiding. Mandy, where are you? Mandy?"

She cautiously stood up from behind the bed, clinging to her doll and blankie, her eyes dilated with fear.

"Are you okay, Mandy?" the woman asked.

Mandy slowly nodded, keeping her eyes fixed on the woman.

"It must be scary for you to be here alone, without your mom and dad."

She nodded again.

I looked down at the floor, wondering what was going to happen. The woman seemed very nice, very kind, sort of like my grandmother, on my dad's side, but...

"How about if I stay with you until your parents come back. We could leave the door open and the lights on."

I looked at Mandy, our eyes met, and she nodded, so I said, "Okay."

"Mandy, if you have a book you'd like me to read to you, maybe I could sit on the bed and we could look at it together. Would you like that?"

Mandy smiled for the first time, came around to the other side of the bed, closer to the woman, set her blankie and her doll down, went to the coffee table by the window that looked out onto the lake, picked up a book from a small pile, carried it over to the bed, set it down near the edge and climbed up. The woman sat down on the other side of the book, and I sat down close to Mandy. But just as the woman picked it up, a man with gray hair, in pajamas and a black robe, appeared in the doorway, looked at the woman, and at Mandy and me, and back at the woman and arched his eyebrows.

She said to Mandy, "Just a minute. I have to talk with my husband." She got up and went to him, and they stepped into the hall and talked, their voices too low for me to understand. He walked away and she returned. She sat down on the bed, picked up the book, looked at the cover and said, "Hans Christian Andersen." She flipped through the pages, smiled at Mandy and asked, "Which story would you like me to read?"

"The Little Match Girl."

The woman checked the table of contents, turned to the story, gave Mandy and me another smile and began reading, while Mandy held her doll and blankie close to herself.

The woman had read only a couple pages, when Mom and Dad appeared in the doorway and stopped, startled. I saw Mom clinging onto

Dad's arm, as if she might lose her balance were she to let go, her eyes dilated and her mouth hanging open. I'd already seen her like that enough to know she was stoned, a word I'd heard them use a few times.

"Who are you?" Dad asked.

And Mom asked, "What the hell are you doing here?"

The woman retained her composure and said, "I'm staying in the next room. I heard a little girl crying and screaming and knocked on the door to see if she was okay." She glared at Mom and Dad and asked, "Why weren't you here?"

And then the woman's husband and another man, with blond hair, wearing slacks and a long sleeve shirt, appeared behind Mom and Dad. The blond man exclaimed, "Excuse me!"

Mom and Dad started and turned around.

The blond man asked in a stern voice, "Can you step outside, please? I need to talk to you."

Mom and Dad followed him into the hall, while the man in the robe looked at his wife and nodded at the door, suggesting they leave. She shook her head and said, "In a minute. I want to introduce you to Mandy." She smiled at Mandy, and then looked at her husband and said, "She's quite a book lover."

"Hi, Mandy," the husband said, with a big, warm smile, as I heard the blond man, confronting Mom and Dad, declare, "That's what the people in both rooms said."

"And who are you?" the woman's husband asked, smiling at me, raising his voice over the intense exchange between Mom and Dad and the blond man.

I said, "Nicky," and the husband was about to say something, when the blond man announced, "You have to leave in the morning."

Dad sighed and answered, "Okay."

But Mom exclaimed, "How dare you treat us this way."

The blond man said, "Checkout time is 10:00."

The husband moved away from me and seemed to sneak past Mom and Dad toward the blond man.

"We're never coming back here again!" Mom yelled.

The blond man answered, "That's your right."

Mom shouted, "This is so unfair!"

"Keep your voice down, or I'll call the police."

Mom screamed, "I'm going to tell everyone I know what an asshole you are. I'm going to warn people about this lodge. You're going to pay for this!"

"Keep your voice down!" the man said.

Dad took Mom by the arm and said, "Come on," as he pulled her toward the room, while the blond man repeated, "Checkout is 10:00."

As Mom and Dad paused inside the door, the woman said, "I think it's time for me to go, kids," and forced a smile.

"Yes, it is!" Mom shouted. "Get out!"

"Have a good night and sleep well," the woman said to Amanda and me, and then slipped past Mom and Dad, joining her husband and the blond man in the hall.

Dad closed the door and stood behind Mom, who was shaking her head as she said, "What a disgusting asshole." She looked at me and asked, "Why did you let those people in? I told you we'd be back. So why did you let them in?"

I glanced over at Mandy sitting next to me. She was clinging to her blankie and her doll, looking down, avoiding Mom's glare.

"Why did you let them in?"

"Mandy was scared," I said, my voice trembling. "She woke up and there was no one here but me."

"So why didn't you calm her down?"

"She was really scared, Mom. She couldn't stop crying."

"You know what that man told us a few minutes ago? We have to leave tomorrow. We have to leave because you kids were making so much noise." She glared at me. "They're kicking us out!"

Dad put his arm around her and said, "Come on. Let's call it a night. Get ready for bed. I'll tuck the kids in."

Mom shook her head and muttered, "That... that fucking... "

Dad held her tight and rubbed her back to try to calm her, and then she pulled away and went over to the chest of drawers, got her pajamas out, and went into the bathroom, shaking her head and muttering something to herself.

Dad sat down next to Mandy, put his arm around her shoulder, bent over so he could see both of us and said, "I'm sorry this happened. But Nick, your mom's right. You shouldn't have let those people in. What if they wanted to kidnap you? Or worse? Don't ever let a stranger into a room. And Amanda, you have to trust us. If we say we're coming back, then we're coming back."

I looked over and saw Mandy peering up at him. She looked terrified. A terrified little girl.

"Okay," he said. "Get back under the covers and try to get some sleep. I'll tuck you in."

We did what he told us, and he bent over and kissed each of us on our foreheads.

He turned off the overhead light and the light next to our bed, went over to his and Mom's bed and turned on their lamp.

Mom came out of the bathroom, stopped by Amanda's side of the bed, kissed her, murmured something, and then came to my side, whispered she loved me and kissed me, too. She got in bed with Dad, and he turned their light off.

It wasn't long before I could hear Mandy's steady breathing and knew she was asleep. I rolled over on my side, facing Mom and Dad's bed, and could see Dad's face in profile in the moonlight. They remained silent for a while, and then Dad said, barely loud enough for me to hear, "Maybe we should stop doing drugs. And hanging out with people who do."

Mom didn't answer.

"That desk clerk did exactly what he was supposed to do—throw us out. That's what happens when you're at a party that makes so much noise the neighbors call the front desk. It's just a matter of time before we get into trouble with the police. That could damage our careers."

Mom murmured something.

Dad stared at the ceiling. Or maybe his eyes were closed and he was sleeping. And then I fell asleep too.

In the morning, Mom apologized to Mandy and me in a very ambiguous way, simply saying she was sorry for what had happened. I listened, trying to appear as if I took her seriously. That sort of thing had happened before and it would happen again. Dad would always protect Mom, and they would blame me, or Mandy, or both of us.

I continue staring at the water, thinking of the gravitational power of my love for Mom, Dad, and Mandy that continues to draw me back, and the memories that motivated me to flee, until I'm startled by a large dark shadow flowing across the smooth surface and heading for the shore. I look up and see a bald eagle, its huge wings spread as it glides toward a giant white pine, where its outstretched feet grab hold of a branch far above the ground. After settling into stillness, it eyes the water below, occasionally moving its white head one way and then the other. I continue gazing at the bird, awed by its beauty, and then look around the inlet at the lily pads and blossoms, at the shore with reeds and scattered rocks, and at the grassy banks and the pine, fir, aspen, and birch trees, and feel like I'm waking up again.

I look off to the side and see Ethan, Dad, and Grace in the other canoe, seventy or eighty feet away, toward the end of the inlet, where the water lilies and the reeds are thickest, and hope that my son is happy being with his grandpa and that his grandpa is talking to him and making him feel loved. I watch them—Dad in the stern, his eyes hidden beneath his gray flat-brimmed hat, holding his rod, staring at his bobber floating on the water, seeming to have sunk into his world of silence, and Ethan in the middle, with his rod, looking at the lily pads, and Grace in the bow. It's been a while since they reeled in their last catch, and I wonder if Ethan's getting bored. Fishing for about two hours is a long time for a little boy. Grace turns her head and appears to say something over her shoulder, and Ethan laughs, looks at her and responds, and the two of them giggle. And Grace turns further and calls "Tom, Tom," and Dad seems to wake up and look at her as she says something I can't hear, and he nods and smiles, and I feel relieved.

And then Luke shouts, "I got a bite!"

I flinch, look at him, sitting in the middle of the canoe, and see his bobber has disappeared, his line is pulled taut, and his rod is curved and swerving as the fish tries to pull away.

"Whoopie!" shouts Sarah from the bow, her eyes beaming from beneath the brim of her straw hat as she smiles back at Luke. "Hang on to it, kiddo."

The fish continues to yank Luke's bent rod in one direction and then the other, while Luke pulls with all the might a nine-year-old can muster, and it's clear he has hooked something a lot bigger than a sunny.

I cry, "Steer it over here," and hold the net just above the water, ready to scoop up the fish once Luke gets it close enough.

While the rod continues to swerve back and forth, and I'm hoping the tense line won't suddenly go slack, Luke manages to force the fish toward the stern and pull it to the surface, and I glimpse its head, plunge the net into the water, scoop up the fish and see a pike, its body curved in the bottom of the net. I drop the fish into the canoe, disentangle it from the net, pick up the line and hold it up so Luke can see his pike, a foot-and-a-half long, as it flips back and forth, and I shout, "What a catch!"

And Sarah says, "We'll take a picture of you with your fish as soon as we get back to shore."

Luke beams with pride and joy as I work the hook out of the side of the pike's mouth, attach the fish to the chain stringer, which already has a few sunnies and a bass attached to it, and slip the stringer back into the water. I glimpse Grace paddling toward us, turn and see the canoe about ten feet away, Dad steering it so that it pulls up parallel to ours. He congratulates Luke on his catch and then says to me, peering from beneath the sagging brim of his hat, "I don't know about Luke, but I can tell you, this boy"—he nods toward Ethan in the bow—"is bored. I think it's time to call it a day."

"Yeah. Over two hours, that's a long time for the kids. And we still have to clean the fish."

"Yeah," he nods, with a chuckle.

"You take the lead," I say. "We'll follow."

He nods again and begins paddling, and once the canoe is about fifteen feet ahead of us, Luke and Sarah and I follow. We move along the shore, its interior concealed by the trees and their shadows, and head for the opening of the inlet. When we reach it, we navigate our way around the tip amidst the scattered rocks that protrude above the lake's surface and those just beneath, the water so clear we can see the pebbles at the bottom. Having rounded the curve, where the canoe scrapes across the lake bottom, we're back in deep water and heading down the long channel that leads to yet another large inlet, and another.

When Mandy and I were teenagers, we'd set out with Dad early in the morning on our trips to explore the wilderness, and we'd often go down this channel to an inlet where there was a portage to another lake, and Dad would carry the canoe, while Mandy and I would carry the paddles and the backpack, with our food and water. And then we'd paddle around that lake, and the next one, encountering beautiful animals, like that huge bull moose, with gigantic antlers that spread about five feet, standing in the shallow water, dipping its mouth to drink, and the pack of wolves that we surprised as they scurried about on the shore and then froze when they saw us, and stared, and suddenly turned and disappeared into the woods, leaving me with the feeling they might've been nothing but a dream.

And on our way back we would return through this channel, the same way we're going now. It seemed so big back then, but now it feels narrow and short, maybe two hundred feet wide and a quarter of a mile long. We'd sometimes land on one of the two islands at the other end of the channel, get out, go for a swim in the deep water, lie on the huge, flat granite slabs on the island, dry off in the sun and talk—like that time Mandy told me she knew all about my girlfriend, the one who looked so sexy in that skimpy bikini at the Highland Park swimming pool, everyone was talking about her. And I asked, "Jealous?" And we laughed. And I turned my attention toward the lake and looked for Dad, and looked, and panicked because I couldn't see him. And then I saw his head, barely above water, at least a hundred feet away, like he'd let himself go, drifting off, leaving us alone. I screamed, "Dad! Dad!" But he didn't respond. I had the feeling his head could disappear as suddenly as a bobber. Just like Mom had disappeared from our lives.

"Dad, can we go on one of those islands and go swimming?"

Startled, I look away from the islands and see Luke smiling at me.

Sarah pauses and looks back to see how I'll respond.

"Luke," I shake my head, "the water around those islands gets deep really fast."

"Grandpa said he used to take you and Aunt Mandy to islands when you were kids. And you'd go swimming."

"We were older than you. And you know, we have all these fish to clean when we get home."

"And," says Sarah, "I want to get a picture of you with your pike, before your dad and Grandpa clean it."

"Do you want to help us do the cleaning?" I joke.

Luke wrinkles his face into a frown and drawls, "No."

I laugh. "Well, sometime maybe Mom and I can take you and Ethan to one of the islands and we can go swimming. But you'll have to wear your life vests. Okay?"

"Okay."

We enter the open lake and turn toward the inlet where our cabin is located, and I feel relieved that we've avoided taking the boys to the island with Dad. We'll be home soon. Mandy is probably waiting for us on the balcony, and she'll come down and greet us at the dock. Sarah and Grace will want to get their phones and take pictures of the boys with their catches, above all one of Luke with his big grin holding up his pike. I look around and smile at the beautiful world and feel the warmth of the sun and the happiness of my family.

Day 4, Tuesday

Alone in the cabin, sunk deep into one of the armchairs, I set the novel I'm reading on my lap and gaze at the windows that look out upon the open space above the bluff... I'd rather spend the day here. Sitting in a canoe, in the same place hour after hour... I shake my head at the thought. When you actually catch a fish, that can be exciting... for a few minutes. But then, you're back to just sitting and waiting. In silence. If you talk, you'll scare the fish away. I guess that's what we think. But maybe we don't talk much because there's not much to talk about. Or we're willing to talk about. Or maybe we just get lost in our thoughts.

Tomorrow, I'd like to go on a trip. A real trip. Explore the lakes. Maybe with Nicky. He's strong, he can portage the canoe from one lake to another. He's done a lot of canoeing, and he doesn't get lost. The last time we explored the Boundary Waters lake-to-lake was years ago, with Dad. When we discovered that pictograph. What lake was that? Or maybe it was the Kawishiwi River. We were paddling past a granite cliff that rose out of the water. I happened to look up and saw a bull moose, with huge antlers, painted in a reddish brown on the flat stone wall. The moose was walking away toward the side. A few feet behind, a four-legged animal was stalking it. The animal had a long tail that made it look like a large cat, but it must've been a wolf. And a few feet above the animals hovered a tall male figure, standing straight, with his arms stretched out on either side. I stared at the pictograph, stunned by this reminder that Native Americans lived here in the Boundary Waters hundreds of years before we Euro-Americans arrived. This was their home. They decorated their walls with pictographs that honored the hunters and the animals they killed to feed their families.

The image of the hunter and the hunted reminds me of the illustrations of animals and people in the children's books that I read when I was little. Or that Mom read to me. Fairy tales that featured rats and mice, dogs and cats, wolves and deer, and little boys and girls. Some of those stories were more like monster tales, in which children might be threatened by wolves or snakes, or monstrous versions of predators. Mom seemed to enjoy reading them to me, and sometimes she'd tag one of her own stories onto the one narrated in a book and carry me off into a weird world, where I'd see crazy creatures and hear bizarre sounds. She loved scary tales about labyrinths. They'd frighten me so much I'd cling to her, as if I might otherwise get pulled into one of them.

And sometimes I did. In one of her tales, I felt I'd become a terrified little girl, walking down a dark hall that keeps on turning, and turning, following a receding glimmer of light. I can't see far ahead, and don't know what I'm walking toward, but behind me is gloom. And then I hear something following me, some creature growling, scraping the floor with its feet, moving faster and faster. I look behind, but see nothing. I hear a raspy voice snarling, "Run little girl! Run, run, run!" And I start running down the dark hall toward the light, until I turn a corner and freeze. There's a door, opened just a crack. I walk toward the door and slowly push it open all the way, and there's a woman, whom Mom—as she tells the story—refers to as Mother. She's wearing a fur coat and sitting in a rocking chair, on the other side of the room. Mother looks at me and smiles, and I breathe a sigh of relief. She extends her hands and says, "Come here, little one." Not knowing her, I hesitate. She repeats, in her soft, seductive voice, "Come here. Come on." I walk toward her, focusing on her warm smile, until I'm close enough for her to pick me up and cradle me on her lap, her soft fur coat caressing me. She smiles down at me. And then the creature that's following me, its paws thumping the floor, its claws scratching the wood as it runs, leaps into the room, and I see a wolf. It bares its teeth and growls, its eyes already piercing me. Terrified, I cling to Mother. But when I look up at her, I see her mouth wide open, revealing huge fangs. She's going to bite me! Just as I'm about to jump off her lap, I see the wolf, right in front of me, and it has Father's face. I was trembling as I experienced the story Mom was telling me, but she laughed, her eyes bulging dramatically, and snarled, "My parents were monsters!"

Maybe Mom was a bit of a monster herself for telling her little girl a story like that. A story she repeated until it lost its effect. And maybe she didn't realize that a little girl has difficulty separating her identity from her mother's. I had a really hard time with that. In all those monster stories she told me—stories imbued with the aroma of her vodka martinis—I always felt I was the little girl. I was Mom. And I might have suspected that her parents were the monsters, even though I never got to know them.

I remember being at their home just once. Mom, Dad, Nicky, and I were sitting in their living room with them. Very little conversation. Lots of silence. No hugs and kisses when we arrived. Nothing that felt like love. Mom just sat in her chair, chain-smoking, and then crushed her last cigarette in an ashtray and said, "It's time to go." I didn't see fangs in Grandma's mouth, and Grandpa's face didn't resemble a wolf's, but I can see how Mom could have come to think of them as monsters.

Mom could also be cold and silent, but not like her parents. And she wasn't really cold. She was distant... lost inside herself. Probably inside memories and feelings that possessed her and led her back to the world of that little girl running down the dark hall. But Mom loved me. And when she wasn't lost inside herself, she'd look at me, and I could see love glowing in her eyes. She'd hug me, kiss me, tell me funny stories, and we'd laugh. Her martinis might've helped her laugh. She had to have them pretty much every afternoon, after she finished working, and every evening. Sometimes she'd sway as she'd stand and smile at me and say things like, "Look at my lovely little darling girl." And she'd laugh. And I'd feel so happy. I can still feel that happiness she gave me. It really was a gift for life. It'll always be with me.

But sweet, loving Mom... unstable, wobbly Mom... could lose her balance and come crashing down on me. She was so hypersensitive. Easily offended, easily hurt. And my loving Mama could quickly morph into that hurt little girl... or a monster. Like that time when I was in third grade, and she and I went to school one day to attend the parent-teacher conferences, while Dad stayed home with Nicky. I hung out with my friends, until I saw it was Mom's turn to meet with Mrs. Hargrave, and then I joined her. Hargrave had said students could be present when she met with their parents, and Mom wanted me with her. Hargrave smiled a lot as she told Mom what a good student I was, and Mom smiled down at me, so proud. And then Hargrave talked about how creative I was. She explained that she'd had her students write a story and read it to the class. It had to be at least a page long. Well, she said, Amanda read this very long, strange story about a woman who leaves her daughter at their house in the country one day, while she walks to the market in town. Hargrave paused and looked at me and asked if I'd like to read the story to my mother.

I shook my head, *No.*

Hargrave gave me a faint smile, nodded, and then looked at Mom and handed her the story and said, "Here, I think you'll find it very interesting."

I watched Mom as she stared down at my story...

> Once upon a time, a mother is walking to town. It is hot. She is sweating. She meets an old woman with long gray hair. The woman is standing in front of her cabin. She says, "Hey, would you like something to drink?" The mother thinks she looks familiar. The mother wipes away the sweat on her face and says, "Yes. I'm burning up." The woman takes her into her kitchen. The mother sits down at the table. The woman stands by a counter with her back turned toward the mother. She pours a potion into a mug. She hands the mug to the mother. The mother notices the woman has long claws, instead of fingernails. They scare her. She feels like she's remembering something but doesn't know what. She tries not to look at the nails as she drinks the potion. It tastes strange. She starts to feel dizzy and stands up. She sways back and forth. She knows she's been drugged. She tries to run away. The old woman grabs her and claws her arms. She claws her again and again. The mother screams, "Let me go!" She

> finally escapes. She hears the woman scream, "You're my daughter. I'll get you someday. I'll never let you go." And the mother realizes that's the woman she's been running from all her life. When she gets home, she collapses on a chair. Her daughter screams, "Mama!" She runs to her and crawls up on her lap. She sees the blood and says, "Mama, what happened?" Mama stares straight ahead. The daughter begs to know. Finally, Mama says, "Nothing happened. This is a dream." Mama sets her down and leaves the room. When she comes back, she's wearing a sweater with long sleeves. There's no blood on her hands. Mama's cuts are gone. Mama looks down at her little girl and says, "It's just a dream."

Mom continued staring down at my story in silence. And then, she looked up at Hargrave and said, with a strange smile, "Amanda is a very creative storyteller."

Hargrave, who hadn't taken her eyes off of Mom, responded, "That's a strange story for an eight-year-old girl to write."

"My daughter loves to read strange stories. She's a big fan of the Brothers Grimm and Hans Christian Andersen. We have their complete works at home. She's read those books cover to cover."

Hargrave nodded and said, "An eight-year-old girl? Hmm. That's pretty impressive." She fell silent as she stared at Mom. Finally, she said, "Well, maybe your daughter will become a writer someday."

"Maybe."

Hargrave smiled at me. "Do you want to be a writer?"

"Maybe," I said, echoing Mom, though I'd never given any thought to it. Feeling the tension between Mom and me, I mumbled that I wanted to go play, and Mom said, "Go ahead!"

Not long afterward, Mom found me sitting alone, too upset, too anxious to talk to friends. She pulled me toward the car and ordered me to get in. She didn't say a word as she sped us home. As I headed for the house, I could hear her walking behind me, and I thought of the woman in my story, struggling to escape from her mother. I tried to open the door, but found it locked. Dad and Nicky were gone. I'd be all alone with Mom. As soon as we entered the living room, she grabbed me by the shoulders, spun me around, riveted me with her eyes and said, "Why did you write that story?"

"I don't know."

"You don't know? Really?"

I looked down, ashamed, scared and trying to avoid her eyes, but she wasn't going to let go of me.

"I want to know. Why did you write that story?"

I continued looking down, on the verge of tears.

"It's a story about the scars on my arms, isn't it."

I nodded.

"You want to know how I got those scars, don't you. Don't you!"

I raised my head just enough to see her eyes glaring at me.

"Well, I'm not telling you. You're too young to understand. But someday you'll figure it out. Until then, don't you ever again write a story about my scars. Do you hear?"

I bit my lip, trying not to cry.

"Do you hear?"

I nodded.

"I'm a lot more than just these scars." She looked down at her arms, as if she could see the scars beneath her sleeves, and then at me and shook her head. "How I got them is my business. Not yours. From now on, you tell your own stories. Not mine. Understand?"

Afraid to say anything, I nodded my head.

"Do you have homework to do?"

I shook my head.

"Then go outside and play."

I left Mom standing there in her silent rage, escaped to the back steps, stopped and looked around the yard at the flowers, the crabapple tree and the swings. I went over, climbed onto one of the swings and began pulling with my legs, and as I coasted back and forth, I wondered again how Mom had gotten those scars. Was it something her mother had done to her? Or someone else? Some monstrous person? Or were there animals that could've done that? And why did she get so upset? It didn't make sense.

Mom often left me wondering, and my wondering generated the stories I told. It would've been very difficult for me to tell stories that didn't have something to do with her, that weren't about her, for the simple reason I couldn't separate myself from her. After telling me all those weird, creepy tales about animals and monsters, about mothers, fathers, and children, that all seemed to have something to do with what haunted her, why would she be surprised that I would tell similar stories? Crazy stories motivated by the questions she left in my mind.

Mom will always be with me. There's no escape, even though she's been gone for over thirty years. Sometimes I feel like she's stalking me, determined to teach me a lesson, and other times she's inside me, whispering, warning me to look out, that person's a monster, a monster who's going to deceive me, manipulate me, use me, and hurt me. Turn me into a sex object. A sex slave. You need to be in control, I can hear her say, somewhere in the back of my mind. I do need to be in control. But I also need to be loved. I need love that is unconditional. Isn't that what real love is? Unconditional? If a child does something wrong, the parent might punish the child, but the child still feels she is loved. And the love from a lover, a spouse, or a partner, shouldn't that be unconditional too? You should be able to trust your mother, your father, your lover. But if you can't...

I couldn't trust Mom. When you're an adult, you begin with some distance between you and the person you might fall in love with, but when you're a child, you don't have that distance. And if the love you need disappears, the love from that person you love so much you can't separate yourself from her, then... you're nothing. When Mom ended her life, she nearly ended mine. I was the little girl who couldn't separate herself from her mom, who was nothing without her mom, and then Mom was gone... Gone...

Who was I? Who was the person I would become? I hated Mom so much for what she did to me. For abandoning me, leaving me lost in pain. I didn't exist for her. Wasn't worthy of her love. There was no love. I had to recreate myself. Had to become a separate, autonomous being. My pain would suck me in and draw me close to her, and I'd relive the memories of her holding me, tucking me into bed, reading to me, and kissing me goodnight. And every time I felt close to her, felt her warmth, her love, I'd experience her loss all over again, and I'd be the lonely little girl, the little girl who was nothing, who had no identity now that her mother was gone. None. And I'd be furious. I'd hate her all over again, swear at her, throw things, break things, scream, "Mom! Mom! You abandoned me! How could you do that to me?" And I'd cry and wail. The only way I could be happy was to create a wall between her and me. And to build that wall, I had to stop thinking of her, stop remembering her. Distance myself. Be a girl... a woman, who doesn't need—and will never need—her mother.

Be the opposite of her. Don't try to be theatrical the way she did. Don't try to be the queen. Oh, Mom, the way you used to dress. So haughty. So sexy. You so wanted to be the center of attention. You always tried to control people. Manipulate them. Dad, Nicky, and me—you seduced all three of us. You loved to recite lines from your favorite poets in the most dramatic way, and from your own poems, sometimes laughing, like you were putting on a show for us. And you liked to let everyone know you were a mom, and you had such a wonderful husband and wonderful kids... whom you abandoned when you killed yourself. Asshole! Sometimes, when you'd been drinking, or using drugs, you could get a little scary. You might push Nicky's hair back with your hand, look into his eyes and go, "Aww!" Like you had a crush on him. And then you'd hold him close and look at Dad in such a way that he might feel he had reason to be jealous. I haven't played any of your games. Don't drink. Don't smoke. Don't use drugs. And I tried not to have any relationships with boys.

But I needed love. Above all, after I started menstruating. I didn't have a mother to guide me, and Dad... he had the best intentions, but he couldn't help me the way a mother could've. A mother who loved her daughter. So, I did what I've always done—I read articles and books. I thought I was destined to be with a man. But after all those horrible relationships with men, in which I always ended up being the weak one, the one desperate for love, the one who always capitulated... And I was reminded of what I'd already learned from watching Mom—that women could be just as manipulative and exploitative and cruel as men. And when I was about to give up on ever having an amorous relationship, a real love relationship, I met Tony... He loves me, but he is also driven by his other love, his other passion—writing. Everything in him goes into his plays. Just as everything in me goes into understanding what happened when I was a child.

I gradually realized that Mom had cut herself. But why? And why did she commit suicide? Why did she do it the way she did? By carbon monoxide inhalation, while holding a glass of vodka in her hand, and wearing her mother's fur coat. How can I understand this... this horror story... that sometimes I feel I'll never escape. Trying to figure this all out... trying to come up with an answer… That's how I became Dr. Faust. That's what motivated me to become a psychologist, a therapist, this unending quest to understand her. I know I'll never really know her. I'm missing a lot of pieces of the puzzle, and the ones I have put together... they provide me with an interpretation of who she was, but... That's all we have of the people in our lives—interpretations. Nothing but interpretations... that could be wrong.

Day 6, Thursday

I stand in front of the living room window, staring at the thick downpour drenching the trees and shrubs and pummeling the surface of the lake below, and trace the scar above my eye with my fingertips, as I remember riding back today from Ely to the cabin, with Dad and Grace... Nicky's car was nothing but a blur ahead of us. I doubt we ever went more than twenty miles per hour. I was so anxious. Even though I was sitting behind Grace, I couldn't stop looking for a deer that might leap onto the road.

We should've stopped by the lodge this morning to check the weather report before driving to town. There were some gray clouds, but they didn't look ominous. And then it started to rain when we got to the Wolf Center. Not pouring, but enough so the wolves didn't want to come out, and the boys could only watch them lie in their dark dens, barely visible, at the other end of the yard. After five days here in the cabin, and four days of fishing, those little guys needed a break, and a trip to the Wolf Center and the Bear Center in Ely seemed like such a good idea. But then this damned deluge obliterated our day. Unbelievable!

A hand touches my arm, and I look over and see Grace.

"Are you okay?" she asks.

"Yeah. Just a little stressed from all this rain."

"Oh, we had such a wonderful day planned with the kids, and then, ugh!"—she shakes her head—"this had to happen." She stares at the downpour for a few seconds and then smiles at me. "Oh, well, we can still have a good day."

I see love in her eyes, the love she brings to all of us. But her blue eyes move me to wonder again how Dad could have ever mistaken her for Mom.

She turns around, I follow her move, and we look at the boys, sitting at either end of the couch, on the edge of the living room, Luke holding a picture book about a soccer player and Ethan a graphic novel, also about a soccer player. And I look over at Dad, reading the Ely newspaper, settled in the armchair closer to the window and turned partway toward the couch and partway toward the other armchair where Nicky sits, immersed in his book about the Russian-Ukrainian War. He always travels with a book, always studies what's going on in the world. Sarah emerges from the kitchen and walks toward us as she looks over at Nicky, Dad, and the boys, and out the window at the storm, and then at Grace and me, and arches her eyebrows while shaking her head and stops next to us to murmur, "I wonder what we can do, so everyone can have a good time."

Ethan drops his hands, lets his book fall on the couch and stares at the floor, bored. Dad snaps the newspaper wide open, catching everyone's attention, and then closes the paper, folds it and begins reading again. Ethan picks up his book, flips through it, and stops and stares at a page, still looking bored.

Sarah murmurs to Grace and me, "You know, the boys love playing board games. We brought one with us that we played during the pandemic."

"A board game might be the best way to get them out of their funk," Grace says. "What's it called?"

"*Catan.*" Sarah looks around at everyone seated in the living room and says, "Hey, guys!" They look at her. "Who would like to play *Catan*?"

Luke looks at Ethan, who lightens up and shouts, "Me!" And Luke shouts, "Me, too."

"What's *Catan*?" Dad asks, dropping the newspaper on his lap.

"It's a board game," Nicky says. "We played it during the pandemic, when we were staying home a lot. It's fun."

"Yeah, so, what is it?" Dad asks. "What do you... "

"It's a game about settlers," Nicky says. "There's all this land that is unoccupied, and settlers take it over and build towns and cities and—"

"And no wars?"

"Nope. No wars."

"Sounds like a fairy-tale version of history. Settlers take over a land that just so happens to be empty. How about that!" He laughs, and then puts his hand on his heart and chants, "'A land without a people, for a people without a land.' How sweet! Was this game created by a politician? It sounds like propaganda." He laughs again and shakes his head.

"Does this mean you don't want to play the game?" Sarah asks.

"I don't play games that propagate lies."

Sarah says, "Okay," while Nicky sighs and arches his eyebrows and shakes his head. She smiles at him and says, "Sweetie, do you want to play?"

"No. I got enough of it during the pandemic. I'd rather read my book."

She looks at Grace, and Grace says, "Yeah, I think it would be fun."

Sarah looks past Grace at me. "Only four can play. If you'd like, you can take my place."

"No," I say, "I think I'd rather read, too."

Nicky looks up and gives me a sympathetic smile.

Sarah turns away and walks behind the couch toward the hall that leads to her and Nicky's bedroom, at the back of the cabin, and I leave Grace, walk past Nicky and Dad, climb the stairs to the loft and my bedroom and find the book I'm reading on the nightstand. I pause to stare at the queen-size bed, so huge I almost feel lost in it at night, its size a constant reminder that I'm alone. But I remind myself I'm not alone. I have Tony. And in a few days, I'll be back in New York with him. I imagine him greeting me at the airport and taking me in his arms, until the sound of the rain pelting the roof and the windows draws me back into the present. I stare at the blurred world beyond the glass and shake my head and leave. Descending the stairs, I see Nicky and Dad still seated in their armchairs, and the boys, Grace and Sarah at the dining room table, where they're setting up *Catan*. Nicky glances up at me as I pass, a reflective look on his face, and plunges back into his book. I stop at the couch and gaze at Sarah, seated at the head of the table, and at Ethan, on one side, facing Grace on the opposite side, who has her hand on Luke's shoulder as she bends close to talk to him. Sarah shakes the dice, the boys watch her hands, and I can feel their excitement as the dice hit the table and roll.

I turn around, plop down on the couch and open the novel that Tony recommended to me. He described it as "introspective psychological fiction." I begin reading, hearing the occasional roll of the dice and exclamations from the boys behind me. And then Dad crunches the newspaper, shattering my attempt to concentrate. He folds the paper a couple times, whacks his thigh with it, stares at the window and says, "This damned weather. I can't believe it. After five years, I finally get to see my grandkids. I want to do things with them, and then we get this goddamn storm."

Nicky lays his book on his lap and looks to his side at Dad. "Yeah, I know. It's frustrating."

"The pandemic in 2020, I can see that. Maybe. Maybe." He glares at Nicky. "But in 2021, you cancelled your flight because of the wild fires. They never got close to the resort. I don't even recall seeing any smoke." He looks past me in the direction of the table and asks, "Do you, Grace?"

"Do I what?"

"Do you remember seeing smoke anywhere near our cabin from the fires in 2021."

"No. Why do you ask?"

He looks at Nicky. "But *you* felt they were a threat."

"Tom," Grace calls, "if you want to spend time with the boys, you can come here and take my place."

Dad continues glaring at Nicky, and as I watch them, my stomach knots.

"Like I told you, Dad," Nicky says, with a defiant look, "Sarah and I are not taking the boys anywhere where there are fires. If the winds had shifted, those fires could have posed a real threat. Above all with the drought. And it's not just the fires, there's also the smoke. Smoke can damage your lungs, and I don't want my boys' lungs damaged. Sorry, Dad, but Sarah and I did the right thing."

"Did the right thing? Huh! Did the right thing?" Dad shakes his head. "Yeah… Well, with climate change, we're probably going to get a lot more drought and fires. When I think of the world my grandchildren are going to inherit... Fires in the boundary waters, drought across the planet, famine, extinction of thousands of species. We're in the sixth extinction now, and the big question is whether or not humans will be among the species going extinct. And what are politicians doing about this? What are they doing? Nothing! Climate change? Aw, it's just a hoax!" He clenches his jaws and shakes his head, his eyes glaring with rage.

I think of going back up to my room and escaping the mounting tension, but my eyes remain fixed on Dad and Nicky, and I can't move.

"You're right, Dad. Climate change is an existential threat, and we're not doing enough about it."

I hear mumbling behind me, look over my shoulder and see Sarah, a panicked look on her face, herding the boys toward the hall, while Grace stands still, her eyes on Dad. She and Sarah can feel what's coming.

I look back at Dad as he says, "But you're a member of the House. You could do something about it."

"I've tried. But I'm just one of four hundred and thirty-five voices. Okay? It's frustrating, but that's reality."

"Reality? Huh! And is it really just because of the fires that you didn't come here and spend time with us two years ago? What about 2019? Why didn't you come then? Huh?"

"Dad... " Nicky shakes his head. "I had my own issues I was dealing with."

"Like what? What's more important than being with your family?"

"I was trying to create a life for myself and *my* family, that's what."

"And that's more important than being with your family?"

"My family isn't just you, Grace, and Mandy. My first responsibility is to ensure the health and well-being of the family that Sarah and I have created." He pauses, catches his breath, seems to reflect, and says, "As you might have surmised, I had a rough time building my career. I worked on my boss's staff for years, worked my way up to chief of staff, so after he decided to run for the senate, he'd support me when I ran to replace him in the House. Being a staff member, that's tough. There are a lot of people who can't take it and quit. I was *not* going to quit. I was determined to become a member of Congress and determined to try to make this a better country. And you know why?"

"Why?"

"Because of *you*. When I was growing up, I'd hear you rant about all the ways this country is failing its people. We're the richest country in the world, but we have insane rates of poverty and homelessness, suicide, murder, and massacres—all symptoms of a sick society."

"You can't drive around Minneapolis without seeing homeless people begging in the streets."

"And you'd always raise the question, Why can't we do what they do in Western European countries? Provide free daycare, free college education, free housing for the homeless, and a national healthcare system that provides healthcare for everyone. Everyone. People of every income level. Do you remember how you'd go on and on about all that stuff?"

Dad nods, but his face is expressionless as he stares straight ahead.

"And for some insane reason, I grew up thinking that *I* had to right all the wrongs in the world. *I* had to—"

"And there's the racism," Dad mumbles. "You forgot to mention the racism."

"Okay. And the racism, too."

"The murder of George Floyd."

"Yeah. As you know, Dad, I live in Portland and—"

"Memorial Day." Dad shakes his head, gone in his world. "It was insane. We saw over and over the video of that police officer kneeling on Floyd's neck, while Floyd screamed, 'I can't breathe! I can't breathe! Mama, I can't breathe!'" Dad glares at Nicky. "That man was dying, but the cop never showed any concern." Dad's eyes drift toward the couch, focusing on nothing. "Grace and I participated in a demonstration the next day, and the day after that. And the tension in the city just kept on increasing. And that night, everything blew up. Jesus Christ! The violence! Lake Street... " He looks at Nicky. "You remember Lake Street?"

Nicky takes a deep breath and nods.

"Lned with businesses and shopping centers... runs from east to west in Minneapolis."

"Yeah."

"Cars all up and down that street were set on fire. Mobs burned and looted buildings. Some places, it looked like entire blocks were on fire. Smoke filled the sky. And the buildings that didn't get burned were covered with graffiti. A lot of this was done by some really weird people who'd shown up." Dad stares past Nicky, as his memories envelop him. "Like the Umbrellaman, dressed in black, walking down a sidewalk, wearing a black mask, holding a black umbrella over his head in one hand

and a huge hammer in the other, smashing the windows of every building he passed. Turned out to be a member of the Aryan Cowboys. And the Boogaloo Bois, in their Hawaiian shirts, some far right group hoping to start a new civil war. And the Accelerationists, a bunch of neo-Nazis who wanted to accelerate the end of our government and bring chaos, so they could take over and create a new white nation. It was like a war, and we were living on the edge of the war zone. Every afternoon, around five, helicopters would start flying overhead... fly back and forth all night long. And I'd hear that constant whacking of the helicopter blades... and the chugging of the motors... just like in... like in *Apocalypse Now*. And that character—the main character, who wakes up to the sound of helicopter blades whacking just above his room. *Whack! Whack! Whack! Whack!* And the sound of the motors chugging. Sounds that beat against my brain, drove me fucking crazy and made me feel like everything was closing in on me. And every night, I thought of Bobby... Bobby, where are you? Why did you leave?" Tears trickle down Dad's cheeks. "Why?" His voice trembles. "Why?"

I'm about to jump up to go to Dad, but Grace rushes past me, stops by the side of his chair, and crouches next to him, placing one hand on his shoulder and the other on his wrist. She leans toward him and whispers something in his ear. He shakes his head and says, "No." She looks into his eyes and says, in a soft, coaching voice, "Honey, you're really upset. Let's go to our room and talk. Okay? Or maybe just rest a little. Come on."

Dad shakes his head. "That feels like hiding." He takes a deep breath and clenches his jaw. "I'm not going to hide." He looks toward Nicky on his other side. "Not coming here to be with us for years, that's hiding. A way to avoid talking. And maybe thinking about things that we should talk about."

Grace gives up, passes in front of me, sits down at the other end of the couch, and shakes her head and sighs.

"Listen, Dad," Nicky says, his voice hard as steel, "if you're going to start something again like what you put us through five years ago, then I—"

"What I put *you* through?" Dad looks as if he's about to explode. "What I—"

"Look, I don't want my boys to have to deal with all the trauma in this family! All this fucking trauma that's been part of our lives for as long as I can remember. I don't want them to have to grow up with that, the way Mandy and I did."

"What about what you put *me* through?"

"Dad, you're the one who loses it all the time. You start shouting and—"

"I start shouting because of the pain I have to deal with. The pain of having two children who move far away from me, who don't include me in their lives, and who don't come home to be with me."

"I'm here now."

"And you didn't bring your children home for four years. And before that, it was rare you brought them home." Dad glares at Nicky. "When you needed me, I was always there for you."

"No." Nicky shakes his head. "No. Much of the time, you were gone. Lost inside yourself. I never thought of you as someone who... someone whom I could turn to when I needed help. When I felt alone. In pain. Abandoned."

Dad stares at Nicky, his mouth hanging open, as if he's about to say something, and then slowly lowers his eyes and looks down.

Grace leans forward on the couch and says, "You're right, Nick. There's a lot of pain, a lot of trauma in this family." She looks at Dad and then back at Nicky. "I think we all need to learn how to listen to one another... and understand what everyone has gone through. And is still going through. Your dad has suffered so much over the last few years. Because of the pandemic, he had to transition from teaching in a classroom to teaching online. He hated that. Just hated it."

Dad nods in agreement, wiping the tears from his cheeks.

"Teaching had always been good for him. He complained a lot about academe, but he loved teaching. It had a kind of therapeutic effect for him. Interacting with his students, with his colleagues—that helped him to not feel so alone. Gave him a sense of purpose." She pauses again, looks over at Dad, and then at me and back at Nicky, as if making sure the two of us are taking seriously what she's saying. "That's why he retired in 2020. He never wanted to teach online again."

Dad shakes his head and mumbles, "Never. Never again."

"And then, after the George Floyd murder, his life became hell. He talked to you about the violence in the city, hearing those helicopters flying over our house every day and every night, and feeling like he was in a war zone. And the way all that brought back memories of his lost brother. After those helicopters started flying," she shakes her head, "he couldn't sleep."

Dad mumbles, "Fucking helicopters."

"He joined a group of neighbors on WhatsApp. They'd stay up at night and report any suspicious activities in the neighborhood, any unknown people hanging around. Looking out for all the bad guys... the Accelerationists and the others... And he thought about his brother... and your mom... "

Dad covers his eyes with his hand, and I look away and feel the dread I felt that day when Nicky and I walked down our street toward our home... and saw the gurney bearing the black body bag roll out of the garage... And looked up and saw Dad crying... and realized Mom was dead.

"Believe me," I hear Grace say, "I know how much her death affected your dad. The loss... the pain... and not knowing why it happened."

"The pain... the anger," I murmur, as my emotions surge. I look at Nicky, and then at Dad, and say, "I still feel anger toward her. Still hate her. How could she do that to us? Did she not love us? Did she not care about us? Did we not mean anything to her?"

"You have to understand that your mother's suicide is not something she did to you," Grace says. "It's something she did to herself."

"Oh, I understand." I shake my head, pissed that Grace would assume I didn't know that. "I understand. I know Mom's pain, her psychache was so great, she could only think of how to end it. She wrote in her journal about hearing her mother's voice in her mind telling her she was a sick woman, she'd always been a problem, and now she was a burden to her family. And she wrote about being alone, and hearing that voice, and never being able to escape it, because it was inside her. And she wrote about how beautiful death is. Its voice, so seductive. Never again would she hear her mother's voice. Never again feel pain. Never again suffer." I look at Grace. "If you're in that state of mind, if your feelings are that intense, you can't see anyone else. You can't think about how your decision might affect the people you love. So you don't even write a note for those people. You don't feel a need to explain what you're going to do. What you've probably fantasized doing for... for months. Maybe years. Probably from the time she started cutting herself." I take a breath as I remember my own fantasies of suicide, of entering a world in which there is no pain, no suffering. "Yes, I understand you, Mom... I understand you."

"The fur coat she was wearing when I found her... "

I look at Dad and see his eyes staring at the couch, at the space between Grace and me.

"Her mother's coat," he murmurs. "She loved to wear it. Loved to feel the soft, warm fur. She said it felt like love. The love she so desired..." He shakes his head. "That coat, the dress she was wearing, the bottle of vodka, the martini glass... it was like she was at a party, celebrating."

"Celebrating what?" Nicky cries.

Dad looks at him.

"The end of her life?" Nicky asks. "Her disappearance?" He shakes his head, and for the first time since we were kids, I see tears in his eyes. "She abandoned us. All of us." His voice trembles. "And look at what it did to us. A life of"—he shakes his head—"a life of pain. Trying to escape. Being anywhere but in that Goddamn house... " He looks at Grace. "And even if I could calmly remind myself, Well, she didn't intend to hurt us, she was just incapable of thinking of us, would that... ?" He shakes his head. "No. The thing is, when I feel the pain... when those feelings of being abandoned and unloved come back... when I feel hatred for her...

reminding myself that she didn't intend to hurt any of us is not going to change a damn thing. When I'm in that state—and that's generally the state I'm in when I think of her—I cannot calmly tell myself, Hey, Mom was just too overwhelmed by her pain and her depression to think of us. You shouldn't feel any anger... No, that doesn't work."

"When she hurt herself," I say, "she hurt us, too. And when she ended her life—"

"She ended ours." Nicky stares down at the floor. "Ended the lives we might've had."

I nod. "That last year, year and a half, part of her just disappeared. It was like she was two people—our Mom, who still loved us, and that other person, distant and cold. No love. I so wanted my mom, but... " I shake my head. "Sometimes we didn't know which person was there. If we asked anything of her... "

"She had a temper." Nicky looks at me. "That cold, unloving woman... she had a hell of a temper. I remember, not long before Mom killed herself... I remember going into the study to tell her our cat, Lisa, was sick. She had vomited in the living room. But Mom, it was like she was in a trance. Sitting at her desk, staring down... not at the desk, but at something—or nothing—beyond it. I was afraid to say anything, but I was so scared about Lisa. She was hiding under the couch and wouldn't come out. Finally, I said, 'Mom, Lisa's sick. She vomited in the living room.' Mom didn't respond. It was like she couldn't even hear me. So, I said, 'Mom. Mom? Mom!' And she looked at me and yelled, 'What do you want! Can't you see I'm busy?' The way she glared at me... it was like she hated me. I almost fled the room. But then I remembered Lisa, and I told her again that she had vomited, she was sick. And then, her reaction... " He shakes his head. "It was weird. It was like Mom came back to life. She looked at me and said, 'What's the matter with her?' And I said, 'She vomited, and she's hiding under the couch. I'm scared she's sick.' And Mom... she looked really concerned and said, 'Let's go see her.' She got up and walked with me to the living room, resting her hand for a while on my shoulder, and when we reached the couch, she got down on the floor, where she could see Lisa, and managed to extend her hand far enough to touch her. She started petting her, until Lisa came a little closer, and then Mom pulled her out and picked her up. We sat next to one another on the couch, and Mom held Lisa on her chest, just under her chin. She petted her and moved her cheek back and forth across Lisa's soft fur. And I could hear Lisa purring."

I smile as I see Mom, happy, rubbing her cheek on Lisa's fur.

"Mom looked at me and asked, 'When was the last time she vomited?' I told her I didn't know. She said she couldn't remember the last time either. But Lisa was purring, so she was probably fine. The way Mom smiled at me, it made me feel like she'd never been gone. And that woman who yelled at me," he shakes his head, "that wasn't Mom, that was someone else."

As I gaze at Nicky's face, seeing the tears in his eyes, I remember those nights when I watched Mom, sitting on the rocking chair, staring out the window... silent and still.

Nicky takes a deep breath, sighs, looks over at Dad and says, "This is why it's difficult for me to come home. The memories. I'm always going to relive them. Re-experience the disappearance of Mom... replaced by that frigid woman. And your disappearance, too... Sometimes I hate Mom. Sometimes I hate you. And sometimes I think the only way to go on living is to put up a wall between me and my past and never return."

"Nick," Dad pleads, "please don't do that. I know I might've failed you at times. I was overwhelmed by my loss... our loss. But I love you. I love Sarah, I love my grandkids. You mean everything to me. Everything. If I were to lose you, I couldn't go on living."

"Dad, I have to think of my family. I can't drag my kids into this." He shakes his head. "I can't." He takes a deep breath, sighs, closes his eyes, and, after a few seconds, opens them and looks at Dad. "After Mom's death, I felt guilty, as if somehow I was the cause of her suicide. I couldn't understand why. What did I do?" He shakes his head. "But I felt guilty about being alive. Like somehow, I didn't have the right to live, because she'd died. That makes no sense, but that's how I felt."

I feel Nicky's despair and remember that feeling of guilt. And remember, too, the fantasy that I could be with Mom forever, if I ended my life. No more separation. No more pain. I mumble, "We were so young when she killed herself. So vulnerable."

"And you were gone," Nicky says, staring at Dad. "You weren't able to help me, because you were lost. I had to create a wall between Mom and me, so I could live." He pauses, and the look on his face hardens. "And I need to create a wall to protect my family and me. Because I don't want my kids growing up haunted by a past that sucks them in and ruins their lives."

"I don't understand," Dad says. "Instead of concentrating on everything that went wrong, everything bad, why can't you focus on how much your mother loved you? On what was good about your mother? Maybe think about the way she read books to you at night when you were little, before she put you to bed. And when you were reading your books, the way she'd sometimes go over and give you a kiss. The way she'd push you on the swing, so you could reach for heaven with your feet. The way she'd hold you and hug you and kiss you. She loved you. Both of you! She loved all of us!"

"No, Dad," I exclaim, "that doesn't work. If I think about all the good things about Mom, sooner or later I remember her becoming that other person, sitting in a rocking chair, staring out the window. Gone." I pause, look at Nicky through my tears, then back at Dad. "I had the same problem Nicky had. Feeling guilty, like somehow I'd caused Mom's death, and it was wrong for me to go on living. And the solution I'd fantasize was to kill myself, so I could be with her. It's a miracle I didn't. If you hadn't arranged for me to see a therapist, I probably would've. She helped me deal with Mom's death. So, I thank you for that. But even after having seen a therapist for a year, I still felt guilty... still had suicidal ideations... still felt alone, abandoned, and lost... And you were gone."

"I was too angry, too confused, to listen to that therapist," Nicky says. "And with you gone, Dad, I just wanted to smash everything in that fucking house. Just blow it up. Maybe you would've paid some attention then... The other thing I wanted was to get the fuck out of there, get as far away as I could. So I became a nomad."

"You think I wasn't aware of what the two of you were going through? I did everything I could. Everything! Everything! to help you and be supportive. I could see your suffering, but... what you seem to have never understood is... " Dad shakes his head. "*I* was suffering, too. *I* felt lost. Abandoned."

Grace tries to intervene with a calm voice. "Your father lost two people he dearly loved, who meant everything to him. Whose loss damaged his life forever. A loss he can never forget. You have to forgive him if he wasn't always able to be there for you."

Nicky stands up, looks down at Dad, and says, "Like I said... I don't want my kids to grow up haunted by a past that ruins their lives. I need to create a wall to protect them, protect Sarah and me, so my family can be happy." He turns away, walks past Grace at the other end of the couch, and heads down the hall.

Dad's shoulders tremble as his head falls forward and he sobs. Grace moves over to his side, kneels, and puts her arms around him. I look away, touch the scar above my eye, and feel the pain as I gaze out the window and through the rain at the dark clouds.

Day 7, Friday

I hear the boys laughing, shouting and splashing water, feel the side of my face resting on a warm fabric and open my eyes to see my hand, resting on a blanket, and, beyond the edge of the blanket, grass, reeds, and tree trunks. Wondering where I am, I raise my head and see the boys playing in the lake, a few feet from shore. I lay my head back down, close my eyes and remember the rage that burned in me as I walked down the hall in the cabin the night before, pushed open the door to the boys' room, and saw Luke curled up on Ethan's bed, on his side, facing me, but not looking at me, not looking at anything; and Sarah, sitting next to him, her head bowed, her hands resting on her legs, appearing exhausted and depressed; and Ethan, sitting on the edge of his bed, on the other side of Sarah, facing the wall, the wall next to which I was standing. Sarah looked up at me, her eyes begging for help.

"What's going on?" I asked.

She got up, came to me, and exclaimed in a whisper, "You guys were talking so loud!" She shook her head. "They heard a lot of what the three of you said." She looked at the boys, then back at me. "We need to go to our room and talk."

"Okay." I looked at the boys and said, "Your mom and I are going to our room. We'll be back in a few minutes."

Ethan glared at me and asked, "When are we going home?"

Luke looked at me, his eyes asking the same question.

"We're going to talk about it."

"We'll be right back," Sarah said.

Ethan scowled at the wall, while Luke laid his head down, appearing hopeless.

As soon as I closed the door to our room behind us, Sarah spun around and said, "I tried to get them to read their books, but there was no way. Their attention was glued to the door. And then they started asking questions. 'Why were Dad and Grandpa and Aunt Mandy so angry? Who is that mom they're talking about? Why do they hate her?' And then Ethan asked, 'Did she kill herself?'" Sarah shakes her head. "I didn't answer. I'm not going to lie to him. *You* have to start answering those questions. If you don't, they're going to ferment inside those boys, and someday there'll be a huge explosion… Nick, they don't know anything about your mother. They don't even know Grace isn't their biological grandma. They're so upset. What are you going to do?" Sarah stared at me, beseeching me for a response.

"I suggest we go into town. Have dinner. I'll call the airlines and see if I can change our departure from Saturday to tomorrow. After dinner, maybe take the boys to see a movie and get their minds off all the shit they've experienced here. And then tomorrow morning, we pack up and leave. Okay?"

"No. No, Nick. Before we go into town, *you* have to answer their questions. Building a wall of ignorance around them isn't going to protect them anymore. They have to know."

"They're too young."

"They have questions. They need answers. And if they don't get them—"

"No! I'm not going to drag them into all this trauma. I told you before, I don't want them to have to deal with all the shit that Mandy and I had to deal with growing up."

"So, what are you going to tell them?"

"I'll tell them... I'll tell them that... that Grandpa and Aunt Mandy and I had a disagreement, we got a little angry, and... and everything's fine."

"Everything's fine? And what about the mom killing herself?"

"If they ask that question, I'll say that we weren't talking about anything like that at all. Those were words heard out of context."

"Really?" She shook her head.

"Yeah. The woman didn't kill herself. She was killed in a car accident. Words out of context."

Sarah's eyes fixed on mine. "Unbelievable."

"I'm protecting my kids."

"Our kids."

"Okay. Our kids. Let's go." I guided her toward the door and followed her to the boys' room. They stared at us when we entered. Both of them were sitting on the edge of the bed. I walked over, squatted, and looked them in the face. Ethan continued staring back at me, while Luke looked back and forth at me and Ethan. I said, "Guys, your mom told me you were upset about the conversation you overheard. I understand. Aunt Mandy and I got into an argument with Grandpa. But things are okay now."

Ethan asked, "What about the mom who killed herself?"

I shook my head. "There was no mom who killed herself. We did mention a mom who was killed in a car accident years ago. And we were very upset about it."

"What mom?" Ethan asked.

"A mom you don't know. She died a long time ago. Grandpa and Aunt Mandy and I knew her. It's still kind of upsetting for us. But it's not something that should concern you."

Ethan, who had been staring at the floor, looked at me and asked, "When are we going home?"

"We're going to go into town and have dinner. And I'm going to call the airlines and see if we can change our departure time, so we can leave tomorrow, instead of Saturday. Okay?" I forced a smile.

We headed down the hall. As we passed the living room, I heard Dad's voice ask, in a mournful tone, "Are you leaving?"

I froze. Sarah and the boys came to a halt behind me. I glanced over and saw him sitting in the gray light, in one of the armchairs, gazing at me, and Grace in the other armchair, her eyes also fixed on me.

"We're just going into town to get dinner. Maybe see a movie." I paused for a few beats. "We'll be back."

I could see a look of despair in Dad's eyes, even as he nodded.

We stepped outside and stopped. The rain had finally ended. Dark heavy clouds blocked the sun, and the whole universe was dark. The only sound I heard was the dripping of water from the cabin's eaves and from the branches of nearby trees so drenched their limbs looked like they were sobbing. I reminded myself we needed to get going. We navigated our way around the huge puddles and got in the car. As I drove us to town, I wondered, Why did I tell Dad we'd be back in such a way as to suggest he had nothing to worry about? That there was no problem? I glanced over at Sarah. She continued staring straight ahead at the windshield, and the boys remained totally silent in the back. I could feel the tension.

We went into the first restaurant that came up, took a table, and put in our order. Sarah mumbled, "Let's just get out of here," and rummaged through her purse until she found a pen and a piece of paper I could use to jot down our new plane reservation. I went to the bar, ordered a shot, and called the airlines. After being put on hold for a minute, and tapping the bar with Sarah's pen until the bartender started staring at me, I was finally connected with a representative, who informed me that the flight leaving for Portland the next day had only two available seats. "Oh, fuck!" I exclaimed, and then apologized to the woman who'd given me the bad news. I returned to the table where the boys gloomed while picking away at their fish and fries. Sarah stared at me. I sat down and ate a little of my walleye as I whispered to her that we couldn't leave the next day. She asked me about getting tickets on a different airline. I said I'd thought of that, but even if it were possible, I didn't want to throw away that much money. She shook her head in disgust.

When the waitress stopped by to ask us how our meal was, I asked her if she knew what was showing at the theater. Her eyes bulged as she exclaimed, "*Oppenheimer*! I've heard it's a great film." Her enthusiasm vanished when I mumbled, "Oh, shit!" There was no way we could deal with the atomic bomb and Hiroshima on top of everything else.

It started raining again on the way back, gusts of wind whipping the trees, flashes of lightning piercing the darkness and illuminating the road. We parked in front of the cabin, where the light above the door shined like a beacon, and dashed inside. I turned off the lamp that had been left on in the living room, and we tiptoed back to our rooms. After the boys settled down, Sarah and I got in bed and turned off our lights. Exhausted, she rolled away and fell asleep lying on her side. I lay on my back, staring at the ceiling, reliving the day, wishing I could sleep so I could deal with what lay ahead as well as possible. I kept on checking my watch, trying to escape the memories that wouldn't let go of me. Finally, the rain ended.

I gave up on falling asleep, got up, went to the living room, stopped in front of the windows and stared at the dark forms outside in that black world, forms that seemed to lurk there like phantoms of all the problems in my life that always come back. I shook my head, turned on the lamp next to one of the armchairs, sat down and picked up where I'd left off with the book on the Russian-Ukrainian War. Huh! War seems to be the theme of our lives. I was relieved this morning, when I woke up feeling Sarah's hand on the side of my face and opened my eyes to see her smiling down at me. She apologized for her anger the day before and suggested we just try to get the boys through the next two days as well as possible. I whispered, "Yeah." And she kissed me.

* * *

I feel the warmth of the sun on the side of my face, open my eyes again, gaze at the grass and tree trunks and hear Sarah say, "Oh, you're awake!" I turn my face toward the other side and see her sitting next to me. "Yeah. Took me a while to figure out where I was."

"Did you have a good nap?"

I roll over on my back and look up at her, as she smiles down at me. "How long have I been asleep?"

"Oh," she nods, a serious look on her face, "probably a couple hours."

"A couple hours! Really?"

"I don't have my phone with me, so I don't know for sure, but... "

"Oh my God!" I stare at the white cumulus clouds in the blue sky and shade my eyes from the sun with my hand.

"You were so tired this morning, you looked like you had a hangover."

"I did have one, but not from drinking." After reflecting for a few beats, I say, "It was a miracle I was able to portage the canoe." I remember balancing it, its weight pressing the yoke down on my shoulders, my hands gripping the gunwales as I made my way along the narrow path that twisted and curved back and forth, ascended and descended a few slopes, some of which had large rocks I had to walk around. "God, that was tricky. The slopes were steep enough so that a couple times the bow poked the ground, or the stern clunked on a rock behind me, and I nearly lost my balance." I sigh. "But I made it." I smile at Sarah. "We made it. You had quite a load, too."

"Yeah. That was a lot! The backpack, the paddles and the bag, with the blanket and towels."

"You're always the sweet mom. I could hear you behind me, encouraging the boys, 'Come on, come on guys, we're almost there.'"

She smiles in response.

"I'm happy we're here."

I close my eyes and soon feel myself drifting off. I remember reaching the end of the path, flipping the canoe down, taking a deep breath, letting it all out and looking at the lake, at the still water glowing in the sun, not another canoe in sight. I pushed the canoe about halfway into the lake, the bottom scraping on the shore. Sarah helped me load everything, and then I straddled the stern, while she gripped the gunwales and worked her way to the bow. I slid the canoe a little further into the water, had the boys climb in and get settled in the center, sitting on their cushions, and then pushed off. As I started paddling, I already felt calmer. The land separating this lake from the one where the cabin is located provided a wall to protect us from Dad... from all that fucking trauma that's never going to end. Never. Maybe I was nuts to think I needed to portage to another lake, but, irrational or not, I felt more relaxed. It would be easier to talk with Sarah. Unload some of the shit I'm carrying inside. Decide what we should do. Luckily, we didn't have to paddle far before I recognized the shore and remembered the campsite that I'd once used.

Not wanting to fall asleep again, I open my eyes to the sun and look up at Sarah gazing at the lake. I sit up next to her and watch the boys laughing about something as they pass in front of us, swimming on their backs side by side.

"They seem to be in pretty good spirits," Sarah says, "in spite of everything."

"Yeah. It feels good to see them happy. And safe." I see the shock, the pain on Dad's face, when I told him I needed to create a wall to protect us—from him. "Last night was awful."

Sarah looks at me. "You think Mandy's okay?"

"I hope so." I remember Sarah, the boys, and I walking down to the dock this morning and discovering one of the two canoes was gone. Baffled, I looked back up at the cabin, saw Dad and Grace on the balcony, at the top of the bluff, watching us and realized that it must've been Mandy who'd taken the canoe. I wonder again where she went... what she might be doing... might've done to herself. I don't want to think about it. "I was hoping we'd find her here, but that was crazy. She could've gone in several directions. Maybe down the Kawishiwi River." I continue watching the boys as they stand next to one another in the water, submerged up to their lower backs, talking about something.

"I'm concerned about her," Sarah says. "She wasn't there at breakfast this morning."

"Yeah."

"Once someone in a family commits suicide, there's a good chance another family member will, too."

"I know. That's one of the reasons she and I stay in touch with one another. To be supportive."

"Mandy is so compassionate." She falls silent for a few beats. "I've always thought her decision to become a psychologist had something to do with your mom's suicide."

"Oh, it did. She wanted to understand what I've tried to understand—Why? Why did Mom do it? And maybe she thought a psychologist's knowledge and experience would protect her from suicide." I shake my head. "The thing is, according to what I've read, the suicide rate among psychologists is even higher than among the general population. Mandy might've thought that studying Mom's life and her death, understanding all that, might help her build a wall to protect herself. She obviously wants a wall. Wants to be the opposite of Mom. No drugs. No smoking. No alcohol. And no kids."

"But there is no wall. It doesn't seem possible."

"Mandy's research into Mom's life drew her closer to Mom, to her pain and suffering. I don't think that's how you build a wall."

"Maybe we should go look for her."

"Go look for her?" I shake my head. "There's over a million acres in the Boundary Waters. No, if she's not there when we get back to the cabin, then we report her missing." I glance over at Sarah and add, "She'll be there." I look back out at the lake and the boys, who are on shore now, putting on their swim masks, and think of the lie I just told her, knowing she might not be there. I worry all the time about

Mandy reaching that point when she can no longer live with the trauma from Mom's suicide. And when she talked yesterday about what Mom had written, that death is so beautiful, so seductive, because you'll never feel pain again, never suffer again, I wondered if that's what she feels at times. She's so obsessed with Mom's suicide. No suffering… no depression… ever again.

I find myself watching the boys diving under water, exploring what's below the surface.

Sarah asks, "Do you think never bringing the boys back will build a wall to protect them?"

"I don't think we have a choice. We can't put their sanity at risk."

"Maybe they'll wonder why we stopped coming to see your dad and Grace, and then start doing research. Like their aunt. And get sucked into everything we want to protect them from."

"Maybe. But when I think of the alternative, not bringing them back is the right thing to do."

As I watch the boys plunge under water and resurface, gasping for air, I wonder if Sarah is right, if they will become obsessed with understanding what happened in their family. Why Grandpa was so unstable and Aunt Mandy so distant at times. And eventually they'll learn who their real grandmother was, and they'll wonder why she committed suicide. Ethan's eleven. The age I was when Mom killed herself. And Luke is the same age Mandy was. Both of them are going to ask questions. Maybe it's already too late.

The boys are heading for shore, their masks in hand, a happy look on their faces as they trudge through the water. They gingerly cross the mix of pebbles and sand.

Ethan exclaims, "We're hungry! What's there to eat?"

And Luke echoes Ethan with, "I'm starving!"

"Here are your towels," Sarah says, as she hands them to the boys, smiling at them.

Ethan wipes off his face, wraps his towel around his shoulders, and asks again, "What's there to eat?"

Sarah and I make room between the two of us. She sets paper plates on the blanket, a large piece of cheese on one of the plates, and begins slicing it. "Well," she says, "we have this cheese. And here," she pulls a box out of the cloth bag, "we have some wheat crackers. And apples and bananas." She sets everything on the blanket.

The boys sit down with us. We quickly finish the cheese and crackers, and each of us grabs an apple or a banana.

I finish chewing on a bite of my apple and say, "I was hoping that huge breakfast would keep you guys full until dinner. Those pancakes, and the eggs and bacon, and the fruit."

"Breakfast was a long time ago," Ethan says.

"Yeah," Luke chimes in. "The pancakes were really good."

"The pancakes, or the maple syrup?" Sarah asks, with a grin.

Luke grins and says, "Both."

Sarah and I laugh, as I think about how important she and the boys are to me. I need to do everything I can to protect them. From Mom and Dad. From all the shit I carry inside. I look up at the sun, which is still a long way from the treetops. I need to encourage the boys to continue swimming, playing, doing whatever, until it's time to leave. I want to arrive at the cabin around sunset. A quick dinner, and then off to our rooms.

* * *

We enter the inlet, where the sun glows just above the trees on the shore across from our cabin, and pass the tip of the small peninsula that conceals the bluff on which our cabin rests. Paddling toward the dock, I search for Mandy on the balcony and on the path descending toward the shore, but don't see her. The anxiety I've tried to suppress all day grips me, and I grip my paddle and push the canoe faster across the still water. And then, as we glide further into the inlet to the other side of the dock, I see her lying on a blanket. Sarah smiles back at me and says, "There's Mandy!" I nod, "Yeah," and sigh. She's alive! She sits up, looks at us and stands to greet us as the canoe glides toward her. The bow scrapes across the sandy shore, the canoe grinds to a halt, Sarah climbs out and, with Mandy's help, grabs the bow and drags the canoe as far as they can onto shore. The boys hop out, and they all drag the canoe further. I get out, finish pulling the canoe on shore, remind the boys to carry the fishing gear they didn't use to the cabin, and turn and see Sarah giving Mandy a hug. She appears a little surprised, as Sarah pulls back and says, "I was so worried about you."

"We both were," I say, as I approach Mandy to give her a hug, too.

"Why?"

"You seemed to have disappeared," I murmur, as I hold her, relieved she isn't gone.

"Yeah," says Sarah. "We didn't see you at breakfast, and then when we came down to the dock, one of the canoes was gone."

"I just didn't want to be around the cabin today, so, when I got up, I had a bowl of cereal, grabbed my book and a blanket and left. I paddled down the river to a campsite, lay on my blanket and read. It was good to get away. But then I got hungry, decided to go into town, have lunch in a restaurant, and treat myself to a movie."

"Oh! You saw *Oppenheimer*?" I laugh, shaking my head.

"Yeah. Very intense."

"I'm sure," I say.

"How did you get into town?" Sarah asks.

"I asked Grace if I could borrow their car, and she gave me the keys. They'd just gotten back from a trip to the supermarket."

"Huh!" Sarah exclaims. "That was very nice of her."

"Yes, it was."

"Well," I say, "we went into town last night for dinner, and we were thinking of seeing a film, but when I learned they were showing *Oppenheimer*... " I shake my head. "On top of everything else we've been dealing with... No way!"

"Yeah," Mandy responds, as she peers into my eyes. After a few beats, she says, "Well, Dad and Grace prepared dinner for all of us. That's why they went to the grocery store."

"Really!" Sarah exclaims. "That was also very nice of them."

"Are they waiting for us?" I ask.

"No," Mandy says. "They left a note, telling us they went for a long walk. And we should go ahead and eat without them."

"Huh! An attempt to make amends. How often did we see him do that when we were growing up?"

Mandy nods. "Yeah. But sometimes he didn't. He didn't even know he'd hurt us."

"Yeah."

"He suffered every bit as much as we did."

I nod. "Well, we don't have a lot of time. The sun will set soon. So, we have a quick dinner and go find peace in our rooms."

"Yeah," Mandy says and turns to head up the path. I gather up the cloth bag that Sarah set on the shore, join her as she waits for me, and we follow Mandy, already several feet ahead of us.

"What do we do if your dad and Grace arrive before we can hide?" Sarah asks.

"I'm a politician. I know how to be civil toward people I don't agree with."

"And our boys?"

"They don't want to be anywhere near him."

She shakes her head. "You're still angry."

"Anger is part of our lives. Always has been, always will be." After a few beats I mutter, "There's no end to this."

We reach the top of the bluff, and I see Dad's car parked on the side of the cabin next to mine and wonder how long we have to eat dinner before he and Grace return. Before Dad tries to make amends, so he can hurt us all over again. We enter the cabin and find Mandy standing next to the table. "There it is," she says, as she nods at the note on the table.

I walk over, pick it up and recognize Dad's handwriting. Some of the letters look as if his hand was trembling while he wrote.

> Dear Amanda, Nick, and Sarah,
>
> We've eaten all the fish, so Grace and I went shopping. We prepared dinner for you. You'll find in the fridge two

roast chickens and steamed corn on the cob. You can warm them in the microwave. And a salad. We'll be back around sunset. Bon appétit!

Love,

Dad and Grace

I hand the note to Sarah, look at the table, which is set for five, and think, This is the perfect setup. We all sit down, start eating, and Dad and Grace appear. And we have another fight. How about that!

I hear a door slam shut, a machine humming in the kitchen and realize Mandy is warming up food in the microwave.

Sarah hands the note back to me. "I'll go get the boys." She heads for the hall.

"Wait a minute!"

She stops and looks back at me.

"This is a setup. As soon as we start eating, Dad and Grace are going to walk through that door. You know that, don't you?"

"Life has to go on."

"What?"

"Life goes on." She turns and heads down the hall. As I watch her, the microwave door opens and slams shut again, and the machine hums. Mandy comes around the corner of the kitchen and walks toward me and the table with a large plate bearing a roast chicken. She sets the chicken down near the head of the table, asks if I'd like to carve it, and returns to the kitchen. And then Ethan and Luke come rushing down the hall toward me, ready to eat, with Sarah right behind them. The boys grab the two chairs on one side of the table and plop down.

Sarah looks at me. "Are you going to carve it? They're hungry."

I look at the boys and see them eyeing the chicken.

Mandy sets a plate piled with corn on the cob on the table, looks at me and says, "Aren't you going to sit down?" She nods at the head of the table.

"Okay. All right." I sit, feeling something weird is going on.

"And Sarah, do you want to sit at the other end?"

"Okay."

I look at the boys to my side and Sarah at the other end, pick up the butcher knife next to the plate with the chicken and start carving. When I finish, I pass the plate to the boys, they serve themselves and pass it on to Sarah. Mandy sets the salad on the table, sits down on the side across from the boys, serves herself, and joins us as we devour our dinner. No one talks. The snacks we had in place of lunch didn't do much to satisfy our hunger. As we finish, Mandy clears the table and brings us smaller plates. She goes back to the kitchen, returns with a pie, and announces, "Grandpa and Grandma got us something for dessert, too. Raspberry pie, from the bakery in Ely." She sets it in front of me and asks me to cut it. And then, looking at the boys, says, "Grandpa and Grandma also got ice cream. Who wants ice cream with their pie?" And the boys scream, "I do." Mandy gets the ice cream. After I cut the pie and put the slices on the plates, she scoops on the ice cream, leans across the table to hand the boys their dessert, and then serves the adults. The boys dig in, and I start eating as soon as Mandy hands me mine, savoring the ice cream with the sweet raspberry filling, until I'm scraping up with a spoon and a fork the last of the white cream, with streaks of sweet red sauce.

And then I hear feet walking up the steps and see Dad's face through the window in front of me as he approaches the door and enters, followed by Grace. He looks around at everyone, then comes over, sits down next to me, at Mandy's side, and eyes me. I hardly notice Grace as she sits down on Mandy's other side.

I glare at Mandy. "Oh, for Christ's sake! Did you collaborate in this setup?"

Mandy looks at me, the boys and Sarah, and then back at me. "Grace and I talked today before I went into town. We agreed that the boys need to learn they have a grandmother, a grandmother who was a wonderful wife and mother. And they need to learn what happened to her and why they don't know her. They need to start getting to know her. If we don't help them with this, it could become something that haunts them. And we need to start doing all of this before you and your family leave."

"You've got a lot of nerve! Maybe... just maybe you should've asked my permission to do this. They're not your children."

"But we're all part of one family."

"You don't have the right to do this!"

"Nick!" Sarah's exclamation jolts me. I look down the table at her. "Mandy's right. I think all of us need to talk, and we need to talk with the boys about this. About everything."

"So, you're also involved in this plot!" I shake my head and grit my teeth. "Instead of letting them stay here, where they'll get hurt, why don't you take them to their room."

"Because that doesn't protect them." She takes a deep breath. "I've been thinking about this for a long time. Mandy and I talked for a few minutes in the kitchen, but I'd already made up my mind." She pauses and pierces me with her gaze. "I'm their mother."

I can't think of anything to say to her, except I feel betrayed. I look at the boys. Ethan glares back at me, as if wondering, What are you crazy adults doing now? While Luke leans back into his chair and stares down at his lap, avoiding my eyes, as if he were ashamed as well as scared. I look back at Ethan, see he's baffled and afraid and remember what Mom's suicide did to Mandy and me. How difficult it was to talk about it. How it separated us from Dad, and sometimes Mandy and me from one another, and from our friends and everyone else, and isolated us in a world of pain. And shame. And made me feel I was an outsider, a creep, a weirdo, and I remember listening to Radiohead's song and crying. And I feel something I haven't felt in years. I feel I'm still the little boy I was thirty-two years ago, after Mom died. Still that creep, that weirdo. I remember what I wanted then, when I was growing up—just to be normal, just to be like everyone else... to have a mother, who hadn't killed herself... and to be loved by that mother... to be someone special for her. I feel tears welling up. I shake my head. This is so damned embarrassing! Right in front of my boys.

A hand takes hold of my arm, and I see Dad's face, his eyes peering into mine. I shake my head. "I can't put my sons through this. I can't!" I stand up and say, "I can't do this," and head for the door and burst out into the encroaching darkness, rushing away as if I could flee my pain and my fear.

I walk on the gravel road, hearing Sarah cry, "Nick! Nick! Wait! Wait for me!" And then I hear nothing. And all I see is the road between the trees. Mom is still with me. I can't let go of her.

Sarah grabs my arm, but I keep on walking. She cries, "Nick! Please, stop." She pulls so hard she stops me, and I spin around and see her looking up at me, tears in her eyes as she pleads, "Please listen to me! Please!"

Ethan has stopped a few feet behind her, his mouth hanging open, panic in his eyes. And Luke, standing a few feet behind Ethan, looks terrified.

"Nick," Sarah says in a soft voice. "Nick... let's go back to the cabin."

I look at her, look into her eyes that are pleading, Please. Please come. And I see her love for me. I begin walking with her. I wrap my arm around her shoulder, take Ethan's hand, and Sarah takes Luke's as we head toward the cabin, where Dad, Grace, and Mandy stand in front of the door, watching us. Dad and Grace step aside, Mandy holds open the screen door and Sarah and the boys and I enter the cabin. Sarah guides me toward the couch, where we sit down with the boys. Dad and Grace sit down in the armchairs, while Mandy brings a chair from the dining room and sits down near Dad.

Mandy looks at each of us and then focuses on the boys. She takes a deep breath and begins. "We need to talk about something. Something we should've talked to you about a long time ago." She pauses, nods and says, "Yeah?" as if she sees in their eyes a desire to know. "If you have any questions, please feel free to ask. Okay?"

I look down at Ethan next to me and over at Luke on the other side of Sarah and see both of them have their eyes fixed on Mandy.

"Your dad and I had a mother named Helen. She was Grandpa's wife. She was your grandma. Grandma Helen." She pauses for a few beats, and then continues. "When your dad was the same age as you are, Ethan, and when I was your age, Luke, our mother—your Grandma Helen—ended her life." Mandy pauses. "She killed herself. She committed suicide."

"I was right!" Ethan exclaims. "I did hear you and Dad and Grandpa arguing about a mom who killed herself."

"Yes, you were right, Ethan. You did hear that. And as you could tell from the sound of our voices, your grandpa, your dad, and I are still very upset about this. It really hurt us."

"Why did she do that?" Luke asks.

"We don't know. She didn't leave a note behind that would've explained why. So, we will never really know. But we think she might have been suffering from sadness. You know how sadness feels."

The boys nod their heads.

"We think she might have been suffering from a terrible kind of sadness called depression. The sadness that people who suffer from depression feel is so horrible... so extreme... that they sometimes become unaware of the people around them. Even the people they love. They isolate themselves in their minds from other people, and feeling alone makes them even sadder. And they become so sad, so isolated, so alone that everything in life seems meaningless. And they might even think their own lives are meaningless. So, that's what we think Grandma Helen was suffering from."

"That's awful!" Ethan exclaims.

"You're right," Mandy nods. "That is awful." She smiles at him with compassion. "But I want you to know that Grandma Helen was also a wonderful wife." She looks at Dad. "Wasn't she."

He nods and says, "Yes," as he wipes tears from his face.

"And she was a wonderful mother. She loved your dad and me very much. And she made us feel loved. She was so kind and... " She shakes her head, as she pauses and takes a breath. "She loved to play games with us... and read to us... and take us to movies and plays for children. And every Halloween she would help us get dressed up like fairies and monsters, and famous actors and rock stars." She looks at me and says, "You remember?"

I smile and nod.

"One year I was Patti Smith and you were David Bowie."

I nod again. "And one year she dressed you up as a witch... with lots of deep black eye shadow and black lipstick. Made you look scary. And instead of fingernails, you had long sharp claws, like a wolf's."

"Yeah," she says, grinning and shaking her head. "That's not one of my fondest memories." She looks over at the boys. "But I do have a lot of fond memories of your grandma."

"If Grandma was so happy," Ethan asks, "why did she kill herself?"

"During the last year of her life, she got that extreme sadness that's called depression."

"Why did she get it?" he asks.

"We don't know. There could have been a number of causes." She shakes her head. "It's hard to say."

"Can Mom get depression?" Luke asks.

I glance over and see him on the other side of Sarah, clinging to her arm, and think, Oh, Jesus Christ, Mandy! You opened a door you should've left closed. He's going to be scared from now on.

"My mom didn't feel that her mom and dad really loved her. And I think that might have been part of what caused her depression. I think your mom feels that her parents loved her very much. Is that right, Sarah?"

Sarah nods and smiles. "You're right."

"And you two are *really lucky*," Sarah says, as she looks back and forth at Ethan and Luke, "because you have a mom and a dad who love you very, very much. Love is something that we pass on from one generation to the next. It gives us strength."

"How did Grandma Helen kill herself?" Ethan asks.

Oh, fuck! I sigh and shake my head.

Mandy takes a deep breath and lets it out. "That's a good question, Ethan." She glances at me as if to reaffirm that Ethan asked a good question. "When Grandpa found her, she was in their car, parked in the garage, with the motor running. The doors were closed, and the garage was full of exhaust. Exhaust from cars includes carbon monoxide, which is a very deadly poison. Grandma Helen died of carbon monoxide poison."

"Can carbon mo-nox-ide kill us when we're in the car?" Ethan asks.

"Not if the car is outside. For there to be carbon monoxide poisoning, the car has to be in a small building, like a garage, with all the doors and windows closed, and the motor has to be running for a long time." She studies his face, as if trying to see what he's thinking. "Does that make sense, Ethan?"

I look down at him, waiting for him to respond. Finally, he says, "Yes."

"Good," Mandy says. "Do you have any more questions?"

I look over at Luke and back at Ethan. Both remain silent. I look at Grace, Dad, and Mandy. Their eyes are on the boys.

"Well," Mandy says, with a sigh of relief, "I hope this was helpful."

Everyone remains silent. I pull Ethan and Sarah close.

Dad stands up and says, "This has been... a lot." He nods. "I'm going to bed."

Grace stands up and says, "I'll come with you." She thanks Mandy and walks down the hall, following Dad to their room.

I watch them until I hear their door close, and then look at Ethan and over at Luke and say, "I think it's time for all of us to get to bed." Feeling Sarah's eyes on me, I look at her and see her compassion. I sigh and say, "I think it's time we get to bed."

She nods, looks down at Luke and over at Ethan and says, "Come on, guys. It's time."

Sarah thanks Mandy, and we get up, go down the hall and enter the boys' room. I close the door behind us and look at the boys, as they put on their pajamas, and at Sarah.

She says to them, "Don't forget to brush your teeth. Go on." She opens the door, they head for the bathroom in their bare feet, and then she looks at me and says, "That was a lot." She gives me a faint smile, hoping perhaps that I share her feelings.

"Yeah. It was."

"Unless they have questions, I think we should just encourage them to get some sleep."

"Yeah. If they can sleep after all that."

She looks me in the eye. "We can talk about it, if you want."

"When we get to our room."

"You're angry, aren't you."

"When we get to our room."

The boys return, hop into their beds, and we kiss them goodnight, turn off the light and go to our room.

She shuts the door behind us. I turn, and we face one another.

"Of course I'm angry," I say. "Why wouldn't I be? Do you think our boys are going to be able to process all of this? You think they're not upset? Not going to be haunted by their dead grandma?" I shake my head.

"I think it's better they learn everything from their grandma's daughter, and her son, who can explain what happened, rather than overhear arguments that leave them asking questions and afraid of what the answers might be. Ethan was obviously relieved to find that he did in fact hear what he thought he'd heard, and then he got an explanation."

"Yeah, got an explanation. And will forever have in his mind the image of his dead grandmother, sitting in a car, in a garage full of fumes of carbon monoxide. And did you hear what Luke asked? 'Can Mom get depression?' Of course she can. We all can. And what's he going to do with that? Is he going to worry for the rest of his life that if you get really sad, you might kill yourself? Or he might get depressed and kill himself?"

"I'm sorry, Nick, but I really feel that it's better to talk about these things openly than to argue about them behind closed doors. We can't undo what your mother did, but hopefully, if our kids know and understand what happened, they'll be able to live with it."

"Live with it! Huh! They'll live with it, all right. For the rest of their lives."

"Not the way you and Mandy have."

"That's true. Because next year, we aren't coming back."

"Oh, you decided. You're going to build that wall. Well, I don't think it's going to protect them."

"I think it's the only way."

She sighs, shakes her head, walks over toward our bed and starts getting undressed. She puts on her pajamas, hangs her clothes on a hook, and sits on the bed. "I'm exhausted. I've got to get some sleep." She gets under the covers. "Do you mind turning off the overhead light?"

I do what she asks, and she thanks me and closes her eyes.

I get undressed, lie down and stare at the ceiling in the dark. I should be exhausted, too, but I'm not. Or I'm too upset to feel my exhaustion. Everything I've been through... we've been through... over the last few days... I reach for Sarah's hand lying next to me, but just as I touch it, she rolls over on her side, her back turned toward me. And I feel even more alone. More isolated. And I think of Mom. That she could be with us, she could play with us, or watch us play, but still feel alone. And I could see her isolation in her eyes, as she sat just a few feet away. Her distant gaze. Present, but gone. And I remember the black bag being wheeled out of the garage…

Not able to stop thinking, stop remembering, I get out of bed, walk to the front room, stand in front of one of the windows and stare at the lake, at the moon in the black night glowing above the trees on the other side of the inlet, and at the silver light shining on the still surface of the water, and I feel there's something about the beauty of that light that excites me and gives me hope. And I can feel my love for Sarah, Ethan, and Luke. Feel that we can live and be happy in this world.

"It's beautiful, isn't it?" That's Mandy's voice.

I turn and see her sitting in one of the armchairs facing me, barely visible.

"You couldn't sleep?" she asks.

"No."

"Me neither."

"Why did you pull that stunt tonight?"

"Stunt?"

"You know what I'm talking about. Getting Sarah, the boys, and me to sit down and have dinner with you, and then in walk Dad and Grace. And then you tell my sons all that... " I shake my head.

"All that truth? I did it because I want this family to come together. I'm concerned about Dad losing his son, his daughter-in-law, and his grandsons. I'm concerned about losing you, too. And I don't believe that silence and walls are the answer. They don't lead to anything good. Not for me, not for you, not for Dad, not for your sons, not for any of us."

"I want Ethan and Luke to be able to forget about all of this."

"That's not going to happen. If you do choose to build a wall and not bring your family back, sooner or later your sons will be asking questions and demanding answers. And if they can't get them from you, they'll find another way."

"She wasn't their mother, she was their grandmother. And losing a grandparent is not the same thing as losing a parent. I want to ensure the mental health of my family."

"And what about your mental health? What about your love for your parents? Your love for me?"

"I... I, ah... "

"You can't build a wall and not feel you've lost people who mean a lot to you. Do you want to live with that feeling? What is it going to do to you?" She stands up, walks toward me, stops next to me, looks out at the moonlight on the lake. "Rather than building walls, I think it would be good for us to meet more often. Maybe get together for Thanksgiving. Or Christmas. Or both. Provide your children with a loving family."

"They have a loving family. They have Sarah and me. And I will always protect them from this past that fucked up my life. And yours."

I turn and head back down the hall to my room, lie down next to Sarah, close my eyes, and try not to think about everything Mandy has said, yet it all comes back. But I'm not getting up again. I'll lie here until I fall asleep, even if I have to stare at the ceiling all night long.

Day 8, Saturday

I close the door to the cabin and head for the lodge to pay the bill, walking along the gravel road, unable to stop seeing Nick's eyes glaring at Amanda as she talked to the boys last night. Nick just wants to get his family out of here. That was clear yesterday morning, when I was standing on the balcony with Grace, watching him and Sarah and the boys load their canoe. He looked up and saw us. Didn't say anything. Didn't wave. Nothing. Just pushed off and paddled away. When Grace told me about her conversation with Amanda, I thought maybe their plan would work. But seeing the glare in Nick's eyes last night… No, they're never coming back. And if Nick isn't coming, Amanda won't either… If I never get to see my kids and my grandkids again, why should I go on living? Grace always reminds me we have one another, but... If I could just forget Helen and Bobby... If they would never enter my mind again... If I could build walls in my mind the way Nick thinks he can... But that doesn't work... I know they all think I'm a crazy old man, who has all these obsessions about corrupt politicians and the disasters they create—the wars and massacres and poverty... and climate change.

Grace reminds me all the time I can't control the world. She's right. I know she is. When I seem really frustrated, she encourages me to write articles and letters to the editor and release some of the steam that's built up. And sometimes I do. And it helps. A little. Makes me feel I've done something good. But if life is just loss upon loss upon loss, then why try? But I have Grace. I have her love. She gets me to go to music clubs, and to theaters to see plays and films, and sometimes we get together with friends. And it seems like we have a good life, until something triggers my damn temper and I go on a rant. But she always stands by me… tries to convince me things will get better. I need to believe that. Believe that my kids will come back next year. And my grandkids. When I said I didn't know if I'd reserve the cabin for next year—because why reserve it, if it would be just us? She said, "No, no, reserve it! And trust that they will come." But will they? Ah, shit! There was so much tension in the cabin.

I could hear the sound of voices in the middle of the night coming from Nick and Sarah's room, and footsteps moving around upstairs. Amanda pacing... Oh, fuck! Just pay the bill and get this over with.

Seeing the path that departs from the road, leads toward the lake and cuts across the plots in front of the cabins, providing a shorter walk to the lodge, I descend the gentle slope, walk along the side of the lake, between the docks and the cabins, and notice some guests taking bags and suitcases out of their cabins and putting them in their cars. And then I see a man and two little boys on a dock, the three of them facing the side that I'm approaching, and I stop to watch them. One of the boys looks like he's around six or seven, the other a couple years younger. Each of them is holding a fishing rod, standing on either side of the man, who is probably their father. Bent over, and looking at the older boy, the father appears to be showing him how to bait his hook. I watch the father as he holds the hook in one hand, what might be a nightcrawler in the other, and looks back and forth at the faces of his sons as he talks, and I remember watching you, Bobby, the first time Dad tried to teach us how to bait a hook. We were standing on a dock, and Dad was holding the hook for your line in one hand, the nightcrawler in the other, and looking at you as he talked. You seemed anxious. He pushed the hook into the nightcrawler, and it squirmed in agony, twisting and turning. You started to cry. You shook your head, backed away from us, and turned and ran to the cabin. And I ran after you... And then, twelve years later, you were sent to Vietnam, where you were expected to kill people. That war destroyed your life. And it took you away from me. Forever.

* * *

Looking around the bedroom to make sure I've packed everything, I hear the hushed voices of Nick and Sarah. I pause, wondering what they're talking about. Are they going to leave without saying anything to Tom? He should be back by now. But there might be a lot of people checking out, paying their bills, and he's waiting. I look at my watch. It's a little after nine. We're supposed to be out of here by ten... Maybe I should try to talk to Nick and Sarah. But I don't know what to say. Everything that's happened over the last few days concerns the relationships of Tom and Helen and their kids and grandkids. I feel like an outsider. If they don't want to talk with me, then maybe I shouldn't try talking with them. It sounds like they're leaving. I'll wait until they're gone, then I'll walk to the lodge, and hopefully meet Tom on his way back.

I can't hear Nick and Sarah anymore. I wait a couple more minutes, then sling my purse over my shoulder, pull the door open, look down the hall and, seeing no one, start walking and pulling my suitcase. As I'm about to pass the kitchen, I see Nick ahead of me, on the other side of the screen door, standing on the balcony and facing the lake. I wonder if I should say hello, or just sneak out the side door. But then he glances to his right, seems to hear someone say something, responds with a nod, and looks back at the lake. I move a little closer.

"So," he says, "I woke up this morning, thinking about last night, and this strange thought came into my mind... " He takes a deep breath and sighs. "If I were to let go of my anger about Mom's suicide, it would be like letting go of her. Like I've finally allowed her to die... All these years, I've been holding onto my anger, maybe as a way to hold onto her, trying to keep her alive. But she's gone and... I've never been able to accept that."

I take a few steps closer and stop when I hear Amanda's voice respond, "There's nothing harder to accept."

"And I thought about Dad. One of the things that's always made me angry about him is his anger, but his anger might've been his way of hanging onto her, too. That might sound crazy, but... "

"No. No, I don't think it does."

"He couldn't bear losing her either… And now… This is strange, but I feel closer to him."

"Yeah. Letting go is one of the hardest things in the world. But you're not letting go of your love for the person you lost."

"You might be right about what you said... about creating a wall. That just bottles up all the anger. And it accumulates and... We need to talk. Get it out of us. I suspect the more we talk, the more we can let go of our anger, because it comes from our refusal to forgive, and getting our emotions out there, sharing them with our family, might help us forgive."

I move close enough to the screen door to see Amanda nod.

"I've always avoided talking with the boys about Mom. I need to talk to them." He pauses for a few beats. "Ethan said something this morning that really surprised me."

"What?"

"He said he remembered seeing a picture of Grandpa and a woman on the wall in Grandpa's bedroom. A picture of just their faces. He said Grandpa and the woman were young, and they both had really big smiles and looked happy, like they were in love. And he wondered who that woman was. You remember the picture?"

"We saw it every day of our lives growing up."

"Yeah. I told him she was Grandma Helen. He nodded, like he was processing something, and then he looked at me and smiled." Nick shakes his head. "Ethan hasn't been in Dad's house since he was six years old."

"Wow! Five years ago." She pauses for a few beats. "That memory was a hole in the wall."

"Yep! I guess no wall is impermeable."

"You know, it's amazing how supportive Grace is of Dad. Of all of us. Like when we're talking, we say Dad's house, not Dad and Grace's house. And Mom keeps on coming up. And nevertheless, Grace is always supportive. He's really lucky. We're all lucky."

"Well," I say, "I feel embarrassed."

They spin around, surprised to see me standing on the other side of the screen.

"I was on my way out, and I heard you talking, and I was going to say something, but you seemed so engaged in your conversation, I didn't want to interrupt you. I apologize. I didn't intend to eavesdrop."

"That's okay, Grace," Amanda says, and Nick smiles at me as he opens the screen door and makes room for me. I leave the suitcase and my purse behind and step out onto the balcony, between the two of them, and smile back at them.

"I just want to say about your dad that I'm very lucky to have a man who is capable of loving me the way he does. I learned a long time ago that your mother would always be a part of our relationship, and that's not a bad thing." I smile. "Now, concerning the picture of Helen and your dad, you could stop off at the house before you go to the airport, and we could show it to the boys."

"I'd love to, but after we get done having brunch in Ely, we've got that long drive back to Minneapolis, and I don't think we'll have time to stop off at the house before we go to the airport. I have to return the car, and then we have to go through security and all that."

I hear the other screen door slam. "Oh!" I exclaim. I look through the screen and see Tom has entered the cabin. "Tom!" He stops and looks in my direction. "Come here, Tom. We're having a conversation."

I open the door as he approaches, a puzzled look on his face, and make room for him to join us and put my hand on his back.

Tom looks at me and at Nick, and at Amanda on his other side, and says, "About what?"

Nick says, "Oh, a few things. Important things—like letting go of anger, forgiving, and empathizing with one another."

"Oh," Tom says, a tense look on his face, as he peers into Nick's eyes. "Does that mean you'll be coming back next year?"

Nick smiles. "I think it does, Dad. And I think we'll have a better time."

Tom brandishes a big grin, looking like he'll burst wide open with joy, and throws his arms around Nick. "I'm so happy! So happy." He pulls back and looks around at Amanda and me and says, "We'll all be together again."

We smile and repeat, "We'll all be together again."

"And we're all set," Tom says. "I went ahead and reserved the cabin for next year."

"Hurrah!" Nick exclaims, and we laugh.

Amanda says, "Dad, I've been thinking. August, next year, that's a long way off. Maybe we should get together for Thanksgiving, too. And you'd get to meet Tony."

"We'd love to meet Tony." He looks at me. "Wouldn't we?"

"Oh, yeah!" I exclaim. "And we've got plenty of space. We could find room for everyone in the house. So, you could all come home for Thanksgiving."

Nick says, "Well, we generally celebrate Thanksgiving alone. It would be great to be with you. And meet Tony. I'll talk with Sarah about it."

Tom looks at Amanda and says, "Maybe Grace and I could fly to New York and see Tony's play. I've never seen a Broadway production." He looks at me. "What do you think?"

Surprised by Tom's sudden interest in seeing the play, I say, "I'd love to."

"A warning, Dad," Amanda says. "Broadway tickets are not cheap."

"Well," Tom chuckles, "it's a special production. *Putin the Great.* We've got to see that."

"We'd love to see it too," Nick says, "but I don't know if we can. It all depends on our schedule."

"Don't worry about it," Amanda says. "The kids will be in school, you'll be in Congress, you'll all be busy. If you can, great. If not, that's okay."

"Well, we'll all be able to get together for Thanksgiving," I say. "And we could show Ethan and Luke the picture of Grandpa and Grandma Helen."

"What?" Tom looks at me, confused.

"I'll tell you about it later." And then I say to Nick, "You know, I can just take a picture of the photo when we get home and email it to you."

"That would be great. Thanks, Grace."

Tom looks around. "Where are my grandsons?"

"They're with Sarah, down by the dock," Nick says.

We move to the railing of the balcony, look down and see Sarah sitting on a chair on the dock, turned toward the boys so she can watch them as they skip rocks across the glowing surface of the still water. The boys seem to be competing with one another to see who can get the most skips for each rock.

And then Nick shouts, "Hey guys! Guys! Up here!"

They stop and look up at us, as does Sarah.

"We're going into town to get brunch."

The boys start running up the path, laughing and shouting, and Sarah follows them. The boys reach the top, run toward the side entrance and clamber up the steps. Ethan comes flying around the corner of the cabin and nearly throws himself at his dad, and Luke follows him. Nick, with his hands on their shoulders, pulls them close.

"Are we leaving now?" Ethan asks, gasping for air.

"In a minute."

Sarah comes around the corner, smiles and stops next to Amanda.

Nick says, "I think we have some good things to talk about."

"Oh?"

I chime in with Nick. "We've got some good things to talk about."

"Well," Sarah says, "I need to talk to you about something, too. The boys have a request. Mandy told them about the time she and you"—she nods at Nick—"and your dad went on a camping trip and came across those pictographs. The boys want to go on a camping trip next year and see those pictographs. And explore the wilderness." She pauses. "And what is the good news you want to tell me?"

"We've agreed we're coming back next year," Nick says.

"And," I add, "it looks like we're going to get together for Thanksgiving, too. Assuming that'll work for you."

Sarah nods, smiling. "Of course it does."

"And maybe Christmas, too," Tom says, beaming with happiness.

"Dad," Amanda says, "we can talk about that at Thanksgiving."

"Yeah," Nick says, "one step at a time. Let's see how things go."

Tom nods. "Whatever you want."

We remain silent for a few seconds, looking around at one another, and then Nick says, "Well, shall we go?"

I hold onto Tom as Nick and the boys pass in front of us, join Sarah and Amanda and head for the cars.

I look at Tom. "Are you happy?"

He grins. "What do you think?"

We both laugh.

"Well, we need to get our suitcases." I open the door for Tom.

As he steps inside, and I'm about to follow, a loon cries, and I freeze. That haunting cry... that beautiful wail… of mourning and loss. I take a deep breath and think, I'm lucky to have this man, even with the past he brings with him.

Discussion Questions

Here are twelve challenging reader's-guide **questions** designed to function almost as a brief afterword—literary, psychologically probing, and suitable for intelligent discussion without sounding clinical. They are grounded in the novel's three-part structure and its movement from Helen's interior life to Tom and Amanda's grief, and finally to the family's later reunion in the Boundary Waters.

1. **The novel is structured in three time periods rather than as a continuous chronology.** How does this fractured structure shape the reader's understanding of memory, family history, and emotional inheritance?

2. **Helen's inner life is rendered with great intimacy, but not always with easy explanation.** How does the novel invite sympathy for her without simplifying or excusing the pain she leaves behind?

3. **Several characters seem to live partly in the present and partly inside earlier wounds.** Which characters are most trapped by the past, and which seem most capable of moving through it?

4. **The Boundary Waters becomes more than a setting; it becomes a place of confrontation, refuge, and revelation.** What does wilderness allow these characters to say—or feel—that ordinary domestic life does not?

5. **The novel repeatedly explores the difference between love as feeling and love as action.** Where do characters fail one another despite loving one another? Where do they succeed?
6. **Helen, Tom, Amanda, and other family members each seem to possess different emotional temperaments—some inward, some caretaking, some avoidant, some searching.** How do these temperaments shape the family's misunderstandings?
7. **What responsibility do family members have to understand one another's suffering?** Is love enough when another person's inner life remains partially inaccessible?
8. **The novel presents silence as both protective and damaging.** When does silence become mercy, and when does it become abandonment?
9. **How does the book complicate the idea of forgiveness?** Does forgiveness in this novel require understanding, or can it exist even when full understanding is impossible?
10. **Objects and sensory details—photographs, a fur coat, birdsong, water, cabins, weather—carry emotional weight throughout the story.** Which recurring image or object most powerfully deepened your understanding of the characters?
11. **The novel asks how trauma passes between generations, sometimes through words and sometimes through moods, gestures, absences, or withheld truths.** What does the younger generation inherit, and what, if anything, can it refuse?
12. **By the end, does the novel offer consolation, reckoning, ambiguity, or some combination of all three?** What kind of emotional resolution does a story like this honestly allow?

Acknowledgements

Whatever success *Day Brings Back the Night* might experience in the future is due in part to the support that I have received from many people. Thanks to my partner, Jane Bassuk; my daughter, Cathy Molenaar; and my sons Neil, Michael, and Daniel and their families for their love and support. My life would be nothing without you. And a special thank you to Michael, whose beautiful songs inspired the lyrics composed by my character, Vincent. Thanks to my beta readers, whose critiques helped me craft the book that *Day Brings Back the Night* became: Jeff Kellgren and Barry Woodward, my friends from graduate school; Claudia Kelly, Amy McCumber, and Victoria Tirrel, whom I met in a writers group years ago; and Bill Burleson, Stephen Parker, and Ed Sheehy, members of a recent group to which I belonged. And a special thanks to Richard Lentz, a psychiatrist and novelist, whose responses were so supportive. Thanks to my editor, Ian Graham Leask, publisher at Calumet Editions, for his patience as I worked through his perceptive editorial suggestions, and Gary Lindberg, co-founder of the press, for his beautiful cover design that captures the essence of the book. And thanks to Cass Dalglish, Junot Diaz, Cary Griffith and Will Weaver for their endorsements. It is wonderful to know that my work is appreciated by such gifted writers.

About the Author

Brian Duren earned a Doctorate in French Literature from the University of Paris, as well as a PhD in French and a BA in English from the University of Minnesota. After a career in academe, Brian became an author of innovative psychological literary fiction. He writes novels with an introspective quality about nomadic characters who travel through time and space, always returning to what haunts them. *Whiteout*, praised by the *St. Paul Pioneer Press* as a "stunning debut novel, worthy of national recognition," won the Independent Publisher Gold Medal for Midwestern Fiction. Nancy Robinson, the Minnesota-based surrealist painter, lauded *Ivory Black* for "putting an imaginary paintbrush into the hands of the reader and leading the way through an experience so real, it seems like more than a dream." Recognizing Brian's Proustian roots, Peter Geye commented about *The Gravity of Love*, "In lyrical, looping, loving prose, Brian Duren has worked toward Proust, that grand master of remembrance. This book is hypnotic and stylish and unforgettable." And Junot Diaz lauded the book as "a magnificent haunting duet of grief, absence, and the unshakable bonds of family . . . a profoundly moving, profoundly human novel…" *Day Brings Back the Night* is Brian's fourth novel.

www.ingramcontent.com/pod-product-compliance
Lightning Source LLC
LaVergne TN
LVHW091039080826
845145LV00002B/551

* 9 7 8 1 9 6 2 8 3 4 7 6 6 *